Advance reviews for *The Last*

"What a fascinating story. I enjoyed every
—**Barbara Erskine, *Sunda***

"Well researched and stylish, full of emotion from past and present, this is an engrossing mystery to keep the reader turning the pages."
—**Anne O'Brien, author of *The Queen's Rival***

"An engaging, beautifully crafted romance that weaves together several intriguing mysteries, both ancient and modern."
—**Alison Weir, author of the Six Tudor Queens series**

Praise for the novels of Nicola Cornick

The Forgotten Sister

"Fascinating… Cornick's rich mystery will serve readers well on a rainy day."
—***Publishers Weekly***

"A gorgeous novel, so fresh and original. And the tension! I was on the edge of my seat."
—**Jenny Ashcroft**

The Woman in the Lake

"I was hooked from the first pages."
—**Gill Paul**

"You just can't put it down. Brilliant!"
—**Katie Fforde**

The Phantom Tree

"There is much to enjoy in this sumptuous novel."
—***Sunday Mirror***

"A brilliant time-slip novel with a great twist in the tail!"
—***Woman* magazine**

House of Shadows

"Fans of Kate Morton will enjoy this gripping tale."
—***Candis***

"A gripping read."
—**BBC Radio**

Also by Nicola Cornick

THE FORGOTTEN SISTER
THE WOMAN IN THE LAKE
THE PHANTOM TREE
HOUSE OF SHADOWS

For a full list of books by Nicola Cornick,
please visit www.nicolacornick.com.

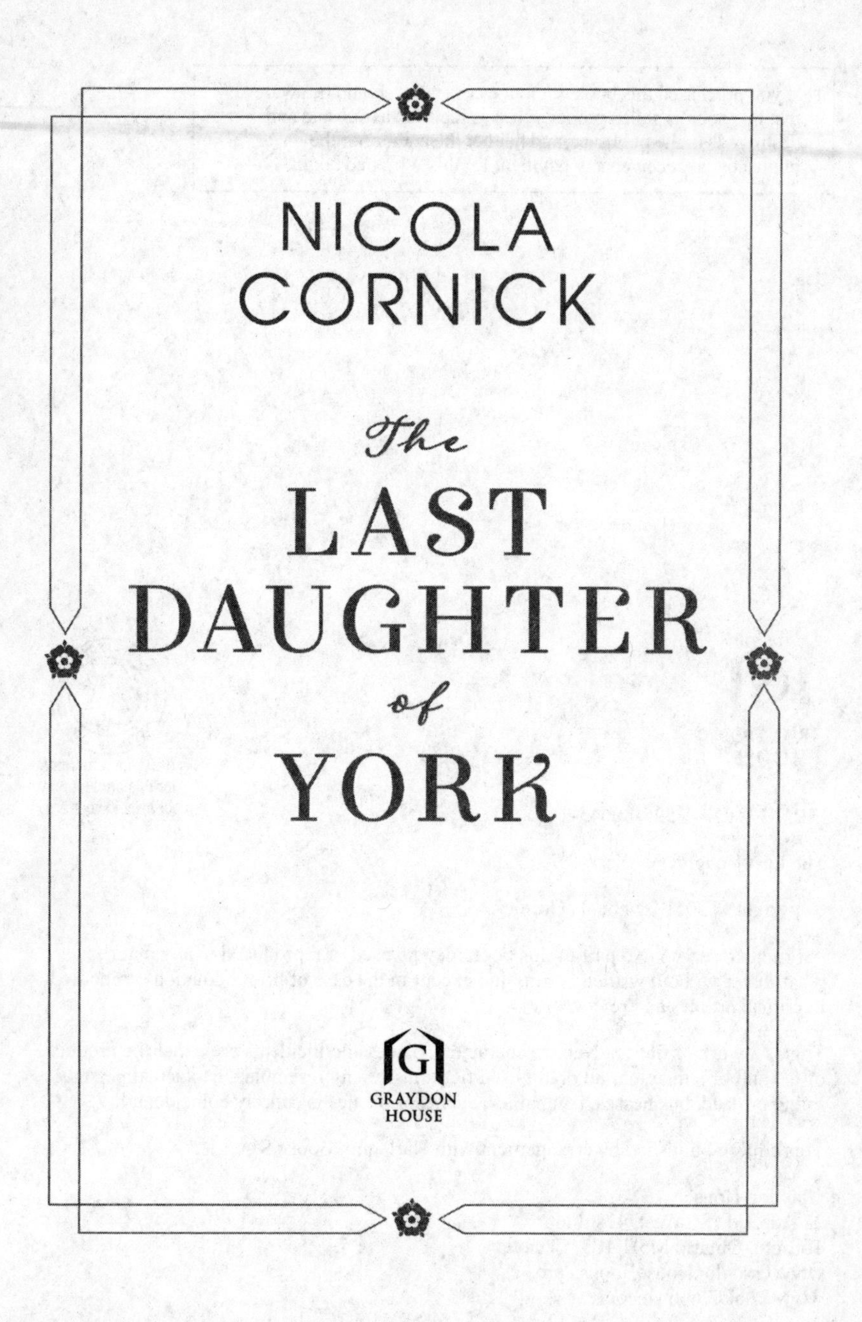

NICOLA CORNICK

The LAST DAUGHTER of YORK

GRAYDON HOUSE

ISBN-13: 978-1-525-80645-2

The Last Daughter of York

This edition published by arrangement with Harlequin Books S.A.

Graydon House
22 Adelaide St. West, 41st Floor
Toronto, Ontario M5H 4E3, Canada
www.GraydonHouseBooks.com
www.BookClubbish.com

Printed in U.S.A.

For Deb

The LAST DAUGHTER of YORK

“TIME IS A STORM IN WHICH WE ARE ALL LOST.”

—William Carlos Williams

Prologue

Minster Lovell Hall, Oxfordshire
Winter, sometime in the thirteenth century

Snow spattered the windows of the old hall, carried on the sharp north wind that spun it into fierce spirals before battering it against the diamond mullions. The wind howled down the chimney, and the snow fell on the hot embers of the fire with a hiss and burned away in an instant. No one noticed. There had been a wedding at Minster Lovell that day and the hall was hot, the guests drowsy with wine and good food, the atmosphere merry. Mistletoe boughs hung from the rafters and meat congealed on the plates. The minstrel sang a soft song of love whilst the bridegroom toyed with his empty goblet and contemplated his marriage bed. Then a shout went up for games and charades, for hoodsman's blind or shove ha'penny or hide-and-seek.

The suggestion prompted a burst of clapping mingled with the groans of the drunkards. The room was split between those who wanted to play and those whose senses were too fuddled. The groom's uncle and the dogs were all snoring, unashamedly asleep. There were no guests on the bride's side; she was a beautiful orphaned heiress, and no one knew where John Lovell had found her. Some whispered that she was really a harlot who had ensnared him, others that she was a witch who had used sorcery to capture his heart. John Lovell laughed at the folly of the whisperers and seemed well pleased with his good fortune. He was a baron, noble but poor; the only item of worth in the entire house was said to be the Lovell Lodestar, a sacred stone that the family had held in trust since the earliest of times. All the food, the wine, the jeweled goblets they drank from and the golden platters crammed with meat had been provided by the bride as part of her dowry. Gossip about her was surely mere jealousy.

"Let's play hide-and-seek." Ginevra, the bride, cast her new husband a coquettish look from beneath her dark lashes. "I shall hide and you may come and seek me out."

A roar went up at her words. There were whistles and catcalls. The wedding guests knew how that would end. No doubt Lord Lovell would find his bride hiding in their bed and then the game would instantly be forgotten in favor of another, more pleasurable one. A mood of faintly debauched anticipation began to seep into the room with the wine tossed back and the singing growing louder.

Ginevra stood, smiling, enjoying the attention of the crowd. For a moment she waited, poised, like a deer on the edge of flight, and then she ran, followed by the cheers and hunting calls of the wedding guests.

John Lovell stood, too, flushed and a little unsteady, barely able to restrain his pursuit until his bride had had time to hide. He listened to the patter of her slippers die away and then with a shout he was off, eager for the conquest. He tripped over furniture, searched behind curtains and clattered up the stairs. Excitement and the thrill of the chase sustained him for the first ten minutes and determination not to be bested for the next ten but after a half hour he rolled back into the great hall, out of breath, a little sullen, his lust frustrated. All the other guests were quaffing more ale and eating more pie. They seemed surprised to see him. Quiet fell over the hall like a shroud. The drunks sobered abruptly.

"Ginevra!" John Lovell bellowed, torn between indulgence and injured pride. "You win the game! Come out!"

There was a moment when the wind seemed to die away, and the sudden hush in the house grew to become a complete and terrifying silence. It was a silence that seemed alive, reaching out from another time to steal them away.

"Ginevra!" John Lovell called again, but this time his voice shook as doubt and fear tightened its grip on him. He marched to the front door, men crowding at his shoulder, and flung it wide. Nothing but blank snow met their gaze, no footprints, no sign of life, nothing but December's cold moon shining on the empty land.

"The Lodestar!" Suddenly John Lovell turned and ran back down the cross passage to the library. Here his father, a most learned man, had kept those manuscripts and documents so cherished by the monks of the early minster church that had stood on the site centuries before. Here was the heart of Minster Lovell, the Lodestar, a holy relic locked away in its gold and enameled box. No one in living memory had seen the stone; no one had dared to look, for it was said to possess miraculous power beyond man's wildest imaginings.

The room was as still and cold as the rest of the house; colder, for it felt as though the very soul of winter had set within those walls. The ancient oaken chest, bound within iron bands that had held the golden box safely locked within, lay open and empty. The Lodestar was gone.

John Lovell slammed the lid of the chest down in fury. His shout of anguish echoed through the house and seemed to seep into the very stones.

The Lovell Lodestar was lost, the bridegroom deceived; the thief bride had vanished.

Chapter 1

SERENA

Santa Barbara, California
Present Day

Serena stretched out on the sun lounger, relishing the sensation of the last heat of the day against her skin. Above her, a sky of a cloudless azure was starting to fade to pale violet in the west. Below her, a long way below, the white sails of the yachts clustered in the harbor. From the kitchen came the scent of garlic and herbs as Polly prepared supper and beside her on the penthouse balcony was a frosted glass of white wine whose icy coolness contrasted deliciously with the heat radiating from the tiled floor.

Polly came out with the bottle, a chef's apron over her chic black-and-white swimming costume. She smiled indulgently when she saw her niece, book discarded on the lounger beside her, sunglasses removed and face tilted up to capture the last rays of the setting sun.

"Supper will be in ten minutes." She waved the bottle. "Would you like a top up?"

Serena opened her eyes and smiled. "I'll have some with my meal, thanks." She groped for her sandals. "Can I help? Make a salad or something?"

"It's already done." Polly put the bottle on the little black steel table at Serena's side and sat in the fat, cushioned chair opposite. "You stay here awhile longer. You look so much better, hon. You look…happy."

"Why wouldn't I be?" Serena ignored the tiny shadow that crossed her mind at Polly's words. "This is an amazing place, Aunt Pol."

Polly's face eased into another smile. "Better than Bristol?"

"Better than anywhere." Serena yawned, stretched. "Thank you so much for inviting me."

"You've been working hard," Polly said. "You deserve a break."

"I can't remember when I last took a holiday," Serena admitted. "If you hadn't encouraged me…"

"Nagged you, you mean." Polly sounded rueful. "I know it's full on running your own business, but sometimes people function better after a rest and you do drive yourself hard."

"That's true." Serena stretched luxuriously again. "You're a wise woman, Aunt Pol."

Polly picked up her wineglass. Her gaze was fixed on the distant horizon where the sea seemed to slip into infinity.

"It's lovely to have you here," she said. "It reminds me of when you and Caitlin were children, and we all went to Oxfordshire for your school holidays and spent time together at Minster Lovell—" She stopped abruptly, the warmth falling away from her expression. "Sorry," she said. "I don't know why I said that. It's nothing like those times."

Suddenly the sun seemed to have lost all its heat. Serena reached for her wrap, shivering.

"I do understand what you mean," she said slowly. "It feels…easy…like those old holidays did. There were no shadows, no ghosts looking over our shoulders."

Polly hesitated and Serena knew what she was thinking. She never normally talked about the past or her sister, Caitlin. Her aunt was wondering why this time was different—and whether it was safe to pursue the conversation. Everyone was very careful around Serena on the subject of her twin. She had experienced so much trauma when Caitlin had disappeared eleven years before that she had suffered from dissociative amnesia. No one wanted to open up those scars again, but as a result they tiptoed around the subject and Serena knew she colluded with them. She'd built a wall of silence around Caitlin that became more difficult to break down every day.

"I never think of Caitlin as a ghost," Polly said, surprising her. "She was too alive, too vivid. I mean—" She caught herself, glancing at Serena again. "She probably still is. We don't know she's dead. Hell." She took a big gulp of wine. "I *really* don't know why I started this."

There was a silence. Far below, there was a splash of water and the faint cries of children's voices. Far above, an airplane arrowed into the blue.

"I think about Caitlin every day, you know," Serena said. She met her aunt's eyes. "Every single day I remember her, and I wonder. I wonder if she's alive and if so, where she is and what she's doing, and why she wouldn't want to contact us, and a million other things. And then I think she must be dead because how could she leave us all like that without a word and never get in touch with us again? How—why—would she be so cruel? That's not the Caitlin we knew." She pulled the wrap tighter about her. "I have the same conversation with myself over and over, and I never find any answers."

"I'm sorry, hon," Polly said. She leaned forward and touched

Serena's arm. "I shouldn't have mentioned it. I've spoiled the moment."

"No, you haven't." Serena smiled at her although she could feel tears pricking her eyes. "We should talk about Caitlin more. We did at the start."

When her sister had first disappeared, the family had drawn together, closer than close, a bulwark against the horror of the outside world. Eleven years on, though, things had changed. The case was cold. Serena's lost memories of the night her twin had vanished had never been recovered. Her parents, diminished somehow by years of stress and loss, only spoke about the superficial—their latest bowls club successes, the dinner they had enjoyed the previous week. Serena's grandfather had slipped into dementia. Only Polly, who possessed the same bright spark and indomitable spirit that had lit Caitlin, remained the same. Serena knew that time passed and that people changed. It was natural. Sometimes, though, she felt that for all the changes in her own life, a part of her was still trapped in the moment of Caitlin's disappearance, unable to recover those memories and in some ways unable to move on.

The buzzer on the oven sounded and they both jumped.

"Come on in," Polly said, getting to her feet with what Serena could only think was relief. "The chicken should be ready now."

Serena picked up her glass and followed her aunt inside, blinking as her eyes adjusted to the cool darkness. Polly, originally from England as she was, had worked in real estate in California for the past twenty years and her sense of style was enviable. The penthouse had 360-degree views and exuded modernity with neutral shades, lots of wood and chrome, and bold splashes of color in paintings and soft furnishings. When

Serena had first arrived, she had been almost afraid to move in case she ruffled the pristine surface of the apartment, so different from the chaotic mix of her own flat back in Bristol. It was odd; she was so organized in her working life and yet her living space overflowed with books, magazines, clothes, stuffed toys, all sorts of bits and pieces. It was some excuse that she had so little space, using the spare room as an office and squashing everything else into her living room and bedroom, but somehow there was an impermanence to it as well.

Jonah, her ex, had told her bluntly when he had left that her whole life was rootless and that it was her choice to be like that. "You don't commit to anything," he had said as he had shoved the last of his shirts into his bag, already halfway out of the door and miles away mentally, "whether it's people or places or jobs. You complain about feeling lonely, but you won't let people close to you. I've tried, Serena. But you were always determined to push me away." He'd stared at her for a moment then, his dark hair ruffled, glasses askew in the way she had once found so endearing. "It's not me," he said. "It really is you." And he was gone, to move in with his colleague Maddie, as it turned out, because Maddie was apparently so much more fun to be with and was prepared to commit to him.

His criticisms had been harsh and, Serena thought, untrue. She'd worked really hard over the past five years to make her company successful. She and her friend Ella specialized in arranging bespoke historical tours and were starting to get the business on a sound footing at last. It was true that she *had* moved around a lot in the past ten years and she had lost touch with almost all the friends she'd had from her childhood and college years, but so did a lot of people. She had had a couple of unsuccessful relationships but again, that wasn't unusual. It was only when she thought about Jonah, which she did less and less since the split, that a tiny doubt crept into her mind that on the issue of people at least he might have been right and that she didn't really want to commit to anyone. Losing Caitlin, the person who had once been closer to her than anyone else in the world, had inevitably taken a toll in terms of how much she was prepared to invest in a relationship. She had the self-awareness to know that and absolutely no idea how to change it.

The glass dining table was set with bright blue plates and crisp napkins. There was fragrant chicken with salad and a creamy herb dressing, chilled white wine... Serena relaxed again. She had another two weeks in California with Polly. Ella was handling the business with the help of a temp and sent her cheerful updates on how well it was all going without her. Tomorrow she and Polly were taking a trip to Gaviota State Park and she'd also penciled in a visit to some of the wineries and, most exciting of all, a day trip to Hearst Castle. Even though history was her job, she never ever got tired of it.

Her phone rang. She ignored it as she took another forkful of salad.

"It's your mother," Polly said helpfully, reading the screen upside down.

Serena felt two sensations hot on the heels of each other: irritation and a whisper of dread. Both were instinctive and both were unfair. She knew it wasn't her mother's fault that she found her needy and felt the pressure of being an only child.

The only remaining child.

"I'll call her back later," she said.

"It's the early hours in the UK," Polly said. "Maybe there's some sort of emergency?"

The chicken seemed to turn to ashes in Serena's mouth.

She stared at Polly for what seemed like forever as the phone buzzed on and on. She refused to frame the thoughts that were hovering at the edge of her mind. Then the phone stopped abruptly and the silence sounded very loud indeed.

"Serena—" Polly said, but then her own phone started to ring with the same brash insistence.

"Don't answer it." Serena's sense of dread increased.

Polly looked exasperated and ignored her.

"Hello, Jackie. You're up late tonight. Is everything all right? How's Paul?" Polly always exaggerated her British accent when speaking to her sister-in-law. Serena was never sure whether it was deliberate or not. Her aunt and her mother did not get on particularly well, although they did a good enough job of pretending that they did for the sake of family unity.

"We have nothing in common," Polly had said once when Serena had asked her about their relationship. "It's not even that we dislike each other, there's just nothing to build on."

Serena thought that like everything else, the differences, the cracks in their relationship, hadn't been so obvious before Caitlin had vanished. Or perhaps she had just missed them. She had been only seventeen when she lost her twin and as far as she remembered, pretty self-absorbed. She could see that Polly, the independent, childless career woman and her mother, the stay-at-home housewife who felt slightly defensive about it, might not have had that much in common.

There was a tide of words from the other end of the phone. Polly was frowning. "Wait," she said sharply. "Slow down. I don't understand..." Then more quietly: "Yes, of course. She's here."

She passed the phone across the table to Serena, who took it without a word. She already knew what it was that she was going to hear. Superstitiously she wondered whether it had been the mention of her sister's name earlier that evening that had somehow invited Caitlin to invade her peace; invited her back into her life to banish the tenuous contentment she had found in the last couple of weeks.

"Mum?" she said.

Her mother's voice sounded crackly and broken over the vast distance:

"The police have just left," she said. "They've found Caitlin. They've found a *body*. Serena, you've got to come home."

Serena's heart started to race. Her stomach knotted. How was it possible, she wondered, to have anticipated this, to have *sensed* that her mother must have devastating news, and yet still to feel so sick and hollow and unprepared? Over the eleven years since Caitlin had disappeared, not a day had passed when she hadn't wondered when, *if*, they would ever know the truth of what had happened to her. Yet now that she stood on the edge of discovery, she felt as though the world had dropped away beneath her feet and left her in free fall.

Her mother was still talking, the words tumbling over each other, interrupted by sobs. Serena didn't stop her, didn't really listen to the words, only the tone and the emotion. Her mind seemed to have frozen, stuck on that one thought:

"Caitlin's body has been found..."

"You still there, love?" It was her father now. He sounded exhausted, confused and old. Serena could hear her mother still crying in the background.

"We don't have many details at the moment, just that the police have identified your sister from her dental records. We don't even know where she was found. How soon can you get here?"

Serena swallowed hard, trying to focus. It seemed so difficult. All she could see in her mind's eye was a vision of Caitlin, blond hair flying as she ran, arms outstretched, smiling and full of life.

"I'll come straightaway," she said. "Tonight. Tomorrow. As soon as I can get a flight." She could see that Polly had already reached for her tablet and was searching for the next flight from Los Angeles to London. Serena's mind started to race. She would need to hire a car when she got to Heathrow to take her from London to Gloucestershire. Could she do that now, or should she wait… She felt a desperate impatience to be on her way home, but at the same time, a sliding horror that this was happening again, the police, the questions, the tantalizing and terrifying gaps in her memory…

"Have you told Granddad yet?" she said.

"No." Her father sounded shocked that she should suggest it. There was a pause. "We thought perhaps it would be better not to…" His voice strengthened. "He wouldn't understand anyway, not with the dementia."

"He might," Serena said. There was a very hard lump in her throat. "Someone is going to have to tell him, Dad."

There was silence at the end of the line, strong with denial. Polly put her hand over Serena's, her gaze intent and concerned, and Serena unclenched her fingers from the tight knot they had formed. She smiled shakily at her aunt.

"Well, we can talk about that when I see you, Dad," she said. "I've got to go. I need to get a ticket, pack… I'll let you know when I'm arriving." She tried, not entirely successfully, to stop her voice from wobbling. "I love you," she said. "Give Mum a big hug from me. I'll see you soon."

She pressed End and cut off the sound of her mother's crying. The warmth seemed to flow back into the apartment, bringing with it the sunshine and the faint sounds of the world outside, but everything was different now, out of reach. In her mind she was already on her way home, back to England and the horror that was waiting.

"Shit," Polly said. "I'm so sorry, hon. How awful. Do you want to talk about it?"

Serena shook her head. "I'm sorry, Aunt Pol, I can't. I don't really know how I feel yet." She clenched her hands. "I just want to get on and *do* something."

"Of course." Polly sighed. She squeezed Serena's arm and stood up. "There's a flight leaving LAX at eleven that has some space. If we hurry—"

"Great." Serena jumped up, abandoning the chicken salad. She had lost her appetite completely. "I'll get my stuff together."

Polly wrapped her in a hug. "I wish I could come with you, hon. I want to support you."

"You've got work," Serena said. "You can't just drop everything, I know that. I'll be fine. Really."

"You'll be supporting everyone else," Polly said, suddenly fierce. "Your mother's in bits, and Paul never was very good in a crisis."

Serena tightened the hug for a moment before letting Polly go. She gave her aunt a watery smile. "Dad does his best," she said, knowing that Polly's unsentimental assessment of her brother was right. "I'm sure he'll be a big comfort to Mum, and I'm happy to talk to Granddad. Actually, I'd rather I did it than that they tried to tell him about Caitlin." She rubbed her eyes. "I'll ring you every day, okay? That would really help."

The worry lightened a little in Polly's eyes. "That would be great, hon."

As she threw her holiday clothes haphazardly into her suitcase, Serena started to feel more grounded again. It was a relief to have something practical to concentrate on. She was always able to ward off the dark, Caitlin-shaped thoughts with action. In the aftermath of her sister vanishing, she had talked to everyone: to family, the police, counselors and psychologists, and tried so hard to recover the memories of that night that she had lost through cognitive amnesia. The psychiatrists she had seen had told her that her memory could return at any time or not at all. Dissociative amnesia was completely unpredictable, and in the event, no treatment had made any difference at all. No memories had come back to her, and she had ended up exhausted and emotionally battered by the endless effort at recall. Not only had it felt as though she had lost those hours, more importantly, it had felt as though she had completely failed her sister.

Her hands still full of T-shirts and shorts, she froze for a second, possessed by the agonizing thought that she had in some way betrayed the trust that Caitlin had placed in her. She had always been the stronger one.

You should have found me, helped me, saved me.

She squashed the rest of her clothes into the bag and forced the zip to close. There would be questions, memories and hard truths to face up to now. She was not at all sure she was ready, but she had no choice.

Chapter 2

ANNE

Ravensworth Castle, Yorkshire
January 1465

In the winter of the year 1465, when I was five years old, my uncle, the Earl of Warwick, the Kingmaker, came to Ravensworth one night, and set my life on a course I could never have imagined. It was late, and the torches were lit in the courtyard and the fires hot in the hearths for there was deep snow on the ground. I was asleep when he came, and the first that I knew of it was when my elder sister Elizabeth shook my arm roughly to awaken me. There was an odd expression on her face, of mingled envy and pity.

"Mother wants you," she said. "You are to go to the solar."

"Go away." I burrowed deeper into my nest of blankets and furs. Beside me my other sister Alice turned over in her sleep, pulling the covers away from me. I pulled them back.

Elizabeth was having none of it. This time she poked me in the ribs, hard enough to banish sleep completely. "Our uncle is here," she hissed. "Get up!"

"I need the privy now you have woken me," I grumbled. I slid from the bed and scurried across the chamber, the cold stone of the floor chilling my bare feet before I had taken more than a couple of steps. The icy draft in the dark little corner garderobe was vicious, straight off the snow-covered fells outside. My teeth were chattering as I came out and stumbled back toward the sanctuary of the bed. I had no intention of going to find Mother in her private rooms; it mattered little to me that Uncle Warwick was here. I was a child and I wanted to sleep.

"Anne."

It was my father's voice, soft and warm. A candle flared and then he was scooping me up and wrapping me in a fur-lined cloak, carrying me out into the corridor. I heard Alice's sleepy voice. "What is it? What's happening?"

And Elizabeth's short answer. "They want Anne. They always want Anne."

My father smelled of his familiar scent, and the cloak was soft and warm. I slid my arm about his neck and clung closer. I adored my father, so equable and indulgent in comparison to my high-tempered mother. But Mother was a Neville born, which was to be special and important. This we all knew and understood, just as we knew she was stronger than my father whatever men say about the wife being subject to the husband's authority.

The adult world after candles were out in the nursery was a strange and dazzling place. There was noise and light, the bustle of a castle awake whilst we, the children, slept. It made me feel both very grown-up and at the same time, at a disadvantage. I wriggled in my father's arms, suddenly wanting my independence.

"I can walk," I told my father. "I'm not a baby."

He laughed, but there was an edge of regret to it. "No," he said. "You are a Neville." He placed me on my feet as we reached the door of the solar, carefully wrapping the cloak about me so that it trailed behind me like a train. It was a rich azure blue, and I drew it close as I entered and felt like a queen.

My mother and her brother were standing heads bent close together as they talked at the fireside. They drew apart as we entered the room, giving the impression of two conspirators. The room was hot and bright, and the air smelled of wine and spices, making my head spin a little. The sense of a strange, adult world grew stronger. I had no place here and yet I had been summoned.

My mother's blue gaze was sharp as it swept over me as though looking for fault, but my uncle smiled.

"My daughter Anne, my lord." My father was suddenly formal. Holding his hand as I was, I could feel something tense in him. He might be lord here at Ravensworth, but in this company he would forever be an outsider. He had been chosen as my mother's consort; an ally, a liege man to the Neville clan who were the growing power in the North. Vaguely I understood this although I was too young to grasp the complexity of it.

I wondered whether I should curtsey to the Earl. It felt odd when I was in my nightclothes, but I did it anyway, drawing back and settling the cloak about me again so that it covered me modestly and warmed my bare feet.

My uncle Warwick seemed charmed. He crouched beside me. I had never been so close to him before, for he had previously paid no particular attention to his sister's brood of children, particularly not the girls. He was too busy, too important.

Like my mother—like me—he had the clear blue eyes of the Nevilles, but the rest of his face reminded me of a hawk, it was so fierce and predatory. People accused the Nevilles of pride and arrogance, and it was written there for all to see, in the hard line of his cheek and jaw and the cold assessing gleam of his eye. He was a great man, second only to our kinsman King Edward, or he had been until the previous year when the King had married secretly and raised up a whole raft of his wife's relatives to the nobility. Uncle Warwick hated the Queen because of the influence she held; this was something else that I knew because I had overheard my parents speak of it. People will speak freely before children, just as they will before servants, thinking us deaf perhaps or too young to understand.

"How do you do, Mistress Anne," the Earl of Warwick said. "You have a great look of the Nevilles about you."

I was clever enough to recognize this as a compliment. "Thank you, my lord," I said.

"What age are you?"

"I am five years old, my lord."

He nodded. "Tell me, Mistress Anne, what do you know of marriage?"

My father was standing behind me. I felt him make an instinctive movement and saw the moment my mother caught his hand and the words on his tongue died unsaid. I looked the Earl of Warwick in the eye.

"Marriage is an alliance of wealth and power, my lord," I said, and he burst out laughing.

"Well said, little maid." He stood up, still smiling. "I like her, Alice," he said to my mother. "She is both comely and clever. You have chosen well."

My mother nodded. I could feel my father's anger stiff within him, but my mother ignored it. She too was smiling at me. Her approval, unlike my father's love, was a cold thing, but still I basked in it for it was rare.

"You are to wed, Mistress Anne," Lord Warwick said. This time he did not trouble to stoop to my level but looked down at me from his great height. "I have the King's ward in my care, a boy of eight years or so called Francis Lovell. He is handsome and rich and kind, a good match for you. Would you like him for your husband?"

I correctly guessed that this was not a question that required an answer since it had already been decided. I dropped another curtsey.

"My lord."

"Good. So be it. We shall hold the nuptials next month—" He looked at my mother. "At Middleham."

"Why not here at Ravensworth?" My father spoke for the first time. Silence followed his words, but it seemed to twitch with matters unsaid.

"If you wish it." After a moment the Earl gave a careless shrug. "I thought to show my sponsorship of the couple—" he smiled at me again "—by hosting the celebration."

Silence again, then my mother stepping smoothly in to break it. "We can discuss these matters in the morning. You'll stay the night, Richard? It's late and too inclement to travel back. Let me show you to a chamber."

My uncle inclined his head. "Thank you." He picked up his goblet. I saw his throat move as he finished his wine in one swift gulp. He gave my father a brief nod and followed my mother out. I knew then that he wanted to talk to her alone. My father watched them go. He did not move.

I tugged on his hand to recall his attention back to me. "May I go back to bed now, Father?"

He smiled then and ruffled my hair. "Of course, sweeting. I'll take you."

My sister Alice was asleep again as he tucked me in beside her and bent to kiss my brow. "Nothing will change," he said, and it sounded like a vow, but I was too tired to ask him what he meant.

A moment after he had left, Elizabeth popped up beside the bed, her face lit from below by the candle flame, both her long hair and her dangling ribbons in danger of catching fire.

"What did they want?" she demanded.

I yawned. "I am to marry a boy with a saint's name," I said sleepily.

"Why you?" Elizabeth groused. "I am the eldest. Even Alice is older than you."

I snuggled down, already on the edge of sleep. "You marry him, then," I said. "I don't mind."

Elizabeth was wide-awake, however, and full of spite. "Uncle Warwick saves his own daughters for better matches," she said, "whilst he barters us away. I heard Father say he means them for the royal princes. Not for nothing is he called the Kingmaker."

"Then I pity them," I said. "Cousin George can be *horrid*." I wriggled crossly, wishing she would take her grumbling elsewhere. I rolled over and turned my back. "Go away. I want to sleep."

Nothing will change, Father had said. I had always trusted him.

Life was so simple when I was but five years old.

Chapter 3

SERENA

Minster Lovell, Oxfordshire
Present Day

Serena woke while it was still dark, the sound of a discordant peal of bells in her ears. She lay for a moment half-asleep, half-awake, pulled from a dream. Her mind, dazed by travel, stress and jet lag, took a few moments to catch up. She knew she was back in England and for one crazy second, she thought she was in her flat in Bristol, and that Jonah was in the bed beside her, his presence a constant and a comfort. Then she realized that this wasn't her flat, and remembered that Jonah was long gone and their past together had been tidied away along with all the other emotional detritus she'd swept under the carpet and that she was in Oxfordshire, at the Minster Lovell Inn. It felt unfamiliar and odd; the vast acreage of the four-poster spread around her, the old cotton sheets smooth and cool. Though the room was pitch-black, she could hear the sounds of the ancient building settling around her, the creak of a floorboard and the sighing of the old beams. She felt anxiety skitter down her spine, wondering once again whether she had done the right thing in coming back to the place where Caitlin had disappeared.

Curling up on her side, Serena thought that in some ways it was actually pleasant to have some peace. She'd spent the previous three days staying with her parents in Gloucestershire. It had been an excruciatingly difficult time. Her mother, never particularly resilient, had crumpled completely when confronted with the proof that Caitlin was dead. Her father, Paul, was not resourceful in a crisis, either. He meant well, but that phrase in itself damned any pretense that he was capable of holding things together. It had been Serena who had spoken to the police, who were still in the earliest stages of the investigation and very reticent in disclosing any details. All they would say was that Caitlin's body had been found not far from where she had disappeared at Minster Lovell, it was currently unclear how long ago she had died and that they would like to discuss the case in more detail with all members of her family in due course. It all felt very cold and procedural.

Serena had kept Polly updated on progress each day and had rung her the previous afternoon before she'd left Gloucestershire. Their calls had been a lifeline, she thought, the only thing keeping her sane and grounded.

"I'm going to Oxford to talk to the police tomorrow," she had told her aunt, visualizing the early-morning sunshine pouring into Polly's penthouse as they spoke. "They want to give us the latest news on the investigation and also to go through the events of the original inquiry into Caitlin's disappearance." She'd glanced toward the door of the sitting room, which was ajar, her parents pretending to watch a news program whilst eavesdropping on her conversation. "We all agreed that it was probably best I handle that."

"You mean Jackie and Paul can't cope with it," Polly had said bluntly. "I'm sorry, hon. This must be so hard for you."

"They're both in shock," Serena had said, defending her parents, as she always did. "It's unbelievably tough for them to face this after so many years of hoping for a miracle. They will have to be interviewed at some point, but they just need a bit more time to come to terms with it all. Besides, I was there when Caitlin vanished. It might help jog my memory to talk it through again." She took a deep breath. "So I thought I'd stay in Minster Lovell for a few days whilst I talk to the police. I'm heading over there this evening."

"What?" Polly's incredulity came down the telephone loud and clear. "Is that really a good idea?"

Serena laughed. "You obviously don't think so! Look, Aunt Pol, I do understand your concerns and I appreciate them." Her voice warmed. "I know you're trying to look out for me. But if I'm going to go raking over the events of Caitlin's disappearance, and let's face it, I don't have much choice as the police want to discuss it, I might as well do it properly." She dropped her voice further, aware that her mother's ears were practically out on stalks. "I've thought for a while that if I went back now, as an adult, it might prompt me to remember what happened that night that Caitlin disappeared. The only reason I haven't done it before was because I was scared. Too scared to face up to it."

Polly gave a gusty sigh. "You'd moved on and now this has dragged you back."

"I hadn't really," Serena said honestly. "I might have moved on in my life, but in my head Caitlin's disappearance is somewhere I just don't go and that has affected everything—my relationships, my sense of who I am… It's like a shadow over me all the time. It feels as though a part of my life is…not missing, but unfinished, somehow, and I owe it to myself as well as Caitlin to try one last time to recover those memories."

"Okay," Polly said cautiously, "but do you really need to *stay* there? I mean, it's only an hour and a half from where you live. Surely you could stay in Bristol and just go over if you feel the need to tramp around the hall and the ruins?" Her tone suggested that she thought this was a particularly bad idea.

"I thought of that," Serena said, "but I want to be as close to the manor as possible. There's something about being on the spot where it all happened... I think it might help me."

There was a long silence at the other end of the phone. "Well, you've clearly made up your mind," Polly said, "so I won't waste my breath. Where will you be staying?"

"There's a few nice places," Serena said, "but the Minster Inn is closest to the manor and the ruins of the old hall."

"You're really going for this, huh?" Polly sighed again. "Then all I can do is wish you luck. Make sure you ring me every day, okay? And if anything happens, if you start recovering your lost memories, get the hell out of there and call a therapist. This feels dangerous to me."

"I will," Serena promised. She had had plenty of therapy eleven years before, and it had helped hugely with the shock and the grief of Caitlin's loss, but nothing had stirred the lost memories of that night. She wasn't sure that anything ever would now, not so long after the event. Yet she owed it to herself, and to her sister, to try.

Sleep had gone for good now. Her mind was too active. Serena yawned, fumbling for her phone on the nightstand to check the time. The bright light from the screen made her squint and showed that it was ten minutes past six. The glow from the phone cast the rest of the bedroom in shades of light and dark, outlining the bulk of the huge wooden wardrobe, an armchair and the table that held various well-thumbed old copies of local magazines describing the glories of the Cotswolds. The table also held a rickety lamp and a more efficient-looking torch. When she had arrived at the Minster Inn the previous night, she had discovered that the torch came as a standard amenity.

"There's no street lighting and we get power cuts sometimes," Eve, the landlady, had said cheerfully. "There's a hot water bottle and an extra blanket in the wardrobe if you need them. After all, it is only March."

Serena could hear the ancient plumbing cranking itself into action as she flicked off the phone and lay back in the big double bed. Six fifteen on a chilly March morning. She started to run through the plan of the day in her head. She had an appointment in Oxford at twelve thirty with Inspector Litton of the Thames Valley CID and after that she planned to visit her grandfather at his care home in Witney. Until then, her time was her own.

Time to think, time to explore, time to remember.

Serena lay for a moment staring up at the faded canopy of the four-poster. Even if Polly had not been happy with her decision to stay at Minster Lovell and neither had her parents, she knew that she was right to follow her instinct. They wanted to protect her and she understood that. They had been trying to do that ever since Caitlin disappeared. But she was an adult and had to make her own decisions and live her own life. When Caitlin vanished, Serena's whole existence had shattered. She had been only seventeen, and the machinery of investigation had swept her up and caused her to feel even more isolated and grief-stricken. It was hardly surprising that once the police inquiries had finished, she had never wanted to talk about Caitlin again. The problem was that it was not so easy. Her twin could not simply be ignored or forgotten. Caitlin's bright spirit shadowed her wherever she went and whatever she did.

Serena sat up and slipped out of the bed, her feet sinking into the thick bedside rug. She padded barefoot to the window. Last night she had arrived in twilight, eaten scampi in the basket and gone to bed with indigestion. This morning, before she headed into Oxford, she would explore the village and the ruins of the hall for the first time in over a decade.

A little shiver tickled down her spine. She pulled back the heavy velvet curtain and peered outside. It was just starting to get light, a tiny sliver of gold on the eastern horizon breaking through a bank of pewter cloud. Night still clung close, however, and in its shadows the ruins of the old Minster Lovell Hall looked unfriendly. When she had been a child, Serena had loved the romantic tumbled towers and moss-covered walls in the meadows beside the pretty little River Windrush. She and Caitlin had stayed as often as they could with their grandparents, in the old manor house that had been built within the ruins of the medieval hall.

Minster Lovell had seemed an impossibly magical place in those days, atmospheric and steeped in history. It had inspired Serena to study for a history degree at university, and when Caitlin had disappeared, she had thrown herself into the past as a way to escape the intolerable nature of the present. A series of jobs in the heritage industry had followed before she and Ella had struck out on their own with the bespoke tour company. Now, though, as she looked at the place that had shaped so much of her life, the lowering bulk of the ruined hall in the morning light seemed threatening rather than inspiring.

The shadows of the past pressed close. Caitlin's body had been found somewhere close to here. She felt a shudder rack her.

Deliberately she remained standing by the window, her gaze fixed on the ruins, until she felt the flutter of fear that was inside her subside. The past could not hurt her now. It was over. And she couldn't afford to be scared if she wanted to remember.

She allowed the curtain to fall back across the window and climbed back into the nest of sheets, blanket and eiderdown, drawing her knees up to her chin and hugging them close. The jet lag that had added another layer of stress to her return home had eased slightly over the past three days, but she still felt simultaneously exhausted and wide-awake, her head aching with tension. With a sigh, she lay down again and fell into the sort of light doze that only seemed to make her feel more sluggish when she woke up again two hours later.

A shower helped her and she went down for breakfast. There was a scent of bacon fat and stale beer in the air, the staple background of the country pub. Piped music played, too faintly for Serena to identify the song. She had a day-old copy of the *Guardian* to read but Eve, the landlady, seemed keen to chat.

"Do the church bells still chime during the night?" Serena asked her when Eve brought her the plate of bacon, eggs, sausage, toast and all the other elements that made up the Minster Inn's full English breakfast. She was the only occupant of the breakfast room and wondered if she was the only guest. She'd never been in the pub before; at seventeen she and Caitlin had been underage although she suspected that Caitlin, who had been going out with the barman, had slipped in now and then for a drink.

"There haven't been any church bells since 2012," Eve said

briskly. She was about fifty, small, with short dark hair and dark eyes, neat and quick of movement, efficient as she unstacked all the breakfast dishes from her tray. "They were banned for being too noisy. Some of the villagers didn't like them." Her sharp gaze appraised Serena thoughtfully. "You must have imagined hearing them. Either that or you're fey. They say that only those who are haunted can hear the ringing of the church bells."

Only those who are haunted… Serena repressed a shiver. It was an odd turn of phrase, and she didn't like it. If anyone in Minster Lovell was haunted she definitely was. She remembered again that Caitlin's body had been discovered somewhere nearby and pushed the thought away almost violently.

"I probably dreamed it," she said, deliberately light. "I've still got jet lag."

"Lucky you." Eve's eyes sparkled. "Have you been away on holiday?"

"California," Serena said, "just visiting family."

"And now you're here…" Eve paused, inviting more conversation. Evidently, she thought a bit of personal information on her guests was fair exchange for the cooked breakfast.

"My grandfather lives near here," Serena said. "I'm calling in to see him later."

"Are you from hereabouts, then?" Eve put her hands on her hips. "I don't recognize you and I've lived here forever."

"My grandparents owned Minster Manor before it was sold to the heritage trust," Serena said. She didn't recognize Eve, either. "They lived there for about twenty years and my sister and I used to come and stay for our holidays. It was a while ago." She smiled at Eve, deciding to change the subject. "I don't remember the pub looking as good as this, though. I only ever saw the outside. You've made it really nice. It's a classic country pub, very charming."

It was certainly the case that Eve had gone to town on the whole traditional Old English image. There were horse brasses tacked on to the beams, a post horn and a chamber pot nestling together rather incongruously on the windowsill, whilst through in the bar Serena could see a motley collection of china toby jugs, a pair of dueling pistols, antique candle-holders and a rather tarnished sword hanging on the wall.

Eve gave a snort of laughter. "It's falling apart, really, but my family has been in the village forever, and I feel I sort of owe it to them to keep going. The place is a money pit, though, and with so many people doing private rentals these days, times are tough for pubs like this. Still—" her tone softened "—there's always the food service. That does well. And I'm glad you like it here."

She bustled away with the tray, leaving Serena with her coffee, good, strong cafetière-brewed coffee she wanted to drink slowly. She picked up the paper, but didn't start to read; instead, she gazed out of the diamond-paned window and thought about the holidays that she and Caitlin had spent with their grandparents at Minster Lovell Manor. The best time had been Christmas and February half-terms, when there had been frost on the rushes down by the river. She could remember the crunch of it beneath the soles of her boots and later, the pleasure of thawing out in front of the huge roaring fire in the parlor, having crumpets and hot milk. In the autumn there had been tumbling leaves and pale blue windswept skies, and in the summer, they had swum in the river and played hide-and-seek amongst the fallen stones of the ruined hall.

In those days Minster Lovell had been enchanted. Now it

was spring—a damp and chill spring—yet to burst into new life. A placed haunted by Caitlin's death.

A series of cars crawled past the window, taking the twisting road over the little stone bridge in a queue. A minibus drew up outside and disgorged a group of teenagers with huge rucksacks. They looked miserable.

"Duke of Edinburgh Awards." Eve had reappeared. "Poor little sods. Or perhaps they're helping out at the archaeological dig at the church. Either way, I'm sure they'd rather be inside on their games consoles." She tilted her head at Serena. "I forgot to ask, did you sleep okay, apart from hearing the bells?"

"Yes, thanks," Serena said. "It was very cozy."

"I didn't put you in the haunted bedroom, just in case." Eve looked wistful, as though she would prefer to terrify her guests so that there was a good story to tell in the morning.

"Thanks," Serena said. "I appreciate that. I imagine the place is stiff with ghosts."

Eve sat down edgeways on the chair opposite, perching in a rather determined fashion. Serena put the newspaper down and poured herself another cup of coffee. She already knew most of the local legends from her childhood, though she suspected she was about to hear them all again. She and Caitlin had scared each other sleepless telling ghost stories on dark nights in the creaky old hall.

"The pub's ancient," Eve said, "although we only have the one ghost here in the building. But the village—" She made a gesture that implied Minster Lovell was the paranormal center of the universe. "Well, there's a lot of supernatural activity around here. The place attracts dark energies."

"Does it?" Serena said noncommittally. She wasn't a great believer in the supernatural. After Caitlin had vanished, the family had been targeted by plenty of people who had claimed they had special powers to find or communicate with her spirit; Serena had been so repelled by this that she had shied away from anything remotely paranormal ever since. Eve, however, was not deterred.

"Yes! There's a ghost of a knight on horseback, who challenges people to race him to the bridge, and a Gray Lady, and a monk who wanders the ruins of the old hall and another ghostly lady—this one's green—and a ghost dog."

"I love dogs," Serena said. "I wouldn't mind seeing a ghostly one. What sort of breed is it?"

"No one's asked that before," Eve said. She sounded annoyed that she didn't know the answer. "It's some sort of hound, I think, long and lean rather than big and shaggy. It belonged to Lord Lovell, the guy who disappeared during the War of the Roses."

A bell rang, away down the passage. Eve jumped up. "That'll be Ross come to change the barrels over. Don't rush to finish up here," she added. "Will you be wanting dinner tonight?"

"I'm not sure what I'm doing," Serena said. "Can I let you know later?"

"As long as it's by two." Eve whisked away.

The guy who disappeared during the War of the Roses…

The words struck a discordant note with Serena, reminding her again of Caitlin. It was a curious coincidence that this was a place where more than one person had vanished over the years. She remembered her grandfather telling her about Francis Lovell, who had owned the old hall in the fifteenth century. He had been the closest friend of King Richard III, and he had disappeared after the Battle of Stoke in 1487. Serena smiled as she drained her coffee cup. Her grandfather had always said she got her love of history from him, and certainly she had been obsessed with Francis Lovell's story when she had been in her early teens. She had been obsessed with Richard III for that matter; he had been one of her first historical crushes along with King Arthur, Robin Hood and Anne Boleyn.

But Francis Lovell had been special, not least because she and Caitlin had been friends with a boy called Jack Lovell who had lived in the village. Serena had often wondered secretly whether Jack was Francis's descendent, but she had never asked because she hadn't wanted to appear uncool. She had cherished a number of adolescent dreams about Jack, maybe because she was so obsessed with Francis and had somehow conflated the two of them. It was a little embarrassing to remember it now, as teenage crushes so often were years later, but it had been very intense and real at the time. Even now she could remember that the infatuation she had had with Jack had felt so real it had been physically painful.

Serena turned the empty coffee cup around in her hands, feeling a surprisingly strong pang of loss. It was just nostalgia for the golden days before Caitlin's disappearance, of course, but she regretted now the way that she had dropped Jack so ruthlessly along with all her other friends at Minster Lovell, in the aftermath of losing her sister. She hadn't been able to begin to deal with her own emotions in that devastating time, let alone cope with anyone else's, but looking back it felt harsh.

She set down the coffee cup and got to her feet, dusting the toast crumbs off her jeans. She wasn't sure she would ever be hungry again after that breakfast. In a funny sort of way, it felt as though it had helped fortify her for what was ahead of her. The day was certainly going to be a challenging and stressful one.

The pale sun was gilding the ruins of the old hall now, softening the harsh gray stone to shades of cream. The shadows of bare branches danced against the walls, the early-morning light glinting on the river. Serena hesitated. The manor house where her grandparents had once lived was owned by a heritage trust now and open to the public to visit from 9:30 a.m. during the winter season. Her plan had been to take a tour that morning before heading into Oxford, but suddenly it seemed impossible to move, impossible to take that final step over the threshold of her past. Suppose she did start to remember what had happened the last time she and Caitlin had stayed there? Suppose she did not?

Fear gripped her. For a second it had a stranglehold on her throat and she could hear nothing but the thud of her heart. The minutiae of other people's lives going on around her faded away: the distant voices of the students as they set out on their hike, Eve talking to Ross down the corridor, a clank of barrels being unloaded, a constant faint drone of traffic from the main road at the top of the hill.

"All finished now?" Eve, like a jack-in-the-box, popped up in the doorway, making her jump. It broke the spell. Serena rubbed the damp palms of her hands down her trousers. Everything would be fine. If she remembered any details of the night Caitlin disappeared, then that would be helpful, to her and to the police. If she remembered nothing, then she was no worse off than she was now.

"Yes, thank you," she said. She could see that Eve had the vacuum cleaner in tow and was keen to get on. "I think I'll go for a walk."

Up in her room, she pulled a padded jacket from the heavy

mahogany wardrobe and slipped it on over her jeans and navy-and-white-striped jumper. The wardrobe, and a massive, carved wooden chest that took up almost all of the opposite wall, gave the room a dark and oppressive feel. Serena pulled the coat close, taking some sort of comfort from its warmth. She'd paid a flying visit home to the flat to grab a few clothes on her way to Minster Lovell; her packing for her US trip hadn't been remotely appropriate for England in March.

She fumbled her phone into her coat pocket and zipped it up, changed her sneakers for hiking boots and went back downstairs. The sound of the droning vacuum cleaner reached her from the breakfast room. There was no one else about.

Serena stepped out of the pub door and into a puddle. It must have rained overnight although the ragged gray dawn had now given way to something brighter and more hopeful. The wind was chilly and made her eyes smart. She wished she had thought to bring a scarf, hat and gloves as well. She'd have to pick them up later. Her hair, long, fine and mouse brown, darker than Caitlin's had been, was already tangling and blinding her. She brushed it away from her face impatiently and pulled up the hood of the jacket.

A horn blared and Serena took a hasty step back. The pub was right on the corner where the road narrowed to cross the humpbacked medieval bridge over the river. Standing here on the edge of the tarmac was asking to be mowed down by commuters who were in too much of a hurry to appreciate either the view or the tourists, so instead she slipped around the side of the building into the car park. Her small blue car was the only vehicle there, tucked away in a corner beneath a sprawling ivy-clad fence, and for a moment Serena experienced an almost overwhelming urge to jump in it and simply drive away, running from the past yet again.

Instead, she crossed the car park to a wooden gate that opened directly onto the water meadow and set off, not toward the village, but across the fields toward the ruined hall. The River Windrush, a small and picturesque tributary of the Thames, was narrow here, and slow, winding lazily in a series of loops amongst the dead stalks of bulrushes, bugle and ragged robin. A path cut through the grass. It was dry immediately under foot although Serena sensed the mud below. She walked slowly, listening to the splash of the river and the quacking of the ducks beneath the bridge.

The edge of Minster Lovell Hall land was marked by a clump of tall trees, poplar and sycamore and plane. There were also some ancient oak trees garlanded with mistletoe in their high branches. Serena remembered her grandmother, who had died when they were in their early teens, warning her and Caitlin not to eat the berries because they were poisonous. Serena's mother had thrown a fit when she had heard and suggested the mistletoe should be cut down, whereupon their grandmother had retorted that the plant had been sacred to the druids and that they had no right to destroy something that possessed mystical powers. Serena's mother wasn't remotely mystical, but she had recognized defeat when she saw it and the mistletoe stayed. Serena felt a rush of pleasure to see that it was still here.

The poplar and oak trees encircled a large square, shallow pond overgrown with weed and grasses that Serena remembered well. In the summer holidays she and Caitlin had played here, hunting for shards of pots and the slivers of tesserae from the mosaic floors of the Roman villa that was said to be hidden beneath the pool. Now Serena could see nothing in the murky green waters. Rooks and jackdaws rose in a cacophony from the treetops as she passed. There was no path as such anymore; her footsteps led her between the pond and the river and right into the ruined hall itself, all fallen stone and jagged ledges.

Serena stopped, took a deep breath and tested her reaction. This was where she had been found on the night that Caitlin had disappeared, huddled semiconscious in the corner of the tower. Apparently, when someone had touched her shoulder to rouse her, she had screamed hysterically, but she remembered nothing of that. She remembered nothing at all before the moment she had come round in hospital in Oxford, asking what had happened.

She walked slowly over the grassed courtyard toward the range of buildings on the other side. These had been the kitchens and stables—there was a sign board in front of her that the Trust had installed to give visitors an image of how the now-crumbling buildings had once appeared—and to her left soared the high walls of the great hall and the chambers beyond. Serena had half expected to feel a rush of panic by now and some recognition that something so traumatic had taken place here that her mind had blanked it out. She waited for her heartbeat to accelerate and her chest to tighten as it had done in the past when she had experienced panic attacks. Nothing happened. Both her mind and body seemed indifferent to this place, recognizing nothing strange nor familiar about it.

Then she saw the manor house. It was sheltering in the western corner of the ruins, next to the church, small and square, gray, with lichened stone and a slate roof and diamond-paned windows. A shaft of sunlight cut through the trees like a blade. Immediately, the green of lawn and hedge lit up as though illuminated, displaying a neat box parterre and sculpted yew trees.

Home.

Serena felt the visceral pull of it, the roots that anchored her to this place and to her past. It was a shock to feel it so strongly. *This* she recognized. She had turned her back on the place and had run from family tragedy and the horror of Caitlin's loss, but the ties connecting her to Minster Lovell Hall were too strong to be broken. Instead of fighting the sensation of inevitability, she relaxed into it and let the sense of coming home wash through her. It felt incredibly comforting. Tears stung her eyes. She had not been expecting that at all.

The house looked very different from the way she remembered it. When she had visited in her childhood and teens, the gardens had been wild and tangled, an adventure playground of overgrown pathways and ponds and hidden sunny corners. The house too had had a more tumbledown air about it, but everything looked so much better cared for now that it belonged to a heritage charity. Her grandfather had sold it about a year after Caitlin's disappearance, when hope of her return had died and his health was fading with it. Serena's grandmother had already died five years before that. There had been nothing to keep him there.

Ten years of renovation and conservation had wrought a huge difference. The place sparkled, beckoning the visitors in. Serena felt a pang of loss, as though the changes that had swept away the dust and decay had also brushed aside something precious—those golden sunlit hours with Caitlin, lying on the lawns reading, playing hide-and-seek between the trees, so many other memories… Until that last summer when both she and Caitlin had been moody teens in their different ways, and for a little while it felt as though the whole structure of their twinship had become frighteningly fragile.

There was a small sign by the gate with an arrow pointing around to the side of the building and the words Estate Office and Information Center printed neatly below. That, Serena assumed, was where she would find the ticket office and possibly a guidebook. It would be interesting to see how Minster Heritage had interpreted the history of the site.

"Serena? Serena Warren?"

Serena froze. For a moment she thought she had imagined the sound of her name, that it was no more than an illusion conjured by the past. Then a shadow drifted across her and she realized she was not alone.

She turned slowly.

A man was standing beneath an arched doorway at a right angle to her. The sunlight was behind him so that he appeared no more than a silhouette. Above him soared the remaining wall of the great hall with its huge pointed window and weathered stone tracery. He took a step toward her, out of the shadow of the door, and the light fell on his face. Immediately, she recognized him. It was Jack Lovell.

Serena's heart did a little flip, but before she could start to analyze her feelings, something shifted in her mind, like brightly colored kaleidoscope pieces breaking up to reform in a new pattern. The scene—Jack Lovell walking toward her through the ruins—was so familiar that she was sure it must have happened before, and yet she couldn't quite grasp it… And before she could see what the pattern was, the images had gone.

She watched as he approached her. He'd certainly changed.

Gone was the lanky boy she remembered, who had always been absorbed in his books. He had grown up tall and broad shouldered, wearing the same sort of outdoor gear she was dressed in: boots, jeans and padded jacket. He had a lean, intelligent face, and when the wind ruffled his thick dark hair, he raised a hand to smooth it down again. Serena recognized the gesture and again felt that tiny skip of the heart. How odd that she had been thinking of him only that morning, and here he was.

"Jack," she said. She felt dumbfounded, too surprised to pick her words. "My God, what are you doing here?"

Jack looked amused and immediately Serena felt as self-conscious as she had been around him eleven years before when she had had her crush on him.

"Sorry," she said. "I mean… How are you? It's been such a long time…" She could feel the color crawling into her cheeks. Could she sound more gauche?

"I'm very well, thank you," Jack said. "I didn't expect to see you here, either." He held out a hand formally to shake hers, and Serena felt the warmth of his smile. She might not have kept in touch with Jack, but she knew that these days he worked as an investigative journalist, specializing in high profile cases of corruption and miscarriages of justice. This easy charm, cloaking an authoritative manner, was part of his professional armory. She'd caught a few of his programs on TV, and he'd been very compelling on-screen. She could see that the camera would love him.

She realized her hand was still in his and pulled it away hastily.

"I come to Witney to visit my grandfather as often as I can," she said, a little at random. "He's in a care home there. But I don't come to Minster Lovell usually because of Caitlin—the memories, you know—it's too hard..." She stopped, hot and embarrassed, conscious that she was talking too much because she wanted to smooth over the awkwardness of their meeting. Why couldn't she just shrug it off; say that it was nice to see him again and simply walk away? She'd mentioned Caitlin now, but she really didn't want to talk about her sister. Jack was as good as a stranger now, not someone to confide in, and her feelings about being back in Minster Lovell were too personal to share.

"I saw in the press that Caitlin's body had been found," Jack said. "I'm very sorry."

"Thank you," Serena said. She could feel him watching her, his dark gaze steady and rather too insightful for comfort. She didn't want to get drawn into a discussion. "It's been a difficult time," she said carefully.

"I imagine it must be exceptionally hard for your whole family," Jack said. He shifted a little. "Now we've met up," he said, "I wonder whether you could spare me a moment? There's something I wanted to ask—"

"Jack!" A woman scrambled through the ruined doorway and hurried toward them. She had a bulging rucksack and an air of preoccupation. "I thought we were meeting at the church," she said, ignoring Serena completely as she swung the rucksack off her shoulders and dumped it on the ground. It had a logo with Minster Archaeology written on it in bright blue letters. "Do you want to see the dig site or not?" she went on. "We need to get in there before the rest of the forensics team arrives."

Serena saw a flash of what looked like impatience in Jack's eyes, swiftly gone. "Yes, of course," he said. Then: "Zoe, you remember Serena Warren?" He stressed her name slightly.

"Serena, my sister, Zoe. She was a few years younger than us, so you may not have seen much of her back in the days when we all hung out together."

"Hi," Zoe said, barely looking up from fiddling with her rucksack to give Serena a quick nod. "I'm sorry to be blunt, Jack, but since this is, strictly speaking, a police investigation as well as an archaeological dig, and you're not meant to be here, you don't really have time to chat with your fans right now."

"Zoe," Jack said, and there was steel in his tone this time, "Serena is Caitlin Warren's sister."

Zoe's mouth fell open. She straightened up slowly, her face suddenly scarlet. "Shit," she said. "I'm so sorry. I hadn't realized that the police had invited you to attend today. They told me they hadn't spoken to Caitlin's family yet about her burial site—"

Serena felt Jack shift beside her. "I think we're at cross-purposes," he started to say, but it was too late. Serena was remembering the conversation she had had back in Surrey with the local police constable, a bashful young trainee fresh from college who had turned his hat round and round in his hands whilst talking to her:

They located your sister's body not far from where she disappeared in Minster Lovell, Miss Warren. I'm sorry that at present we can't give you any further details yet about her burial…

Serena felt coldness seep through her. Her sense of shock was visceral. She started to shake. Jack was saying something else but she cut right across him, surprised to discover that her voice was quite steady.

"Do I have this correct?" she said to him. "You're here to see my sister's grave, for some reason before we, her family, have been given *any details* about her death and burial?"

Zoe made a strangled sound. "It's my fault, not Jack's," she said, scrabbling the windblown dark hair away from her hot face. "I invited him because I knew he'd been Caitlin's friend, and there were some odd circumstances about the whole thing that I thought he might be interested in from a professional perspective—"

Serena swung around on her. "You make it sound as though this is some sort of amateur investigation," she said coldly, "instead of a police inquiry." She turned back to Jack. "My God, Jack," she said, "is this even *legal*, let alone ethical? I…" Her voice cracked. "I can't believe this."

"Serena," Jack said. "It's not how it seems. I'm very sorry. Look—" he ran a hand through his hair "—can we go and get a coffee and talk this through? Please let me explain."

"No," Serena said. She knew she had to get away. She could feel her self-control held on the thinnest of threads, all the tension and emotion of the past few days suddenly piling in on her. She didn't want to break down in front Jack or Zoe, but particularly not Jack. The contrast between his calmness and the dangerous anger she felt inside was too stark and was fed by the knowledge that everyone, it seemed, knew more about Caitlin's death and burial than her family did.

The hurt filled her chest, and she felt as though she couldn't breathe. "I'd rather not talk about Caitlin," she said. "Not to you. Not now, not ever. Goodbye, Jack."

Chapter 4

ANNE

Yorkshire
February 1465

My wedding took place at Middleham Castle on the Feast Day of St. Valentine. I was five years old.

"It could not be a more auspicious day!" my nursemaid, Cicely, declared, as she and a number of the other women in the household prodded and pinned and sewed me into the gown that was to be my wedding dress. "The coming of spring—a day for love and romance! Keep still, Mistress Anne, or this needle will prick you and draw blood, which will be impossible to clean off the gown."

Cicely was only young, perhaps no more than sixteen years herself, though to me at the time that seemed ancient. She had cared for me since I had left the wet nurse, and I loved her for her good nature and her kindness. Her talk of romance I ignored, for whilst the other girls whispered and giggled about men and love tokens, I had no interest in such matters. I knew that marriage for a Neville was about alliances not affection. Even so, I hoped that I would like Francis. I thought I probably would. He sounded nice.

I had been to Middleham Castle before, so my mother told me, but I had been too young to remember. Traveling now in winter—for the snow had yet to release its grip on the high fells—was an experience all in itself as the wagons and packhorses scrambled up over the moors, sliding through mud and ice, we children thrown around as much as the luggage in the carts. I longed to ride, but was considered too young, though I had sat a horse from the time I was the smallest child.

"You must travel by coach to your wedding," Cicely said, trying to make me feel important, but the truth was that as I bounced about in the ruts and ditches, I was of as little consequence as the rest of the baggage.

Richmond, which we reached early in the afternoon, was a busy market town with a castle that belonged to our cousin King Edward. Father wished to stop there to eat, and to water and rest the horses, but the castle was woefully in disrepair and Mother turned up her nose at taking shelter there. The pale winter light was already fading and the frost was starting to set hard on the grass as she gave the order to continue on to Middleham. I heard Father swear under his breath to have his wishes countermanded, but he turned his horse to ride back and chivy the wagon train to follow. People came out of the cottages and shops to watch us pass by, staring at the gaudy banners of Fitzhugh and Neville, the packhorses with their stuffed saddlebags and their heaving sides, the men-at-arms on their powerful destriers. I clung to the sides of the wagon and stared back, drinking in the bustle of the marketplace where the scent of horse dung and sweet wines mingled with the cold air from the hills. I craned my neck, looking back as we went out through the town gate and the smoke and noise was left behind once again.

It was night by the time we arrived in Middleham. Our exhausted cavalcade dragged itself up the hill to the castle, which crouched as a dark shadow against the moonless sky. Here, though, unlike in Richmond, there was a brazier burning by the gate and soldiers stepping forward smartly to escort us inside. My uncle came out to meet us, which was a signal honor.

"We had quite given you up for the night," he said lightly, kissing my mother on the cheek. "What can possibly have taken you so long?"

It was not a real question, more a barb directed at my father, who flicked the dust off his sleeve and affected not to hear it. My aunt Anne, so richly garbed that she looked like a walking tapestry, then came forward to welcome us in her cool way. I was never sure whether she was unbearably proud or simply shy; despite the vividness of her gown, she was like a shadow in the bright glare cast by her husband. Though the Warwick title and fortune had originally been hers, the glory and show was all his. Behind her bobbed my two cousins Isabel and Anne, both older than I and frighteningly grown-up in my eyes; in the hierarchy of the Neville cousins they were so far above me that they would normally ignore me. Now, however, I was the bride and that required some small acknowledgment. They dropped polite curtseys and immediately backed away again, boredom etched on their faces. A moment later they were giggling together and turned their backs on us. My sister Elizabeth slipped her hand into mine and gave it a squeeze.

"Prideful," she grumbled under her breath.

I smiled at her. We sisters all squawked and squabbled at home, but we stood together against all comers, even our own family if they stepped out of line.

"I think Anne is shy," I said in mitigation of my younger cousin.

"What's Isabel's excuse?" Elizabeth sniffed.

I wondered where Francis Lovell was. He had not come to greet me, which seemed rather discourteous when we were to marry in two days' time, but perhaps he was still at his lessons. My uncle's household was renowned for the education he gave his pages, everything from mathematics to music, Latin to the art of war. No doubt Francis would be fearsomely clever.

The conversation of the adults flowed around me and over my head, and suddenly I felt very tired. The torchlight swam before my eyes—so many torches, illuminating every elegant and costly corner of my uncle's domain. It felt as though we had stepped into a minstrel's tale.

I yawned and gripped Elizabeth's skirts to keep my balance as I swayed on my feet. My uncle noticed and broke off his conversation to sweep me up into his arms. He smelled strongly of wine and musk, very different from the comforting scent of my father.

"The little maid is asleep on her feet," he said. "Let me show you to your chambers."

I was so tired and hungry that all was a blur after that; being carried up a turret stair to a fine chamber warm with a fire and sweetly scented with fresh rushes; a basin of water to wash, a bowl of broth and some rye bread and cheese to blunt my hunger. I was already drowsing by the time I had finished, and then Cicely was there to put me to bed between sheets that smelled of lavender, and it seemed that although it was my wedding that we had come to Middleham to celebrate, I was the least significant person in the castle as I slid straight into sleep.

★ ★ ★

The following morning, I woke early. It was impossible to stay quietly in bed when we were in so strange and new a place; I could barely keep still let alone stay in my chamber. Cicely was sleeping in a truckle bed beside mine, but she did not stir when I slipped from the room. I had made sure to climb out of the opposite side of the bed and to tiptoe away, but I knew Cicely to be a heavy sleeper. She had also taken some wine the previous night. Her breath smelled of it and she was snoring, her mouth open.

I had always been a confident child—that Neville arrogance again—and though I had probably dressed myself somewhat haphazardly, I had no second thoughts about setting out on my own to explore the castle. Indeed, I felt quite excited. The corridors bustled with people—servants, carrying steaming pails of water, others with fresh, sweet-scented rushes for the hall. A thin, hungry-looking clerk with a face like a hunting dog passed by deep in conversation with a self-important priest. An ample woman swept past me without a glance, a set of keys jangling at her waist. There were soldiers and huntsmen, chambermaids and scullery boys, there was the smell of cooking and the equally strong smell of animals. There was noise and color and people who were far too busy to notice one small, quick and curious child as I climbed spiral stairs and traversed sprawling corridors.

The castle was a warren, and it was only by chance that I stumbled out of a door in the south range of buildings and found myself beside the tiltyard. I had heard that there was to be a tournament and joust to celebrate my wedding to Francis, though no one had thought to ask me if that was the entertainment I preferred. They were already preparing the ground, erecting the barriers and building the pavilion for spectators. A group of tents mushroomed across the field behind the castle, accommodation for those knights and squires for whom there was no space on the castle. Grand as Middleham was, not everyone could be accommodated within its walls. The presence of the Earl had ensured that everyone who wanted advancement had flocked to the town. I wondered at their determination and ambition, to be prepared to freeze in the winter snows for a moment of my uncle's attention.

Hardly any men were out in the yard in the half-light of a cold February dawn, however. I saw two knights practicing swordplay over by the stables and a squire leading out a horse whose breath was clouding the frosty air. I almost missed the boy who was over by the archery butts releasing arrow after arrow into the target with a concentrated intensity that had something chilling about it in the cold morn.

Another boy emerged from around the side of the stables, more a young man, this, of fifteen or sixteen years. He looked vaguely familiar to me. He strode across to the butts and put a hand on the boy's arm. I saw the tension tighten in the bow and the way the boy loosed the last arrow before lowering his arm and turning to his companion. There was a brief conversation, then they walked slowly together toward the stables.

"That is my brother Francis and Richard of Gloucester." A girl had appeared beside me, wrapped up tight against the cold in a gown and several shawls. Seeing her so cozily attired made me realize that my feet in particular were as blocks of ice. A few years older than I, she was tall and fair with the most expressive gray eyes I had ever seen. She watched the two boys out of sight and then turned to smile at me. "You are Anne Fitzhugh, are you not? I am Joan Lovell. We were not introduced last night, which I think was a great oversight on Lord Warwick's part, but I suppose he had more important matters on his mind."

I tore my mind away from the memory of Francis Lovell sending arrow after arrow into the eye of the target with such concentrated intensity. "How do you do, Joan Lovell," I said. "They told me that you and Francis are twins."

"Yes," Joan said. Then: "I am the elder, of course."

It explained, perhaps, her brisk air of organization and the slightly protective way in which she spoke of her brother.

"Francis is diligent in his practice," I said, "to be out at the butts so early on the day before his wedding."

A faint frown wrinkled Joan's brow. "Since our father died, all Francis has done is fight with sword or bow," she said. "He is angry, and he takes out his feelings on the archery butts."

This was not good to hear. "Why is he angry?" I said.

Joan took my hand. "Why, you are so cold!" she exclaimed. "Come inside. I will take you to meet my mother and sister, and we shall have some black currant juice to warm us and I will tell you all about Francis." She drew me back through the archway and tucked my hand through her arm. "We are housed in the round tower," she said. "It is this way."

I hung back, belatedly remembering that no one knew where I was. "I should go back," I said. "My nursemaid will be fretting over my absence."

"She was still asleep when I went to your chamber just now," Joan said with a giggle. "I was looking for you to make your acquaintance," she added. "I told your mother that you would be with me, meeting your new family." She propelled me along the corridor, dodging the people heading in the opposite direction. "I am still finding my way," she said, chewing her lip as she checked which doorway, which staircase to take. "Middleham is much larger than Minster Lovell. It confuses me."

"It is larger than Ravensworth, too," I said consolingly. "My uncle has to have a larger castle than anyone but the King."

Joan giggled. "I like you, Anne Fitzhugh," she said. "We shall be friends."

"Why is Francis angry?" I repeated. "Does he not wish to marry me?" It had not occurred to me that Francis would dispute the Earl of Warwick's decision on our future any more than I would. He was the King's ward; Edward had handed his knight's training to Lord Warwick and with it his entire future. It was the order of things.

Joan stopped, pulling me into a dark corner beneath a spiral stair. It smelled queasily of a mixture of damp stone, latrines and ale. Not all corners of Middleham were as fragrant as my aunt might have wished.

"It is not your fault, Anne," she said earnestly. "Francis hated our father. He was cruel and spiteful to us all, and we were helpless to resist him. Francis could not bear to see how he treated our mother, but what could he do to protect us? And now Mama is to marry again—so soon!—and Francis has been sent here and has been told he must wed you… He is acutely conscious of his powerlessness in all things and it angers him."

I had never thought of a child's situation in such terms before. I had accepted my marriage because it was common enough amongst the nobility to be wed at a young age, and it was precisely because I was so young that I had never questioned the way that we had no power. Children were moved like pawns on a chessboard, yet I could see that for a boy in particular, as he grew older, the lack of control over his own destiny might well be deeply frustrating. As for the thought that the late Lord Lovell might have been cruel to his family, that was also disturbing to me, with a father as indulgent and kind as mine. I felt suddenly as though I was on the edge of many dark ideas that I could not understand. I thought of the arrow thudding into the target, of the repressed fury in Francis's frame, and I shuddered. I hated to think that I had a part, no matter how unwitting, in adding to his misery.

Joan squeezed my hand as though she understood. "I am sorry," she said. "It is better that you knew, for Francis will never tell you himself. He is very close with his secrets and confides in no one. And you must not fear—" she sounded earnest again "—for he is the kindest of brothers and will, I am sure, be the kindest of husbands, too."

"We shall not be living together for many years yet," I said, retreating in my mind to the safety of my familiar life at Ravensworth. "It does not matter."

Nevertheless, I hung back a little as Joan led me up to the chambers she was sharing with her mother and her young sister, Frideswide. Suddenly, I was not so content for this marriage as I had thought.

It was easy, however, to distract me with pastries and warm black currant juice. We sat before the fire, and Lady Lovell, who seemed a gentle and somehow faded woman, told me of Francis's home at Minster Lovell in Oxfordshire. Frideswide, who was no more than a baby, sat on her mother's lap and stared at me with her big gray eyes. Francis made no appearance, and I wondered whether the first time I met him would be when we were standing before the altar tomorrow.

But no. I had drained my cup and was about to leave, when there was a rap at the door and a certain amount of bustle, which in my experience always heralded someone important. I wondered if my mother had come to retrieve me in person, or even if the Earl of Warwick himself had come to check on the comfort of his guests. Then the door swung inward and the room seemed to be invaded by men. They brought with them the smell of fresh air and leather, and a sort of purposeful feeling that suggested that their business was always so much more important than that of women.

Lady Lovell thrust the baby into the arms of a servant and stood up, smoothing her skirts.

"Sir William—" She sounded flustered. "You should have warned me you planned to visit—"

Joan pinched my arm. "It is Sir William Stanley," she hissed in my ear. "He is to marry Mama."

Stanley was not alone. Lady Lovell's confusion only deepened when she saw that the King's brother, Richard of Gloucester, was of the party and with him Francis, and any number of other young squires from Warwick's household. The scene in the room now reminded me of nothing so much as a fox getting in a henhouse as Lady Lovell scurried about to make her unexpected guests welcome. I was, once again, completely forgotten, at least until Richard of Gloucester pushed his way through the throng to find me.

"Cousin Anne!" He took my hand and kissed it formally. We were not, strictly speaking, cousins, but we were of course related, both with Neville mothers, and that counted for everything.

"My lord." I dropped my prettiest curtsey. I had not met Richard often, but I liked him. He was not dazzling like his brother King Edward, nor arrogant without cause like his other brother George. He was quieter, more thoughtful. I remembered the way he had gone to find Francis that morning where he stood alone with his anger out in the cold of the archery butts. I was glad Richard had befriended Francis in his lonely exile here at Middleham.

"You will be wishing to meet your future husband, cousin," Richard said, drawing Francis forward as though he had arranged this meeting specifically to please me. "What good fortune that we find you here."

We stood looking at one another, Francis Lovell and I. I saw a thin boy with tousled fair hair that was a shade darker than Joan's and whose face was just starting to lose the roundness of childhood. His eyes were the same gray as Joan's, too, but whilst her gaze was so clear and warm, his was shadowed with something that made him look older than his years. I felt my heart contract, but not with fear, more with pity. Then, to my surprise, he smiled at me. I will never forget that smile. It banished the darkness from his eyes and lit his whole face.

I felt myself relax. *We can be friends. Everything will be all right.*

I smiled back at him and put my hand into his. "I am very happy to meet you, Francis Lovell," I said.

Chapter 5

SERENA

Minster Lovell
Present Day

Serena walked away from Jack and Zoe and she didn't look back. Her chest still ached with fury and pain. Surely Jack should *know* how difficult this was for her. Could he not *see* how she felt? How dare he come here and ask questions, as though this was some sort of news story rather than the hideously complicated and hurtful history of her twin's disappearance and death.

She pushed open the wrought-iron gate that led up the path to the front door of the manor house, pausing for a second with her hand on the cool metal. For a moment she felt a little dizzy. She did not want to share her quest to find Caitlin with anyone else. This was too personal, her secret, her burden. Yet somehow Jack was here before her, asking questions, doing his own investigation. Perhaps it was petty of her, but she felt possessive of Caitlin. Whatever there was to find out, she wanted to know first. The knowledge that Caitlin's body had been found at the church and that Jack knew before the police had got around to telling the family was incredibly hurtful. She wondered if the entire village knew.

Looking back over her shoulder at last, she saw that Zoe had gone, but Jack was still watching her with that concentrated, perceptive gaze. Once again, she felt a tug of memory and a persistent sense that in some way, Jack held the key to something crucial that she had forgotten. She shook her head, turning away again, and concentrated instead on the manor garden in front of her, on the sound of the sparrows in the old apple tree, where the faintest of fresh new green shoots stood out against the gnarled bark, and on the sparkle of the dew on the neat box hedge. If anything could help to soothe her, it had to be this place.

It felt peaceful and Serena felt the ache in her chest ease. A moment before she'd been on the verge of ringing the police and complaining about Zoe and Jack, but now she let the quiet of the garden wash over her and take away some of the pain. It was natural to want to lash out because she was hurting, but it wouldn't do any good. She was meeting with Inspector Litton in a few hours. They could discuss it then.

She followed the direction sign around the side of the building, rounding the western end of the building and found herself in the courtyard. Here, once again, things had changed; the old lichen-covered cobbles were scrubbed clean and the stable doors mended and repainted. The archway that had once led through to the orchard and walled garden was blocked by a wooden gate. Renovation in Progress, the sign read. No Entry.

An elderly man was rolling up the blind in the shop, a big picture window revealing a room filled with soft furnishings in tasteful heritage colors: cushions in pastel spring blue and yellow china mugs with flower patterns, throws and picnic baskets. Serena pushed open the door and found herself amongst racks of postcards and local history books, toys, scarves and gardening paraphernalia, ornaments and jewelry.

"Hello!" The receptionist, whose name badge proclaimed him to be a volunteer by the name of Nigel, looked pleased to see her. "We've just opened. Would you like to look round the house?"

"Yes, please," Serena said. She took out her purse.

"Have you been here before?" The man was inserting her ticket into a neat little guide leaflet.

"Yes," Serena said. Then, feeling she should make more of an effort, added, "it was a long time ago, though. The house wasn't open to the public then."

"It's a lovely little place," the man said. "A Tudor farmhouse really, incorporating some earlier parts of the medieval hall. It's all in the guidebook if you would like to buy a copy?" He waved a thicker, glossier book hopefully in her direction.

"I'm all right, thanks," Serena said. "I'll enjoy walking around and just soaking up the atmosphere."

"The self-guided tour starts through the door and on the right," Nigel said, emptying a bag of change into the till with a clatter. "There are information boards in each room and arrows signposting which way to go. You can't get lost."

"Thanks," Serena said, stifling a rebellious urge deliberately to do the tour in reverse order. "I'll see you later."

Nigel raised a hand in farewell and turned his attention back to the till, and Serena stepped back outside and obediently followed the arrow that said Entrance, pausing for a moment to read a board that told her what she already knew: Minster Lovell Hall was no stately home despite its name; when the old hall had fallen into ruins in the sixteenth century, a small part had been carved out and retained to serve as a farm. It was this unpretentious stone building that remained, with its gray walls, mullioned windows and uneven floors, upgraded a little over the centuries as the family who lived there upgraded themselves as well, from yeomen farmers to gentlemen. The place had passed through a number of hands down the centuries.

Serena couldn't remember when her grandparents had bought the place. She wasn't sure if she had ever known. It had been their home from her earliest childhood, but she did remember her mother once saying that the house had been in a terrible mess at the beginning and that her grandparents had lovingly restored it over the years. She knew it hadn't been the place where her father and Polly had grown up—they had been born and lived in a London suburb—so perhaps her grandparents had moved around the time she and Caitlin had been born, or a little bit before.

The back door from the yard led into the kitchens, and for a moment Serena thought she was entirely in the wrong place. The 1990s cupboards that had once been so shiny and modern, together with the gas cooker and the stainless-steel sink, had gone, as had the lino and almost everything else she remembered. The room had been stripped back to bare white walls and old timber beams. The information board stated that the kitchen and scullery were part of the original Tudor house, possibly incorporating elements of the medieval hall. Only the huge old fireplace was familiar to Serena. The room had a chill to it, perhaps from the emptiness or perhaps something more—a sense of abandonment that places sometimes had when they had once been busy and were now silent and unused.

A stone-floored passageway led into the room Serena remembered as the sitting room, but which her grandmother had always called the parlor. She was amused to see that the heritage trust had also chosen to use this terminology, pointing out with some pride the stone-mullioned windows, the oak paneling and the elegant plaster ceiling that had been painted white to reflect the light into the room.

A figure passed the window, making Serena jump. A couple in outdoor clothing with two young children, one in an all-terrain buggy, were making their way up the path toward the Information Center. Serena wondered how her grandmother, so proper, so fastidious, would have taken to people invading her home. Professor Warren, as Serena's grandmother insisted on being addressed, had been a Classics scholar and lecturer at Oxford. Richard Warren, in contrast, had appeared to have very little formal education and was, Serena thought, as much a doer as a thinker. Her grandmother had been quite brusque and sharp, whilst her grandfather was gentle and thoughtful, yet somehow the pairing had worked. Serena realized now that she was older just how much Pamela Warren must have had to struggle to establish herself at Oxford in the 1960s. It had still been a male bastion, and that probably accounted for her grandmother's hard edges. Polly had inherited some of her mother's drive to succeed, but with a softer, warmer approach.

So quiet was the house that Serena heard the click of the gate closing behind the visitors and the excited high-pitched chatter of the elder child as they made their way across the courtyard. She sat down on an upright chair of dark wood with spindly legs and a cane base. It quivered, too fragile to be used. Once again Serena was reminded of Caitlin. Caitlin, whose memory was as insubstantial as gossamer. She could visualize her twin perched on this very chair, swinging her legs, as she chattered about something that excited her. Caitlin had always been enthused, never able to keep still for long.

The hall looked exactly as she remembered it. Serena realized that her grandfather, or the lawyers acting on his behalf, must have sold off some of the contents along with the house. There were the same thin, faded rugs on the floor, the heavy Victorian furniture, the grandfather clock with the painted lion on its face, the eyes moving left and right at each tick. She and Caitlin had screamed and run away the first time they'd seen that. It had given her nightmares; she'd thought the lion would jump down from the clock in the middle of the night, find her in her bedroom and eat her.

Serena waited, weighed the memories, but felt no emotional response to them other than a pang of nostalgia. It was as though she was watching a series of images unspool through her mind rather than reliving the experience. In their worst fights, Jonah had told her that she was cold and emotionless. She didn't mean to be, and she didn't think that she was really, although she certainly hadn't been able to give him what he had wanted. But it was true that after Caitlin had gone, leaving a wake of emotional devastation behind, Serena had emerged with her ability to feel deeply somehow impaired. She wanted to love; she felt as though she was short-changing herself and other people, yet it didn't come. She'd brushed off her former friends and had only over time discovered an ability to reconnect with her family and those closest to her. This, she thought, was natural, but perhaps Jonah had been right that she wouldn't give her love easily in case it was snatched away again as devastatingly as it had been with Caitlin. Or perhaps, she thought with a grimace, she simply hadn't loved Jonah enough. He hadn't been the right person for her. Either way it wasn't simply her memory that was missing. When Caitlin had gone, she had taken a fragment of Serena's soul with her.

She thought of Polly fretting over whether stepping back inside Minster Manor would trigger all her lost memories and cause her grief. Well, that hadn't happened. Clearly, she needed more of a stimulus to remember anything significant. All she felt was the ache of happy times that had been lost—and that odd sensation that Jack Lovell was in some way a key to the past.

With a sigh, Serena walked down the south corridor where there was a second, smaller parlor that her grandfather had used as his study, opened the door and stood for a moment in the patch of sunlight that flooded the room.

This had always been her favorite place in the entire house. It had been a room filled with all the treasures that had intrigued her—her grandfather's books were an eclectic mix of fiction, natural history, folklore, civil engineering, biography and many other topics, and they had piled up on the shelves and overflowed at random onto the floor, utterly dissimilar to the serried ranks of classical scholarship on her grandmother's shelves. The room had also held photographs of Serena's grandparents looking impossibly glamorous at dinner dances and parties in the 1950s, and then there were bottles of colored sand and costumed dolls from package tour holidays in the 1970s, a giant metal key, a plastic model of a medieval castle, a strange stone compass and various other random items. The room had also housed an ancient gramophone player, and Serena could remember the repetitive scratch of the needle, poised to pour out the notes of "Elizabethan Serenade" into the room from an ancient 78 record.

Now there was no music, only a blackbird singing from the

bough of a yew outside the window… Serena blinked. The musty smell of closed rooms was suddenly strong. The room was nothing like the study she remembered for it had been re-created as a second parlor, the "Tudor Parlor" the information board told her, with a couple of tapestries on the walls and some rather uncomfortable wooden furniture softened by piles of cushions. Some dark portraits stared down from the walls. Serena wondered whose ancestors they were; they certainly weren't hers.

The oak staircase to the right of the parlor led to the first floor and the bedrooms. As Serena climbed the stairs, she felt her heartbeat increase. It felt as though this, at last, was bringing her closer to Caitlin. Here they had shared a room, whispered together after the lights were out, tiptoed across the uneven floorboards to climb onto the window seat and gaze out over the garden on the nights of the full moon.

A door opened abruptly to her left, spilling a family out onto the landing and making Serena jump almost out of her skin. She had thought she was alone in the house. A small boy dressed as a knight with a plastic sword ran past her and into the room, his footsteps clattering over the floor. Behind him came a girl a few years older in a long dress and a cone-shaped headdress, also brandishing a plastic sword. Both children flung themselves up onto the big four-poster with shrieks of excitement.

"They love it here." A man, grasping the hand of a third child, threw Serena a slightly harassed smile. "It's great that they can dress up and play on the furniture. Most places don't allow, it but I think it makes history come alive."

Serena smiled politely. There was a clothes rack in the corner of the room laden with different costumes. The girl had swapped the princess outfit for a cavalier's frilly shirt and plumed hat. The boy was still bouncing excitedly on the scarlet tapestry–covered bed. Any connection she might have felt to the past was severed by the immediacy of noise and activity dragging at her attention. She would have to come back again when it was quiet.

Serena was halfway down the stairs when she saw a girl in a green coat. She was on the bottom step, her hand on the smooth oaken rail. In that moment, the door into the walled garden opened, letting in a dazzling, diamond-lozenge shape of sunlight and with it, the honey scent of buddleia and roses. Serena heard laughter and voices:

Caitlin! Wait for me!

The girl paused. Then, with a patter of footsteps and a flash of emerald green she whisked away through the door, leaving Serena with the impression of long blond hair and smiling green eyes.

Serena's heart started to pound in her throat so violently she was afraid she would pass out. She gripped the banister until the unyielding wood made her fingers cramp. She could still hear the girl's laughter and see that mocking flash of green:

Catch me if you can…

She felt as though she had been running after Caitlin all of her life.

Serena stumbled down the stairs, almost tripping over the threadbare carpet runner, and rushed to the door, her hot palms coming up against the cool glass panels. She fumbled with the handle, but it did not turn. She tried again, but the door remained obstinately closed. Then she saw the sign, the same one that had been on the gate from the courtyard. No Entry. Renovation. Work In Progress.

Serena banged her hands against the door frame. "Caitlin!" Her voice was shaky, barely more than a croak. She tried again, louder, and the name bounced off the walls of the hall and came back at her like an echo.

"Caitlin…"

There was no one in the passageway, and she could see no one out in the garden. Nor were there any roses or buddleia or summer flowers, because this was March and it was the pale mauve of pulmonaria that mingled in the borders with the peeping yellow of primrose.

Serena shivered. The sun had gone behind a pile of gray clouds and the air looked chill. A blackbird called in alarm from a tumbling ivy, but the garden was empty.

Gradually, Serena's breathing returned to normal. She felt cold. Upstairs, the voices of the children still echoed along the corridor, but there was no one down here with her; no one but the ghosts of herself and her twin sister whom she had alternately been running from and looking for for ten long years. Caitlin, who had disappeared one hot July at Minster Hall and who, at some point between then and now, had died.

Chapter 6

ANNE

Ravensworth Castle
July 1470

In the summer of the year 1470, when I was ten years old, my father raised a rebellion against the King.

There had been much talk of revolt in the previous twelve months. My uncle, the Earl of Warwick, had lost patience with the way the Queen's kin, the Woodvilles, had the King's ear and the pick of the richest noble marriages. He had been the first to rise up in protest, along with the King's brother George, Duke of Clarence, who had an eye to taking the throne himself. The North had been quick to follow their lead, anger and dissent flaring up like so many small fires that burned themselves out fast and fierce, but left a smoldering resentment. The summer of 1470 was hot and the countryside felt like a tinderbox. The lake ran dry and all the fish died. We could neither eat nor pickle them quick enough. No sooner had Lord Warwick been pardoned than he rebelled once again, and this time my father supported his betrayal.

Even at so young an age I had been aware of the swirl of rumor, the messengers who had come and gone by night, the secret meetings and the whispers of treason. The world felt unsteady, as though it might tip over at any moment and tumble us all into the unknown. And then it did.

I had not been able to sleep that night for there was tension coiled tight about Ravensworth, although perhaps Joan and Frideswide Lovell did not feel it as they were both dead to the world when I slid from the bed that morning. They had come to live with us after the death of their mother, and I was happy to have their company. Joan in particular had become a fast friend to me. Then, the previous year, Francis had also joined us. His education in Lord Warwick's household alongside the King's brother had ended with Warwick's treason, and as he was my husband, it was deemed appropriate that my father should take over his knight's training. What he thought of Ravensworth after the grandeur of Middleham I did not know for Francis, fourteen now and on the cusp of manhood, was as close with his feelings as he had ever been.

It was a beautiful morning the day my father led his troops away. The air was soft and warm in the chamber and the light was already spilling across the floor, though I could tell by its paleness that it was still early. Yet despite the gentleness of the day, I knew that something was wrong. I could also hear the hum of the castle awake, the muted noise of men and horses, of an expedition being prepared. As I slipped into my clothes as quietly as possible, I felt my heart start to race.

The turret stair was dark, the torch burning low now the night was spent. In my haste to descend, I stumbled and almost fell. Some sort of desperation possessed me. I had a sense of urgency and fear that something terrible was going to happen and that I had to stop it or it would be too late. My chest was bursting with bright pain as I ran into the courtyard and found it empty.

I was too late. Clustered by the gate were the grooms and servants who had been left behind. I saw my mother, too, her red hair loose and blowing like a flag in the breeze, her dignity gathered about her as befitted the lady of Ravensworth. The steward, Grimshaw, and the captain of the guard, were both paying stiff attendance to her. They knew who ruled here. And away over the hills to the west I saw a line of horsemen flying the Fitzhugh standard, bright azure blue and gold, as sunlit and hopeful as the early-morning sky. I blinked away tears of frustration and disappointment. My father had left without saying goodbye to me.

"What are you doing here?"

It was Francis who had come upon me. I did not want him to see me crying.

"He left without saying goodbye," I said foolishly, scrubbing the tears away. "How could he?"

To me it was the most heinous crime, for I worshipped my father and thought that his love for me was identical to mine for him. I could not comprehend that I might get lost within the vastness of his other concerns. It was a shock.

Francis sighed. "He will be back."

I turned on him fiercely. "How do you know? He is in rebellion against the King. He might *die*."

Francis looked at me properly then. The gangly youth I had first met four years before was starting to fill out his frame and look like a man. It occurred to me that had he been a year or so older, Father would most certainly have taken him with him as one of his squires. His gray gaze was clear, and, I thought, kind in the face of my hopeless attempts to hide my grief. He put a hand on my arm and drew me gently away from the curious gaze of the servants and men at arms.

"Here..." There was a corner of the courtyard where the early sun cut through the battlements and warmed the stone. He took off his cloak and made a cushion for me to sit. They were closing the gates now, and I shivered. For all the physical reassurance provided by the wall and towers of Ravensworth, I did not feel safe. The linchpin of my security was gone.

"You knew about the rebellion." Francis settled beside me. He had the hard cobbles to sit upon, but showed no discomfort. "I did not realize you were aware of it."

I cast him a look of contempt, made unkind by my misery. "I am not a child," I said, although manifestly I was. "I know that my kinsman Warwick has fled abroad and thrown in his lot with the old King Henry and his faction, and that there is to be a great uprising here at home to persuade King Edward to renounce his evil Woodville counselors and restore the Earl to favor."

"And that is what will almost certainly happen," Francis said. "The last part, at least. No blood will be shed. It is all a game—Lord Warwick will be restored to power and your father will come home."

"Just because that is what happened last time does not mean it will happen again," I argued. "If it is a game, it is one of the most dangerous kind. Surely the King must chafe against these constant challenges to his authority? I know that I would were I him. Even the ties of respect and family loyalty will break one day."

Francis looked at me now as though I had surprised him. Perhaps he thought I was too young to have such opinions or too female to express them. If that were the case, I thought, he had learned little in his year with us at Ravensworth. My mother had opinions, ideas and plans. Her daughters followed her example.

"What?" I said tartly. "Did you think I have no mind to think on such matters?"

Francis laughed. "I think you are as clever as the rest of the Nevilles," he said, "and may very well grow to be equally as dangerous. You have a better grasp of such matters than commanders five times your age." He tilted his head to one side and looked at me, really looked at me as a person now, not a child. "How old are you, Anne?" he asked. "Ten? Eleven?"

As he was my husband, he should have known the answer to that, but I let it pass.

"I am almost eleven," I said, "and I know things because I watch and listen. I think on things. It is not a pastime reserved for men."

"It's uncommon," Francis said, then, with a gleam of amusement in his eyes, added, "in anyone, man or woman. We would all be spared a great deal if men thought first and acted second."

"Or if they aired their grievances openly without threat or blame," I said.

"Now you ask too much," Francis said wryly. He half turned toward me and settled his shoulders more comfortably again the stone of the wall. "You are right, of course," he said. "Sooner or later the King will tire of Lord Warwick's power games and then…" He left the sentence unfinished, but I understood what he meant. Sooner or later Edward would strike back with violence, not diplomacy. *Let this not be that time*, I prayed fiercely. *Let Father return home safe.*

"You must know Lord Warwick well," I said. "You were his ward. Do you like him?"

Francis was silent for so long that I wondered whether he had not heard my question or more likely, had chosen not to answer it. Eventually, though, he stirred and glanced sideways at me.

"Your uncle is not a man you like or dislike," he said. He drew his knees up to his chin and wrapped his arms around them. "You have seen him," he said. "You know what I mean. He is either loved or hated. There is nothing in between. He dazzles people. His men adore him, as do the common folk hereabouts. That is why he can always command their loyalty. Gloucester says—" He stopped abruptly, cutting off whatever he had been about to share. I watched him curiously. I knew that Francis had formed a close friendship with Richard of Gloucester, the King's brother, when they had both been in Warwick's household, forged from the same kind of loyalty and respect that had once bound the King and the Earl of Warwick.

"The Duke of Gloucester says..." I prompted and waited.

"Gloucester says that the King will never be able to rule as he wishes whilst any baron has such power as Warwick," Francis said. "He says Edward must act now to finish this once and for all because Warwick made Edward and will never accept any loss of power except at the point of a sword."

I looked down and swallowed hard. Francis covered my clenched hands with one of his. "That does not mean that harm will come to your father," he said.

I knew he was trying to be kind, and this time I accepted his comfort.

"I fear for him," I said. "How could I not? And why..." I swallowed the tears again. "Why would he rebel simply because the Earl of Warwick commands it? I thought *we*, his family, were more important to him than all else."

I pressed my back against the sun-warmed stone of the tower and closed my eyes, tilting my face up to the breeze. It carried the scent of heather from the moors. It would have been quite lovely had we not been locked inside the castle, like rats in a trap, and had I not wanted to cry for what I saw as my father's betrayal.

"When you belong to a great family such as the Nevilles," Francis said, "matters of loyalty and statecraft are forever in the balance." He shifted a little closer to me. "It will define your life, Anne," he said, "as it has done your mother's. She is a Neville first and your father's wife second. Her loyalty is to her brother ahead of the King. As for your father, he knows his place is to support her and her kin before all else."

Father put that loyalty ahead of his own children, I thought. He put Lord Warwick before his allegiance to the King. To me that felt wrong, and I knew that the sting of it would stay with me forever. In that moment I swore that if there were a child needing my protection, their needs would be more powerful than any other force in the world.

"The way that men's allegiances shift and bend confuses me," I admitted. "It is a great thing to be loyal to one cause, I believe, but what if it is the wrong one?"

"In the end," Francis said, "you answer to your own conscience—and to God alone." His tone lightened. "Your father and I," he said, "are in very similar situations. Both of us are mere barons married into a powerful dynasty."

Despite my unhappiness, I gave a splutter of laughter. "You will be a rich man one day, Francis Lovell! You will be loaded with titles when you come fully into your inheritance. You are no *mere baron*."

Francis did not join me in my laughter. "Sometimes," he said, "I wish I were."

It was the first time I had seen the matter from his perspective. In my mother's family it was a given that ambition, money and status were to be celebrated. They were the glittering prizes. They were the reason my uncle would never relinquish his power by choice. Francis, though, had never been asked what he wanted. From the earliest age he had been used as a pawn on a chessboard, married off to me to bring more wealth and influence into the Neville family and tie another man to our dynasty's cause. I could scarcely be surprised that Francis, more man than boy now, might chafe against his position and consider where his loyalty should lie.

"What would you have done?" I asked on impulse. "If you were older, old enough to fight, would you be riding out now with my father? Would you support his cause?"

He did not hesitate. "No," he said. "I would not."

I was shocked. He had been Warwick's ward, then come to live amongst my family here at Ravensworth. Surely his first loyalty must be to us?

"I gave my oath to serve Gloucester years ago," Francis said with the ghost of a smile, seeing my disapproval plain on my face. "When I was the same age that you are now, Anne. I will never break that allegiance, just as Gloucester will never break his to the King."

"George of Clarence has betrayed his brother the King," I said. "Why would Gloucester not do the same?"

"Because not all men can be bought," Francis said a little grimly. He stood up and extended a hand to help me rise.

"Come, let's take some breakfast. Everything always seems better after food."

I accepted his hand and scrambled up, reaching for his cloak and dusting the dirt and moss from it before I passed it back to him. He tucked my hand through the crook of his elbow and it felt good to let it rest there, a small flicker of warmth to ward off the hurt of my father's actions.

The bustle of the great hall, the familiarity and smell of hot food also went some way to ease my unhappiness. Mother presided from the top of the table, and though there were fewer people and conversation was muted and heavy, the air of purposeful activity was very much as usual. We took our cue from her, calm and dignified in the face of all danger and uncertainty. She acted as though it was nothing that her husband and her brother were in open revolt against the King and so, under her firm hand, the tension eased a little.

Some five days later, I was with Mother when a messenger burst through the castle gates, bespattered with mud and smelling high of horses and sweat. I had been learning how to preserve dried apples in honey, and my fingers were still sticky with it when we heard the commotion of galloping hooves and men shouting. My mother looked up, sharp as a hunting dog scenting danger, and swept me out of the stillroom and into the courtyard, where Grimshaw came panting up to us:

"News from London, madam. The King's army marches on the North against your husband."

To me, London was as remote as Calais or Scotland. I had traveled little beyond Yorkshire, but I knew of course that all great matters emanated from London. I looked up at my mother's face and in that first second, before the words sank in and I felt the familiar clutch of fear for my father, I saw her expression. There was a gleam of satisfaction in her eyes. She looked pleased.

A moment later I wondered if I had been mistaken. "That is ill news indeed," she said, raising her voice a little so that everyone in the yard could hear her. "Send word to warn Lord Fitzhugh at once. See that the messenger is fed and watered and then send him in to speak with me privately."

She walked away, leaving me standing in the middle of the courtyard wondering whether I should follow in her wake. Already word was rippling outward, spreading through the corridors and chambers, men and women coming running to hear what news the messenger had brought. I traipsed slowly through the crowd, unnoticed, still puzzling over what I had witnessed.

The King was marching against my father's army and my mother had appeared *glad*. Then a second later she had declared it ill news. Had I misread her expression? Had I misunderstood? I could not make sense of it.

I watched as the Fitzhugh messenger came out to take the word to my father. He was in so great a hurry that he was still pulling on his jerkin as he leaped into the saddle, his horse's hooves striking sparks from the cobbles in its eagerness to be away. The excitement in the yard swelled and rolled like the waves of the sea, dying away as the man rode off hell for leather. Grimshaw ordered everyone back to work sharply; people melted away.

I let myself out of the postern gate and walked slowly down toward the river. It was quiet here but for the calling of the waterfowl. The sun rippled over the surface in dazzling bars of light. I washed my sticky hands and dried them on the skirts of my gown, then walked slowly back, head bent, toward the postern. I did not see the men until I had almost run straight into them—the master of the stables, the captain of the guard and a groom, who was not in Fitzhugh livery, leading another horse that was a great deal less showy than the first had been. Both man and horse were so plain, in fact, that they would disappear against the dun of the hillside.

I think I startled them. I heard the stable master swear and he shot out a hand to catch my arm, but then the captain stopped him.

"It is Fitzhugh's daughter," he said. "She'll not betray his cause."

The stable master released me and gave me an enormous wink. "Nothing to see here, little maid," he said, and the groom swung himself up onto the horse and rode away softly, keeping in the shadows of the overhanging willows, tracing the course of the river until he was out of sight, heading east, toward the coast.

The men wandered back to the stables as though I had been dismissed, forgotten, my silence assured, and I was left to walk back alone. I plucked the dry grasses from beside the path, shredding them through my fingers as I walked, thinking on all that I had seen. One messenger had left with a full fanfare, another in secrecy. What did it mean?

As I stepped back inside the yard via the postern gate, Francis fell into step beside me.

"I've been looking for you," he said. "There has been a messenger from London—"

"I know," I said briefly. I stood on tiptoe and put my lips to his ear. "I need to speak to you," I whispered. "In secret."

His brows went up in surprise at my tone, but he nodded. "All right." He took my hand. "Your mother summons us all to the great hall. She is to address the whole household. After that we may talk."

This was very serious, I knew. A summons to all the occupants of the castle only happened in times of war or grave danger. I could feel my nerves tighten as I contemplated what my mother might say. The King's army was marching from London, that much I knew. What might that mean for us here at Ravensworth? The nobility of England had been fighting since I was born, but now that battle had come directly to my door and I was afraid.

Joan and Frideswide came running to join us, and we all piled into the hall. My mother stood on the dais looking every inch a Neville as she dominated the room. She held up a hand to quell the babble and command silence.

"I have news of my husband and your lord," she said. "His men hold Carlisle fast against the Earl of Northumberland's force." There were a few ragged cheers at that, which she allowed with a smile before continuing. "We have word today, though, that King Edward's army is marching north and has almost reached Doncaster. The situation is grave. We do not know whether he intends to join forces with Northumberland, or come here to Ravensworth. We must be prepared for a siege."

The mood changed in an instant, a low muttering running through the room. I felt Francis stiffen beside me and tugged on his arm. "What does this mean?" I whispered. "Does the King plan to take Ravensworth in revenge, whilst Father is absent?"

Francis shook his head. His mouth was set in a grim line. "I doubt that," he said. "The King does not make war on women and children. Like as not he will cross over to the west and come up upon Carlisle to engage your father's troops."

I shuddered. "Then there will be a battle?"

"Perhaps," Francis said, and he was frowning.

I felt sick. Either way, the threat was real now. I loved my father and knew he was a good soldier. He might be holding Carlisle against the Earl of Northumberland, but the King was a different matter. Edward was a talismanic leader. Surely, he would not lose.

The hall was growing noisier, voices rising as men discussed the news. Mother let it run for a moment and then asserted her authority effortlessly, raising her voice again above the confusion.

"I have sent a messenger to warn Lord Fitzhugh," she said. "Meanwhile, we must prepare ourselves. You know what to do. Send word to the villages to be ready to bring everyone within the castle walls. Fetch fresh supplies. Grimshaw will direct you. Go with God and with my gratitude."

They were cheering her again and she looked like a heroine, tall and proud, her eyes burning with the cause, with love and loyalty. Grimshaw bustled forward with a huge ledger and self-important air. I took advantage of the surge forward to tug on Francis's arm and inclined my head toward the door. "Come with me."

He followed me out into the corridor and I grabbed his hand, pulling him along until we came to a small chamber off the tower stairs. I ducked inside and closed the door. It was cold and bare in there, but at least we were alone. Privacy was almost unknown at Ravensworth.

Francis was looking amused. "What is this all about, Anne?"

Quickly, I told him everything I had seen and heard earlier. "It makes no sense," I said. "Mother was *glad* to hear the news of the King's advance. I know she was. I saw her face. It was as though—"

"As though that was what she had wanted all along," Francis finished for me. A light leaped in his eyes. "Of course. They planned this. They planned to draw Edward out of London. They *want* the King in the North."

"Are you mad?" I gaped at him. "How will that serve?"

"It leaves the south open for the Earl of Warwick to take," Francis said. "It's a trap."

"The second messenger," I said, grabbing his arm in my excitement as I saw where this led. "The one I saw riding for the coast..."

"Yes," Francis said grimly. "Four days at sea would take a messenger to Calais, where your uncle waits for word to invade. Whilst Edward is so far north, Warwick will take London."

We were silent. It was odd that until now I had not truly grasped the scale of the whole plan. I suppose I was too young to see beyond my own immediate concerns, the danger to my father and the confusion into which the rebellion had thrown my world. Now I realized that this was huge, a power play with no lesser aim than replacing King Edward with the old Lancastrian King Henry. It was my first real insight into the vast, complicated game of chance in which my birthright gave me a small role.

"What can we do?" I asked Francis, and I was not even sure what I meant, only that I felt completely lost.

"Nothing," Francis said. "It is too late." And we stood there, hands clasped, as adrift as two children could be in an adult world.

Chapter 7

SERENA

Minster Lovell
Present Day

Serena was deep in thought as she made her way back across the courtyard to the Information Center and shop. Had she really seen Caitlin's ghost or was it her imagination, stirred up because the manor was where she had last seen her sister? Was her mind desperately trying to prompt her to remember what had happened? And what was the connection to Jack Lovell, and the persistent feeling he had some significance to the memory as well? Jack, like many of her other friends, had been around the summer that Caitlin had disappeared. Had she forgotten something important to do with Jack along with the other events that had been swept away by the trauma of Caitlin's disappearance…?

"Serena!" A voice penetrated her preoccupation, and she realized that someone was blocking her path, a woman who was short, slender except for a baby bump, her striking red-gold hair pulled back under a scarf. She had her hands on her hips and gave every indication of refusing to move.

"I called and called," she said accusingly, "and you completely blanked me!" Her face broke into a huge smile. "How are you?"

"Lizzie!" Serena dropped her bag on the cobbles and enfolded her friend in a huge hug. "I'm so sorry," she said. "I was in another world."

Lizzie Kingdom had been another friend from her teenage years. They'd met at a church nativity locally when they had been little more than toddlers. Serena and Caitlin had been staying with their grandparents for Christmas whilst Lizzie's family had lived in the next village. Serena had been one-half of the donkey in the nativity play, Caitlin had been the innkeeper, but Lizzie had been an angel; she had sung like one, but with her scowling expression had looked rather more like a small devil. Serena smiled now at the memory.

Their respective parents had thrown them together in school holidays in the hope that they might entertain each other, and Serena and Lizzie had developed a sort of wary friendship. It had not been easy to get close to Lizzie, who was prickly and sometimes unfriendly, especially after the death of her mother, but Serena had kept in touch with her through the years and to her slight surprise the friendship had developed into the sort of comfortable connection where they could pick up where they had left off, no matter how much time had elapsed. Even when Lizzie became a celebrity—and then crashed out of the limelight equally spectacularly—they hadn't lost touch. Lizzie was the only friend that Serena had talked to after Caitlin had disappeared. Perhaps because Lizzie had suffered her own traumas it had been easier to talk about it with her. She'd even texted Lizzie when she had got back to England the previous week; Lizzie was the only person she'd told about the discovery of Caitlin's body.

"You didn't say that you were coming back to Minster Lovell," Lizzie said, brushing soil from her gardening gloves and dusting down Serena's jacket. "Oops, sorry—I've made you all dirty."

"It's fine," Serena said. "You look amazing," she added. "Really well. Pop star turned gardener obviously suits you. You said the horticulture course was going well, but I didn't realize you were working here."

"I do some shifts as part of my placement," Lizzie said. "It's nice helping out here, very mindful and relaxing. And with Arthur and the baby as well…" Her voice softened, her eyes sparkling with an emotion that made Serena feel a pang of something close to envy. "Well, sometimes I can't quite believe how lucky I am." Her expression changed comically to horror. "Sorry," she said. "That was *so* crass of me! Here you are because your sister's body has been found and I'm going on about how wonderful my life is. Oh, God—"

"Lizzie—" Serena repressed a smile "—forget it. I'm so happy to see you and very glad everything is going so well."

"Thanks." Lizzie's eyes misted over and she squeezed Serena's hand. "Look, have you time for a proper chat?" She glanced around the empty courtyard. "It's quiet now. The season hasn't got going yet. No one will miss me from the kitchen gardens for a little while, and I can make up the time later."

"If you're sure that's all right," Serena said. "I wouldn't want to be responsible for getting you the sack."

"I don't think they'd do that," Lizzie said with a wicked little smile. "There are still a few perks about being an ex-celebrity." She held open the door of the Information Center for Serena and led the way through the small shop to a neat and bright café area. She eased her bump behind a table and settled on one of the cushioned wooden benches with a heartfelt sigh. "It's nice to rest for a bit. I'm in a tired phase."

"I'll get the drinks," Serena said. "What would you like?"

"Tea and a scone please," Lizzie said. "Thanks so much."

Serena went over to the counter where a lanky youth in a blue-and-white-striped apron was setting an ancient tea urn hissing as it came to the boil.

"Two teas and two scones, please," Serena said.

"Morning, Stuart," Lizzie called across from the window. "This is Serena, an old friend of mine. She used to live here."

"For real?" Stuart gave Serena a thoughtful look from beneath a thick cut dark fringe. "I can't imagine anyone actually living in the manor."

"It was my grandparents' house," Serena said. "My sister and I spent our holidays here when we were children. It was very different," she added. "There was a fitted kitchen and a 1970s avocado bathroom suite in those days."

"Cool," Stuart said. "I like retro. They should have left it when they did the renovations. The seventies are history now, aren't they?" He put a silver teapot under the urn spout and turned the handle. The machine hissed again. "I'll bring it over in a minute," he said.

"Thanks," Serena said, handing over the cash and eyeing the scones with pleasure. It wasn't that long since her full English breakfast at the pub, but she was feeling unexpectedly hungry. A lot seemed to have happened in a short space of time.

"I was very sorry to hear about Caitlin," Lizzie said as Serena sat down opposite her. "I imagine it was horrible not to know what had happened for such a long time, but equally horrible to have her death confirmed."

"It's closure in a way," Serena said, "but I don't think I've processed it yet. Once I've seen the police later today and we've got all the details it might be easier to come to terms with it. We've been waiting so long to know what happened." She paused. "My parents are in pieces. It's horrible for them."

"It can't be exactly easy for you, either," Lizzie said dryly. "Tell me to butt out if you like, but why did you come here? To Minster Lovell, I mean? Doesn't it make you feel worse?"

Stuart clattered up with a tray laden with a big blue china teapot, unmatched flowered china mugs, a milk jug, two plates, scones and butter.

"Oh, wow!" Serena said. "I recognize some of this stuff from my grandparents' kitchen!"

"We got a job lot when the house was sold," Stuart said. "I like the fact they don't match but they all look good together."

Serena picked up one of the teaspoons. They were collector's items she remembered from a wooden board that had hung on the wall in the manor kitchen. There had been about thirty of them, all silver-plated with enamel coats of arms on the handles. This one was from Blackpool with the unmistakable picture of the tower painted on it. The other had the name Shrewsbury on it and featured a blue background with three snarling leopards' heads.

She waited until Stuart had decanted everything and headed back to the counter before she replied to Lizzie's question. She didn't mind talking to Lizzie—in fact, it helped to have someone to confide in—but she felt sensitive about the whole of the village knowing her business. Then she remembered Jack and Zoe and the fact that Caitlin's body had apparently been found nearby. Probably the village was already six steps ahead of her in knowing what was going on.

"I came back because I hoped it would help me to remember what happened the day Caitlin disappeared," she said. She rubbed her forehead. "A part of my life's missing, Lizzie—a really important part. I want it back. Plus, I feel I owe it to Caitlin, you know? I want to do my best for her."

Lizzie nodded. "I do understand," she said. "The two of you were always so close. Plus, Caitlin was special. She was..." She paused.

"A bright, shining light?" Serena said with only a hint of edge to the words.

Lizzie laughed. "People always say that when a teenage girl dies, don't they? Their death rewrites the narrative of their life. The difficult stuff, the bad stuff, gets written out."

"Unless it's so bad it can't be ignored," Serena said. "In Caitlin's case, though, it was all true. She really was lovely." She wondered whether Lizzie could hear the unspoken thought beneath her words, the sense of trying to live up to a younger twin who was prettier, sweeter-natured, simply more appealing in some indefinable way than Serena felt that she was. It had been so complicated for her, feeling protective and jealous of her sister at the same time.

Lizzie looked at her. "People like Caitlin can be a bit bland, to be brutally honest," she said. "There wasn't much to her. I mean, she was good at games and she was popular, but she didn't seem to have any plans or ambitions." Lizzie shrugged. "She was just fun and frivolous and sweet... I sometimes wondered whether she had a dark side that none of us ever knew about, because no one could be so cute."

"I don't think so," Serena said doubtfully. "But you're right, of course, Caitlin wasn't perfect. We did quarrel sometimes and I always felt terrible about it, as though I was being cruel to a kitten."

Lizzie laughed, which made Serena feel obscurely better. "Even kittens have claws," she said, "and not even Caitlin was a saint." She reached for the pot, pouring for them both, splashing milk and tea haphazardly into the blue mugs. "I mean it, you know," she said. "I do wonder whether Caitlin was going through a bit of a rebellious phase that summer. Don't forget that she was always slipping off to drink in the pub and shag that hot bartender, Leo."

"I remember," Serena said. Something touched her mind like a shadow, a doubt that perhaps she hadn't known her twin as well as she had thought she had. "What happened to him?" She added. "Leo, I mean."

"I think he moved away," Lizzie said vaguely. "We all did in our own ways, didn't we? No one wanted to stay—after."

"I really envied Caitlin bagging someone like Leo," Serena said. " He was older than us and he was gorgeous. It was all very hot and heavy between them. Caitlin was precocious in that way, whereas I was still in the teenage crush phase of emotional development. I was so jealous of her. She was always prettier and more fun…" She sighed. "Oh, you know what I mean."

"People are always drawn to the obvious," Lizzie said. "You're just as attractive, just more subtle. I guess at that age we were all growing up at different rates and you were still living through your books and your imagination rather than in real life." She gave Serena a wicked smile. "And Jack Lovell was well worth crushing on even if he was a bit gawky in those days."

Serena was annoyed to feel herself blushing. "Well, he's got an entire TV audience swooning now so he's doing fine."

Lizzie smiled and picked up her mug. "Do you think that being here has stirred any memories for you yet?" she asked.

Serena grimaced. "It's stirred something, though I'm not

sure whether it's just my imagination. I thought I saw Caitlin just now. I was on the stairs and I was sure I saw her running out of the garden door." She took a deep breath. "I didn't, obviously. It must have been my mind playing tricks because I was so immersed in the past, but it's the sort of thing that might help me remember that night."

Lizzie gave a little shiver. "Spooky," she said. "Are you sure this is a good idea? You never know what this might trigger in your mind."

"That's what my aunt Polly says," Serena said, "but it's better than not knowing." She spread butter lavishly on her scone and topped it with jam, then cream. "Mmm." She took a bite. "Heaven."

"Stuart's very good at baking," Lizzie said. "You should try his chocolate cake." She tilted her head and looked at Serena thoughtfully. "What *do* you remember from the night Caitlin vanished? Is there anything at all?"

Serena frowned into her mug. She had gone over this so many times, with the police, the therapists and in her own mind. The answer was nothing. She remembered nothing at all of the evening of July 25, 2011.

She did remember something of the day that had preceded it. Her parents had been abroad, and she and Caitlin had been staying with their grandfather for a week. The school holidays had only just started. That afternoon she and Caitlin had been swimming in the river. Afterward, Caitlin, in her tiny little striped bikini, had stretched out languidly in the dappled shade under the birch trees, as though she was in California rather than Oxfordshire. They had drunk ice-cold lemonade and chatted in a desultory fashion whilst the air hummed with the sound of bees and the river rippled past. Later on, Caitlin's boyfriend, Leo, had dropped by for a while—he and Caitlin had hooked up the previous holiday—and Serena, feeling like a spare part, had wandered off and left them together. She'd been miserable and listless—she could still remember the feeling now—because Caitlin's glowing prettiness had made her feel clumsy and ugly. Caitlin had always been the more outgoing one, the twin the boys fancied. They had not been identical, and Caitlin's hair was blonder than Serena's, her eyes were green unlike Serena's hazel color, and even her bone structure seemed more delicate than her twin's.

Serena had heard her grandmother talking about it when she had been about six years old.

"Serena's so *sturdy*," her grandmother had said, and it had not sounded as though this was a good thing. "Everything about Caitlin is finer."

Finer. Leo had obviously thought so, too. He'd been all over Caitlin, literally, and Serena had smarted to be so obviously unattractive in comparison. She felt sad to remember now how cross and jealous she had been. If only she had known that soon Caitlin would no longer be there to be envied; if only she had realized how unimportant teenage sibling rivalry was compared to the void of losing her sister.

After she'd left Caitlin and Leo together, she had walked across the field to the old dovecote just to be on her own. But the ground had been hard and dry and she'd only been wearing flip-flops, which was how she had managed to trip and twist her ankle. She'd limped back toward the house feeling hot and out of sorts, and then… That was where the memories faded into a sort of mist that was completely opaque. It filled all the corners of her mind and she could not penetrate it. Except that now, as she visualized walking through the ruins of the old hall, she thought she had met someone…the memory flickered and she felt a small flare of warmth inside, as though the meeting had been a good one.

She frowned. It was the first time she had remembered that someone else had been there that afternoon.

"What is it?" Lizzie had seen the change in her expression.

"Nothing, really," Serena said slowly. "Just a few more memories of the day Caitlin disappeared. I'd forgotten some little details." She paused, chasing the image, trying to give it form and substance, but the mist was back, unrevealing, supremely frustrating. She shook her head as though the physical movement might dislodge the memory somehow, but the blankness just pressed closer. "It's hard to separate out imagination from memory after all this time," she said with a sigh.

"It's a start," Lizzie said encouragingly, seeing her disappointment. "It does look as though being here is helping you."

Serena nodded. "I think it is." She thought again of the sense of recognition she had felt when she saw Jack Lovell, the idea that he, in some way, held a clue to the past. "You mentioned Jack Lovell just now," she said. "Did you know he was here in Minster Lovell at the moment?"

"Yes, of course," Lizzie said, draining her mug. "He's staying with his grandmother for a few days. Jack and I are practically related," she added. "His grandmother Avery is my next-door neighbor and godmother. We're all very cliquey around here. Everyone knows everyone else." She set her mug down. "He's a good guy, Jack. I know he comes across all hard-nosed and analytical on the television, but he's on the side of the angels."

"Is he?" Serena toyed with her spoon. "I met him this

morning snooping around the ruins of the hall. I gathered," she added dryly, "that his sister was showing him an archaeological investigation where they had also found some more recent remains—Caitlin's."

Lizzie's eyebrows shot up. "Wait, what? Sorry, am I missing something here? You didn't tell me that Caitlin had been found here at Minster."

"I didn't tell you because I didn't know," Serena said. "As far as I can gather, the police hadn't told anyone yet. Jack, it seems, had inside knowledge."

Lizzie's frown cleared. "Zoe. Yes, of course. She's a forensic archaeologist. She's been working on the dig at the church here with Minster Archaeology." She gave a gusty sigh. "Oh, dear. That's a pretty serious breach of confidentiality. She could lose her job for that if you make a complaint."

"I realize that." Serena finished the last of the scone and sat back with a sigh. "I haven't decided what to do about it yet. And why is Jack Lovell interested in Caitlin's death anyway?" She reached for the empty tray. "I wish I'd asked him now, but I was too upset and angry to think straight."

"Understandably," Lizzie said. She studied Serena for a moment. "We were all close friends," she said after a moment. "Perhaps he feels like you do, that he wants to learn the truth."

"Has he told you that?" Serena asked. She realized she sounded sharp and immediately regretted it. "Sorry," she said. "It's just that I feel...possessive of Caitlin. It isn't particularly admirable of me—" she raised her eyes to Lizzie's "—but I do."

Lizzie nodded. "That's fair enough. She was your sister and you were the closest to her. Besides, you have a desperate need to regain your memories. I get that." She sighed. "Just don't discount the fact that other people have their own memories and experiences of Caitlin, too. And of course Jack didn't speak to me about it." She sounded faintly offended. "I'd have told him to talk to you if he had."

"Sorry," Serena said again, chastened. "I'm a bit on edge. I know you would."

Lizzie smiled and patted her hand. "No problem. But I am a bit worried about you. If you start recovering any memories, give me a call straightaway."

"You sound like Polly," Serena said. "She said if that happened, I should get out of here and call a therapist."

"I have one on speed dial," Lizzie said. She checked her watch. "I'm sorry. I'm going to have to get back to work in a minute. Why don't you come over to The High for a meal and we can catch up properly?"

"I'd like that very much," Serena said. "Thanks."

Lizzie started to stack the crockery, reaching for Serena's mug and plate. There was a clink as the teaspoon rattled against the china, and she made a grab to stop it tumbling to the floor. Lizzie gave a gasp, recoiling, all the color draining from her face. It was so sudden and unexpected that Serena felt a lurch of fear.

"Are you okay?" she said. She got up quickly, coming around the table to Lizzie's side. "What happened? Is it the baby?"

"I'm fine." Lizzie took a deep breath. "I think she must have kicked. Sorry about that." She sat still for a couple more seconds, head bent, then looked up to give Serena a bright smile that somehow did not convince. Suddenly Serena had a different memory, a teenage Lizzie whom everyone in their friendship group whispered had the uncanny ability to touch an object and read the memories associated with it.

It was odd, now she stopped to consider it, just how natural that had seemed as part of Lizzie's personality and therefore a part of her own life. She wasn't particularly drawn to the supernatural and had shied away from anything paranormal in the wake of Caitlin's disappearance, but stories of ghosts, witches and magic had underpinned her childhood reading and somehow Lizzie's gift seemed a part of that.

"Lizzie," she said. "You don't have to pretend with me. You've just had one of your psychometry experiences, haven't you?"

Lizzie looked up sharply. Her face was still paper white but her blue gaze was sharp. "You know about that?" she said.

Serena sat back down again. "Of course I do," she said. "Remember that day Caitlin showed us her bead bracelet? She was showing off, going on about how beautiful it was. You picked it up and said it was strange she was so pleased about it because actually what she'd really wanted was a purple one rather than a blue one."

"Oh, God, yeah, I do remember that," Lizzie said slowly. A little bit of color had come back into Lizzie's cheeks now, and some of the tension has drained away from her body. "It was really unkind of me to spoil her fun like that." She looked rueful. "Caitlin had annoyed me for some reason, probably by being Little Miss Perfect as usual." She smiled faintly. "But how did you know that was psychometry? It could just have been a lucky guess."

"I was there when Caitlin opened the present," Serena said. "It was a gift from our grandmother. I got the purple one and Caitlin got blue. She wanted mine and was so cross about it."

Lizzie blew out a breath. "Wow. You never said."

"I sort of guessed you didn't want to talk about the fact that you could read objects because you didn't want people to think you were weird," Serena said, smiling, "so I didn't push you. But some of us knew—or guessed. There were other occasions too, when you would touch things and seem to be absent for a moment… I went away and looked it up, and came up with psychometry, the ability to read memories or experiences associated with certain objects."

"Right," Lizzie said. She sounded herself again. "I should have guessed I couldn't fool you," she said wryly. "You always were very observant."

Serena laughed. "I don't know about that, but I did notice that about twenty minutes ago I mentioned to you that I thought I'd seen Caitlin's ghost and you took it without turning a hair, from which I assumed that the paranormal is an everyday occurrence for you."

Lizzie rolled her eyes. "You've got me there."

Serena touched the Shrewsbury teaspoon lightly with her fingertips. In her case there was no supernatural revelation when she did so, only a sense of nostalgia for those days sitting in the warmth of her grandparents' kitchen, the sense of belonging, of peace and comfort, the happiness that her time at Minster Hall had brought before it had all come crashing to an end.

Raising her gaze to Lizzie's, she said cautiously, "What did you see when you touched the spoon? Can you tell me?"

Lizzie's expression fell. "I could…" she said slowly. "It didn't make much sense to me, though it might to you." She gave a little shudder. "It was pretty horrible."

"Then don't talk about it," Serena said quickly. "Just forget it."

"No," Lizzie said. She sat up a bit straighter. "It might be important." She looked at Serena. "I mean you said all the china and stuff came from your grandparents' house so there could be some connection to Caitlin."

"Okay," Serena said uncertainly. "If you're sure."

Lizzie took a deep breath. "When I touched the spoon, I sensed that someone was dying." Then, as Serena caught her breath she added hastily, "Oh, God, no, it wasn't Caitlin. Sorry, that was so stupid of me."

"It's all right," Serena said shakily, as her heartbeat settled again. "I thought—"

"Of course you did." Lizzie touched the back of her hand. "I should have explained better." She sat back in the chair. "When I 'read' objects, sometimes I see a vision and at other times I'll just get a sensation, an emotion, if you like associated with the person who owned them. So, for example, there's a gown that belonged to my grandmother. It's really glamorous, and when I touch it, I can feel the excitement that *she* felt when she wore it to dances and parties. It fills me with her sense of anticipation and wonder."

"How lovely," Serena said. "I had no idea that was how it works."

"Yes, well, that's a nice example," Lizzie said, "but it's not always like that. With that spoon—" she looked at it again but didn't touch it "—I think I shared an emotion felt by whoever once owned it."

"That would have been one of my grandparents," Serena said, frowning. "They used to collect loads of commemorative spoons. This one hung on the wall in the kitchen."

"Okay," Lizzie said. "Well, judging by the emotions I experienced, one of them was once at the bedside of someone they loved—a child, a boy, I think, and he was dying. I felt their grief and their desperation and loneliness. It was as though…" She hesitated. "I think they were very young and felt very alone." She shivered, as though trying to shake off the memory. "Sorry," she said again. "As I say, it was fairly intense and horrible."

"It sounds it," Serena said. "I'm so sorry you had to experience that."

"Luckily psychometry doesn't often happen randomly like that," Lizzie said, "or it would probably have driven me insane by now." She was starting to sound far more like her usual self. "Perhaps you could stack everything up," she added with a smile, "just in case I trigger another insight."

Serena piled up the dirty plates, mugs and cutlery on the tray, all the while thinking about what Lizzie had said.

"I'm guessing that nothing I said rings any bells with you," Lizzie observed after a moment. "No one in the family history who died young as a boy?"

"I know next to nothing about my family history," Serena said, "which is ironic," she added, "since I make a living selling history to people who more often than not are looking for their roots. I'll have to see what I can find out."

She carried the tray across to Stuart's counter whilst Lizzie stood and gathered up her jacket and gardening gloves. They hugged each other. "Do come for supper soon," Lizzie said. "I promise not to serve a side order of psychometric readings."

"I will," Serena said.

Lizzie released her, standing back. "If you're really going to try and find out the story behind the spoon," she said, "there's something else I should tell you." She paused. There was a silence in the café apart from the gentle hissing of the tea urn.

"It felt as though it all happened a very long time ago,"

Lizzie said slowly. "I don't mean decades, I mean…centuries. And—" she met Serena's eyes, and her own were full of puzzlement "—I know where it was," she said. "Like I say, sometimes I see a vision as well as sense the emotion. I saw the room, and the boy in the bed. There were banners on the walls with lions and lilies on them and it was high up, in a tower overlooking a river. It was the Tower of London."

Chapter 8

ANNE

Ravensworth Castle
1470

My father did not fight, nor was Ravensworth besieged. As soon as the King arrived in Ripon, the rebels melted away to their homes and firesides. Father ran away to Scotland and although I guessed that he had never intended to meet the King in pitched battle, I did not know whether I should feel glad that he was safe or ashamed that he was a coward.

King Edward summoned us to Richmond, the tumble-down castle that Mother had so disparaged on my wedding journey five years earlier. It was phrased as a polite invitation, but we all knew that it was not; we were traitors by association. Mother did not see it that way, however, and she was not minded to go.

"Who does he think he is to send for me like a servant or a whore?" she stormed. "I shall not obey."

I caught the exchange of glances between Grimshaw and Barker, the captain of the guard. Normally it was my father who bore the brunt of my mother's Neville rages. In his absence everyone else was feeling the strain.

"Madam," Grimshaw said, forcing respect into his tone, "he is the King."

"And he holds the field," Barker added helpfully. "It would be wiser to comply."

My mother gave them both a look of utter contempt to be lectured on strategy by two men whom she felt knew a great deal less than she.

"Thank you, gentlemen," she said with poisonous sweetness. "I am not sure how I would manage without your advice. Now I suggest that you return to your duties before the castle falls down without you." She swept out of the solar, leaving me looking at Joan, Alice and Francis in bewilderment.

"Do we go to Richmond or not?" I demanded. The idea excited me, and I had been disappointed when Mother had rejected it.

Francis unfolded himself from the window embrasure where he had been leaning, a silent observer of Mother's rage. "Oh, we shall go," he said cynically. "They still play the game of war, Anne, even if there is a truce. What would happen if your mother refused?" He strolled across to my side and sat down.

"The King would either ignore her or he would be obliged to come to her instead," I said.

"Exactly." Francis smiled at me as though I was an apt pupil. "Your mother would be even more furious to be ignored. It would be a terrible slight. She cannot risk that. Nor can she be certain that Edward would come to Ravensworth in person—he might send Gloucester or someone else in his place."

"She would not like that," I said. I felt my lips twitch into a smile at how it would offend my mother's pride.

"Therefore, she has no option but to go to Richmond,"

Francis said, stretching. "That way she will control the meeting to her own advantage."

"It seems stupid and pointless," I said crossly. I glanced out of the window. It was a beautiful autumn day; the hot dry summer had given way to a cooler and fresher season. Golden leaves edged the trees beside the lake, and I could see the smoke from the village chimneys rising dreamily into the still washed-blue of the skies. Suddenly, I wanted to be outside, riding over the hills or walking by the river. The power games of princes and nobles seemed foolish to me.

Elizabeth stuck her head around the solar door. "There you are!" she said when she saw us. "Mother wants us to prepare for the journey to Richmond. We are all to go, you, me, Alice, Margery, every last one of us."

I caught Francis's wry smile and wondered what he was thinking.

"You, too, Francis Lovell," Elizabeth said. "And your sisters."

"Are we taking all the village children as well?" I asked tartly. "Does Mother intend to turn this into a nursery outing?"

"I think that is exactly what she intends," Francis said. He caught my hand and pulled me to my feet. "Come along, Anne—we stand as your mother's armor in this battle."

I understood what he meant when, two hours later, our little cavalcade was assembled in the courtyard and ready to leave. Mother was dressed demurely all in blue and resembled nothing so much as the Virgin Mary in the stained-glass windows of the chapel. The fact that she was also pregnant only served to emphasize her soft and womanly appearance. She had elected to travel in a litter when normally I knew she would have ridden, pregnant or not. A small dispute arose when I insisted that I wanted to ride alongside Francis. Elizabeth and Alice had already scrambled up into one of the covered carts along with Frideswide and Joan. They looked particularly annoyed when a small white palfrey was led out for me. This, too, was one of Mother's designs, I knew. I was the best rider amongst her daughters and knew, without vanity, that I looked both pretty and skillful in the saddle.

Francis knew it, too. "I'll give you a silver groat if you gallop off and get covered in mud," he whispered in my ear as he lifted me up into the saddle.

"I'd do it for two," I whispered back, "but nothing less."

This time the roads were dry and the old leaves and oak apples crunched beneath the horses' hooves. The wind from the hills was soft, and the sun shone palely on our little party. Only a handful of men at arms accompanied us and those only for safety, not show. My palfrey was a timid little beast and would not have galloped anywhere even had I wished her to, but it was pleasant to be outside rather than thrown around in the cart with the others.

The huge battlements of Richmond dominated the view as soon as we topped Kirby Hill and looked down into the valley of the River Swale. Glancing across at my mother, I saw that her gaze, too, was fixed on the castle, and there was a steely light in her eyes. Then she settled herself more firmly in the litter and we started the descent into the town to the postern at Friars Wynd.

There were men in royal livery here; I felt a little shiver down my spine to see the soldiers guarding the gate, and the sun picking out the badges of the white rose *en soleil* and the sunburst that was King Edward's own device. A shout went up as we were sighted, and the gate was barred as a soldier spurred forward to meet us.

"The Lady Alice Fitzhugh to see her cousin the King," I heard Mother say, with just the right mixture of authority and deference, and the young captain, blushing as he saw her pregnant state and the young children peeping from the cart, made haste to escort us through.

The town seethed with people and with the febrile air that always came with a royal visit. This time though there was no feeling of excitement or celebration that came with a royal progress, no garlands in the streets or wells running with wine. Even though the rebels had backed down, this was a town at war. Looking across at Francis I could see that he felt it, too. He sat all the straighter in the saddle, grim-faced, tension emanating from him in waves. Yet he rode with the lightest hands and looked every inch the young lord. I felt proud of him.

By the time we reached the castle, we had gained quite a retinue of people who had ascertained that here was a personage of some importance who might be their means of entering the castle and approaching the King. The captain cleared the path through the melee for us as though he were Mother's personal herald. The result was that by the time we were ushered into the great hall, it felt as though Mother were honoring Edward with a visit rather than responding to a summons issued to a traitor's wife. No doubt this was precisely what she had planned. I admired her strategy.

Edward was finishing dinner as we came in. The hall was dimly lit, showing a bare wooden table strewn with platters of cooked meats and poultry that looked as though it had been fallen upon by the dogs who were now squabbling over bones amongst the none-too-fresh rushes of the floor. There was no finesse here and no fire in the grate to offset the chill of the towering walls. This was a campaign headquarters; the fact that the King and all his captains were in armor only served to emphasize the fact.

Mother was not impressed. "It takes more than a royal presence to turn this place from pigsty to palace," she murmured to me as she approached the dais. She gestured to us to fall in line behind her, a train of children following her as though she were the pied piper. I had wondered whether she would ask Francis to offer her his arm, but now I saw that no one was going to be invited to share this moment with her. We were all acolytes, not equals.

Mother sank into the deepest curtsey as she approached the King, and we all followed suit. Francis had given his stiffest bow. I sensed that he detested being tarred with the rebels' brush. I had never seen him look so grim. There was a moment of stillness and I saw Edward toss aside a chicken leg and wipe his mouth on the back of his hand, then he jumped down from the dais with as little formality as a boy, took my mother's hand and raised her up.

"Cousin Alice..." He kissed her cheek. His smile was broad. "It is such a great pleasure to see you again."

It was not the first time I had met Edward Plantagenet—we were distant cousins, after all—but it was the first time I had seen him since I was grown-up enough to appreciate him as a king. He looked disheveled and weary from the forced march North, but there was about him a vivid energy that crackled like the lightning in the summer sky. He dazzled. It was hard to drag one's gaze away.

"Your Majesty..." My mother kept her eyes cast down. I heard the quaver in her voice and would have sworn her hand trembled in the King's. Glancing sideways, I caught Francis's eyes and bit back a smile at the cynical twist to his lips. Such an accomplished act from my mother and such regal generosity from Edward. He drew her hand through his arm, patting it as she allowed herself to lean against him for support.

"I fear the journey has overset you," he murmured. "It was thoughtless of me to ask you to come here at this time of year and in your condition. Forgive me." He raised his voice. "Have the fire made up, and food and wine brought for my cousin! I fear we are very rough here—" he turned to her again "—but you light any hall with your beauty and presence, cousin. Come and sit by me."

It was true that my mother was still a very good-looking woman and looking as she did like a Madonna in the blue dress, she was well-nigh irresistible. We all watched as she graciously accepted a cushioned seat at Edward's side. More torches were lit and the fire glowed; fresh food and drink was brought. She made sure that we were all shepherded close to the warmth as well: "My chicks," she referred to us sweetly to the King, and inquired after his own brood of children.

"Lovell!" Richard of Gloucester had ceded his place beside the King to my mother, and now came across to greet us. He smiled and nodded to me, but I could tell that he wanted to talk to Francis. It was more than a year since they had met. I could also tell that Francis was desperate for a sign of Gloucester's forgiveness, for the recognition that this rebellion was none of his doing and anathema to him.

Gloucester was not as easy to read as his brother the King, a man—for he was a man now—who did not reveal his emotions easily. For a moment, as he looked at Francis, his gaze was unfathomable. Then he laughed and slapped Francis on the back.

"Come and take wine with me. We need to talk."

"Your Grace." I could feel Francis's relief. It did not surprise me when he turned away without a backward glance and the two of them walked off, talking and laughing together, whilst I was relegated to my place amongst the children.

As a result of our cousinly visit to Richmond, the King issued us with a royal pardon for our treason. Francis and I were included in it—as though we had had any say in my father's rebellion—and though I knew it was for form's sake in Francis's case, I felt for him to be so tainted by association. Worse news was to follow, however. Just as we had anticipated, by the following month my uncle, Lord Warwick, had returned and forced Edward into exile. Old, mad King Henry was back on the throne. The Kingmaker had reclaimed his power.

Father also returned from exile in Scotland. He came back to a hero's welcome. By now winter was pressing in over the fells and moors with a coating of hoarfrost on the bracken, muting the bronze and golds of autumn. It was a cold day as we lined up in the quadrangle to greet him. Our breath mingled in the air, and I shivered inside my woolen cloak and slid my hand deeper into Francis's warm grasp. I could not help but remember how different it had been when Father had left, slipping away like a thief. Now he dismounted to cheers and slaps on the back; he kissed my mother heartily and then hugged Elizabeth, who squealed with pleasure. His gaze fell on me, and I tried to smile and to show the same excitement as my sister, but my smile felt stiff and forced. Father's glance moved to Francis, who gave him the barest nod of acknowledgment.

"Sir," he said.

The air around us seemed to chill further. I knew that Francis would never forgive Father for the decision he had made to support Warwick and tar all of us with the brush of treason. More personally I knew Francis's greatest bitterness lay in the fact that Father's betrayal had forced him to break his oath to Richard of Gloucester that he would always support the King's cause. Even though Gloucester had proved at Richmond that he bore Francis no malice, the damage had been done.

Father registered Francis's coldness with a raised brow. His gaze slid to our clasped hands, and then he caught me up in his arms and swung me around, tugging me from Francis's grip.

"Are you pleased to see me, sweeting?" He gave me a smacking kiss on the cheek, before placing me back on my feet.

"Yes, Father." I could sense both excitement and anger burning in him. He was not going to allow a mere boy to show him disapproval. Father slid an arm around me, drawing me away, toward the rest of the family, away from Francis, ostentatiously shutting him out. When I looked back over my shoulder, Francis had gone.

King Edward was not a man to stay long in exile. Within six months he had returned to take back his kingdom. At Barnet, in the thick mist of mid-April, both my uncle Warwick and his brother Montagu were killed. Two weeks later Edward had defeated the Lancastrian forces again at Tewkesbury and was once more undisputed king.

Mother was in deep grief for the loss of her brothers, but I never once saw her cry. Her anger and sadness glittered behind her eyes, sharp as a whetted sword. We trod even more softly that spring. The atmosphere at Ravensworth was ran-cid, like a curdled pudding. Father lived in fear of the King's retribution for his part in Warwick's rebellion and had been working secretly to try to secure safe conduct for us all back to Scotland. One morning, I overheard the most terrible argument between my parents—raised voices in the solar as I was about to go in. Instead, I skulked in the corridor outside, like a spying servant.

"You may run away and hide if you wish!" Mother was shouting. "I'd rather rot in prison than beg reluctant charity from King James of Scotland!"

She might as well have added that she was a Neville, and they ran toward danger rather than away from it.

"Your mind is addled with Neville arrogance," Father bellowed back. "Stay here, then, and see what clemency the King shows you this time!"

I pressed myself back against the wall and clung there as though Ravensworth's solidity could give me comfort. The rough stonework scored my fingers. The solar door slammed open and Father strode out, swearing under his breath. He almost passed me without noticing, but at the last moment he stopped. The angry light in his eyes frightened me for it looked murderous. He blinked as though for a moment he had no idea who I was. Then:

"Anne." He dropped down beside me. The harshness had gone. He looked the same as he had always done, rugged, dependable, the solid core of my life.

"Sweetheart." He put an arm about me and drew me close. The familiarity, warmth and reassurance enveloped me. I so wanted matters to go back to how they had been before the rebellion then; I wished it fiercely, with all my heart.

"I am going away," Father said. "It will not be for long. You will all come to join me soon."

I clutched at his shirt. I knew what I had overheard and it was not this.

"Will you not stay instead?" I said. "Please? For me?"

He laughed. There was an edge of bitterness to it. "I cannot," he said. "I would if I could, but it is not possible. I'm sorry, Anne." He pressed a kiss on my hair. "I shall think about you every day," he said. He put me from him, straightening up. "Be good for your mother and I will see you all soon."

They were his last words to me. His world was vast, full of heavy matters, of power and politics and action. My ten-year-old world was so small in comparison and he occupied so much of it. Perhaps he did think of me every day or perhaps he never thought of me again. I do not know. I do know that from that moment forward, I missed him dreadfully. I ran away to hide in a corner of the stables to cry. It was the only place I could find that afforded me any privacy and even then, one of the grooms appeared, whistling, and I had to run away again. Eventually, I took refuge in my room, pleading a headache. By now the whole castle had heard that my father planned to leave for Scotland again, and the atmosphere was tight with tension as though there were iron bands about the walls squeezing the breath from us all. Men walked silently and breathed lightly for fear of what might happen next, and I pulled the covers over my head and refused to come out.

It was late afternoon when Francis came to find me. I had taken no food, which may have been the indication he needed that the situation was desperate indeed. He strode into the bedchamber and pulled the covers off me. I gave a squawk of outrage.

"Get up," Francis said. He looked unusually severe. "This is not like you, Anne. You are made of sterner stuff than this."

I surprised myself with a watery giggle. "You look so strict," I said. "What will you do if I refuse? Order me as my husband?"

For a moment Francis looked taken aback, then he laughed, too. "Perhaps I will," he said.

"I shall save you the trouble," I said. I slid from my bed. It had cheered me a little to see him, and suddenly I wanted to be out breathing the fresh air.

"May we go outside?" I said. "I don't want to be within walls whilst everyone laments my father's departure."

Francis's jaw set more squarely. I knew he wanted to criticize my father, but he merely nodded. "Of course," he said.

We went to the mews where the falcons were kept, and he showed me the lanner that had been a gift from the Duke of Gloucester. It was a beautiful, fierce creature with pitiless yellow eyes and slate gray wings.

"When you are old enough, we will get you a merlin to fly," Francis said. "Would you like that?"

I assented, but not with a great deal of enthusiasm. I felt as though all my happiness had been squashed out of me. "So, your friendship with Gloucester is repaired," I said. "I am glad."

Francis's lips twisted. "I doubt your father's latest action will endear him to the King and Gloucester any more than his rebellion did," he said. Then: "I am truly sorry, Anne. I know you love him."

"I thought he was a great man," I said forlornly, "only now I see he was no more than a coward."

Francis put the bird carefully back on its perch and stripped off his glove with equal deliberation before he turned back to me. "Come and sit here with me," he said, taking my hand and leading me over to the bench along the wall. He sat forward, his elbows on his knees.

"People are imperfect," he said. "Sometimes they will not live up to the expectations we have. Sometimes they will fail us utterly." There was a darkness in his eyes as though he was looking back into the past, and I realized he was not speaking of my father but of his own, the man who had shown his wife and children nothing but cruelty. I felt ashamed then, for my father had never physically hurt us and had only deserted us because my mother had refused to go with him. We had never had to bear the pain of his violence.

"*You* will not disappoint me," I said, still childish in my certainty. "You will never fail me."

Francis looked at me sideways. "You cannot know that," he said. There was a self-deprecating smile on his lips. "I am very far from perfect."

He stood up abruptly as though he did not want to confront those imperfections. "Come," he said. "It is almost time for supper. I hear there is to be sturgeon tonight."

"I don't like the bones," I said, and he laughed.

"Would you rather have pottage with the babies?" he asked, pulling me to my feet, and I laughed, too, for he was right in that I was still very much a child, though on the cusp of changing. He held me for a moment, his gaze searching my face, and then he released me.

"You'll grow up soon enough," he said lightly, and nothing could have emphasized more the gap between us. It felt as though his four years forever gave him the advantage on me and I was running to catch him.

One day, I thought, that would all change. But for now, there was supper and if I did not care for the sturgeon, then the cook would give me pigeon pie instead, because I was his favorite.

We flew the lanner almost every day of the next two weeks, under the watchful eye of Henzey, the falconer. Henzey was rough in manner with people, but gentle with the birds. The lanner, whom Francis had named Astor, watched him with its fierce yellow eyes and recognized his authority. It returned to the lure every time. Francis, too, had a natural skill for the sport. He and the bird seemed to understand one another.

As I watched Astor climb into the fresh blue sky of spring, a tiny speck against the pale horizon, I think I sensed that this was the last of my time to spend with Francis, at least for now. With Father gone there was every reason for the King to give Francis's wardship to another noble so that he might complete his education. So, when the messenger arrived to summon Francis to court, I was not surprised and I hid my grief so well I think no one knew.

Francis came to see me before he left. He was already cloaked and booted for the journey and looked very fine. He also looked like a man—for that was what he was now—who could not wait to begin a new adventure. There was an energy and excitement that blazed from him. He could barely wait to go, and I wondered whether it would always be my fate to wait behind.

"I am to go to Ewelme," he told me, "to join the household of the Duke of Suffolk. He holds my wardship now."

I had already heard as much, though not from Francis himself. Gossip spread as swiftly through Ravensworth as a fever did; we had all known from the moment the messenger had arrived.

"It is a good choice for you," I said. "The Duke is a thoughtful man and a learned one."

"He is also brother-in-law to the King," Francis said.

I smiled, unsurprised that it was proximity to the center of power that appealed to him for the opportunities that it would offer. In only a few years' time, Francis would come of age. I knew that he burned to take possession of the estates that were his and that the more powerful allies he could gain now, the better. There would be no more association with rebel households and attainted traitors. Francis could fulfill the loyalty he had promised to Richard of Gloucester years before.

"Nevertheless," I said, "it is Duke John's discretion that is a good model to follow whilst you complete your studies."

Francis's eyes lightened with an answering smile. "You are so wise, Anne," he said. "Sometimes I forget quite how young you are. I will miss your good counsel."

It was a compliment of sorts, but it also reminded me that he saw me as a friend, a sister. I was still too young for him to see me as a wife. *One day…* I told myself again, and hoped it were true. I almost asked him not to forget me, but pride held me silent. I didn't even ask him to write, for I knew he would not.

"I wish you Godspeed," I said, standing on tiptoe to kiss his cheek. "Until we meet again."

I watched him ride off, and I thought of the falcon rising higher and higher into the blue of the sky. It might come back, or it might vanish forever.

Chapter 9

SERENA

Oxford
Present Day

The interview room at Thames Valley Police in St. Aldates, Oxford, had no windows and was brightly lit in an artificial imitation of the sunny day outside. Despite the determined fluorescent lighting, Serena found it bare and chilling in its functionality. She took the seat that was indicated, a hard, plastic chair that looked as though it had been borrowed from a primary school classroom.

"Thank you for coming in, Miss Warren." The police officer leading the investigation into Caitlin's death, who had introduced herself as Inspector Litton, had a cool, emotionless manner and disconcertingly light blue eyes. She sat opposite Serena, behind a substantial desk. "We thought you would like to be apprised of the progress in the investigation into your sister's death."

"Of course," Serena said, thinking how rare it was for any real person to use the word "apprise" in conversation. "Thank you."

"Our deepest condolences," put in the sergeant. He was

lean and lanky, with an expression like a sad spaniel, and he paced the room behind Serena. She could hear the repetition of his footsteps, but could not see him; she wondered if this was designed to intimidate her, which it didn't, though it was irritating. He had shaken her hand firmly, told her he was called Ratcliffe and given her a disarming smile, but it had done little to put Serena at ease. The place, the situation, the ghastly reality of Caitlin's death, made her feel as though her nerves were as tensely wound as a violin string.

"I'm afraid it's still not possible to say at this stage how Caitlin died," Inspector Litton said, "although it seems that there *may* have been foul play. There was a broken bone in her neck, but we'll know more when further tests have taken place. At the moment we're treating the death as unexplained." She opened the desk drawer and took out a fat brown folder, resting her right hand on it. Serena noticed her neat manicure and the very large diamond ring on her fourth finger. She wondered if it was a relic of a broken engagement and, as an afterthought, whether Inspector Litton was right-handed, in which case the ring would surely get in the way when she was writing.

"We were told that Caitlin had been identified by her dental records," Serena said hesitantly. The thought filled her with nausea, but she knew she had to understand the process in order to explain it to her family. "Is that common practice in cases like this?"

Inspector Litton's gaze rested on her face with forensic sharpness. "Generally, dental evidence is used in cases where other means of identification, such as fingerprints, are destroyed," she said precisely. "Teeth are the strongest part of the human body and survive when other features are too damaged to be of help."

Caitlin, Serena thought. *Too damaged to be identified by other means…*

Her stomach gave another sickening lurch. It was almost unbearable to think about. Had her sister been hit by a car, or involved in an explosion of some sort? Yet she knew that Caitlin had been found in a grave, and at the church in Minster Lovell, according to Zoe Lovell. That suggested that someone had buried her. Darker, more disturbing thoughts started to spill through her mind. *Foul play…*

She sat forward urgently. "I understand that Caitlin was found at Minster Lovell," she said, "buried in or near the church? Is that correct?"

Inspector Litton's brows snapped down. "Who told you that?"

"I'm staying in the village," Serena said. "I saw the police tape—and heard a few rumors." She hesitated, remembering her conversation with Lizzie. It had been horrible to discover the news from Zoe, but it wouldn't achieve anything to get her into trouble. There were more important things going on. "You know how it is," she said vaguely. "People talk."

Inspector Litton looked annoyed. "There has clearly been a breach of protocol here," she said stiffly. "I apologize. We wanted to wait until we had all the information before we told next of kin the details of Caitlin's death. However, as you already have some of the information…" She opened the brown file.

Serena felt a pang of shock to see a big, bright photograph of her sister's face on the top; Caitlin, with her wide smile and her green eyes and her flyaway blond hair, so vibrant, so vividly alive. She gave a violent shudder. What had happened to take her sister from that shining image to a corpse that had needed to be identified from dental records? It felt obscene, horrific. Tears sprang to her eyes, surprising her in their suddenness and intensity.

The police sergeant placed a glass of water in front of her; she focused on the ripple in the surface until it had stilled. She didn't think she could drink anything, although she appreciated the gesture.

"Caitlin's bones were found in St. Kenelm's Church in Minster Lovell in a burial plot from the eighteenth century," Inspector Litton said, shuffling the photograph to one side and pulling out a folder of clear blue plastic. A pile of papers spilled out from it, a mixture of photographs of the church, notices about fundraising efforts to reroof it and restore the tower, some diagrams of the renovation work and a few pictures of what looked like archaeological trenches.

"They're doing some renovation work on St. Kenelm's at the moment," the inspector said. "You may have noticed that there is an archaeological dig going on there as part of a conservation project."

"I'd heard about it," Serena said carefully.

Inspector Litton nodded. "The restoration work on the church necessitated the removal and reinterment of a couple of burials," she said. "As part of the project, Minster Archaeology was analyzing some of the graves and their contents. One was of particular interest. It was an early eighteenth century burial marked in the church records as being of an unidentified skeleton found in the ruins of Minster Hall during building repair work."

"The archaeologists thought it might be Francis Lovell," Sergeant Ratcliffe put in unexpectedly. "Right-hand man to King Richard III. There's a story that he fled to Minster Lovell after the Battle of Stoke Field in 1487 when they tried to put the Pretender Lambert Simnel on the throne of England in place of Henry VII. The story goes that Francis Lovell starved to death at the hall when the faithful retainer who was hiding him died. The legend states that when the workmen opened up a sealed room in 1708, they saw his figure sitting at the table and the moment the air got it, he crumbled to dust."

"In which case," Inspector Litton said, "there would have been no need to bury his body, would there?" She glared at Ratcliffe. "Really, Sergeant, I don't think we need a history lesson, do we?"

"I remember hearing a version of that legend when I was a child," Serena said. "It's part of the folklore of Minster Lovell, like the story of the Mistletoe Bride. The Lovell family owned the hall for centuries." She turned back to Inspector Litton. "I'm sorry, I don't understand. Are you saying that Caitlin's body was found in the same grave as this 1708 skeleton?"

"There was only one burial in the grave," Inspector Litton said. She looked up. "The only body in the coffin was that of your sister, Miss Warren."

There was a silence in the room. Serena could hear the sounds from outside in the street, the dull muffled constant of the traffic, the faint rise and fall of voices. It was odd to hear the sounds of the world passing by when there were no windows onto the outside. She felt doubly numb, isolated from life and adrift from Caitlin.

"Do you mean that someone removed the original burial and put Caitlin in its place?" Serena felt a rush of irritation that Inspector Litton seemed to be making this so difficult for her. It wasn't a game; why did she have to guess? Could they not simply tell her the facts? She glanced at Sergeant Ratcliffe, who had resumed his pacing across the floor. There was something watchful in his face that chilled her.

They think it was you… They are waiting for you to give yourself away…

She wasn't sure where that taunting whisper had come from and it terrified her because, with the gaps in her memory, how could she be sure it wasn't true? She was certain she had not hurt Caitlin—she felt it in her very core—but she had nothing to put in place of a theory that suggested she had.

"That would be the logical explanation," Inspector Litton agreed. "However, there are one or two anomalies." She paused and Serena, nerves tightened to screaming point, wondered if she was meant to start guessing again. Then Inspector Litton carried on.

"First, it's unlikely that someone disposing of a body would go to the trouble of removing the original one when there was plenty of room in the coffin," she said. "And if they did, where is that original body now?" For once it was a rhetorical question. "There is also the curious circumstance," the inspector added, "that there is no evidence to suggest that the grave had been disturbed since it was sealed in 1708."

Serena rubbed her forehead, which was tight with tension. "Are you suggesting, then, that this isn't actually Caitlin's body after all?"

"No," Inspector Litton said. "This *is* Caitlin Warren on the basis of her dental records. Naturally, when they opened up the tomb, the archaeologists assumed the body dated from the eighteenth century. The general state of the decay suggested it had been interred for roughly three hundred years and that she had been dead for longer than that. However, the radiocarbon dating suggested that this was the body of a young woman who had died early in the twenty-first century."

"Then there must be some mistake," Serena said. "The forensic tests must be wrong. Otherwise what you are telling me is that Caitlin died some time during the past eleven years but was buried in 1708, which simply isn't possible."

"I am aware," Inspector Litton said tartly, "that it makes no sense." She tapped her fingers crossly on the brown file. It was obvious she was a woman who detested a mystery and worse, Serena thought, she felt this whole conundrum was making fools of the police. "I agree there can only be two solutions," the inspector said. "Either this is *not* Caitlin and the forensic tests results are wrong, or it *is* your sister and someone found a way to tamper with the tomb whilst making it look as though it hadn't been disturbed."

"Both scenarios raise further questions," Sergeant Ratcliffe said, "which we are keen to answer."

I bet you are, Serena thought. She could see now why the police had been slow to discuss the details of Caitlin's death. They made no sense.

"Further to the identification of Caitlin," Inspector Litton said, "there were some fractures to the body, old breaks, predating death, that is. Can you confirm whether your sister ever broke any of her bones, Miss Warren?"

Serena felt another uprush of nausea. This all felt horribly procedural with no room for sentiment. Perhaps it was the inspector's determinedly dispassionate manner, stripping all sense of personality from Caitlin. Or perhaps it was the sergeant's pacing which was giving her a headache. Sweat prickled her skin. She grabbed the glass of water and gulped down a mouthful.

"Caitlin broke her arm when we were about seven," she

said. "She fell off a swing. I was pushing her. It was…" She paused, remembering. A sudden gust of wind, Caitlin teetering on the edge of the seat, the wild swinging of the chain… It had been horrible at the time, the type of random childhood accident that years later when the fuss had died down, Caitlin had teased her would scar them both for life. Little had she known what other scars would be dealt them.

"Left, or right?" Sergeant Ratcliffe asked.

"What?" Serena said. "Oh, I think it was her left—yes, it was, because she couldn't write for a while. We're both left-handed," she added.

Inspector Litton nodded, her expression giving nothing away. "Anything else?"

"Not as far as I recall," Serena said.

The inspector opened a drawer in the desk and took out a small, clear plastic bag. She laid it on the desk in front of Serena. "Just one more thing. We wondered whether you might be able to identify this. Have you seen it before?"

It was a relief for Serena to have something tangible to focus on. She rubbed her eyes and leaned closer. The bag contained a broken gold chain, its remaining links dented, and a little gold pendant with the half-moon letter *C* and some sort of pattern engraved on it.

"Yes," Serena said. She cleared her throat. "It's Caitlin's. She had a necklace with the letter *C* on it. I have a matching one with an *S*."

Inspector Litton was leaning over to look more closely at the design. The harsh light shone on her impeccably highlighted hair. Serena felt scruffy in contrast; some people were always so well-groomed, regardless of circumstances. Right now, she felt as though she had been dragged through hell, which in a way she supposed she had.

"There's a figure engraved on it," the inspector said. "Is that a Tudor rose?" She glanced at Sergeant Ratcliffe, who bent over to take a look.

"It's the rose *en soleil*," Ratcliffe said. "The White Rose of York is superimposed on the sun in splendor. You can see the rays shining out from behind it. It was the emblem of King Edward IV."

"Does that have any significance for you, Miss Warren?" Inspector Litton asked. "You're a historical consultant, I believe?"

"I run a travel company offering bespoke historical tours," Serena said, noting that Inspector Litton had evidently looked into her background, no doubt as part of the investigation. "I studied the fifteenth century a little, but I'm not that knowledgeable on the period. The matching necklaces were a gift from our grandparents when Caitlin and I were about twelve," she added, "so perhaps the symbol meant something particular to them. I don't think they ever mentioned it, though."

Inspector Litton nodded. "The chain was found buried with Caitlin's remains," she said. "You may remember that the missing charm was found in the ruins of Minster Old Hall on the night your sister disappeared. The links had broken."

"Yes," Serena said. "I do vaguely remember that. Or rather," she corrected herself, "I remember someone telling me that part of Caitlin's necklace had been found that night. I have no memory of the actual night itself."

Inspector Litton gave her a tight smile. "So I understand," she said. "Apparently, you were suffering from dissociative amnesia." She drew another colored folder from the pile. This one was a rather garish pink and full of photocopies of what looked like hospital reports. Serena recognized them, the dog-eared record of all the tests and treatments she had been through, as dry as dust when described on paper, but so frustrating and painful in real life. She could feel her heart rate increase and tried hard to keep her voice steady.

"I still am," she said.

"Of course," Inspector Litton said politely. She checked the notes. "The police psychologist who treated you at the time believed that you had witnessed a trauma, but that your mind had blocked it out in order to protect you," she said. She looked at Serena with her cool blue gaze.

"Do you think that was the case, Miss Warren?"

"I have no idea," Serena said. "I'm not a doctor." She tried not to sound too snappy. It was difficult; she might not remember the actual events of the night, but the sight of the notes conjured up an acute sense of loss and grief, as acute as it had been when Caitlin had first gone missing.

"That is the medical diagnosis," she amended. "I've no reason to doubt it."

Again Inspector Litton gave her a long, thoughtful stare. Serena willed herself to say nothing. The silence stretched out. Then the inspector smiled.

"Perhaps the tragic discovery of Caitlin's remains will jog your memory," she said.

Serena bit her lip. Inspector Litton made it sound as though she had left her keys in the door by accident rather than blocked out the hideous trauma of her sister's death.

"Perhaps," she said. "If I recall anything useful, I will of course let you know."

Inspector Litton snapped the folder shut. "I'm afraid that we will need to go over your statement from the time of Caitlin's disappearance," she said, "now that we are reopening the case." She checked the small, jeweled watch on her wrist. "We'll be in touch to make another appointment." She stood up. "We will also need to interview all the other witnesses," she added. "Perhaps you could pass that to your family and let them know we will be contacting them?"

"Of course," Serena said numbly.

"Excellent." Inspector Litton nodded her thanks.

"I'd like to be present if you decide to interview my grandfather," Serena added, feeling inordinately protective. "I'd rather you didn't—he's very frail and confused these days. No doubt you are aware that he suffers from dementia?" Her worst nightmare was that Dick, in his confusion, might say something that was misinterpreted.

"We are aware of that," Inspector Litton confirmed. "Whilst I realize Mr. Warren was ruled out of any direct involvement during the first inquiry, the discovery of your sister's body changes matters somewhat. We'll be reviewing the DNA evidence amongst other things." She made a slight gesture. "We do have to consider all possibilities, Miss Warren," she said with the inexorable logic that Serena was starting to detest. "One of those possibilities is that there was some sort of accident and that someone Caitlin knew hid her body, fearing the consequences of what might happen…" She let the sentence hang, and Serena thought again:

She means me. They think I was responsible. The headache tightened in her temples and she blinked and rubbed her eyes hard, feeling how gritty and tired they were. It was intolerable not to remember, to search her mind and come up with nothing other than the clinging cobwebs of lost memory. Instinct told her that she would never, ever hurt her twin, but doubt was insidious, sliding into all those misty corners of her mind.

The silence stretched out until it felt as though it might snap, then Inspector Litton sighed. "Thank you for your time, Miss Warren," she said. "If you think of anything that might be helpful..."

Serena stood, too, and gathered up her jacket and bag. She realized her hands were shaking and felt an almost panicked desire to get out into the fresh air. Sergeant Ratcliffe escorted her politely through the maze of dark corridors and up the steps into the wide concourse of the police station.

"Interesting symbol on the necklace," he said chattily as they crossed the foyer toward the door. "Is your grandfather a history buff?"

Serena forced herself to concentrate rather than to bolt for the door. "I suppose he was in the past," she said. "He wasn't an academic, but he always loved to read about all sorts of historical periods. He was the one who instilled in me a love of history. He never talked to me about the fifteenth century, though, or at least not as far as I remember."

"I'm interested in genealogy myself," Sergeant Ratcliffe said. "I've traced both sides of my family tree back to the early eighteenth century. There's not a single famous ancestor anywhere," he added mournfully. "Coal miners and agricultural laborers on both sides."

"Ironically, I've no idea about our family history," Serena said. "My grandfather was adopted, and he never talked about his background."

"Shame it's too late to ask him," Ratcliffe said, then blushed rather endearingly. "Sorry," he said. "That was insensitive of me. I only mean that we often miss the chance to find out family stuff from our elderly relatives before they die… Not that he is dead, of course, just…" He broke off, sounding even more awkward.

"Just unable to communicate properly," Serena said, feeling like smiling, despite herself. "Quite."

"Sorry," Sergeant Ratcliffe said again. "Dementia is a very cruel illness." He held out a hand to shake hers. "Thank you for coming in, Miss Warren," he said. "We'll be in touch."

As soon as Serena stepped outside, the noise and life of the city hit her like a punch. She walked down toward the river and once she had reached the bridge over the Thames, stopped and allowed herself to be quite still, feeling the warmth of the sun, letting the sound of voices ebb and flow around her, feeling the tension drain from her. She felt an overwhelming urge to lose herself amongst the shops and streets, to revel in the crush of people and traffic rather than go back to the countryside and the stifling silence. She could have a meal, go shopping, see a show… Anything to drive from her mind the image of Caitlin's bones being uncovered in an eighteenth-century tomb.

Except that she knew she could not simply hide from what was happening. She needed to go and talk to her grandfather and tell him about Caitlin, particularly as the police had indicated they might want to interview him. There was no easy way to broach a topic like this, and she shuddered to think of upsetting him, but it was too important not to discuss. A wave of guilt swept over her at the thought that if only she had not blocked out her trauma, she could have spared Dick all of this, spared all of them the uncertainty, the lack of knowing. But as always, when she tried to force the memories to come, the mist swept in to fill the empty spaces and it felt even more difficult to grasp after the truth.

She walked slowly back to the park and ride stop, feeling completely cut off from the people around her, trapped inside her own head. To escape from the endless beating up of her memory, she focused instead on the other mystery: the fact that Caitlin's body had been sealed in a vault in the eighteenth century, yet she had died only eleven years previously. Those facts were not compatible.

There were some odd circumstances about the whole thing, Zoe Lovell had said of the burial, and Serena could see precisely what she meant now, although odd was an understatement. Perhaps she should speak to Zoe; she didn't really want to involve either Jack or his sister in this, but perhaps there was no alternative if she wanted to learn more of the truth.

A shuttle bus came along, and Serena went up onto the top floor. It was quiet and empty, before the end-of-day rush. The leafy streets of North Oxford slipped past as the bus lurched up toward the A40 junction, crossed the roundabout and turned off into the park and ride car park at Peartree. With a sigh, Serena took her car keys from the bag and went down the stairs to the lower deck, thanking the driver as she stepped down. There were only four other people heading back to their cars. It felt cold, and a sharp little breeze blew the litter across the concrete, wrapping it around her ankles.

She rang the retirement village on the drive to Witney to let them know that she was on her way. There was already a car in the parking bay in front her grandfather's neat one-bedroom flat when she arrived, so she parked in the main car park and walked through the gardens, past the perfectly manicured bowling green and planters full of spring bulbs. It was a tranquil place, and Dick seemed very happy there, but as always, Serena's relief that he was in a place where he could have full-time care for his dementia was tempered by the sense that his family had in some way failed him because they could not look after him themselves. The memory of the grandfather she had known down the years, with his energy and vitality, his enthusiasm and his pin-sharp mind, rubbed up against this other Dick Warren, who sometimes felt like a lost stranger. She was the only one in the family who went to see him regularly.

"Darling, what's the point?" Serena's mother had said when she'd asked her why they so seldom went to Witney. "He doesn't recognize us most of the time. The dementia has robbed him of coherent speech and most of his memory."

"But *we* remember *him*," Serena had argued hotly, and seen her father at least turn away in shame because he had never been good at handling emotion and difficult situations.

"Mr. Warren has been looking forward to seeing you." One of the uniformed staff—young, smiley and with a name badge identifying her as Bella—was waiting to let Serena in at the front door. The flat smelled of polish and fresh flowers. Serena could hear the sound of low voices drifting in from the terrace. Evidently, Dick had a visitor already and it seemed he was having a good day; sometimes he was very chatty. It was one of the things about the illness that baffled Serena and seemed so particularly cruel. On one day her grandfather would recognize her and show flashes of his old self. On another he would be lost and drifting, a silent loner locked in his own world. She was glad that today he was more his old self, though undoubtedly that would make telling him about Caitlin all the more painful.

She followed Bella into the airy living room. The big double doors that led out onto the patio were open. Dick was sitting outside on a smart beige rattan sofa, a rug over his knees.

A dog sat beside him, a black Labrador that was graciously allowing him to stroke its ears. Its eyes were half-closed in pleasure, and it was pressed against Dick's side.

It was actually the dog that Dick was addressing, speaking softly as he rubbed its gleaming head. For a moment, Serena assumed that this was some sort of pet therapy; judging by Bella's beaming face it was a big success. Then she saw the man sitting opposite Dick on a matching armchair.

It was Jack Lovell.

Chapter 10

ANNE

London
June 1472

Time flew by on leaden wings. Soon after Francis had gone to Ewelme to the household of the Duke of Suffolk, Joan and Frideswide left Ravensworth to join him there. I felt their loss as acutely as I had Francis's own departure, for we had been good friends. At least Joan wrote to me even if her brother did not and in this way, I became acquainted with their lives at one remove.

Mother, meanwhile, was busy making marriage alliances until it felt as though there had been nothing but weddings and babies for the past several years. I had been married longer than any of my siblings, but my life was the only one that saw no change. I still shadowed my mother in overseeing the dairy and poultry, the spinning and weaving, the preserving and distilling. I visited the sick in the village, I walked and rode, I discussed sermons with Mother and my sisters, and did some poor embroidery, for I had no talent with the needle. I read books with increasing enjoyment. But I fretted. I felt as though the world had moved on and left me behind and that I would be trapped in this round forever as the seasons came and went.

It was Joan Lovell's marriage that changed everything. Her husband, Sir Brian Stapleton, was a distant cousin of the Duke of Suffolk. New alliances were being formed as King Edward shored up his power. Sir Brian had lands in the North, but the wedding was to take place at Ewelme. So, for the first time, I traveled south to Oxfordshire. I was bursting with the excitement of all the new experiences.

I found the soft land of the south very rich and green, though a touch too gentle for my tastes. Ravensworth was a proper castle, a fortress, and I liked the uncompromising strength that seemed to flow from the rugged moors and the heathland that surrounded it. The southern manors, like their setting, were far less rugged. Francis, though, loved this part of the country.

"Wait until I show you my estate at Minster Lovell," he told me. "It is the most beautiful spot. The river runs slow in lazy curves and the meadows are lush with sweet flowers and grasses..."

"You will be telling me that the sun shines all the time," I teased him. I was pleased to see him after a while apart and relieved that he seemed no different and that we picked up our easy friendship with one another. For his sake I tried to sound excited at the prospect of living out my future away from the moors and valleys of my home, but I felt a pang of anticipated grief. Francis's life was so much more exciting than mine, for he was starting to take up the duties that came with his titles and estates, but there was no mention of a time when we might live together. My future still felt as remote as the moon. And whilst I was glad that we were still comfortable with each other, I would have welcomed a change in the way that he viewed me. Being seen by Francis in a sisterly light was not what I desired anymore.

From Oxfordshire we moved to London for the wedding of Richard of Gloucester to my cousin Anne Neville. London was different from anywhere I had been before. It was a vast, untidy sprawl of dark and dirty streets, tiny crowded houses with dank thatch atop, a pall of smoke hanging over it all. The noise was relentless. Even at Westminster, set on the edge of the river away from the sounds and smells of the teeming city, it felt as though we were in another world, a world that hummed with power and purpose. I did not like it. It was strange to me and unwelcome. It spoke of men's ambitions and the dangerous games they played. I was too straightforward for such a world. I disliked pretension and pretense equally and besides, there could be nothing but discomfort in a place where rivalries old and new lurked so close to the surface.

The marriage was solemnized in St. Stephen's Chapel, and the banquet that followed was quite the most elaborate of my life. Once I had eaten and drunk my fill—and I was hungry for it had been an equally long and elaborate wedding service—I was bored. No one spoke to me as I was young, female and of no consequence, and I was seated with Frideswide Lovell and various other children near the bottom of the table. Early on, Gloucester had gestured to Francis to join him and their friends, and he had gone with a word of apology to me, but clearly glad to escape the nursery atmosphere. Rather than sulk to be left behind, I turned my attention to watching the wedding guests. The King presided, enjoying demonstrating his benevolence to his favored younger brother. Women apparently found him handsome, but I thought he was in danger of losing those good looks as they blurred with overindulgence. Beside him the Queen was the very opposite, her ice-cold beauty as sharp as daggers. She was pregnant again, and it gave her an air of complacency, but at the same time she kept a close eye on her husband as his gaze roved over all the women. Gloucester himself was a different matter, as thin and pale as an aesthete, my cousin Anne at his side, a fragile English rose whose stem looked as though it might snap at any moment.

I became aware that the King had beckoned Francis over to him and was speaking urgently in his ear. I saw them both glance down the table toward me, and then Edward gestured to a girl who was seated a little way down to his left. She was a few years older than I, and at that age I felt the difference sharply for she was comely and full-grown whilst I was still half-maid, a half-woman. She was dark where I was fair, knowing and bright-smiling. I realized now that she had been watching the King keenly, awaiting her summons, and now she slipped gracefully from her seat and went to curtsey to him. She smiled and dimpled prettily at Francis when they were introduced, and I felt a prick of jealousy as keen as a spur.

I looked across to where my mother was seated and saw that she, too, ever-watchful, had seen this byplay. And in that moment, seeing her expression, I understood. I knew that the King had taken the opportunity of his brother's marriage feast to suggest to Francis that he annul his marriage to me so that he could marry elsewhere. Even now he was whispering in Francis's ear that he could be rid of me to form an alliance that the King favored, and to a woman he could bed at once and did not need to wait for.

Edward was acting procurer to Francis right under my nose.

There was a blatancy to it that stole my breath, and yet at the same time I felt a dull thud of inevitability. Ever since Father had rebelled, I had had it half in my mind that my marriage might be annulled. Tainted by his treason, I was no longer the prize I had once been. Father was dead and my brothers both too young to be influential. Francis could now do much better, and as the marriage had not been consummated there was nothing to stop the King's plan.

I felt quite powerless for a moment then, trapped in a vision of myself excluded from the future I had thought would be mine. I got to my feet and stumbled clumsily from the table, for my eyes were swimming with tears. I was tired and lost, and did not know what to do. Frideswide Lovell saw me and tugged on my gown to stop me in my tracks.

"I go to find the privy," I lied, blinking back my tears through pride. "I shall not be long."

It was little surprise given my distress and the fact that I could not see properly, that I was soon lost amidst the maze of rooms and corridors, ignored by scurrying servants who were laden with platters for the feast and had no time to spare to direct me. Nor did I have any clear idea of where I might go. I simply wanted to escape the crowds for a little while and gather my thoughts and my dignity in private.

I found a room that was aside from all the noise and bustle. It was bright with lamplight and the embers of a fire glowed warm in the grate. At first, I thought it unoccupied, but then I saw that a woman was sitting at a spinning wheel. I thought she looked beautiful the same way a witch in a fairy story is beautiful and frightening at the same time, a creature of the elements, barely real. The light gleamed on her dark brown hair and her fingers flew nimbly over the wool. She looked up when she saw me hovering in the doorway and the wheel slowed. The austere beauty of her face lightened into a smile, although it was not a warm one. There was still something cold about her.

"How do you do, little maid?" she said. "You look tired. Would you like to come in?"

I slipped into the room and sat in the little wooden chair by the fire, watching her all the while as the wheel turned and she concentrated on the spinning, lips pursed, eyes following the run of the thread. There was something about the room and her presence that made me forget my fears for the future. I felt soothed and calmer than I had all evening, tucked away from the noise and the threat of men's powerful games.

"There's blackberry juice in the jug," the woman said after a moment, inclining her head toward the sideboard, "should you care for a drink."

I poured a beaker for myself and looked at her inquiringly to see if she would like one, too. She smiled at that. "You are a well-brought-up child," she said. "Thank you. What is your name?"

"I am Anne," I said. "Who are you?"

"Ginevra," she said simply. "Lately tirewoman to the Duchess of Bedford."

The Duchess of Bedford had been the Queen's mother, the infamous Jacquetta of Luxembourg, who had been roundly detested by my uncle Warwick for her ambition and cupidity. When he had displaced the King a few years before, Warwick had accused both the Duchess and her daughter of witchcraft. This woman, I thought, might pass for a witch in a fairy tale, the beautiful stepmother who tried to poison the princess through jealousy. Then I laughed at my own foolishness, for

I was twelve years old, not a baby to be enchanted by stories of magic.

I poured a beaker of blackberry juice for her, too, and sat down again by the fire. It was so peaceful here in this little chamber, the warmth of the fire and the rich sweetness of the drink making me drowsy. I could happily have fallen asleep.

"I've been at the wedding feast," I said, yawning. "It goes on and on most tediously."

Ginevra laughed at that. "Poor child!" she said. "You sound quite worn-out by it all."

The spinning wheel clicked and creaked. I wondered what it was like for her, sitting here, working whilst others made merry in the hall. I wondered why she had not been invited. The ladies of the court were in general gently born and she looked too fine and rich to be a lower servant.

"How did you come to wait upon the Duchess?" I asked on impulse. "Were you already known to her?"

Ginevra smiled, a small smile that spoke of secrets. "I knew her from long ago," she said. "When I was in need of help, she was gracious enough to offer it to me."

This told me very little, but I had been taught not to pry and so I asked no more. I thought that perhaps I should go and leave her to her work but a strange lassitude had come over me and I did not seem able to summon the energy to move.

"Shall I tell you a story to cheer you?" Ginevra asked. Her busy fingers never hesitated on the spinning wheel. "It is a tale of another wedding, one that happened long ago." Her voice changed; a hint of bitterness crept in. "It is a goodly tale for a night like this."

I slid a little deeper into the chair, curling up against the fat cushions. I was not averse to hearing a story. It fitted the warmth of the room and the sudden sleepiness that had come over me as the blackberry juice warmed my veins.

"Once upon a time," she said, "many, many years ago, there was a beautiful manor set beside a little river that ran sweetly between the rich fields of corn. The lord was a handsome young man, his family noble and well respected. When he found a bride, there was much rejoicing and all the nobility of the realm gathered to celebrate. It was winter and a storm was raging outside, but within the ancestral hall the wedding guests feasted and made merry. What they did not know, however, was that the bride with whom the young lord had fallen madly in love was no lady, but a thief come to rob the house of its most precious treasure."

I sat up a little straighter. "How could this be?" I demanded.

"She was young and beautiful and to all appearances rich," Ginevra said simply, "and the lord was…a man like any other."

I understood what she meant. In fact, the story made me think of the Queen and how it was said she had seduced the King into marriage because he was so desperate to bed her.

"Poor fool," I said, "to be so deceived."

"Perhaps the bride deserves some of your pity, too," Ginevra said. "Thieves are often made, not born."

This had not previously occurred to me. I had a simple enough understanding of right and wrong, learned from my tutors and the Bible. I did not know then what it was to starve for want of a loaf of bread, or freeze for lack of a warm blanket.

"What made her so, then?" I asked, my curiosity stirred. "What excuse can there be for a thief?"

"She had lived by her wits since she was a child," Ginevra said. "She and her sister were orphaned young. When you have to fend for yourself, you cannot afford to be too high-minded. She fell in with a bunch of rogues, and whilst they offered some protection—" she made a slight gesture "—the price was high."

"They wanted her to steal for them," I said.

She nodded. "The manor held a treasure of great worth," she said. "No one had seen it in generations, for it was locked away in a golden and jeweled box, and men were forbidden to touch it for fear of releasing its power. It was said to be a relic of some sort and had been beloved of the ancient druids and revered by the great King Alfred himself. It held the key to knowledge and learning, but it also held a darker power from a time before Christianity. It was also known to be closely guarded. Only someone who held the trust of the lord and access to the muniments room would have the chance to take it."

I shuddered at the dark specter of the treasure's power. "Yet the thief dared all to take it," I said. "She must have been brave."

"Or desperate," Ginevra said. For a second, I could have sworn I saw a glitter of tears in her eyes. "She had bargained her freedom upon it," she said simply. "She was a serf—a slave—and her sister the same. They belonged to the man who ran the gang of thieves. He told her that when she delivered the treasure to him, they would both go free."

This seemed to me a very dark and unhappy fairy tale, not a happy story for a wedding eve. I no longer felt warm and sleepy, but cold inside and I wished she had not started it.

"Did she succeed?" I asked, hoping that the story would have a happy ending.

"She did," Ginevra said. "When the guests became drunk on good food and wine a cry went up to play a game of hide-

and-seek. That gave the bride the chance she needed. Quick as a flash she offered to be the one to hide."

"I like that game," I said. "If you are clever, you can find a hiding place no one else will discover."

Ginevra looked at me. Her eyes were very dark and impossible to read. "Sometimes you may hide too well," she said, "and no one ever finds you."

"Then you win the game," I said.

She laughed. At some point her hands had fallen idle and the click of the spinning wheel had died away to leave nothing but quiet in the room, broken only by the hiss and snap of the fire.

"There are some," she said, "who say that that is what happened to the Mistletoe Bride. They say she hid in a wooden chest, and that although the bridegroom and his guests hunted for her for days, she was never found. Only years later was her body discovered in the trunk, a sad and withered corpse dressed in the tattered rags of her wedding gown. That is the legend men tell on dark winter nights."

I shuddered again. "That would be harsh punishment," I said, "even for a thief."

"Those who tell that tale do not know the true story, of course," Ginevra said. "They do not know it was never the bride's intention to hide, that she planned to steal the treasure and to run."

I was starting to warm to this thief who had the sense not to become trapped in a chest and the courage to try to free herself and her sister—even if her actions were morally dubious.

"What did she do?" I asked. "When the game of hide-and-seek started—what was her plan?"

"First, she ran to the muniments room where the old books

and documents were kept," Ginevra said. "There, she pried open the iron bars on the trunk where the treasure was stored, for the wood was old and rotten and gave easily. Then she snatched up the golden box in which it lay, and then—" She stopped. I was holding my breath and almost burst with frustration.

"Yes? Did she open the box? Did she touch the treasure?"

"You are impatient," Ginevra said, laughing. "No, she did not. She jumped into the muniments chest and hid away."

"So, she *did* hide," I said. "She became trapped in the box just like the story said."

"She hid only as long as it took for the groom and his men to hunt for her," Ginevra said, "and then when they set out to search through the snow, she climbed out of the box to make her escape."

"That was clever," I admitted, "and courageous."

Ginevra nodded. "Once the hue and cry had died down, she imagined that she might escape via the river. She stowed the golden box beneath her gown and crept through the silent house and across the snow-filled courtyard. There was a water gate in the wall and a boat tied to the staithe…"

"She escaped by water!" I said, but Ginevra was already shaking her head.

"Perhaps she might have done," she said, "had she not opened the box."

"She should not have done that," I said. I felt a sickness in my stomach as though this were a true story and not a fiction. I wished with all my heart that the Mistletoe Bride had not succumbed to her curiosity. Curiosity was dangerous.

"The box was a beautiful piece of gold set with jewels," Ginevra said, "and would fetch a good price, but not enough to buy her freedom. So she looked within." She took a breath. "But when she saw what it contained, she thought she had been cheated, for the treasure was so small and plain a thing that it had to be worthless. She took hold of it, intending to cast it aside, but then she felt as though she was falling, far, far down through the dark, so far that she thought she would never step out again into the light. And when she did—" Ginevra's voice was so quiet I had to strain to hear her "—when she did, she was in a different place, in a different time."

"An enchantment!" I said. "The treasure was enchanted, just as she had heard! She stole it and it took its revenge upon her."

Ginevra took a little golden pair of shears from her belt and cut the woolen thread. The snap of the blades sounded loud in the quiet room and, somehow, very final, as though she were drawing a line under the story and the Mistletoe Bride's fate.

"It did indeed," she said with a faint smile. "She has had plenty of time to repent of her crime."

"If the treasure had the power of enchantment," I said, "and had taken her to another time, could it not have taken her home again?"

Ginevra looked at me. Her gaze was dark and inward-looking. "Many times she tried," she said. "She took hold of it and wished with all her heart to return to her sister, back where she belonged. But the magic the treasure possesses is old magic. It is not so easily bent to the will." She looked me straight in the eyes. "The treasure must be returned whence it came," she said. "I see that now. Only then will the circle be closed."

She picked up her box of wools and closed the lid, dousing the brightness of the colors within. She stood, unhurried and graceful. "It is time for me to go," she said. "I have a commission for you, Anne Lovell. Return here in a half hour and the treasure will be waiting for you. I want you to care for it. Take it to Minster Lovell when you go there. Take it back where it belongs."

She stooped to kiss my cheek and her lips were as cold as snow. I put out a hand to catch her sleeve. "Wait!" I said. I wanted to ask her how she knew my name, whether she was the Mistletoe Bride and so many other questions. But I was too late—she had gone. It was odd, but as soon as she left the chamber the fire seemed to dwindle and die to ash and the candles dim. The wheel sat silent, the cut thread trailing. A melancholy mood came over me then. It had been a strange hour; for a little while, listening to Ginevra's fairy tale, I had forgotten about Francis and the King's plans for him, but now I felt downcast once more. Although I did not want to go back to the feast, I knew that by now Mother would be seeking me and I had no desire to be upbraided by her.

Slowly, I got to my feet and wandered out into the corridor, finding my way back to the great hall more by luck than judgment. To my astonishment, it was as though no time had passed at all, though it seemed to me I must have been closeted in that little chamber with Ginevra for an hour or more. The sweating pages still ran hither and thither with platters high with food, the wine still flowed and Francis was bowing politely to the lady the King had just introduced to him. He looked up, caught my eye and smiled and then he excused himself and came down the room toward me, guiding me back to my chair and seating himself beside me.

"I am sorry to neglect you," he said. "I came back as quickly as I could."

"I thought that the King was proposing a new match for you," I blurted out, my indignation at Edward's behavior overriding my recent experience with Ginevra. "He seemed most anxious to acquaint you with that lady." I jerked my head in the direction of the girl who was now smiling charmingly as she was introduced to another young knight, like the tempting prize she was.

Francis's eyes crinkled at the corners when he smiled. It gave his expression a warmth I loved. "Lady Jane Conyers," he said. "She is vastly wealthy, so I am told."

"And vastly pretty," I said dryly.

"And already a widow who is a favorite with a number of gentlemen at the court," Francis said, even drier.

"Oh," I said. "I see. The King wishes to find her a husband…"

"In repayment for services rendered," Francis said smoothly. "Alas, I could not help him. I pointed out to him that I already have a wife and am very content with her."

I looked again at Lady Jane and felt a flash of pity for her, bartered away when the King's lust for her had been sated. She mattered nothing to Edward other than as a commodity to buy a man's loyalty through warming his bed.

"I commend your loyalty to me," I said a little stiffly. I wanted to ask if that loyalty also extended to him not taking a mistress, but I did not dare, did not really want to know the answer. I knew that Francis, at seventeen, was the same age that the Duke of Gloucester had been when he had first fathered a child. If I had no wish to think of Francis annulling our marriage to take a new wife, I was equally unhappy to contemplate him taking a mistress to while away the years until I could fulfill my wifely duties.

Francis took my hand. It looked small in his, a child's hand still. He turned it over and kissed my palm, closing my fingers over the kiss. "I will wait for you, Anne," he said. "I will always wait for you."

And now, at last, the feast was finally coming to an end and Gloucester and his bride were preparing to leave. The guests started to fragment into different groups, my cousin Anne's ladies sweeping her from the room to prepare her for the bridal bed whilst a more ribald party assembled around the Duke. Mother, evidently awakening to the way in which the night was sliding into impropriety, came over to take me away.

She was in high good spirits, having mended her fences with her cousins of York. "We are all of Neville blood," she told me, conveniently forgetting that one branch of the Neville family had risen against another not so long ago, "and kinship is stronger than all else."

"I am glad," I said, "for I feared that the King might look to overset my marriage to Francis."

She stopped then and caught me by the shoulders, turning me so that the light from the torches fell on my face. "You are very loyal to him," she said.

"I love him," I said simply, and it was true, for I did love Francis. I pressed my fingers against my palm, feeling the imprint of his kiss there.

"He has been a part of my life for almost as long as I can recall," I said. "I would miss him sorely if we were to be parted." My feelings were more complicated than a child's affection whilst less than the emotions of a grown woman since I was still betwixt and between. One day soon, though, I sensed, that love might grow and change.

"No one can break the bond of marriage without your consent," Mother said reassuringly. "You need have no fear. Nor would I ever permit that to happen."

She threaded her arm through mine as we resumed walking. "Gloucester's marriage will strengthen our hand still further," she said. "He is a good friend to Francis and will reward him well. The Woodvilles will soon be in eclipse."

For Mother, I thought, everything was measured out in ambition and achievement, and if it was at the expense of someone else, so much the better.

"I met a servant who was tirewoman to the Duchess of Bedford this evening," I said, recognizing that we were following the same corridor that I had trod earlier when I had met Ginevra. "She gave me sweet blackberry juice and told me a tale of a thief at a wedding."

Mother raised her brows. "You should not consort with Jacquetta of Bedford's women, Anne," she said sharply. "Everyone knows that the Queen's mother meddles in dangerous enchantments. Besides, when did you meet her? You were only gone from the feast for but a moment."

I was not really paying attention to her for we had reached the little chamber where Ginevra and I had spoken, and despite half-believing that it had been no more than a fairy story, I wanted to see if she had left the treasure for me to return to Minster Lovell. The door was wide, the room lit only by the flare and shadow of the torches without. There was no fire and no candles, no spinning wheel and no beaker with the dregs of my drink left in it. All had been swept away, vanished as though they had never been, and suddenly I felt tired, so very tired, as though I were awakening from a dream.

"Perhaps I imagined it all," I said, staring blankly into the darkness. "Yet I was sure..."

"You're seeing ghosts," Mother said indulgently, patting my cheek. "It's time to sleep."

I was about to follow her when I saw on the bare mantel what looked like a black arrowhead. I picked it up. It was only about four inches long, with a small hole drilled through the slender shaft, and its surface was pitted and a little rough yet in the palm of my hand it felt smoother than silk.

"What have you there?" Mother asked. Then, seeing it was nothing of value: "You are like a magpie, Anne. Throw it away!"

I looked at the arrowhead. Surely this was nothing but a piece of discarded old iron. Despite Ginevra saying that the treasure was small and insignificant, I had been expecting something a little gaudier—the gold box studded with jewels, perhaps. I was very disappointed. Even so I tucked it within my bodice where the warmth of my skin warmed it, too, and it was lodged against my heart. When I undressed that night, I took it out and rolled it up in one of my smocks and packed it in my trunk for our return to the North.

"It's some sort of lodestone, Lady Anne," Crowther, the farrier at Ravensworth said when I showed it to him. He was an old man who had worked at the castle for much longer than I had been alive. I liked him because he knew all manner of interesting things, which was why I had shown him my arrowhead in the first place.

"What is a lodestone?" I asked. I'd never heard the word. "What does it mean?"

"In the old days a lode was a path or a journey," the farrier said. "A lodestone is said to show you the way, for it points to the North." He shook his head. "I know naught of that but I do know that it draws iron. Look…" He took some of the small nails he used for the horse's shoes and I watched them spin and dance toward the arrow as though by magic. They stuck fast to it, like the prickles on a hedgehog.

"It's enchanted!" I said, drawing back. I thought of Ginevra then, and her stories. Mother had been right that the Duchess of Bedford's women dabbled in devilry. This was the treasure indeed and it possessed some strange power.

The farrier laughed. "It's no enchantment," he said, "unless it is nature's magic. You keep it safe, Lady Anne." He sounded reverent, turning the stone over in his gnarled hands. "That's special, that is. I'll make you a case for it."

I thought he would forget, but he did not—two nights later he presented me with a wooden box lined with blue velvet where the arrowhead fitted snugly. For so plain a piece it looked curiously precious there, gleaming black and shining on its rich cushion. I decided that Crowther had been correct. There was something otherworldly about this lodestone. Its very plainness concealed a heart of magic. There and then I decided that I would keep the relic close by me.

Chapter 11

SERENA

Minster Lovell
Present Day

"What are you doing here?" Serena said. Shock at seeing Jack had given way to a sharp antagonism. First, he'd been snooping around Caitlin's grave at Minster Lovell and now he was here talking to her grandfather. If he had told Dick that Caitlin's body had been found before she had had the chance to talk to him, she really would have to kill him. A hot wave of anger washed over her.

Jack got to his feet unhurriedly, a wry smile on his lips. Unlike her he looked cool and effortlessly in control, which only made Serena feel hotter and more annoyed.

"Hello, Serena," he said. "That seems to be our default greeting."

"Mr. Lovell came to do a talk for some of the residents today." Bella, the carer, sensing an atmosphere, was quick to throw herself into the breach. "Wasn't that kind of him?" She gave Jack a starry-eyed look. "We do a program of talks throughout the year. This month it's about TV stars. The residents love a celebrity."

"Actually most of them hadn't a clue who I was," Jack said self-deprecatingly, "but they did seem interested in hearing about journalism. Most of them think all journalists are scoundrels."

"Far be it from me to disagree," Serena said frostily.

"Mr. Lovell's a patron of our local dementia charity," Bella said. "Definitely a good guy, not a scoundrel." She gave Jack another adoring look that reminded Serena irresistibly of the dog.

She felt a wayward pang of sympathy for Jack's look of acute embarrassment. Despite everything, she could feel herself softening a little toward him. It wasn't every hard-nosed forensic journalist who would bother to visit a local care home. She looked at him, and he raised his brows slightly, as though challenging her to question her assumptions, but he said nothing. The Labrador, which had been watching Serena with its limpid dark eyes, came over and pressed a damp nose to her palm. She dropped down onto her haunches to stroke it.

"She's called Luna," Jack said.

"You're a beautiful girl," Serena said to the Labrador, who wagged her tail in total agreement. She looked up from tickling Luna's tummy. "Does she parachute into hostile territory with you, Jack?"

"Only in circumstances like this," Jack said dryly. "No, she belongs to my grandmother, but she's a regular visitor here."

"The residents enjoy having dog therapy," Bella said perkily. "It lifts their spirits."

"I came over to see Dick after the talk," Jack said to Serena. "You may—or may not—remember that back in the day he coached me when I was in the under 18s cricket team. He taught us fencing, too. Anyway, I appreciate you'll want to talk to your grandfather on your own." He turned back to Dick and offered his hand. "It's been a pleasure to see you again, sir."

"Come back again, Francis," Dick said, looking up, his pale blue eyes bright. "Come back, anytime."

"Thank you, sir," Jack said, smiling. "I'd like that."

"It's good to talk about the past," Dick said vaguely, as though the memory was already slipping away from him. "When Pam was alive, we could remember things together. It's lonely without her. No one else knows the truth." He sounded forlorn.

Serena caught Jack's eye and glared at him. She didn't want him witnessing Dick's vulnerability. She wanted to protect her grandfather from his pity.

"The truth about what, Granddad?" she asked.

"History," Dick said, fretful now. "Lions and lilies. What happened in the tower." For a moment, Serena thought she saw a gleam of slyness in his eyes, as though he knew something she did not and was teasing her, then it faded away again. "Can't talk about it," Dick said. His chin sank onto his chest and he lapsed into silence.

Once again Serena saw Jack watching them and glimpsed sympathy and understanding in his eyes rather than the pity she resented. She looked away from him, feeling a pang of loss. When her grandmother Pamela had died from cancer fourteen years before, she knew Dick had been profoundly, grievously lost and lonely, and only his innate strength and determination had kept him going. Despite her grandmother's brusqueness, Serena had recognized then that Pam and Dick had had a strong bond.

Then Caitlin had disappeared and it was as though the

shock together with the unhealed loss of his wife had come together in one swift, overwhelming blow to rob Dick of his health. He had been utterly devastated when Caitlin went missing and seemed to fold in on himself, physically and mentally. He'd sold Minster Hall to the heritage trust and moved to Witney where the care he needed had increased with each passing year. The dementia had become apparent a few years ago, and it was gaining on him all the time.

Serena took her grandfather's hand. It was going to be even more heartbreaking telling Dick about Caitlin now. She wanted to cry. She wanted Jack to go before he witnessed it.

"I'll see you out, Mr. Lovell," Bella said, with bright incongruousness. "Thanks for calling."

Serena gave Luna a final pat. The dog trotted off after Jack, her paws silent on the thick pile of the carpet.

"I'll go and make us some tea, Granddad," Serena said. "Shall we have some chocolate chip cookies?" She kissed his cheek, adjusting the rug more securely over his lap against the chilly little breeze that had sprung up. Her grandfather smelled faintly of mothballs and more strongly of soap. Serena put her arms about him and hugged him close. His cheek felt cool and rough again hers, but his grip was still firm. She felt a huge rush of love for him and a sense of loss, as she always did, when she remembered how different he had been before the illness. It was another world, another time.

"Serena," he said, and the hot tears burned her eyes as she realized that today he recognized who she was. Perhaps it was one of his more lucid days.

She released him and straightened up, then walked back through to the kitchen. Everything in the flat was spotless and curiously lifeless. When Dick had moved to the retirement village, her parents had persuaded him to buy practical furniture for his new home. The result was shiny and without character, Serena thought, in contrast to all the old bits and pieces she had seen at the hall that morning. She felt a pang for that scattered collection of furniture, books, ornaments and other items that Dick and Pamela had gathered over the years, each with their connections and memories, their story to tell. There was so little left.

One exception was a couple of Dick's paintings, which had hung in the manor house and were now on his living room wall. Whilst the kettle boiled, Serena went back into the living room to look at them. The first was a fairly conventional view of the ruins of Minster Lovell Hall, a sleepy summer watercolor of the meadows and the river beyond. It looked familiar, safe and unthreatening. The other was different, and Serena had always found it faintly unsettling, though she could not explain why. It was a pencil sketch of a huddle of gray stone buildings around a courtyard. A tall tower topped the left-hand corner, and a church spire peeked over the wall at the back. A river lapped at the retaining wall where a small boat bobbed in the shallows. There was a dovecote across the fields to the right, and it was this that gave the clue to the location. It was Minster Lovell Hall before it was a ruin. She had always wondered whether Dick had drawn it from imagination or based it on an old print he'd found. His study had been packed with ancient books, maps and pictures.

On the table were some more recent pencil sketches of flowers, a fat robin and a beautiful soaring sketch of a falcon in flight. Even with the worsening of his dementia, Dick's artistic talent had not deserted him. The strokes were shakier, but Serena thought he still had more of a gift than she had ever possessed. The nurses had told her that this was quite common; whilst people might lose their memories and to a degree their ability to care for themselves or understand normal modes of behavior, often their skills and talents remained with them, whether it was a facility with foreign languages, an ability to recognize plants or a talent for art.

The kettle hissed and clicked into silence, and Serena went back into the kitchen to warm the pot. Whilst the tea brewed, she stood looking out at her grandfather, nodding in his sleep on the sheltered patio, and thought about their family history. It had been in her mind since that morning, conjured up perhaps by her visit to the hall. She knew so little about where either of her grandparents had come from originally or much about their lives before they moved to Minster Lovell. It was odd that both of them in their different ways had been interested in history and yet had not spoken about their own past. Perhaps Polly would be able to tell her more. She would ask her when she rang later.

When she came back out onto the patio with the teapot, mugs and the cookies, Dick was still dozing in his chair, but he woke when he saw her and smiled gently. He seemed to have no recollection that she had been there minutes before, but he seemed pleased to see her and even more pleased to see the cookies.

The tears pricked Serena's eyes. She couldn't begin to imagine how she could tell Dick that they had found Caitlin's body. It felt impossibly cruel, and she remembered how devastated he had been when her twin had disappeared. Yet not to tell him felt wrong and untruthful. And perhaps he simply would not register it. Already his smile was fading, and his eyes seemed to reflect the blankness of someone who had forgotten what they had been speaking of a moment before. Dick's memory, once so sharp and incisive like the man himself, was now a flimsy thing that slipped away without notice, leaving him a shell of the man he had been.

Serena poured strong tea into his favorite mug, which featured a knight in full medieval armor. She'd bought it for Dick as a birthday present years ago when she'd visited Warwick Castle on a school trip. Even now she could remember how inordinately pleased he had seemed when she gave it to him. Now his gaze dwelt on it for a moment before he took his first mouthful of tea.

"Granddad," Serena said. Her voice sounded rough in her own ears. "I've got some bad news." She looked at Dick, who was watching her with his faded blue gaze. "They've found Caitlin's body. I'm so very sorry… She's dead."

There was a silence, but for a blackbird calling plaintively from the yew tree. Dick did not answer. Serena wondered if he had heard her or if the words had made no sense to him. There was no way of telling. She swallowed the tears that thickened her throat.

"Caitlin," Dick said, and Serena put her hand over his.

"I'm very sorry," she said again.

Dick turned his hand over so that he held hers properly, his calloused palm rough against hers. It felt infinitely comforting and yet infinitely sad at the same time.

"It was the lodestar," Dick said suddenly.

Serena was so surprised that she put her mug down with a snap, spilling some drops of tea on the patio.

"What?" she said. "I'm sorry, Granddad—I don't understand."

Dick's gaze had the same opaque quality that Serena had

seen there earlier, but this time the sense of distance felt different, as though he was looking back a long way, into the past, further than the eye could see.

For a moment his fingers tightened around hers. "I should have warned you," Dick said. "I should have told you both."

"Told us about what?" Serena said.

"Where we came from." Dick sounded irritable, as though she was being deliberately stupid. "I should have explained, but you would never have believed me." He sounded sad. "People tell me I don't remember well," he added. "But I remember my childhood right enough. I know who I am."

Serena waited, afraid that if she questioned him, she might break this tenuous link Dick had forged with his past.

"I'll show you," Dick said. He seemed suddenly agitated, pushing aside the rug that covered his legs, trying to struggle to his feet.

"Granddad!" Serena jumped up, afraid that he might fall. "I'll fetch whatever you need," she said. "Tell me where to find it."

She waited, watching the agonizing struggle behind Dick's eyes as he groped to keep ahold of the thought that she could tell was even now slipping away from him. "The pictures," he said at last, "fetch the pictures," and she watched the tension leave his body as he slumped back down into his chair and closed his eyes.

Serena hesitated, hoping he might say more, but Dick sat still now with his face tilted toward the faint warmth of the early-spring sunshine. "The sun will grow stronger again," he said, and a small smile touched his mouth. A moment later he was asleep.

Serena went back inside and picked up the drawings on the

coffee table and studied them. She wasn't sure whether these were the pictures Dick had meant, but other than the ones on the wall they were the only ones she could see. The fat robin looked cute and Christmassy, but there was a different quality to the others if she looked beneath the faltering pencil lines. The hawk, for example, was a fierce predatory creature whose chest was white, but whose wings were flecked with black and gray. Beneath it in shaky capital letters Dick had spelled out GYRFALCON. The flowers in the other picture were painted in splashes of bright yellow, with dark green leaves, and again beneath the picture there was a title. This one read simply: Plantagenet.

Chapter 12

ANNE

Ravensworth
1475

By the time that I was fifteen, I was wanting my own household to govern and space to grow and spread my wings. My mother's matchmaking had proved most successful in the past few years, and two of my sisters were wed and were already mothers; Elizabeth, who married William Parr, had named her first daughter for me and I stood as godmother to her. Anne Parr was a beautiful child, placid and happy. When she first closed her tiny fingers around mine, I felt a sweetness flower within me that I had never experienced before, an ache that was both joyful and poignant in the same moment. Yet, I also felt left behind. I had been married far longer than my siblings, yet somehow it was as though everyone had forgotten I was Lady Lovell.

Francis remained with the Duke of Suffolk in those fallow years that I spent at Ravensworth. Frideswide wrote that her brother was starting to familiarize himself with his estates, the vast parcels of land that he possessed across the length and breadth of the country. Yet he, too, was still in his minority and the King seemed happy for that to be the case, for he was using the income from Francis's inheritance to pay his own debts. Frideswide wrote of Francis's fury that Edward had assigned the income from their grandmother's lands to his wine merchant.

"Francis resents paying off the entire court's drinking bills," she wrote dryly. "Yet his loyalty will never falter. He is to accompany the King to France, being eager to prove himself on campaign."

This news troubled me. Not so much the King's extravagance at Francis's expense, but the thought that he was going away to fight and that I might be widowed before I was a wife.

"It is the way of men," Mother said as we sat that night in the solar, the firelight playing across the stone floor and leaping up the arras to illuminate the scenes of hunting and hawking in bloodred and black. "If there is not a war to fight, they will provoke one."

I looked at her sitting there placidly and incongruously with her needlework. If she had been a man, she would have been first in the field.

"Why the King needs to invade France is a mystery to me," I said. The chessboard was laid out in front of me, but I had no one to play against so I was pitting the pieces against one another. "Surely he had enough with which to occupy himself in his own kingdom?"

Mother sighed. "The King has a claim to the French throne as well as that of England," she said. "It is important that he should assert it."

"Important for whom?" I asked.

"I do not know why you are forever questioning," Mother said with a snap. "It does no good."

"I am curious, that is all," I said. "You want me to have the Neville ambition. It does not come without understanding."

Mother laid aside the needlepoint. Her embroidery, unlike mine, was very fine.

"Men will always be looking to aggrandizement," she said. She beckoned to one of the maids to pour her a cup of wine from the pitcher and one for me as well. This was unusual and an honor that had only come in the last few months since my fifteenth birthday.

"Your Francis, for example," she said. "I hear he has already been engaged in more lawsuits than a man can count in order to secure his lands, and he is not yet of age."

"That is different," I argued hotly. "It is only because the terms of his inheritance are so complicated. To him it is a matter of law and honor that he should pursue them."

"Men speak of law and honor and all manner of high-flown virtue when it suits their purpose," Mother said with a cynicism I had not heard from her before. "You would do well to hear it, note it and judge by their actions, not their words."

I filed that piece of advice away for future reference and watched as she refilled her cup and drank again. It was unusual to see her like this; there was some discontent in her this night that I did not understand.

"So, if men seek out conflict," I said, "what do women do?"

She gave me a sour smile. "They marry and beget children," she said. "And when they are too old to do that, they are forgotten."

I wondered whether that was what ailed her. Mother was over forty years old by now and had been widowed for three years. She was still a handsome woman yet the King had not suggested she remarry and it seemed no one had sought her hand. This, I thought, might well have been because of her cursed Neville temper, which was well-known. I was not sure any man might find the bargain worthwhile, but I had the sense not to say this.

I also wondered whether the sight of all her children marrying and the arrival of the first grandchildren, far from pleasing her, had actually embittered my mother and made her feel the passing of the years. Like Francis, my brothers had gone to train in other households after Father had died, and now my elder brother Richard would soon take up the governance of Ravensworth.

"Women can have power in other ways," I said. "There is the church, and—"

Her laughter cut across my words. She raised the cup in salute. "Can you see me as a nun, Anne?"

I went across to her and knelt beside her. "There is the court," I said. "You enjoyed our time at Westminster."

Her mouth turned down at the corners. Down went the cup with a snap that made the delicate gold quiver and bend. "My services are not required there," she said. "The Queen has no need for me."

I understood then that she had asked and been rebuffed. Edward, for all his talk of kinship and reconciliation, had not wanted the meddling widow of a traitor in the heart of the court. The Queen certainly had no reason to like Mother, either. Her star had fallen; her time was gone.

"That may change," I said, trying to comfort her. "The wheel of fortune always turns."

"That is superstition," she grumbled, sliding down in her chair, "or if not that, then it is treason."

I shrugged, getting up from her side, irritated that she had rebuffed my attempts to offer solace. I thought she was sorry for herself, or in her cups, or both.

"You should pray for Francis," she said suddenly, her fingers flicking impatiently through the little book of illuminated manuscripts on the table at her side. I loved that book. It had been created for my grandfather at Rievaulx Abbey, and the pictures of the lay brothers laboring in the fields and the monks at their prayers were delicate and jewel bright in their coloring. It was a far cry from the energy and violence of the hunting tapestries.

"I will," I said. "I do."

"Should he die and leave you a virgin widow," Mother said, "a nunnery might be the best place for you since you are so keen to extol the religious life."

I was so shocked and hurt in that moment that I could have dashed my own wine in her face. The urge to strike back, to tell her that I was young and comely and clever, and would find another husband where she could not, was so strong. Then I saw the glitter of tears in her eyes, and she held out her arms to me and I went into them. She smelled of wine and sweat and heat and a heavy perfume that could not conceal any of the other smells, and I pitied her then.

"Forgive me," she said against my hair. "Forgive me, Anne. I am old and sour tonight, and when the north wind blows my bones ache." She eased back and looked me in the eye. "You should know," she said fiercely, "that if you need me, I shall always be by your side. You are my daughter and I love you. Sometimes I am fearful for you, that is all. You are so curious, so questioning. I do not know why it scares me, but it does."

I put her words down to the maudlin effect of drink, but I hugged her back nevertheless.

"Don't fear for me," I said. "I am sure I shall lead a life of tedious domesticity."

In that moment, there was a gust of wind down the chimney and a spiral of flame leaped from the hearth and spun toward us, bright, malevolent, and at its heart, nothing but darkness through which moved formless shadows. I felt such dread then that I could not move. It weighed me down with abject terror. The fire caught the arras and started to burn. The maid was screaming and crossing herself, and the sound broke me from my stupor. I picked up the ewer of water on the table and threw it over the flames. There was a hiss and the acrid smell of burning, and then nothing but the drip of water onto the stone floor.

"Witchcraft!" The maid sobbed and I thought Mother was going to slap her. I stepped hastily between the two of them.

"It was nothing," I said. "A spark, no more."

But I had seen the shadows in the flame and felt their evil. I thought of the Lodestar in its velvet box, and Ginevra's words about old magic, and I shivered.

It was September when Francis came back from the French wars. The afternoon was fair, and I had been in the stables playing with the latest litter of kittens provided by Nala, the half-feral tabby whom we kept for her fearsome ability to rid the place of rats. Generally her kittens seemed to be fathered by one or other of the wildcats that roamed the hills around Ravensworth. They were sly, secretive creatures; if I ever saw one on my rides it would stare at me with its pale eyes before disappearing into the woods at the flick of a whisker. This litter had inherited the thick black banded tail of their father, but with some flecks of white and fawn stripes from their mother.

They were extremely pretty and at this age, still too small to do much harm with teeth and claws. Nala was not maternal in any way, having abandoned her offspring to be fed by the grooms whilst she preferred hunting. In a number of ways, she reminded me of my mother. After I had done my duty in playing with them and providing a bowl of milk, I wandered down to the lake in the late-afternoon sunshine.

Here it was quiet, the bustle of the castle left behind. I saw the fowler with a brace of woodcock for supper; he touched his cap as he passed by. The plop of the fish was loud in the silence. The light spun across the water. It felt a soft and dreamy day with the heat that sometimes came as summer slid into autumn. I sat for a while on a fallen log beneath a curtain of willows and thought about very little, content only in that moment of warmth and brightness. Then a shadow fell across me, a twig snapped, and I realized that I was not alone.

A man was standing by the edge of the water, watching me. My heart jumped into my throat and I reached for my knife in the little scabbard on my belt, but in that same moment he stepped into a band of light and I recognized him.

"There is no need to greet me at the point of a blade," he said. He was smiling.

"Francis!" I jumped up, hurrying across to him, putting both my hands into his. He looked different, I thought. It was not simply the spattering of mud on his cloak and boots that showed he had ridden hard and come to find me before he had changed his clothes. There was something else about him, something in his bearing, a new confidence perhaps.

"How are you, Anne?" he said. "They told me at the castle that I might find you here."

"I am well," I said, "and happy to see you." Pleasure burst

inside me and I realized it was true. I drew him down to sit beside me. "I missed you," I said. "What happened? Did you fight?"

Francis shook his head. "King Louis had no stomach for it," he said. "He offered us parley. An alliance was brokered and then we feasted together."

"How very civilized," I said dryly. "If only all wars were to end that way."

Francis's lips twitched. "Gloucester was furious at the treaty," he said. "He considers it dishonorable. He is right, of course, for we were paid to go away and not to cause trouble."

"Surely that is preferable to dying in battle," I said. Sitting here beside him, feeling the solid presence of him next to me, I couldn't imagine that it was ever worth trading peace for battle no matter how it was won.

"There *may* be valor in dying for a cause you believe in, I suppose," I said, "but not for the throne of France. It is not worth it, not when we already have England."

Francis burst out laughing. "You are a pragmatist, like King Edward," he said.

And unlike his younger brother Richard, I thought to myself. Edward did indeed have his weaknesses, but he was a skilled commander and a ruthless man. More practically, he was capable of compromise, whilst there was a rigidness in Gloucester that scared me sometimes.

"How long do you stay in Yorkshire this time?" I asked, aware that my hand still rested in his and that it felt very sweet and right that it did so. It was so pleasant, just the two of us down by the water. I had become accustomed to seeing Francis's time as rationed and valuing it accordingly. I hoped we would have the chance to go hawking and to ride out across the moors before winter set in.

"I must be gone within a week," Francis said. "I came to deal with a matter at my manor at Bainton."

I felt a thud of disappointment. I had thought he had come to see me; I tried to tug my hand from his, but he held on to it.

"And to see you, of course," he said, laughter lurking in his eyes.

Once again, I tried to free myself, annoyed at his teasing. Instead of letting me go, though, he pulled me closer.

"Anne," he said. "I do but jest. You know you are by far more important to me than aught else."

I looked up to see him looking at me. There was a darkness in his eyes I had not seen there before. He raised my hand, spreading out my fingers carefully and linking them between his own. My palm tingled. Suddenly the warm afternoon seemed hotter still, silence wrapped about the two of us, intimate and close.

"I do not know it," I whispered.

"Then you should," Francis said. His expression was very grave. "I've waited for you," he said. "I promised I would."

I understood then, understood why my heart raced and I felt hot and feverish. Exhilaration sparked through me, making me catch my breath. "You need not wait anymore," I said.

Francis drew me close to him, slipping an arm about my waist, and I pressed my cheek against his shoulder. I felt safe there, but I could feel the beat of his heart against my palm and that felt exciting, not safe at all. His lips brushed my cheek and I looked up. His face was very close to mine, so close I could see the intense gray of his eyes and count each individual eyelash, which I did a little dreamily. I raised a hand to touch his lean cheek and recoiled with a slight gasp from the roughness of it. He caught my fingers in his free hand.

"What is it?" His voice had changed, grown husky.

"I didn't realize what it would be like to touch you," I said, not really making sense, except in my own head, where this world of new sensation was entirely exciting.

He smiled. "You've touched me plenty of times in the years we have known each other," he said.

"Not like this," I whispered. "Only as friends."

"And now we are not?" he asked.

"Always," I said, "but now it will be different."

"So wise," Francis said. His lips were but a hairbreadth from mine now, and I could see from his eyes that he was smiling. I think I had stopped breathing entirely.

His mouth touched mine. It was odd; we had been married for ten years and yet this felt like the beginning, as though we were plighting our troth. The light blurred and faded as I closed my eyes. This was so new to me, and different from any of my imaginings. My mother had yet to instruct me on the duties of a wife, having said that there would be time enough when I was old enough to join Francis at Minster Lovell. It seemed, however, that I was old enough now and did not need her advice after all.

I dared to wrap my arms about his neck, to slide my fingers into his hair and kiss him back. He parted my lips with a gentle nudging of his own and suddenly the kiss became very different, full of hunger and tenderness at the same time. I gave myself up to the promise of it and heard Francis groan. We tumbled off the log to lie in the springy grass beneath the sweeping willows, still kissing, entangled in his cloak. Suddenly, it seemed to me that he was wearing a deal too many clothes.

Perhaps it was because I had known him so long that I felt no shyness or perhaps my natural curiosity conquered all. I slid my hands beneath the smooth linen of his shirt and ran them over his back, feeling the ripple of muscle beneath his skin. He gasped and drew back, and I wondered if I had hurt him in some way, but then he brushed the hair back from my face with a hand that shook.

"Anne," he said. Then: "I had not intended for it to be like this."

I pressed my lips to the curve of his neck, made reckless by the knowledge that he wanted me. The skin there was soft and warm, and my heart turned over with love for him.

"How could it be better?" I whispered, touching his cheek, and he kissed me again and I was lost. When his hand slipped inside my gown and I felt it against my bare breast I think I would have cried out, but his kiss captured the sound.

"The first time," Francis said. His voice was not steady. "It may hurt you."

I didn't care. I cared for nothing but him and when he came into me and it did hurt, I still did not care. I felt nothing but desire, and awe at my own power. Afterward I rested my head on Francis's chest and he wrapped the cloak about us, and I felt so happy that it felt as though there was the tightest of bands about my heart.

Everything will be different now, I thought. *The future can begin.*

Chapter 13

SERENA

Minster Lovell
Present Day

"You've been shopping!" Eve popped up from behind the reception desk as Serena pushed open the door of the Minster Inn. She eyed Serena's bags with delight. "Retail therapy. It never fails."

"What? Oh..." Serena had almost forgotten that after she'd left the care home, she'd dropped in to the Woolgate center in Witney. There had been so much to think about and she didn't want to face any of it, so instead she had done a bit of late-night shopping. She glanced down at her tote bags. It had taken her mind off things for a little while, and now she had a new pair of shoes, a scented candle, three birthday cards, a bottle of her favorite perfume, even though she hadn't finished the last one, and a couple of books.

Eve's expression shifted to sympathy. "I read about your sister on the local online news," she said. "They're saying her body was the one found during the archaeology dig at the church. Do they think it's murder?"

Serena felt a rush of sickness. Eve's ghoulish enthusiasm was too much to bear. She was holding Serena's room key just out of reach, as though it would only be handed over when Serena had satisfactorily answered her questions. Serena contemplated snatching it out of her hand and making a bolt for the stairs. "They don't know," she said. "Could I possibly have my key?"

"They're appealing for witnesses," Eve said, as though she hadn't spoken. "Dangerous if you ask me. People misremember all sorts of stuff after ten years. Stirring things up… They'd do better to let it lie."

Serena remembered all the true crime books she'd seen on the shelf on the landing outside her room. Eve was probably a connoisseur of stories like this, and a real live investigation so close to home would no doubt be irresistible to her.

"Serena? Could you spare a moment?" It was Jack. She turned to find him leaning against the doorway, and for once she was almost glad to see him. Luna sat neatly at his side, soft brown eyes fixed on Serena's face.

"Would you like a drink?" Jack said. "The bar's open." He turned to Eve. "If it's no trouble…"

"I'll send Ross along to serve you." Eve was wreathed in smiles now, whether for Jack's benefit or at the prospect of a customer. She bustled off down the corridor, leaving Serena's key on the counter. Serena grabbed it.

"I thought you looked as though you needed some help," Jack said. He nodded to the key in her hand. "No need to have that drink if you'd rather not."

"Thanks," Serena said a little grudgingly. She hesitated. She could see that the bar was empty and it looked cozy and comforting, with a fire leaping in the grate and the lamps lit. She could feel the warmth from where she was standing, and suddenly all she wanted to do was sit down and relax, preferably with a dog on her feet.

"I'd like a drink," she said.

Jack's smile showed such genuine pleasure that she felt as though she had been hit in the solar plexus. She seemed to remember that smile had been her undoing when she'd been a teenager. She'd visited his house one day, and his mum had sent her up to his bedroom. The door had been ajar and she'd seen Jack sitting at a desk, completely engrossed in some political biography. He hadn't looked as though he had wanted to be disturbed, and she'd felt so intimidated by his concentration and his evident nerdiness that she had turned to go, but in doing so had caught his eye. He'd looked up and seen her then, and smiled at her…

"Is everything all right?" Jack's attention now made her feel quite ridiculously hot and bothered.

"Yes, sorry, I was just…um…admiring Luna." Serena brushed the moment aside, and Jack stood back to let her precede him into the bar.

"What would you like to drink?" he asked.

Serena wanted a huge glass of wine, but she knew that wasn't a good idea. The combination of grief, exhaustion and alcohol would probably have her dozing on the table within minutes; not a good look.

"I'll have a cranberry and soda, thanks," she said. She took a seat in a secluded corner beside the fire. Luna gave a little sigh indicative of pleasure and curled up beside her, front paws outstretched, head resting on them so she could watch Jack.

Serena watched him, too, as he stood at the bar in conversation with Ross. Serena watched him chat easily whilst Ross pulled him a pint and topped up the glass of cranberry juice with soda. She supposed it was Jack's stock-in-trade to be able to talk to everyone, but still she envied him that easy confidence. In her work she had little difficulty in building a strong relationship with her clients. It was part of her success. Right now, though, she felt raw and unsociable. It was no surprise, perhaps, but still she resented it.

"So, I wanted to thank you for not bawling me out at the care home," Jack said. He put the glasses down on the table and slid into the seat opposite. "I realize it must have been a nasty surprise for you, especially after our meeting this morning."

Serena slid a hand over Luna's silky head. "I wanted to spare Luna a scene if I could," she said, smiling. "It wouldn't have been pleasant for her."

Jack's answering smile was rueful. "You're more than generous, even if it was only for Luna's sake," he said. "I do realize," he added, "that you could have reported Zoe this morning. It was kind of you not to, so I'm doubly grateful."

"I did think about it," Serena admitted wryly. She took a mouthful of the drink, enjoying the sharpness of the cranberry flavor. "I couldn't see that it would help the situation," she said. "Things are bad enough as they are without making it worse."

Jack grimaced. "Yeah, they are," he said. "And I'm very sorry that Zoe and I inadvertently added to that for you." He shook his head. "She was totally terrified," he said. "She knew she'd lose her job if you lodged an official complaint. She asked me to go after you to persuade you not to do it."

Serena drew circles with her glass on the table. "And yet you didn't," she said. She looked up at him. "Why not?"

"I didn't think it would help," Jack said ruefully. He took a mouthful of beer. "I knew we were out of order. There are no excuses. You were within your rights to report both of us for professional misconduct. I just hoped you'd remember..." He stopped, shrugged, as though there was so much more, but he wasn't going there. "Well, as I say, thank you. Zoe loves her work. She was very reluctant to help me in the first place, and I'd have been gutted if she had lost her job through my stupidity."

There was quiet apart from the hiss and crackle of the fire and the faint drone of the piped music. Luna was already asleep and snoring softly. Serena waited for Jack to raise the subject of Caitlin, to press her to talk about her, but he said nothing. She wondered if that was part of his journalistic skill, to let the silence lengthen until she found it so uncomfortable that she started to chatter to fill it. Then she felt ashamed of herself for being so mistrustful. Jack had been her friend years back. There hadn't been any duplicity about him then, and she doubted that there was any now.

"When I saw you talking to my grandfather today, I thought you might have told him that Caitlin was dead," she said. She had no idea why she felt she needed to be so honest with him, only that it felt important to clear the air.

She saw a flash of expression in Jack's eyes that looked almost like pain. "You really thought I'd do that?" he said. He pushed his pint away as though repudiating her words through the abrupt gesture. "Well, hell."

"I'm sorry," Serena said. She realized she'd hurt him—and that she cared. "I know now that you wouldn't have done it," she said. "It was just that I couldn't see why else you would be there. I didn't know that you knew him. Didn't remember, I mean." She pulled a face. "My memories of that time are... somewhat hazy. I'm sorry."

There was a taut silence, then Jack's expression relaxed slightly. "I heard that you developed dissociative amnesia after Caitlin vanished," he said. "That can't be easy."

"No," Serena said. "It's not great. But I think I've kind of blotted out lots of the stuff associated with my time at Minster Lovell. I'd forgotten about the cricket, for example, but when you mentioned it, I remembered Granddad playing for the village team and hitting a six into the river."

"Yeah." Jack smiled for the first time in a while. "I remember that, too. I was the fielder who had to retrieve it."

"Granddad was very good at sports," Serena said. "Did he teach you at school?"

"He came in to tutor us all in fencing and archery," Jack said. "It was great. Zoe was much better at it than me, though. I was pretty uncoordinated as a kid."

Serena looked at him. "I find that hard to believe," she said.

Jack's gaze lifted to hers and lingered there. Suddenly Serena felt breathless and about sixteen years old again. Then he smiled self-deprecatingly.

"Hopefully I've improved," he said, "but Zoe can still beat me at tennis, which is pretty mortifying since she's four years younger than I am."

"You're still a protective older brother to her," Serena said, thinking of the way he had defended his sister's actions.

Jack took a drink and placed his glass back on the table. "I guess I am," he said. "Not that Zoe thanks me for it normally. She's—" He hesitated. "Well, you saw her, though not at her best, I'll admit. She can be quite tactless, if I'm honest. Zo tends to concentrate more on tasks than on people."

"I got that," Serena said with a smile. "It's probably good to be that focused as an archaeologist, though."

"What about you?" Jack leaned his elbows on the table. Serena had the impression he was deliberately changing the subject, steering them away from potentially difficult ground. "What do you do these days?"

"I run a bespoke historical tours company," Serena said. "A friend and I started it a few years after we left university. It's been hard graft, but it's starting to do pretty well."

"That sounds interesting," Jack said. "So you offer tailor-made holidays for history buffs?"

"Everything from stately home visits to lecture tours with resident experts," Serena said. "We research all the places ourselves. Along with the big, famous houses like Chatsworth and Blenheim we also focus on quirky, lesser-known destinations. People love visiting somewhere a bit different, especially if it has a royal connection—and a tearoom and shop, of course. You'd be amazed at the number of places around the country where Queen Elizabeth I stayed, for instance."

"Or the caves that Bonny Prince Charlie hid in," Jack said.

Serena laughed. "Scotland is *very* popular," she said.

"Did you get your interest in history from your grandmother?" Jack asked. Serena could see why he was so effective as an interviewer; he gave a 100 percent attention and it felt effortless and easy to talk to him. She could feel herself relaxing.

"I think it was more from Granddad's side," she said. "My grandmother died when I was only about thirteen and I never knew her very well, but whilst he wasn't an academic like she was, Granddad had a real passion for history." She finished her drink. "I wish I knew more about his own history now," she said, feeling suddenly wistful. "You know how you seldom care about these things when you're a child?" When Jack nodded, she continued. "Aunt Polly said that Granddad did some film work before he married. When you mentioned archery, it reminded me. I think he was pretty good at riding, too. He must have had such an interesting life, but he never talked about it. I always assumed it was because he was adopted and didn't want to talk about his past, but now I wonder. I've so many questions, you know, and it's too late to ask."

"It's pretty hard to see those you love struggling with dementia," Jack said. "It steals the person you once knew."

"Sometimes there's a glimmer of the old self visible," Serena said. She frowned. "How did you find Granddad today? Did he remember the cricket or any of the other stuff you talked about?"

"I don't think so," Jack said, and there was real regret in his voice. His eyes were kind as he looked at her. "He was a total gentleman, though. He was probably wondering who the hell I was, but he was too polite to tell me to leave him alone."

"He enjoyed talking to you," Serena said. "He's not always that animated." She shook her head. "I only wondered because he doesn't usually mention the past, but today he spoke of my grandmother and mentioned her name. That's unusual."

She hesitated on the edge of confiding in him about her odd conversation with Dick on the topic of the lodestar. They had slipped by slow steps toward intimacy, and now she looked up she realized that there were other people in the bar and that she'd been so engrossed in talking to Jack that she hadn't noticed them coming in. The place had started to buzz with conversation. A few people were ordering food, and the smell of chips wafted out from the kitchens. Serena's stomach rumbled. She realized she'd missed lunch and that the afternoon tea and biscuits she'd shared with Dick were long gone.

"Did you want something to eat?" Jack said, seeing her

distraction and reaching over to lift a couple of menus from the next table, where they leaned against the salt and pepper pots. "The chef here does a great burger, and the chips are pretty good, too."

"I wish I'd known that last night," Serena said. "I had scampi in the basket and it was a bit dry." She stood up. "I'll order. Would you like another drink?"

"I'm good, thanks," Jack said, indicating the half pint left in his glass.

Ross was gone from behind the bar and it was Eve who took the order for the two burgers plus a glass of white wine for Serena. "It's a good job you got in early," she said, nodding toward a group seating themselves over by the bow window. "We've got the book club in tonight. Jack's doing a talk for them tomorrow about the Bowes case—that big financial scandal he uncovered a few years back. Someone wrote a book about it and it's being made into a film. Jack's consulting on the production."

"You're a busy man," Serena said as she came back to their table with cutlery, napkins and big wooden number 3 for the food order. "Today the care home, tomorrow the book club."

"Oh…" Jack looked endearingly self-conscious. "I didn't actually *write* the book myself, but it was an interesting case and the book club members were keen to discuss it, so as I was here for a few days…"

"Don't worry." Serena smiled at him. "I won't give away that underneath that tough investigative journalist exterior you're actually really sweet and generous with your time."

Jack laughed. "I'm hardly sweet."

"That's how I remember you, actually," Serena said, thinking of the geeky boy reading a political biography in his summer holidays who had given her the kindest smile when she had interrupted him. “You were very…thoughtful.”

Jack looked startled. “Really? Was I? I thought I was just a nerd.” He rubbed his hand through his hair. “I didn’t really fit in, not like Leo who was so popular with the girls. I suppose I was good at sports, which helped a bit, but aside from that I just wanted to be in the library, finding out more about politics and finance and big data and stuff like that that bored everyone else to death.”

The food arrived, smelling sensational and reminding Serena that she was ravenously hungry.

“It’s interesting to hear you say that,” she said. “I kind of feel there’s a gap between the boy I once knew and the man you’ve become.” She could feel herself blushing because his gaze on her was so direct, and she felt suddenly self-conscious. “I mean, things change so much at that age, don’t they? How you feel, and what you want to do with your life… Why did you decide to choose journalism as a career?”

She picked up the burger and took her first bite; Jack had been right, it was delicious. She closed her eyes and almost moaned with pleasure.

She opened them again to find that Jack had noticed and was laughing at her. Her skin heated with a mixture of embarrassment and awareness. “Sorry,” she said, “but it’s a long time since I ate and you were right—this is fabulous.”

Jack nodded. “I think without the food this place would fold completely,” he said. “Not many people stay here, but a lot come to eat.” He smiled. “Sorry, you distracted me there. You were asking about why I chose journalism.”

Serena nodded. “With those interests I guess there were a

number of things you could have done," she said. "Why did you become a journalist?"

"I had a bit of a passion for it, I suppose," Jack said, "like you with history. It was as simple as that. I liked words and I liked numbers, so being a financial journalist seemed an ideal combination. I was lucky—I got a break with a local paper in Nottingham and from there went to one of the nationals. I was still interested in politics and business, too, so I started to dig into a few stories..." He shrugged. "I went on from there."

"It feels as though there's a crusading spirit in there somewhere as well," Serena said, looking at him thoughtfully. "A need to find out the truth? Or to do good?"

"Don't make me out to be better than I am," Jack said, and there was a rough note in his voice all of a sudden as though she'd touched a nerve. Suddenly she knew he was thinking about that morning and that he still felt bad about the way she'd discovered his interest in Caitlin's death.

"Tell me more stuff," she said, smiling to lighten the mood. "Just ordinary things," she added. "Interests, friends, the things that people normally talk about when they meet up after ten years."

"Okay," Jack said. He smiled. "You already know I'm twenty-nine years old. I have a flat in London where I'm based when I'm not traveling for work, and I'm currently supposed to be investigating the growth in private water utility companies and the danger that poses to water supply. When I'm not working, I do all kinds of stuff—windsurfing, swimming, skiing. It helps to get out when I've been at a computer all day. I like music, too. I used to play the guitar—badly. You may remember."

"I do," Serena said with feeling. "I thought investigative

journalism was all about confronting dodgy characters in sleazy parking lots," she added. "That's what it looks like on TV."

"Most of the time it's about research," Jack said. "I don't get out much."

"A bit like organizing historic tours," Serena said. "That's ninety percent dealing with admin and guests' questions and dietary requirements, and only ten percent touring fabulous old buildings and historic sites."

"Yeah," Jack said. "The truth is more mundane than the job title sounds."

"But I still love it," Serena said. "And I'm guessing you love your work, too." She took another mouthful of burger. "Friends?" she said succinctly.

"I have a few close ones," Jack said. "Lizzie, of course. When she got together with Arthur it was great, because he and I had known each other since university. There are a couple of other childhood friends from home and a few in London. I have lots of acquaintances." He glanced at her. "I'm pretty straightforward really."

Serena wondered if she could ask about his relationships and then wondered why she wanted to know. Whilst she was thinking about it, Jack read her mind.

"My last relationship finished about six months ago," he said with a faint smile, "in case that was your next question." He raised a brow. "What about you?"

"Oh..." Serena shook her head. "I split up with my ex over a year ago," she said. "He wanted more from the relationship than I was giving him, he said. So he ran off with a work colleague of his."

Jack's mouth turned down at the corners. "Not the most mature way of dealing with it," he said.

"To be fair," Serena said, "there may have been something in it." She hesitated. "I'm not brilliant at commitment. I do push people away." She shrugged, trying to make light of it. "I know all the reasons, just not what to do about it."

Jack's smile was warm. "I always think that insight goes a long way to sorting a problem," he said. He held her gaze for a long moment, and Serena felt a rush of awareness. Then Luna woke up abruptly and starting scratching her stomach, legs splayed out, and they both burst out laughing.

"Classy," Jack said.

On impulse Serena put out a hand and touched his wrist lightly. "Jack," she said. "This morning when I met you and Zoe—"

Immediately Jack's smile faded. He made a movement to brush her words aside. "You said that you didn't want to talk about Caitlin," he said, "and I respect that." His gaze met hers briefly. "I've decided not to pursue it anyway."

"But there must have been a reason why you were interested in the first place," Serena said. "Please tell me what it was."

Jack was silent for so long that she thought he wasn't going to answer, and when he did, he spoke with a deliberate lack of emotion.

"When Caitlin disappeared," he said, "it was a horrible shock to all of us—her friends, I mean, me and Leo and Lizzie and the rest of that crowd we hung out with." He looked at Serena. "I'm not comparing it to what you went through," he said. "I imagine that must have been intolerable, and I don't in any way blame you for dropping us all in the aftermath." Some expression she couldn't read touched his eyes. "But we all cared about Caitlin, Serena. We all felt lost, too, and confused, and cast adrift." She saw his hand clench briefly. "We wanted to know what was happening, and no one was telling us anything. We wanted to find Caitlin, to do anything we could to help."

"You did," Serena said. She put down the remains of her burger, suddenly too upset to eat any more. "You organized search parties and put up posters and did all kinds of things! I know I wasn't there to help, but I heard all about it. You did so much!"

"It didn't do any good," Jack said bluntly. "We felt as though we had failed. We couldn't find her—or help you. Lizzie and I in particular felt..." He stopped, shook his head. "Well, it's water under the bridge now. But that was why, when Zoe came to me and said that they had found Caitlin's body, I wanted to know more about it. It felt like a second chance to find out what had happened, even if it was too late to put things right."

It was Serena's turn to be quiet now whilst she thought about what he'd said. She knew she had been selfish; so wrapped up in her own grief and pain she'd had no space for anyone else's. Worse, she'd never really thought how Caitlin's disappearance might have affected the lives of those outside her immediate family. She'd only kept in touch with Lizzie, the two of them, slightly damaged and spiky, perhaps finding it easier to stay friends.

"I'm sorry," she said. "I had no idea." She cleared her throat. "I mean, I miss Caitlin every day. It's lonely without her. But I never imagined other people might feel so strongly..." She stopped. She was wondering whether Jack had had feelings for Caitlin beyond the friendship he spoke of now. Glossy, vibrant Caitlin had been so much fun and so popular. It would explain why her disappearance had hit him so hard. Suddenly there was a tight lump in her throat. She didn't really want to know, but that was cowardly of her.

"Did you..." She took a deep breath. "Were you in love with Caitlin? I know we were all young, but you can feel things very intensely at that age."

She saw the glimmer of amusement in Jack's eyes and felt her tension ease a notch. "You certainly can," he said. "But no, I loved Caitlin. I'm loyal to my friends. But I wasn't in love with her in the way you mean."

Serena could feel herself blushing. Luna put her paw on Serena's lap, and for a moment she thought the dog had sensed her embarrassment, but it turned out she was just begging for some food.

"I can't give you anything," Serena said regretfully. "Chips are not good for dogs." Luna gave a tiny whinge and lay down again.

"It was worth a try," Jack said with the ghost of a smile. "She is a terrible scrounger."

"She's lovely," Serena said warmly. "I miss having a dog."

"I'd like one of my own," Jack admitted, "but with all the traveling I do it's not possible at the moment. Borrowing Luna when I'm visiting Gran is the next best thing."

Serena nodded, scooping up the last of the chips. "When we met this morning," she said, "Zoe said there was something strange about Caitlin's grave." She looked up. "Was it that her body had been found in a sealed burial from the eighteenth century?"

Jack paused in the act of raising his glass to his lips. "The police told you that?" he asked.

Serena nodded. "They can't explain it, and—"

"All finished here?" Eve had popped up beside the table, reaching across Serena to pick up Jack's plate. "Can I get you the dessert menu?"

"Not for me, thanks," Serena said. "That was delicious, though."

"It's lucky that you're not one of those people who lose their appetite when they're dealing with a death in the family," Eve said cheerfully. "Some people can't eat a scrap when they're upset. I've often wondered what the point is of serving food at a wake. Can I get you coffee? Liqueurs?"

"Just the bill, thank you," Jack said. "I'll get this," he added to Serena. "I owe you."

"We'll split it," Serena said. "You don't need to bribe me. Besides—" she glanced at Eve's retreating figure "—that bit of information about the burial will be all over the village in five minutes so I don't think Zoe needs to worry about being indiscreet. She has plenty of competition."

Jack grimaced. "Eve does seem to have a rather unpleasant interest in anything ghoulish, doesn't she?" he said. "If we are going to talk about Caitlin properly, I don't think it can be here."

Serena checked her watch. It was time to ring Polly; she had lots of questions for her aunt as well as things she needed to tell her.

"When's your talk tomorrow?" she asked Jack. Then when he looked blank, "The book club?"

"Oh..." Jack laughed. "We're meeting at midday."

"Are you free before that?" Serena dropped her voice. "We could walk to the ruins, if you like, and talk on the way over there." She hesitated. "I came back here to try to recall some of my lost memories from the time Caitlin vanished," she said. "It might help to go to the hall with you. When I saw you this morning—" She stopped again, self-conscious.

"What?" Jack said. "What happened?" The way he was looking at her made her suddenly feel very hot. She gulped down the last of her wine.

"Just that it felt as though I was about to remember something from the day Caitlin disappeared," Serena said. "Something to do with you."

"Here's your bill!" Eve trilled, slapping a little silver tray down in front of them. Serena almost jumped out of skin.

"She does pop up at the most inopportune moments," Jack said ruefully as the landlady walked away. "You were saying?"

"Oh, nothing," Serena said. She felt awkward. "I mean, it's probably nothing. I might be wrong. Or it might be nothing to do with Caitlin, but—"

"Serena." Jack stilled the rush of her words with a light touch on her arm. "Let's see, shall we? In the morning?"

He stood up and Luna, who had been dozing with half an eye open, leaped to her feet, too.

"Goodbye, gorgeous girl," Serena said, patting her. "See you tomorrow, I hope. Jack…" She smiled at his expression. "A less effusive goodbye for you," she said, "but thank you all the same."

Jack gave her another of those heart-shaking smiles. "See you tomorrow," he said. "Sleep well."

He went out and Serena headed up to her room to fetch a jacket. The conversation with Polly was another one that she didn't want overheard. She went out into the car park and found a spot with good mobile reception, crammed into a corner near the bins. The position had the benefit of being near the kitchen extractor fan so no one could overhear her. The downside was that the air was thick with the oily smell of fried food, which was nowhere near as pleasant as eating the chips had been.

"Are you okay, hon?" Polly picked up on the second ring. "I've been so worried about you."

"I'm fine," Serena said. She smiled. Just hearing Polly's voice did her good. Her phone call to her parents earlier had been significantly less easy.

"I've seen the police," she said in answer to Polly's next question. "They're treating Caitlin's death as unexplained at the moment." She gave her aunt a very brief summary of her interview with Inspector Litton, but left out the bit about the mysterious circumstances around Caitlin's burial. She was interested to hear what Jack had to say about that tomorrow, but couldn't see any point in telling either her parents or her aunt at this stage. The most likely explanation was that the grave had been opened and resealed in some way so as to appear as if it hadn't been disturbed. She knew nothing about archaeology, but she did know that the most obvious explanations were usually the right ones and no doubt the police would discover how it had been done sooner or later.

"Keep me posted if there's any more news," Polly said. "I'm so sorry you're having to go through all of this, hon. Have you…" She paused delicately. "Remembered anything yet?"

"Not really," Serena said. She didn't think that telling her aunt she thought she'd seen Caitlin's ghost would help. "I went to see Granddad today, though," she said. "He sends his love." This was not strictly true, but she knew Polly felt guilty about living on the opposite side of the world to her father. It wouldn't hurt to tell a white lie.

"Ah..." Polly's voice warmed. "How is he?"

"Much the same," Serena said. "He was quite animated and chatty today, although I'm not sure how much of what I said to him he understood."

"Did you tell him they'd found Caitlin's body?" Polly asked.

"Yes," Serena said. "I didn't want to pretend to him." A shiver ran over her skin as she remembered Dick's words. "He seemed to think it was his fault."

"Poor Dad." There was a catch in Polly's voice. "He was always so protective of the two of you. He adored you both. For this to happen to Caitlin when he was looking after you just about killed him." She sighed. "God how awful—for you to have to tell him and for him to have to hear that. I'm so sorry."

"There was something I wanted to ask you, actually," Serena said. "After I'd told Granddad about Caitlin, he said something along the lines that he should have told us where we came from. I'm not sure what he meant, but I wondered if you know anything about our family history?"

There was a silence at the other end of the phone. Serena wondered whether they had been cut off or whether Polly, firmly if not aggressively modern in her outlook, didn't even understand what she was asking. "I mean," she added, "do you remember your grandparents, for instance?"

"Oh, I see," Polly said. "Yes, of course. They were lovely. They spoiled me and your dad rotten."

"Wasn't that Grandma's parents, though?" Serena said. "Did you ever meet Granddad's parents?"

"Well, you know that he was fostered," Polly said. "I think his parents were killed in the war, during the blitz. We never heard anything about them. We never met his foster parents, either, for that matter. I sort of assumed that they were long gone by the time Paul and I were born." She hesitated. "I think Dad had some sisters…they were all split up as children, and there was a brother who died young as well." Serena heard her catch her breath. "That's funny, I'd forgotten all about that. He only ever mentioned his brother once. Perhaps it had had such an impact on him that he didn't want to talk about it. People of that generation are so much more reticent, aren't they? They bottle things up and hide them away."

"Granddad certainly did," Serena agreed. She was thinking of what Lizzie had said when she had touched the spoon and seen the vision of a child dying. Had that been her grandfather's brother? Had he been there, the child whose grief and loneliness Lizzie had experienced? Yet, Lizzie had said it had been a long time ago, centuries, in fact…

"I don't suppose he ever tried to trace any of his siblings, did he?" Serena asked.

"Not as far as I know," Polly said. "It wasn't the sort of thing you did in those days, was it? Not like now. There wasn't the technology that could help you. It was all about getting on with life and not complaining. Pretty harsh."

"And there's no photos of his family or anything like that?" Serena asked. "I've seen the ones of Granddad before he married, and the ones of him and Grandma when they were young."

"Oh, they were so glamorous!" Polly's voice had warmed again. "You know that he was a dancer? Professional, I mean. Ballroom. I've seen pictures. He worked on the cruise ships and at posh hotels under the name Richard Shrewsbury. It must have been in the 1950s, I suppose. I remember him teaching me to dance when I was a kid and saying it was all in the footwork."

"I thought he worked in films?" Serena said. *Richard Shrewsbury*, she thought. *Like the spoon.* No wonder he'd like the pun of having it on the kitchen wall.

"He did," Polly said. "He was a talented rider and fencer. I think he used to work on those historical epics that were so popular in Hollywood in the fifties and sixties. After he was married, though, he gave up all the exciting stuff and became a teacher and never really talked about it again."

"I had no idea." Serena felt winded. "I mean, I knew some of it—the fencing and stuff, and I've seen some of the pictures, but it sounds amazing. Why would he never tell us about it?"

"I don't know," Polly said. "Maybe because we didn't ask? He's always been a quiet man, hasn't he? I don't mean he was shy, but he was very private."

"I suppose he was," Serena said. "It's weird how you can know someone all your life, and yet not really know them at all. I wish I'd asked him so much more before it was too late, especially as now he seems to want to tell me something."

"That is odd," Polly agreed. "What were his precise words to you, Serena?"

Serena cast her mind back to that afternoon and Dick's reference to the night of Caitlin's disappearance. "He said he should have warned us," she said slowly. "That he should have told us where we came from. And he mentioned something called the lodestar. At least I think that's what he called it. Does that mean anything to you, Aunt Pol?"

"Nothing at all," Polly said. "The lodestar? What is that?"

"I haven't had a chance to look it up yet," Serena said. "I thought I'd ask you first. It sounded vaguely familiar to me for some reason, but I don't know why."

"Sorry I can't help, hon," Polly said. Her voice changed.

"Look, I've decided I'm going to come over. To England, I mean. It's time I saw Dad again anyway, and..." She hesitated. "I don't like you doing this on your own. Could you book me into that pub you're staying in? I'll get a flight tomorrow and be with you on Friday."

"What? Wait—" Serena was taken aback at the abruptness of Polly's decision-making. "This is all very sudden. Are you sure?"

"I've already squared it with work," Polly said. "I want to be there for you whilst this is going on and I miss Dad." There was an odd tone in her voice. "Besides, I have a strange feeling..."

Serena waited, but her aunt's words trailed away. It was odd. Polly never had feelings, at least not of the spooky kind. She was far too down-to-earth for that sort of thing.

"Okay," she said after a moment. "If you're sure. I'll book you a room, and I'll come to pick you up from Oxford station on Friday. Let me know when to expect you."

"Thanks, hon," Polly said. "Now, you take care, all right? And ring me tomorrow? It doesn't matter if I'm traveling. I still want to hear from you."

"Of course I'll ring," Serena said. "Have a safe journey and I love you." She put her phone away, shaking her head a little at the suddenness of Polly's decision. It wasn't like her aunt to be so impulsive, but she knew Polly had wanted to come with her when the news had broken about Caitlin and she knew she missed Dick terribly. Perhaps this might be the thing that prompted her to come back to England for good. Or perhaps, Serena thought, she wouldn't want to give up California, and who could blame her?

The phone rang again as she was heading back into the pub.

"Serena?" It was Lizzie. "How are you? How did you get on today?"

Serena could see Eve hovering in the hallway, ears on stalks. "Hi, Lizzie," she said. "I'm good, thanks. Are you around tomorrow for a chat? It's a bit…busy here at the moment."

"Oh, you mean that landlady is listening in," Lizzie laughed. "Look, why don't you come over for dinner tomorrow evening like we said, and we can catch up properly? Seven o'clock at The High?"

"I'd love that," Serena said warmly. "See you then."

She went upstairs to her room. The uneven treads of the stair beneath the faded carpet betrayed the antiquity of the building. The wooden banisters were painted black to match the beams of the ceiling. It was much quieter up here with the sounds from the bar and restaurant muted. Serena wondered whether there were any other guests besides her. It felt uncannily as though the place was deserted.

Once inside her room she turned on the lamps, slipped off her shoes and propped herself up against the pillows on the bed. It was only eight o'clock but she felt incredibly weary, the events of the day catching up with her and combining with the lingering jet lag to make her feel at once physically exhausted but with a mind that was frustratingly wide-awake. She decided to run a bath and read one of the books she'd picked up earlier in Witney, and then try to get an early night. But before that… Snapping open her phone, she logged onto the pub internet and searched for the word *lodestar.* A number of references came up to a music festival and to a type of boat. The dictionary definition of *lodestar,* she read, was a star that was used to guide the course of a ship, particularly the polestar. Alternatively it was a word used to describe a person who served as an inspiration or guide. It wasn't at all obvious to her what relevance that had to Dick, and Serena wondered again if she had misheard him.

She was about to close down the webpage when she spotted a reference to *lodestone* being another word for lodestar. A lodestone, she read, was a naturally magnetized mineral that had been used in antiquity as the first compass and now had a variety of purposes, particularly in steel manufacture. There were also pictures of polished lodestones that were sold as jewelry. According to the more paranormally inclined, lodestones were said to possess the power to work with you to attract all that you most desired.

Serena turned off the phone and put it on the nightstand.

The power to attract your heart's desire...

What was it that she desired most in the world? To find out what had happened to Caitlin? Or even to have Caitlin back?

A shiver skittered down her spine. Did people really believe that a stone could possess that sort of supernatural power? It felt out of place in the modern world, the sort of thing that belonged with medieval superstition, and for all that she was prepared to accept Lizzie's feyness, she wasn't sure how she felt about magic.

She got up to put the bath on, then paused with her hand on the doorknob. There was another reason that the word *lodestar* had seemed vaguely familiar to her when Dick had mentioned it. In her mind's eye she could see the bookshelves on the landing outside her room, Eve's collection of true crime books mixed in a little incongruously with some classics and children's paperbacks. She was almost certain that one of those had had the word *lodestar* in the title.

She went out onto the landing, flicking quickly over the

bloodstained spines and sensationalist titles of the crime books until she found what she was looking for. There was a small selection of old Penguin books and other children's novels, including a book by Rosemary Sutcliff called *Knight's Fee* and another old favorite, *Moonfleet.* She picked it up and saw her own name in the front of it, written in a childish hand. It was the strangest sensation, like time travel, until she realized that there was a perfectly logical explanation for it—the books, like the contents of the manor and the crockery and cutlery in the café, must have been sold and someone had bought a job lot of them to furnish the bookshelves at the pub. She recognized more of them now—*Children of the New Forest*, *A Traveller in Time*, and some of the Goosebumps series, which had been Caitlin's favorites.

The Lovell Lodestar.

There it was, a slender paperback, blue, with the name printed in bold black on the spine. It wasn't a novel; it looked more like an old local history book. Suddenly shaky, Serena slid *Moonfleet* back onto the shelf and reached for the smaller paperback, and in that moment, she sensed someone watching her.

"Anything I can help you with?" Eve was standing on the half landing, looking at her with a bright and somewhat unfriendly gaze. Serena almost jumped out of her skin. Her hand dropped to her side. Instinctively, she didn't want to draw Eve's attention to the book she was interested in, although she couldn't have explained why.

"No," she said. "Thank you. I was just…looking for something to read." She turned back to her room.

"Aren't you going to choose one, then?" Eve was still there, poised, one hand on the banister, head tilted curiously to one side.

"I just remembered I bought a couple of things earlier when I was in Witney," Serena said weakly. "Good night."

After her bath she briefly contemplated venturing out again and retrieving *The Lovell Lodestar* from the shelf, but she couldn't face the thought of bumping into Eve again. It was ridiculous to imagine that the landlady would have been lurking out there all this time waiting for her, and yet Serena couldn't shake the idea that she was. Instead, she made a cup of hot chocolate and read for a little before falling into a light sleep that was punctured by dreams in which Caitlin was forever running from her, a wraith leading her on into darkness.

To her surprise it was eight o'clock and bright sunlight when she woke, and there was a text from Jack suggesting that they meet by the bridge over the river at ten. She got up feeling more rested and went out onto the landing where the scent of bacon was already thick on the air and the sound of voices from the breakfast room suggested that there were in fact other guests staying at the Minster Inn after all.

There was no sign of Eve. Serena furtively sidled up to the bookcase and looked for *The Lovell Lodestar* amongst the children's books on the second shelf. It wasn't there. She checked along the row, then on the shelves above and below, but it seemed to have vanished. Just to be sure, she ran her gaze over the whole bookcase one more time before she went slowly down the stairs to breakfast.

"I've set your table up by the fire," Eve called out gaily from behind the reception desk. She seemed to have overcome her odd mood from the night before.

A middle-aged couple was sitting in the breakfast room, talking quietly as people tended to do at breakfast in hotels if they talked at all. A copy of the *Times* was folded on the table between them, and they had almost finished their breakfast. They looked up and greeted Serena as she came in before the woman poured herself another cup of tea and made some comment about the weather. It was cold in the breakfast room despite the sun; Serena was glad that she was sitting by the fire, where a small blaze burned merrily and brightly. It seemed to throw out very little heat, but amongst the wood snapping in the grate, Serena could see the pages of a book turning to translucent ash before her eyes, and the black lettered spine that even as she watched, curled and crumbled into dust.

Chapter 14

ANNE

Minster Lovell
1476

Mother took one look at us when Francis and I came back from the lake that afternoon and told him very dryly that he had better set about arranging his household so that I might join him at Minster Lovell as soon as possible. I do not know what it was that gave us away—the grass stains on my skirts, perhaps. However, there was no censure in Mother's words, indeed she seemed relieved, and when the time came for us to repair for the night, she allowed Francis to join me in my chamber, where the giggling maids were shooed away.

Early in the spring I traveled south to my new home. Francis's presence on the journey distracted me from the heartache of leaving all that was familiar, and my own natural curiosity did the rest. Everything was new, and fresh and exciting. As for Minster Lovell, I loved it on sight.

I will be happy here, I thought, and there was no shadow cast over my mind when I thought it, no hint of the secrets that Minster Lovell held.

The manor was quite new. Francis's grandfather had rebuilt it a mere forty years before, and it was spacious and comfortable. Despite that, Francis was determined to put his own stamp on it and planned a tower to the southwest, close by the river, where we might have a new range of apartments. He showed me the plans he had had drawn up. I wondered whether it was the need to distance himself from his father's time that prompted him to create a new place where we might live. The old one was full of memories and for Francis, I knew, those had not been happy.

In the meantime, however, we shared the manor with the ghosts of his past, the high vaulted hall and the beautiful solar, and of course, the bedchambers with a view to the west across the little river and the fields beyond. In addition to Minster Lovell, I was also mistress of a vast number of other properties, including Wardour Castle in Wiltshire and Acton Burnell away to the west on the borders of Wales. Francis promised to take me to visit them all.

It was scarcely surprising that in the whirl of my new life I forgot all about the treasure that Ginevra had entrusted to me to return. The story of the Mistletoe Bride and that evening at the Duke of Gloucester's wedding years before had slipped from my mind like a shadow, a fairy tale that belonged to my childhood. Now I was, of course, grown-up. I did not even remember the strangely shaped arrow until the day when one of the maids was unpacking my remaining trunks sent from Ravensworth and I saw her take out the plain wooden box that Crowther had made for me. She gave it only the scantest glance before discarding it, and as she put it aside, it opened and the little stone arrowhead fell out. She gave an exclamation, picked it up, and was, I thought, about to throw it on the fire.

"What are you doing?" My words were sharper than I had intended and immediately she dropped the arrow and turned a deep unbecoming shade of red. I thought she was going to cry. She had already torn one of my underskirts in her clumsy sorting, and I had reprimanded her. No doubt she thought I might dismiss her now.

"My lady..." she stuttered. "I thought it nothing, a piece of coal..."

"No matter." I retrieved the arrow and gave her what I hoped was a reassuring smile. I was learning that people hung on my every word as the mistress of the house. It was a new sensation for at Ravensworth I had been known since childhood, and indulged, but I had not had the same authority as I did here.

"No harm is done," I said. "Only this little treasure is special to me. It was a gift."

She looked uncertain, as though I might be half-mad for treasuring a small lump of arrow-shaped rock.

"Run along and ask the boy to bring in more wood for the fire," I said on a sigh. "I will finish the work here."

After she had gone, I sat down by the window with the little stone arrowhead in my hand. It was not dull black as I remembered it, but smooth and shiny from contact with the velvet of the box. It felt cold to the touch, but warmed in my palm. It looked exactly what she had believed it to be, no more than a lump of rock, crudely fashioned into that pointed shape. Seeing it through a stranger's eyes, doubts formed in my mind that the stories Ginevra had told me were no more than fantasies made up to amuse a bored child. Even so, I set it back in its box and put it at the bottom of a chest amongst my best clothes, and I determined to discover if there was any truth in the old tales.

"What do you know of the Lovell Lodestar?" I asked Francis one night as we lay together in our bed, drowsy in the aftermath of loving. "Is it true that there was once a sacred jewel that was lost?"

Francis raised himself onto one elbow and looked at me with amusement.

"Who has been telling you those old tales?" he asked. "They are no more than legends."

I wasn't prepared to give up so easily. "I heard that the Lovell family held a precious treasure entrusted to them centuries ago," I said. "And that it was said to possess enchantment beyond man's wildest imaginings."

Francis drew my head back down on his shoulder and started to play idly with my hair, winding it about his fingers before letting it spring loose again.

"It is true that there was a minster church here back in the time of the old Saxon kings," he said, "and that some of the manuscripts and documents were placed in our family's care for safekeeping. They are still here in the muniments room. If you would like to see them, I will ask Fiske to show you." Fiske was his clerk, a man as dry and dusty as the documents in his care. An hour spent poring over Latin in his company was not a pastime I relished, but perhaps I would need to do so if I wanted a clue to the powers of the Lodestar. I thought of the little rock in its velvet box and felt again that sense of disbelief. Had I been taken for a fool? Had Ginevra's story really been no more than a fantasy? Yet Crowther had called my rock a *lodestone* so surely the two, lodestone and lodestar, must be one and the same.

"But what of the treasure?" I persisted. "You said it was a legend, but perhaps there was some truth in it."

"Perhaps," Francis said. He yawned. "There are many tales

of treasures and the like. There may be a grain of truth in them to begin, but over time they become so embroidered that they are as much a fiction as the stories the traveling players tell. The time of the Saxon kings was over five hundred years ago, Anne. Nothing but a few old scrolls remain. But as I say, Fiske can show you."

I sighed, relaxing back into his arms as he started to kiss me. Francis was no scholar, neither was he in the least a superstitious man. Even if there *was* truth in the stories, he would have paid no heed to them. I resolved instead to ask the priest. Despite their calling, or perhaps because of it, I had often found men of the church to be most knowledgeable on matters of myth and legend. They were educated and well-read. If anyone would know of the Saxon Kings' treasure, it would be the village rector.

Meanwhile, I was easily distracted by the touch of Francis's hands on my bare skin and the press of his body against mine. Looking at him, at his face so grave in the firelight and the desire in his eyes, I felt such a surge of love for him and I raised my hand to cup his cheek. "I love you," I said. "I hope it will always be this way between us."

"It will," he said. He smiled that rare smile of his. "Anne," he said. "My love, now and forever."

I woke at some point during the night to find the fire burned out and the room lit only by the full moon outside. I slipped from the warmth of the bed and crossed the floor to the window. The night was mild although outside the sky was clear and studded with so many stars that shone as hard and bright as diamonds. I sat by the window and looked out across the manor and the river beyond, painted in the silver and black of moonlight and shadow. There was the river, a rippling silver mantle beneath the moon, and the water gate and the dovecote edged sharp against the deep velvet blue of the sky.

The April moon, the hare moon, as we called it at home in the North, was a pitiless white, so bright on the river that it dazzled me momentarily. In that instant I saw the picture before me shift and change, as though snow was falling, a blizzard of it that reshaped the scene before me and obliterated all familiarity. I saw a dark figure slip from a doorway into the courtyard and cross to the water gate. She looked cold and furtive, her steps hurried, her footprints erased from the snow as soon as they were made. The wind snatched at her cloak and the snow swirled around her in a fury. I saw her pause as she reached the shelter of the wall and she turned back, looking directly up at my window.

She had Ginevra's face.

"Anne, come back to bed," Francis called to me. He sounded drowsy. I looked over toward him, and when I turned back to the window the vision had gone and the river was still and pale again.

"You're cold," Francis said, as I slipped in beside him. "Let me warm you." And I curled up beside him and he drew me into his arms again.

I spent a fruitless hour with Fiske, Francis's clerk, who had quite clearly never read the old documents in the muniments room, probably because he always seemed extremely busy with all the current work to do with Francis's various estates and complicated lawsuits. He was an earnest young man who wanted to please me, if only because I was Francis's wife, but after we had both become very dusty and frustrated trying to read the faded script of endless land charters, we gave up.

"I am not quite sure what it is you are looking for, my lady," he said helplessly, rubbing his dirty palms together and smearing the dust even further.

I did not really know, either. Naively, I had hoped there might be a big old book that told the story of the Lodestar, and that of the Mistletoe Bride for good measure. I would even have settled for a charter from King Alfred himself to the minster church offering the Lodestar to them for safekeeping and outlining its magical powers. Unsurprisingly there was no such document, or at least not that Mr. Fiske and I could find.

I was not giving up easily, though. Next, I asked the priest, catching him for a moment on his own after Mass one Sunday. This was difficult for I was so seldom alone—if Francis did not want my company then there were a dozen other people clamoring for it, or some household matter or other to attend to. Sundays were particularly difficult because of the parade of neighbors and acquaintances at church; however, I cornered Father Bernard beside a Lovell tomb and asked to speak with him. His gaze flickered to my stomach, as though he was expecting me to announce the imminent arrival of a Lovell heir, and to ask him to pray for me.

"Do you know of an old treasure lodged here from the days before the Conquest, Father Bernard?" I asked. "Maybe it was a relic? It is said to possess miraculous powers."

Father Bernard's eyes bulged. "Indeed not, my lady," he said, his pebbled spectacles flashing nervously in the light. "I know of no such legend. A relic, you say? Miracles?" He rubbed his palms down his cassock. "There are no miracles here."

That I could well believe with such a staid fellow in charge.

"Are you sure?" I persisted. "I met a woman once who told me of a holy treasure that possessed extraordinary powers. It was called the Lovell Lodestar."

Father Bernard looked as though he wanted to cast the devils out of me. "That sounds like pagan wickedness to me, Lady Lovell," he said. "T'would be best to forget all about it." And he scurried away, muttering about enchantments.

"You have been asking all the wrong people," Frideswide said when she came to stay with us a couple of weeks later and she and I were sitting together in the solar, alone for once, whilst Francis and Fiske worked long into the night over the latest of his claims for his lands and manors. I had confided in her that since coming to Minster Lovell, I had heard many fascinating tales of a lost treasure and also of a Mistletoe Bride, married to one of her ancestors. Instead of telling me that my wits were begging or that I was meddling in witchcraft, she nodded.

"I heard those stories, too, when I was a child," she said.

This made me laugh for she was no more than fourteen years now. "What did you mean by the wrong people?" I asked. "How have I erred?"

"They are all men," Frideswide said simply. "Oh," she said, waving one slender hand to clarify her words, "I do not mean that men cannot be storytellers—the minstrels with their tales of love and chivalry prove it can be so—but men like Francis who are soldiers, and men like Fiske—" she wrinkled up her nose, clearly having no great opinion of the clerk "—who is an administrator... And the *priest*..." Her tone was full of disdain. "It is not that they do not countenance such stories, it is that they do not even *hear* them. They consider themselves above such fantasies. They are tales whispered as lullabies to children, or as ghost stories on a winter night."

"So how did you hear of it, then?" I asked. I set aside the piece of embroidery I had been pretending to work, and curled up on the settle. Frideswide sat on the floor at my feet, resting against one of the new cushions I had purchased for the room. I was pleased with my decorations, the rich reds and bright golds of the tapestries and cushions that lifted the gray stone of the walls and made the place seem warmer and lighter. I hoped that it might chase away some of the shadows that Francis and his sisters had experienced here.

"My nurse," Frideswide said, drawing her knees up to her chin, "told me the story of the Mistletoe Bride. It is well-known in the village. There was a woman who married one of my ancestors, John Lovell, but at the wedding feast, during a game of hide-and-seek, she disappeared. They searched high and low for her, but she had vanished. John pined for her—but not a great deal, for he remarried and begot a family soon after. Then, years later, when they opened an old chest that had been left untouched in the muniments room, there she was, no more than a pile of bones in the rags of a wedding dress!"

I shuddered. This was the alternative story that Ginevra had told me, the one she said had not been true.

"Do you know when it was?" I asked. "Who was the bride?" One thing that I had seen when I had spent the hour with Mr. Fiske looking for references to the Lodestar had been the Lovell ancestry, all the way back to Eudes, Duke of Brittany in the tenth century and before. There had, I remembered, been a number of John Lovells on the family tree. Any one of them could have been the John Lovell in question—or none of them.

Frideswide shrugged. "I have no notion of either the date or her name."

"Nor where she is buried?"

"There is no grave for her," Frideswide said. Her gray Lovell eyes met mine. "I think it only a legend," she said judiciously. "A ghost story told to frighten small children."

"So perhaps it isn't true," I said. "Perhaps…" *Perhaps John Lovell himself invented the whole tale of the dead bride in the chest to hide the truth that he had been robbed of his treasure by the bride thief. Perhaps he made it up so that he would not look like a fool and over time, men believed the falsehood, as they are wont to do.*

"Did your nurse also tell you about the Lodestar?" I asked. "The treasure that the Lovells had been given to guard as a sacred trust back in the days of the old Saxon kings?"

Frideswide reached for some nuts, which I had thoughtfully set in a bowl on the table beside her, having noted that she had the appetite of a growing girl.

"The relic of St. Kenelm," she said. "Of course."

I was so surprised that I sat up straight and almost fell off the settle. "Tell me," I said.

One of the hunting dogs pushed open the door of the solar and came over to Frideswide, curling up beside her. They were supposed to be kept in the kennels by the stable, but I liked having their company in the house. Frideswide petted its ears as she talked and the dog made a happy sound deep in its throat, rolling over to invite her to rub its stomach.

"Did you never wonder why the church is dedicated to St. Kenelm?" Frideswide asked.

"I cannot say that I did," I said. I knew it to be an unusual name, but it had not aroused my curiosity beyond that.

I thought I vaguely remembered the name from hearing the *Canterbury Tales*.

"St. Kenelm was a boy king," she said. "He ruled the old Saxon kingdom of Mercia. He was slain by his sister's lover because she wanted to rule in his place, but her plot was discovered and his body found and all manner of miracles took place in his name."

This was standard saintly fare and I wondered at it. Although I had been brought up to believe in holy miracles there were times when, secretly, I doubted the truth of these stories and thought that the church simply made them up. Once, as a child, I had asked Mother if miracles truly occurred and she had told me that the Church said they did and therefore we must believe it. My curiosity, so often unwelcome, had been silenced on that topic ever since.

"St. Kenelm was buried at Winchcombe," Frideswide continued. Seeing my look of query, she waved a hand vaguely. "It is not far from here, I believe, though I am not precisely sure where. The monks at the abbey there brought a relic of St. Kenelm to the minster church here so that pilgrims could venerate it."

"But what was it?" I asked. "What form did it take?"

Frideswide shook her head. "No one knew. No one ever saw it. It was kept in a casket of gold and precious stone, and it was said to possess miraculous power beyond man's wildest imaginings."

There was quiet in the room but for the dog's happy snoring.

"What does that mean, I wonder," I said. Idly, I traced a pattern on the polished wood of the settle. "What are your wildest imaginings?"

"Every man's wildest imaginings are different," Frideswide said gravely. Then she giggled. "That is what my nurse told me. Some imagine fiery beasts that fly, others a power to cure all ills, or an invincible sword, or riches enough to rule the world." She stroked the dog's warm flank. "I did hear tell that a simple youth stole it once, thinking it would make his fortune. They say it drove him mad, and he was found clutching it in his hand, raving of having traveled through time and seen monsters of iron." She looked at me. "I do not know the truth of any of this," she said simply, "but if the treasure existed then it was a relic, a holy object. It should never be used for evil gain."

I thought again of the story of the thief bride. She had only wanted to use the relic to purchase her freedom and that of her sister from a cruel master. Surely that had not been so bad. And yet she had suffered for it, like the simple youth whose story mirrored her own:

She felt as though she was falling, far, far down through the dark, so far that she thought she would never again step out into the light. And when she did, she was in a different place, in a different time.

A dark magic, Ginevra had said. A wild imagining. The power to move through time.

I shivered. I was not prone to wild imaginings myself, and, sitting here with the dog twitching as he chased rabbits in his sleep, and the evening sun shining through the high windows illuminating the gold and red of the Lovell arms on the wall, I felt so content that I did not think I could wish for, or imagine, a better life. I had no need to try to bend the power of the treasure for my own gain.

I thought it would be best to lodge the Lodestar somewhere safe, but the question was where could I put it where it would not be either lost or stolen again. It was a pity that the priest did not want it, but he saw it as a heathen object corrupting the faith. I could not give it to Mr. Fiske to preserve without inviting question. It was difficult to know what to do.

In the end I decided to keep the stone with me and vowed to take better care of it. It had been my talisman since Ginevra had given it to me and I had to become its protector. I would find a thin gold chain to fit through the hole on the arrow's shaft and I would wear it around my neck like a pendant. That way both the stone and I would always be safe.

Chapter 15

SERENA

Minster Lovell
Present Day

"This feels slightly clandestine for some reason," Serena said as she, Jack and Luna went through the little picket gate at the corner of the bridge and entered the water meadows. The morning was finer and brighter than the previous day; little white clouds chased across the sky in a brisk breeze and the sun rippled over the river. "I think it's because whenever I escape from the pub, I breathe a little easier."

She thought about the copy of *The Lovell Lodestar* crumbling to ash in the grate that morning. She was sure that Eve had deliberately taken it from the shelf the previous night. She hadn't forgotten the odd expression in the landlady's eyes as she had looked up at her from the stairs. The way that the book had been lying in the fire had been so blatant, and Eve had specifically directed her to that table. But why she should have burned the book was both odd and inexplicable.

"I know it sounds a bit far-fetched," she said, "but sometimes it feels as though there's something strange about the pub." She shuddered. "I'm the least fey of people normally, but it feels unfriendly to me."

"I feel it, too," Jack said. "Perhaps it's just that Eve seems to have such an unhealthy interest in…just about everything, really. It's rather intrusive but also…" He hesitated. "Inimical, somehow." He gave a shrug as though sloughing off the feeling. "Shall we walk along the river?"

They started along the path through the meadow. Jack's stride was slightly longer than Serena's, and she dropped back a little, which gave her a perfect view of his broad shoulders and ruffled dark hair. He stopped and turned, waiting for her to catch him up, and Serena hoped he hadn't seen her staring.

The dry, dead leaves of the previous year crunched beneath their boots, the whole scene lit in shades of bronze and gold from the rising spring sun. Luna dashed about checking out all the sniffs, kicking up her paws in the leaves.

"Does she ever swim?" Serena asked, looking at the peaceful curve of the river. "Most Labs like water."

"She loves it," Jack said. "One time when I was swimming here, she came in with me, but I think she was puzzled what I was doing in the water. She definitely saw it as her domain."

Jack, Serena realized, was waiting for her to indicate whether she wanted to talk about Caitlin or not. He wasn't going to force the topic. She felt a rush of gratitude at his thoughtfulness.

"This may sound a bit left field," she said, "but bear with me. I wanted to ask you—do you know anything about your family history? I mean—you're called Lovell and you've lived in the village here for years. Do you know if you're descended from the Lovell family?"

Jack laughed. "Dad always swore we were," he said, "but

I don't know what evidence he has for that. As far as I know, until a few generations back our family came from the east coast of Scotland, a tiny place called Lunan Bay. We moved back south a few generations ago and Dad chose to live here because of the name, but as to the precise connection..." He looked around. "It's true that I do love the village. I grew up here, and it feel like it's in my blood somehow."

Serena smiled at the unembarrassed warmth in his words. Jack, she was beginning to see, was completely comfortable with who he was. It was refreshing.

"I don't think Francis Lovell had any children," she said. "But perhaps you're descended from another branch of the family."

"Francis?" Jack said. "The one they tell all the legends about?"

"That's him," Serena said. "Francis, Lord Lovell, was a bit of a crush of mine when I was a teenager," she admitted. "I had a huge thing for Richard III and was obsessed by the mystery of the Princes in the Tower. Francis was Richard's close friend and I found his story fascinating."

"Did he die at Bosworth Field with Richard?" Jack asked.

"No," Serena said. "I think he raised a rebellion against Henry VII after Richard died. He wanted to restore the Yorkist monarchy. He disappeared after the Battle of Stoke Field."

"Of course," Jack said. "There's the old story that he hid out here at Minster Lovell, isn't there? And that they found his body years later." He shook his head. "Rebellion was a risky business, that's for sure." He glanced at her. "What about the princes? What's your theory?"

Serena smiled. "Does it catch your journalistic interest? It would be one hell of a mystery to solve, wouldn't it?"

"Especially following on from the recent discovery of Richard III's remains in the car park at Leicester," Jack agreed. "There's a lot of interest in that sort of thing at the moment." He smiled at her. "I suppose you think Richard was innocent of the boys' murders? I've read *The Daughter of Time*," he added. "I have to say I found it pretty compelling."

"You're just humoring me," Serena said. "Neutrals find the passion that Richard evokes completely baffling."

"No one likes a miscarriage of justice," Jack said mildly. "Killing your nephews is a heinous crime to be accused of."

It was certainly that, Serena thought. There was something so disturbing about the disappearance and death of a child or a teenager, all that innocence and promise snuffed out like a blown candle. She gave a shudder and Jack saw it and stopped.

"A bit too close to home?" he said. "I'm sorry. So many things must remind you of Caitlin."

"They do," Serena said, "and yet the really important bits, the bits I *want* to remember, just won't come to me. It's incredibly frustrating."

"Do you want to talk about it?" Jack asked, and she nodded. He drove his hands into the pockets of his coat and they walked on side by side whilst Serena tried to work out where to start.

"I told you last night that I came here wanting to recover the memories I've lost of the night Caitlin died," she said. "It's really important to me—I feel I owe it to Caitlin, and it might help the police investigation. Also I think that sometimes, for my own sanity, I need to remember what the hell happened so I can get on with my life. There's no closure. It's like a puzzle I've never solved. I've tried to ignore it and that hasn't really worked so I've only got this one option left. It's a case of remember or go mad."

"That sounds a bit extreme," Jack said, "though I do hear

what you're saying. And I get that you feel you owe it to Caitlin even though it wasn't your fault. You do know that, don't you, Serena?" He spoke emphatically. "Whatever happened to Caitlin, it was not your fault."

"I don't even know that, though, do I?" Serena was horrified to feel the tears spring into her eyes. She rubbed them away fiercely. "If I can't remember," she said, hating the wobble in her voice, "how do I know I didn't do something, even accidentally, to hurt her or drive her away—" Her voice broke as she finally expressed the fear she'd kept hidden so long. "When the police were talking about finding Caitlin's body," she said, "I could see that they thought someone might have killed her accidentally and tried to hide her body out of fear at what they'd done. I know they thought it might be me..." She turned away as tears stung her eyes again. "Sorry," she said. "I just wish I could say it wasn't me and know it was true."

She heard Jack swear under his breath. "Serena. Stop this." He pulled her into his arms, his touch as gentle as his tone had been rough. "You *know* you didn't hurt Caitlin," he said. "*I* know you didn't hurt her. No one, knowing you, would imagine it for a second. Now, believe it."

Serena allowed herself to remain in his embrace for a moment, her head against his shoulder, his arms about her. It was immensely comforting.

"Thank you," she said after a moment, reluctantly stepping back and rummaging in the pocket of her jeans for a tissue. "I needed a bit of tough love there."

"Anytime," Jack said with a lopsided grin.

Luna, who had tired of waiting for them and had splashed off to paddle in the river, now came bounding back toward them, threading through the ruined stones of the hall with the skill of a slalom skier. A moorhen whistled on the river and the sun dipped behind a cloud.

Without warning, Serena was back in the moment eleven years before when she had trailed across the dry field from the dovecote, the grass cutting her bare feet, the July heat beating down on her. She could feel the pent-up irritation of her awkward seventeen-year-old self, jealous of her twin sister, knowing they were growing apart because of Caitlin's romance with Leo and she felt left behind, unwanted and dull, her life empty and childish and boring in comparison to her sister's.

She'd been feeling miserable and lonely, but then someone had come… In her mind's eye she could see a dog racing toward her and behind it the figure of a boy…

Luna stopped at her feet, panting, gazing up, and Serena turned to look at Jack.

"Are you okay?" He touched her arm lightly, looking concerned. "Serena? What is it?"

"Oh, my God," Serena said blankly. "It was you." She realized that she was shaking. "It was you I met in the ruins that afternoon, the day that Caitlin died," she said. "I knew there had been someone, but I couldn't remember who it was. Then when I saw you again yesterday it felt strange, as though I'd missed a step in our relationship, and now I realize why." She stopped for breath. "That's what I meant last night when I said that I was trying to remember things, and seeing you seemed to help."

There was a flash of emotion in Jack's eyes. He gave her a wry smile. "Yes," he said. "It was me you met."

"You had your dog with you," Serena said, reaching down to pat Luna whilst the Labrador looked up at her, sides heaving, eyes bright. "He was a spaniel, wasn't he? Loki? He ran toward me, and I looked up and you were there wearing a black-and-green rugby shirt and jeans." She closed her eyes, the images coming thick and fast now. "And your hair was wet… You told me you'd been swimming, further upriver, not where Leo and Caitlin were, but beyond the dovecote. You'd seen me come out and followed me back to the hall."

There was a tension in Jack's shoulders. "I wanted to talk to you," he said. "You looked sad."

"I was in a miserable mood that afternoon," Serena said. Another burst of memories returned to her and with them another rush of emotion. She sat down abruptly on the jutting masonry of a ruined wall.

"I'm sorry," she said. "Oh, God, I was so rude to you, wasn't I, telling you to leave me alone! I was jealous of Caitlin and I didn't want to talk."

"I thought you were sweet," Jack said. He sat down beside her, Luna flopping down at his feet. "Yeah, you were grumpy as hell, but with good cause. Everyone always made such a fuss of Caitlin, how pretty she was, how popular. I wanted you to see…" He stopped. "You were a person in your own right," he said fiercely. "You didn't need to be in her shadow. You were special."

Serena pressed her hands to her hot cheeks, barely hearing his words through her embarrassment. "You kissed me that afternoon. It was my first proper kiss! I was scared it would be awkward, but it wasn't, it was lovely—you were lovely…" She stopped. "Why do I feel self-conscious *now*, eleven years later? That's bizarre."

"You're reliving the experience," Jack said. His eyes gleamed with amusement. "Actually, it's really cute. Do you remember what happened next?"

"No, not yet." Serena risked a glance at him. "We didn't… Did we? I mean… Oh, God, tell me we didn't. No, of course we didn't. Not with the dog there." She spoke in a rush. "All I can remember is a lovely warm feeling—" she pressed a hand to her stomach "—so I guess whatever did happen, it was really nice."

"We sat and chatted," Jack said. "Over there." He nodded toward the archway into the hall. "We talked for ages," he said, "not about anything in particular, about our families, and studying, and what we planned to do in the future. We were just kids, really. Both of us. It wasn't like Caitlin and Leo—all intense and heavy. I don't think either of us were mature enough for that. But it was terribly sweet."

"I remember it all now," Serena said. "You're right—I wanted to be like Caitlin, so glamorous and grown-up. I was always running after her, calling for her to wait for me to catch up, and I was the elder twin! Yet at the same time the way she behaved scared me. I knew she and Leo were sleeping together and that they were totally wrapped up in each other. I didn't want her to get hurt—I wanted to protect her, but I didn't know how."

She glanced up at Jack, but the sun was in her eyes and she couldn't see his expression. "I do remember that you made me see I didn't have to be the same as Caitlin," she said. "I don't recall the precise conversation, but I do remember the feeling it gave me, the confidence and the sense of being myself. It's just a pity it all got swept away with everything else when she disappeared."

Jack squeezed her hand gently and let her go. "I'm glad you've remembered," he said.

"Why didn't you tell me?" Serena said. "Maybe not straightaway, but when we had dinner last night?"

Jack shrugged. He looked slightly uncomfortable. "I did think about it," he said. "But I knew you'd forgotten everything about that day, and I didn't know if it would help or just make things worse if I started telling you what had happened. It felt as though it would be better for you to recover the memories naturally." He looked at her. "If I made a bad call, I apologize. I wasn't deliberately trying to deceive you."

"I understand," Serena said, "and for what it's worth, I don't think it was a bad call. I keep getting little flashes of things that happened. We had some sort of fizzy drink, I think..."

Jack was smiling easily now. "I shared my homemade lemonade with you," he said. "My grandmother had made it—"

"The bubbles went up my nose and we laughed when I sneezed!" Serena said. She took a breath, feeling a little lightheaded. The rush of memories, the sweetness of them and the recovery of a part of her past overwhelmed her for a moment. She hadn't expected anything she remembered to be positive and was taken aback to feel tears sting her eyes for a moment.

"It was very simple and easy being with you," she said, clearing her throat. "I remember talking about the future. You said you wanted to study abroad—in Holland somewhere..."

"Delft," Jack said. He pulled a face. "I thought at that stage I might study architecture," he said, "but I changed my mind."

"You walked me back to the manor," Serena said, "and kissed me again, and asked if you could see me the next day. And then Caitlin disappeared and the next time I saw you I'd forgotten everything that had happened between us." She pressed her hands to her cheeks again, feeling oddly upset even though it had all happened so long ago. "Oh, Jack, I'm sorry! You must have thought I was horrible when I just dropped you—"

"At first I thought you were just too upset to want to see anyone," Jack said. He looked away, across the fields toward the river. "I heard on the grapevine that you were ill, but I didn't realize that you'd got dissociative amnesia. I kept hoping that, somehow, you'd come and see me and that together we'd sort out the whole horrible nightmare—find Caitlin, somehow, and put matters right. It was stupid because of course there was nothing we could do, but I remember thinking that if only I could talk to you everything would be all right. It wouldn't have been, of course..." He stopped and rubbed a hand over his face. "Perhaps because we'd had that one perfect afternoon, I sort of idealized it afterward when everything went so painfully wrong."

"I'm sorry," Serena said again. Impulsively, she took his hand. "It was lovely, wasn't it?" She smiled a little ruefully. "I had a terrible crush on you, you know, and when you finally took notice of me it was like a dream. I can't believe I forgot it."

Jack's lips twitched. "I had no idea," he said. "That you had a crush on me, I mean. I always saw myself as so awkward and nerdy, and you were..." He stopped and shook his head, turning her hand over between his. "I really liked you," he said softly.

His gaze lifted to hers, and Serena wondered, irresistibly, what it would be like to kiss him now, now that they were both grown-up and, she thought, probably a great deal better coordinated than they had been that summer afternoon eleven years before.

"Hold that thought," Jack said as though she had spoken. "I've just seen Zoe over by the buttery door." He gestured to a figure in a fuchsia pink waterproof jacket and the ubiquitous backpack. "She's waving at us. Do you mind giving her the chance to apologize?"

"Of course not," Serena said.

Jack squeezed her hand gently and let it go. "We can talk some more later," he said, "if you like."

"Yes," Serena said. She smiled at him. "I would like that." She watched Zoe trudge toward them. There was something very intense about her, compared with Jack's laid-back manner. "I'm glad Zoe's here, really," Serena said, repressing a sigh. "I wanted to ask her about this weird business of the eighteenth century burial."

"Yes, that is very odd," Jack said. "I asked Zo yesterday whether it would be possible to open a grave and reseal it so that it was impossible to tell if it had been tampered with. She didn't think it was likely."

"The police said the same thing," Serena said. "They felt it would show up under close forensic examination. But I can't see there's any other alternative."

"Hi, Jack, Hi…um…Serena." Zoe, out of breath and pushing the damp stray strands of hair back from her face, had scrambled over the wall to join them. She gave Serena a shamefaced half smile, clearly uncertain of her welcome. "I want to apologize," she said formally. "I'm terribly sorry about what happened yesterday—"

"It's okay," Serena said, taking pity on the younger girl. "Don't worry about it. I need your help, actually." She glanced at Jack and smiled. "As an archaeologist, would you say it's impossible to bury someone in an existing grave without the disturbance being obvious?" She kept the question deliberately impersonal for her own sake as well as Zoe's. It was easier to deal with.

Zoe, too, seemed happier with things on a professional level.

"Never say never," she said, "but I think it would be most unlikely. This particular burial—" She swallowed hard. "Well, we've been all over it several times and so has the police forensics team. To all intents and appearances, it took place in the early eighteenth century."

Serena looked across at Jack. "Yet the body has been positively identified as Caitlin," she said, "so that's not possible."

Zoe's gaze darted from one of them to the other. "Did the police mention the…um…decomposition of the body?"

"Yes," Serena said shortly. She was remembering Inspector Litton's words:

The general state of the decay suggested she had been interred for roughly three hundred years and that she had been dead for longer than that. However, the radiocarbon dating suggested that this was of a young woman who had died in the early twenty-first century.

"They said they were waiting for further tests to be completed," she said. "There must be some glitch in the results."

"It's always possible," Zoe said carefully, "but perhaps you should read this, Serena." She rummaged in the rucksack and took out a sheaf of photocopied papers. "It's not an original manuscript, but it is a typed version of the original. I was going to give it to Jack—" she looked at her brother "—before he said he wasn't interested in the case anymore."

"What is it?" Serena asked.

"It's a witness account of the discovery of a body that was found in the ruins of the hall," Zoe said. "Our body, I mean. Caitlin's. The one in the grave." Again she looked awkward. "The thing is…" She stopped and the color rushed into her face. "It was written in 1708."

"What?" Serena looked at her in astonishment. Beside her

she felt Jack stiffen with the same shock. "You mean there's a *contemporary* written account?"

"See for yourself," Zoe said. She passed the papers to Serena, who moved along so that she was closer to Jack and they could both read them.

Minster Lovell, August 1708

From my window here in the eaves of the vicarage I can see the men laboring in the manor courtyard in the heat of the day. Mr. Coke, who owns Minster Lovell Hall now, has decreed that some of the building should be repaired and reroofed, though as he has no intention of removing here to live, it seems a costly and pointless business. He is allowing the rest of the old hall to fall down. He thinks it looks romantic to see the bare beams reaching to the sky and the masonry crumbling into dust.

Serena looked up. "Is this someone's diary?"

Zoe nodded eagerly. "When we originally found the grave, I looked back through the church documents to see if it had been recorded at the time. Initially, of course, we thought it was a straightforward burial. I found a reference in the files to the interment of an unknown girl in 1708, but then at the records office, I also found this as well from the same year." She pushed the hair back from her face. "It's the diary of a servant at the vicarage at the time. It was in with the Wheeler family papers."

Serena nodded and went back to the diary.

It has been an arid summer. The river runs almost dry and the ground is hard. Mr. Coke's men sweat and swear as they dig; perhaps this is the reason the Reverend Wheeler will not let us take them cool ale to quench their thirst, for their appearance is rough and their language rougher, quite inappropriate for ladies to hear. It would have been a kindness to offer them refreshment, but the vicar has little truck with Christian charity unless it is to his own benefit and why waste his good ale on Mr. Coke's workmen when no one is here to applaud his generosity? The water from the well in the courtyard may be rank, but it is good enough for them.

I live in the vicarage attic along with the two maidservants. Although I am companion to the vicar's daughter, I am in essence a servant myself. Servility does not come naturally to me. Eleven long years have I been here. In that time, I have grown old and Miss Wheeler has turned from the hopeful young girl I once knew into an embittered spinster with nothing to occupy her hands and even less to occupy her mind. She is ill-educated, for the vicar does not approve of learning in women, and so his daughter does nothing but fret about her life, on the absence of a husband and children and on the nothingness of each day, until her complaints threaten to drive us both to madness. The lot of a lady's companion is to be agreeable in the face of all and any provocation, and so I hold my tongue, remind myself that her life is very small and that I am fortunate to have this position.

"Rebecca!" I jump as I hear Miss Wheeler calling me from far below. She sounds cross and impatient. The heat irritates her; everything irritates her. She will want me to fetch her a glass of lemonade, which she could so easily have poured for herself.

I tread lightly down the faded runner of the attic stair carpet, one hand on the rail to steady me against the steepness of the flight of steps.

"Rebecca!" Miss Wheeler is standing in the hallway, flapping her arms at me like an outraged butterfly. "Where have

you been? They have found something exciting in the ruins of the hall. I see them digging madly! Do you think it could be the Minster Lovell treasure? They say it was lost hundreds of years ago and nothing but ill luck came to the family thereafter."

"I doubt it is any kind of treasure," I say, wondering at her childishness.

We stand on the steps, Miss Wheeler and I, watching the sudden buzz of activity in the courtyard of the manor. The workmen are excited. They have uncovered something in the cellars of a tower, something lost and long forgotten. This is an unexpected prize that breaks the monotony of their routine, and they dig with a will now, curiosity speeding their work. Beside me, Miss Wheeler fidgets with anticipation.

"I cannot see," she says. "Rebecca, should we go down there?"

"Certainly not," I say. "That would be most unladylike."

A shout goes up. The foreman comes running across the courtyard and behind him, more slowly, Mr. Coke's agent, Mr. Anstruther, emerges from his office, rubbing the ink stains from his hands and blinking in the sunlight.

Miss Wheeler grasps my sleeve and pulls me down the steps. I realize that she intends us to join the gathering in the courtyard. I try to resist, but Miss Wheeler is hastening us down the path to the gate and into the ruins. The ground is hot and the stones score my feet through the thin slippers I am wearing. I feel the sweat slip down my back and prickle my neck. And all the while she is talking and talking…

"How exciting this is! It looks as though they have found a body! Perhaps it is old Viscount Lovell. Do you know the tale, Rebecca? They say that he was a great friend of that terrible monster King Richard III and that he hid away here after the

Battle of Bosworth and starved to death, locked in a secret room, when the retainer who was hiding him perished..."

I put up a hand to guard my face from the harsh sun. Miss Wheeler had dragged me out in such a hurry that I had no bonnet. I can only hope that the Reverend does not see us or he will rebuke me for immodesty, perhaps even dismiss me. I try to ignore Miss Wheeler's babble.

Blinded by sunlight, I stumble and almost trip over the irregular stones of the path. The workmen do not notice our coming at first, so intent are they on their discovery. One man doffs his cap; others dip their heads. Still they have not spoken.

I cannot relate what it is they have found. Some poor creature whose body is tumbled on a rough blanket, bare bones, jumbled and brittle. She looks as though she might disintegrate with a puff of wind. There is a flash of gold amongst the remains; a man pounces on it like a magpie but the others turn on him and he falls back, abashed.

"Have you found the famous Lord Lovell?" Miss Wheeler trills.

They look up from the corpse and the naked shock in the face of Mr. Anstruther to see us there stirs me from my horror. This time it is I who pluck at her sleeve.

"Come away, Miss Wheeler," I say. "This is no place for us."

Mr. Anstruther hastens to agree with me. "Let me escort you back, ladies," he says gallantly. "I must inform the vicar of what we have found." He shepherds us away with a masterful manner that Miss Wheeler finds is quite impossible to resist. Nevertheless, she is talking all the time, and looking back over her shoulder to watch the foreman marshaling the men to remove the girl's bones from her makeshift grave.

"It looked too small to be the Viscount Lovell," she said with evident regret. "A child, perhaps."

"The surgeon will no doubt be able to tell," Mr. Anstruther says. He sounds grim.

It is a relief to regain the shadow and coolness of the vicarage. Whilst Mr. Anstruther summons the vicar and Miss Wheeler hurries to acquaint the housekeeper with the shocking news, I sit quietly in the parlor and try to regain some semblance of calm. I feel hot, dizzy and in danger of swooning.

There was a row of dots at the bottom of the sheet and then another diary entry below. Serena swallowed hard. She was aware of Jack's hand on hers, warm and comforting. "Are you all right?" he asked.

Serena nodded. Her throat was paper dry. "Caitlin was wearing a necklace when she disappeared," she said. "A gold chain with a little golden rose. They found part of it in the ruins that night and the other part in the grave with her body—" She swallowed hard. "Oh, God, this is so weird! I can't..." She picked up the papers again. "I want to read on."

"Are you sure?" Jack said. He was looking worried.

"Absolutely," Serena said.

September 1st 1708

They are burying the girl's bones today, a week on from when she was found. There is a pitifully small group of mourners. Reverend Wheeler insisted that his daughter and I attend to make it appear that someone cares about her passing. As long as the correct observances are made, the Reverend Wheeler is content. God forbid that the bishop should hear any whisper of scandal or malpractice in this parish.

It seems to me that the only person who genuinely grieves for the girl is Mr. Coke's agent, Mr. Anstruther. I sense he feels pain for the dead girl even though he knows nothing of her.

"Poor child," he kept repeating, when we assembled outside the church, "to die alone and lost."

Miss Wheeler is standing beside him now, shedding a pretty tear every so often whilst checking out of the corner of her eye that he has noticed her distress. Occasionally, she will lay her gloved hand on his arm for comfort. I suspect she sees Mr. Anstruther as her last hope of marriage. For his sake I hope he does not make her an offer. He is too good a man to be obliged to suffer her complaints each and every day. At least I am paid to do so; a minuscule sum, but it is a small recompense.

There are but a half dozen of us in the church. The foreman of the laborers stands in the back pew for the service, looking ill at ease and turning his cloth cap round and around in his big, meaty hands. He knows it is his duty to attend, but his eyes dart about as though he is seeking escape. He looks everywhere other than at the small casket resting before the altar. The workmen are a superstitious breed, and they say that the building work is cursed because of this girl. They live in fear of an accident on the site, believing themselves ill-wished for disturbing a corpse.

"Man, that is born of a woman hath but a short time to live, and is full of misery..." The Reverend Wheeler is in full flood; he adores the sound of his own pomposity.

The girl is being buried in a plain grave. The fragment of a golden necklace that was found amongst her bones will be buried with her. No one wants to risk the wrath of God or any other deity by removing them. It feels as though everyone, whether educated or illiterate, rational or superstitious, feels discomfort at the discovery of her body.

The body is laid to rest, out of sight, out of mind, forgotten once again for all eternity. Now she is safely returned to the ground, we all breathe more easily and as we step out of the church into the bright, hot afternoon sunlight, our spirits lift still further. There is no suggestion that we should mourn the girl any longer; our lives resume. Miss Wheeler and I walk back to the vicarage, Mr. Anstruther returns to the estate office and the foreman of the builders jams his cloth cap on his head and hastens to the alehouse.

Serena looked up from the transcript. Her eyes were full of tears.

"I feel as though I've just read an account of Caitlin's funeral," she said, "but that's impossible. It simply cannot be."

Jack put his arm about her. It felt so reassuring that Serena allowed herself to lean into him. Zoe, tactful for once, was looking the other way, fiddling with the strap of the rucksack. Serena felt Jack's lips brush her hair.

"Sometimes," he said, "when all logical explanations have been dismissed, all you're left with is the impossible."

"In this case," Serena said, "the impossible is that somehow Caitlin was buried in 1708, and that's madness."

"I agree," Jack said steadily. "By all the known laws of physics it's not possible. Yet it seems to have happened. And we're going to keep on working on this until we find out the truth. Come on." He stood up, pulling her to her feet. Luna jumped up, too, shaking herself. "Luna's on the case," Jack said. "We've got work to do."

Chapter 16

ANNE

Oxfordshire
1478

The winter of 1478 was a harsh one. We had traveled to London for the Christmas festivities at court and made our way slowly home to Minster Lovell through the winter snows. It had felt a less than festive season, for the King's second brother, the Duke of Clarence, had been arrested for treason and Edward, it seemed, was less inclined to tolerate Clarence's disloyalty than he had in the past. The Duke's imprisonment had hung over the court like a pall of smoke whilst Edward tried to decide what to do with his glory-seeking brother. Francis, as Richard of Gloucester's close friend, had been party to some discussion on the matter and I sensed the distraction and disquiet in him as we rode.

"Gloucester seeks to intercede for Clarence with the King," Francis confided in me in the privacy of our chamber that night. We were staying with our neighbors, Sir William and Lady Stonor, near the little village of Henley on the Thames and were only a night away from home. I was looking forward to being back in my own bed.

"The King has been remarkably tolerant of his brother until now," I commented as I warmed myself before the fire, thawing out my frozen limbs. "What can have changed?" I was allowing myself to think pleasantly of dinner. The Stonors had been anxious to court our friendship, being nakedly ambitious, so they were likely to provide a splendid meal, perhaps even roast swan, as the Christmas season was not quite over yet.

Francis shook his head. "I do not know why the King has moved against Clarence now. Not even Gloucester knows. Perhaps the King's patience has simply run out, or perhaps..." He remained silent for a moment, staring into the fire.

"Perhaps?" I prompted. I glanced toward the door for I suspected that Elizabeth Stonor might have her ear pressed to the outside of it. One of the things I abhorred about the society in which we moved now was the endless rumor and factionalism that swirled about it like a fetid miasma from the Thames. It choked all that was fresh and clean and free. No one spoke openly; men tested their power against one another and everyone courted favor. I hated it. The Stonors sought our company now because were so close to the Duke of Gloucester. Without his friendship we would be as nothing to them.

"Perhaps Clarence has finally gone too far," Francis said. He looked uncomfortable. "Gloucester thinks that he might have threatened the King."

"Threatened him?" My brows shot up and my voice with them. One did not threaten Edward; it was supreme folly.

"With blackmail," Francis added.

I went across and knelt beside his chair. "About what?" I whispered.

"A marriage," Francis said reluctantly. "Made long ago, before he was wed to the Queen."

I sat back on my heels and let out my breath in a long sigh. The King had a way of wooing beautiful but virtuous women. It was the way in which Elizabeth Woodville had become Queen, withholding herself from him until he agreed to marry her. But what would happen if Edward had already promised the same to another woman and had already been married when he wed Elizabeth?

My eyes met Francis's. It was a measure of our opinion of the King that neither of us denied the possibility.

"Who is the woman?" I asked. "Who do they say is the King's true wife?"

Francis shook his head. "That I do no not know. Nor where and when the marriage is alleged to have taken place. Gloucester is working to discover if there is any truth in the story, and I have pledged him my aid should he need it."

I did not move; did not speak. It was easy to see how such tittle-tattle might take root, and how dangerous it could be. I thought of the King's young family, of Edward, his eldest son and heir; the younger boy, Richard, a chubby child of three now, and the little golden-haired princesses of York. The Queen was almost perpetually pregnant. King Edward would not risk any threat to their future. He would stamp out anyone who tried to blackmail him, even his own brother.

There was a knock at the door. Francis's man, Franke, stuck his head around. "A messenger, my lord. Gloucester's livery."

Francis saw the man alone in the hall whilst I endured an awkward wait with Sir William and Lady Stonor in the parlor. When Francis returned, his face was pale and set.

"We leave at once," he said to me, and although we had only just arrived and I was aching from traveling and longing for hot food and a comfortable bed, I was glad he made no mention of my staying behind. So often it seemed that women missed out on all that was of interest.

"Cousin Stonor," he said, turning to William, "I must apologize for my abruptness. A most urgent commission..."

Lady Stonor was, of course, quite frenzied in her desire to know what was happening. "What in God's name could prompt such haste?" she demanded. "Surely one night's delay can be of no consequence? It is but a few hours to nightfall and the weather is bad and the roads are worse! You will be set upon and robbed, or fall in a ditch—"

"Dear Elizabeth," I said, seeing Francis's deep discomfort and having fewer qualms about lying than he had, "I am so sorry that we must leave your hospitality so soon. No footpads in their right minds would be out on a day like this. I am sure all will be well and we shall reach home in safety." Out of the corner of my eye I saw Francis make a slight, instinctive movement, and knew at once that we were not to return to Minster Lovell that night. The Duke of Gloucester's commission would take us elsewhere.

"Thank you, Anne," Francis whispered in my ear, as I went up to our chamber to oversee the packing of trunks so recently unpacked whilst he went to the stables. "We travel light," he added, "and the servants will not accompany us. Only Franke comes, too."

I felt the tiniest shiver of premonition. "Francis," I said. "What is it? What has happened? Is it to do with the Duke of Clarence?"

He shook his head quickly, for we were easily overheard. "Later," he said. "For now we must make all speed if we are to catch up with our quarry."

As I had guessed, we did not take direction for Minster

Lovell but cut southwestward on paths and tracks almost blocked with snow. This was downland country, high, fierce and wild. It was the closest to Yorkshire that you could find in the soft southern counties, and for all the cold and the hard riding I relished it. The skies had cleared now and were bright with the last light of a winter afternoon. Far above us the buzzards wheeled and called on the wind, a keening sound of plaintive isolation. The snow-shrouded hills stretched for miles with nothing to break the emptiness.

"A man could die out here and no one would find him for days," I remarked cheerfully, "and by then he would have been picked clean by the birds and the beasts."

Francis and Edward Franke both looked at me as though I were the least congenial traveling companion, and I laughed at their expressions. I liked Franke, who was as sound a man as one could ask for as well as very handy in a fight.

"Whither do we ride?" I asked.

"Along the old Ridgeway," Francis said, drawing his cloak closer against the bite of the wind. He had snowflakes on his eyelashes. "And down into Ashbury."

I had no notion of where Ashbury might be or why the Duke of Gloucester might send us there, but I knew that the Ridgeway was an ancient track, built centuries ago across the high hills. It would not be a comfortable ride.

Even I had lost my eagerness by the time we reached the scarp of the Downs above the Vale of the White Horse. The snow had returned with nightfall, more lightly, punctured by moonlight, and we were picking our way along the track at what felt slower than a snail's pace. There was something primeval about this land, especially at night and alone, something unfriendly, supernatural even.

"We should have crossed the hills earlier and made our way along the vale," Franke grumbled. "The land is gentler though the road is longer." He sighed. "No matter. At least we are almost arrived."

He led us down a steep hillside, the horses picking their way with care. They were tired now, too, and reluctant whilst I could scarce feel my legs for the cold and stiffness of the ride. Within a few minutes, though, a squat church appeared on our left, encircled by shrouded white standing stones that only added to the ghostly air. Dimly through the snow we saw a sullen fire burning; there was a brushwood barrier across the path. A man stepped out to challenge us.

"We are travelers seeking refuge at the monastery guest-house." It was Franke who spoke up whilst Francis, I was interested to see, hung back, even whilst he had his hand on his sword hilt beneath his cloak. "Don't keep us standing out here, man—the horses are exhausted and we scarcely less so."

With some muttering, the man dragged the makeshift barrier aside and let us through. The village was wrapped up tight against the night, a meager place, no more than one muddy street with poor cottages and above it the solid church. How could there possibly be a monastery here, I wondered, and what urgent business could the Duke of Gloucester have with anyone in this place?

We picked our way along the street between the blank-faced cottages and turned right down the hill. Franke seemed to know where he was going. I remembered that he had a brother who served the Duke of Gloucester. No doubt both of them were as deep in his confidence as Francis was. I felt a chill then that was nothing to do with the cold of the night. All my life I had been an observer, watching the games of the men and women who brokered power. Now I realized properly for the first time how deep Francis was in those games and how much that was shaping our lives.

At the base of the hill a high wall reared up out of the dark. "We are here," Francis said, and he held my arm lightly for a moment in a reassuring grip.

"I wish I knew what was going on," I grumbled. "Supposing there is trouble? What am I to do?"

Francis laughed. There was an air of contained tension about him, like a soldier on the edge of battle. I realized this was the first time that I had seen him thus, ready for the fight.

"You need have no fear of violence," he said dryly. "This is a house of God."

Franke rapped sharply on the wooden door in the wall, and we waited whilst the horses blew and the snow still fell.

"I could climb the wall," Franke suggested, measuring it with an experienced eye, but then the hatch slid back abruptly and a face peered out, tonsured, wrinkled, with deep-set eyes.

"We seek accommodation for the night," Francis said crisply. "Let us in."

The gatekeeper gaped at us. "Open the door, man," Franke said impatiently. "You heard Lord Lovell."

The door creaked open and we stepped through into a small, torchlit courtyard. There was no monastery here, but I could see now that the place was a manor grange, with a small but elegant little house surrounded by more practical farm buildings. From one of the sheds came the scrape and cluck of sleepy chickens who had no wish to be disturbed. There was the scent of warm manure in the air. A working farm, then, and again I wondered at Francis's business here, in the middle of nowhere.

"Your pardon, my lord. We are ill-prepared for guests." The brother who had let us in was already regretting it, judging by the way in which he was wringing his hands nervously.

"We are easy to please," Francis said pleasantly. "All we require is a warm bed for the night and some food, for we are sharp set from the journey."

I slid from my horse rather than dismounted, I was so cold and stiff. Franke led the horses away to the stables whilst the anxious monk ushered us under a porch, through the enormous oaken doorway, and into the house.

"There are only four of us here," he said, as though to excuse the lack of fuss on our arrival. "We have few visitors in the winter."

The house was a haven. A stone-flagged corridor led almost immediately into a chamber on the left with a roaring fire in the hearth. There was no monastic austerity here. The cushions were soft, the wood highly polished and the silver very fine. An inner door was closed; behind it I could hear the clink of crockery and the low hum of voices. A tantalizing scent of roasted meat was in the air. My stomach rumbled.

"This place belongs to Glastonbury Abbey," Francis said in answer to my unspoken question. "It is a guesthouse for pilgrims and scholars traveling between the West Country and Oxford, a useful staging post on the journey east to London and beyond."

"I have never heard of it," I said, stripping off my gloves and holding out my hands to the fire.

"Not many people have," Francis said. "That is what makes it such a useful place for clandestine business."

I glanced toward the closed doorway. "Is that what is happening now?"

"Not as far as I know." Francis helped me remove my cloak and placed it over the back of a chair by the fire to dry. "All I expect to find here is the Bishop of Bath and Wells, traveling home from London and pausing to collect some important papers from the church coffers on the way. This was once his parish in the days before preferment took him to higher things. He knows the village well."

I looked at him. His gaze was sharp and bright, fixed on the panels of the closed door.

"And Gloucester needed you to catch up with him," I said. "For what purpose?"

"To ask him about a secret marriage he performed here years ago," Francis said with the ghost of a smile, "and to retrieve those selfsame documents he guards so carefully."

"You seek a marriage record," I said.

Here was the answer to one, at least, of the questions that I had asked at Stonor Hall. The King's first secret marriage had apparently taken place here, in a tiny, remote village that was perfect for clandestine business. I shivered a little to think of it and the consequences it might have now.

The door reopened and Franke strode in, carrying a bowl of steaming water and a towel, which he offered to me first. The water was deliciously hot and though I was certain to have chilblains I plunged my hands in with a pleasure that made him laugh.

"The servant tells me there is a garderobe up the stair should you require it," he murmured, "and a comfortable chamber where you might take supper whilst we—" he inclined his head toward Francis "—speak with His Grace the Bishop."

I was about to object to being excluded, but Francis came across to take the towel from me and to wash.

"I think Anne should stay," he said. He splashed water on his face and over the fresh rushes on the floor in the process, shaking his head like a dog so that the droplets flew wide. "Her presence may induce the bishop to behave…differently," he continued, "and the meeting to progress more calmly than it might if only men were present."

I took this to mean that Francis wished to avoid a violent confrontation. Franke realized it, too. His face fell.

"The bishop rides with an escort of five men only," he said. "Two in the stables, two in the kitchens, both as drunk as lords, and one—" he jerked his head toward the door of the dining parlor "—in there with His Grace. I do not know if there are any other guests, but five to two is good odds," he went on. "The holy brothers will not intervene if there is any trouble."

Francis laughed. "You are spoiling for a fight," he said, "but Gloucester felt that would be unnecessary. All he wishes us to do is…ask nicely."

"He also demanded the strictest secrecy," Franke grumbled.

"Anne can keep a secret," my husband said.

"I can," I averred.

Franke's mouth turned down at the corners. "I do not doubt it, my lady," he said, "but this is a murky business."

The nervous monk appeared at that moment with a platter piled high with slices of beef, and nothing would have induced me to leave the room, not even Francis's direct instruction. I would have fallen on the meat there and then had the door from the inner room not swung wide in that moment as well. A tall, thin man stood there, a man with a querulous expression and a grease stain on the front of his robe, which spoke of a dinner too greedily and carelessly consumed.

I had never met Robert Stillington, Bishop of Bath and Wells before, though I had heard much about him. He was a churchman who also enjoyed more earthly pleasures—it was common knowledge that he had a son—and was a politician who had hitched his fortunes to those of King Edward from the very start. He had risen high in royal service and favor. I wondered what on earth could have induced him to turn against the King when he had benefited so much from his favor.

"What the deuce is all this commotion?" the bishop demanded. His gaze fixed on Francis and a curious expression crossed his face, furtive and truculent at the same time.

"Lovell?" he said. He wiped the back of his hand across his mouth. "What is your business here?"

"How do you do, Bishop?" Francis was smiling, but there was an edge to it. "My wife and I—" he drew me forward "—are traveling back to Minster Lovell from Stonor, and sought refuge for the night. The weather is appalling. It is our good fortune that this guesthouse is so handily placed. May we join you?"

Stillington stared suspiciously at me before grunting a greeting and standing back to allow us to enter the dining parlor. The room was in a state of some disarray. The table was littered with the remnants of a meal already consumed. A mastiff lounged before the fire, and a young man in Stillington's livery was sitting with his feet up on the table, picking his teeth. He straightened as he saw us, and his chair returned all four feet to the ground with a crash that roused the dog to open half an eye before it lay back down with a sigh. None of them looked particularly pleased that we had disturbed their privacy here.

The monk placed the platter of beef on the table and hurried to fetch more chairs. The youth in livery slopped more wine into his own cup and viewed us insolently over the rim. Franke looked as though he would punch him given the first opportunity.

More brothers came rushing in with food and wine: soup that smelled fragrantly of mutton and herbs, fresh fish and capon. Francis held a chair for me and filled my cup with wine. Stillington's man, who had not been introduced to us, looked at me with an appreciative gleam in his eye. I smiled back and saw Francis raise his brows. If it was his intention to lull the bishop and his man into a state of intoxication, they were already well on the way and I could play my part.

The food was delicious.

"I like a woman with a hearty appetite." Stillington's man leered at me. I saw Francis make an involuntary movement and flashed him a look to tell him to keep quiet.

"Are there any other guests staying tonight?" I inquired, refilling the fellow's cup. "Any other poor, benighted travelers here?"

"There is no one," the man said, tossing a bone over his shoulder to the dog and taking a great gulp of the wine. "Our company must suffice."

"You have the choice of whichever bedchamber is the most comfortable, my lady." The bishop bared his yellowing teeth in a smile. "We are all entirely at your service."

"That is most generous," I said. "The weather was foul and the journey hard. It is a pleasure to find a good meal and pleasant company at the end of it."

"Your husband is a brute to make you travel in such conditions, madam." Stillington's man gave Francis a scornful glance. He took my hand, pressing a wine-stained kiss to it. "If you were mine, I would treasure you like the jewel you are."

"How pretty, sir." I removed my hand from his and wiped it on my skirt. "However, I assure you that my husband sees very well to my comfort."

Conversation dwindled. The bishop sat hunched like a heron over his food and showed no wish to talk at all. His man was fast slumping into a state of torpor. A half hour and plenty of good food later, I was feeling in a similar frame of mind, but aware of the look exchanged between Francis and Franke, I knew the moment of confrontation was approaching and I pinched myself to stay awake.

"So, Bishop," Francis said genially, pushing away his empty plate and sitting back in his chair with every indication of being entirely relaxed, "I hear you have been very busy of late. Tell us, what manner of business have you been indulging in?"

The bishop's head came up, his eyes darting from Francis's face to Franke and back again. He looked as though he had suddenly lost his appetite.

"I have been traveling," he said. "Church business, my lord..."

"I heard it was the Duke of Clarence with whom you had business," Francis said, suddenly deadly quiet. "What say you to that, Bishop?"

Stillington took a mouthful of wine, slopping some down his robe as his hands were shaking. "Your informant is mistaken, my lord," he said. "I have not seen the Duke for many a year."

"Clarence himself says that you have," Francis said. "He told his brother of Gloucester, and Gloucester told me." He shifted slightly. "The Duke of Gloucester is curious, Stillington. Clarence told him that you possess a secret that threatens the kingdom itself." He fixed Stillington with a very straight look. "What could he mean by that, Lord Bishop?"

Stillington shrank in his chair, folding in on himself. "Clarence is a drunkard," he said, his voice quavering. "He talks from out of a butt of Malmsey. It means nothing."

Beside me, the bishop's man shifted a little and blinked blearily, sensing the atmosphere. His hand moved uncertainly toward his sword hilt. I cocked my head toward him and Franke nodded at me.

"There was a wedding, was there not, Stillington?" Francis continued, as though the bishop had not denied everything. "Years ago, here in the middle of nowhere, secret and intended always to remain so? A young man, hotheaded and eager to bed a beautiful but virtuous woman... He promised her marriage to win her consent to lie with him, and you performed the ceremony."

We were all watching Francis now. I could see now how the King's brother might grasp after this as his way to the throne. Declare his brother a bigamist, denounce his children as illegitimate and Clarence would be within touching distance of what he had most desired for all his life.

Stillington was also watching Francis as a mouse watches a cat. "I do not understand you, my lord," he said, his Adam's apple wobbling. There were bright spots of red high on his cheekbones now.

Francis toyed with his wine cup. "Come, Bishop," he said, "you need not pretend to me. I am the King's man through and through, but are you? Both His Majesty and His Grace of Gloucester asked me to impress upon you how imperative it is that you should remember where your true loyalty lies."

He fixed Stillington with a very direct gaze. "Furthermore, they want the papers you have come here to collect. You are to hand them over to me."

This seemed finally to spur Stillington to action. He jumped to his feet, gesturing impatiently to the manservant, who stumbled up, grasping for his sword. Franke leaped up in response; I stuck out a foot and tripped the manservant who fell forward, connecting with Franke's fist in the process and tumbling facedown in the rushes on the floor. It was all over in a moment. The dog, clearly too old for combat, watched with incurious eyes from his place by the hearth.

"You need to choose your servants better, Stillington," Francis said dispassionately, viewing the man's prone body. "Now, where do I find those papers?"

"My lord..." Stillington was as pale as he had been flushed a moment before. "His Majesty...and His Grace of Gloucester... They misunderstand! I never had the slightest intention—"

Franke took a step toward him.

"The papers," Francis said again.

"In the church!" Stillington babbled. "They are stored in the chest there."

"Hidden in plain sight," Francis said. "Very clever, Bishop."

Franke grabbed Stillington's arm. "Come along, then, Bishop, we will go and fetch them together."

They went out. I heard one of the holy brothers asking questions in a high, anxious tone, and then I heard a babble of noise and shouting explode into the clash of swords. On the floor the servant was snoring in his unconsciousness and the dog, magnificently uncaring, was fast asleep.

Well, Franke had got his wish of a fight. I paused, trying to decide what I could most usefully do. I knew better than to try to intervene in a sword fight and I judged that whilst Stillington's men delayed Francis and Franke, the bishop might get clean away with the marriage documents. I should try to stop him.

I wondered if there might be another way to get to the church. I crossed to the door behind the arras. It was well-concealed by the rich tapestry, a little archway that led directly to a spiral stone stair curving both upward to the next floor and down into darkness. I chose to go up first. It was cold out here after the comfort of the parlor; the icy wind found every crack in the wall and whistled down the stair, making me shiver. On the first floor, a doorway opened directly into a grand bedchamber that was lit by the embers of the fire and one candle. In the shadowy dark I could make out a little oratory with altar and prayer stool. A Bible lay closed on the stand. There was no one there, no movement but the mice that scattered at my approach.

I took the candle and retraced my steps down the stone stair. In the dining parlor the lay brothers were standing around looking lost and perplexed. I carried on down the steps into darkness. No one tried to stop me. I thought the stair would lead to the buttery or perhaps storage cellars, but at the bottom was a stout wooden door that stood ajar. Pushing it open, I entered a narrow passageway that sloped downhill.

Just as at Minster Lovell, there was an old tunnel connecting the manor and the site of the old minster church so here, it seemed, there was also a passage linking the two. The ceiling of the passage was low, and the walls were smooth and chalky white in the candlelight. The floor bore the print of many feet. The sense of being trapped in an enclosed space made me catch my breath, but I calmed myself. It was a warm and sheltered place. There was nothing to fear here. My little candle flame burned steadily. Eventually I reached a place where the path started to incline upward again with steps cut into the chalk rock.

The corridor opened out into a room and there was a change in the air, fresher and colder. I stumbled over the corner of something hard and almost fell. The wavering candlelight revealed it to be a stone coffin, covered in cobwebs, its carvings worn and battered. Rank upon rank of them stretched into the dark. I was in the crypt of the church.

A sharp sound echoed above my head, the noise of a heavy lid falling. I froze. Had the bishop escaped the melee at the monastery guesthouse to race up here and retrieve the marriage lines or was there another of his men guarding the church? I crept up the steps from the crypt into the church and eased open the door a tiny crack. The church was empty and pitch-black but for one lantern lighting the chancel. I waited. Nothing moved. I tiptoed forward. I could see the huge chest where the vestments and silver were kept. The chain that would normally have held the lid fast was hanging loose. I tiptoed closer. There was a sudden movement to my left and from the corner of my eye I saw the fall of a flashing blade. I leaped back just in time, feeling the sword slice through my sleeve, and darted away down the nave. Stillington's man followed me. I could hear his panting breath behind me. He was so close. He made a grab for my arm, and I slipped on the floor and saw the sword come down again, aiming for my throat.

It hit the chain around my neck where I was wearing the Lodestar, the misshapen arrowhead that had become my talisman. The ring of steel on stone was musical, like the sounding of a bell. I saw sparks fly from the tip of the sword and in their light the man's face, his eyes narrowed in shock and sudden horror. The light grew and spread like a great explosion. I raised a hand to shield my eyes from the glare.

Then there was nothing. A silence so loud it hurt my ears. Darkness, impenetrable. I wondered whether I was dead. Then I thought perhaps I was not. I sat up, looked around and saw that I was alone. I touched my throat. There was no wound at all. The Lodestar nestled against my skin, smooth and warm. My assailant had vanished without trace.

The church door crashed open in a welter of snow and noise. Francis and Franke burst in, torches in hand.

"That whoreson bishop!" Franke was swearing, blood dripping from a long slash on his forehead. "He meant to double-cross us all along. The coward, to run like that! Surely he knows that the King will not let this issue go?"

"No matter," Francis said. "If we get the papers—" He stopped as he saw me, staggering to my feet. "What the devil?"

"I came to get the marriage lines," I said. "They are in the chest." I pointed to the chancel where the one lantern flared.

"That's a sword cut," Franke said, pointing to my arm where the blood dripped.

"There was a man," I said, "guarding the chest. He had a sword."

Francis looked around. "There is no one here now."

I shivered. My mind was still grappling with what had happened. Francis was right; the church was empty. I remembered the falling blade and then the burst of light. I'd not heard the man run away, nor seen any place he might have hidden. It was as though he had disappeared from in front of my eyes.

I touched the Lodestar again and felt the slightest of vibrations against my fingertips. My talisman. Surely it had saved my life.

"Franke, give me a strip of your shirt," Francis ordered, recalling my thoughts from the supernatural to the real. "We need to bandage Anne's arm."

"I don't see why I should be the one to shed my clothes," Franke grumbled, but he did as he was bid and Francis bound the cut on my arm so tightly it hurt twice as badly.

"How did you get here?" he asked.

"There is a secret passageway from the guesthouse into the church," I said. "I thought I would get here and stop the bishop if he came to retrieve his documents."

"The guard cannot have gone far." Franke started toward the door. "No doubt he and that cursed bishop have arranged a place to meet. I'll go after them."

"No," Francis said. "There is no point. Get the papers and we will be gone. The King will hunt Stillington down if he so wishes." He placed his cloak about my shoulders and I drew it close, burrowing into the warmth, inhaling the scent from his body.

"We'll return to the guesthouse," Francis said. "Franke, I need you to carry those papers directly to the Duke of Gloucester."

Franke had seen me shivering and gave a brusque nod. "Very well, my lord. We'll get your lady back to shelter and then I'll ride to the Duke." He glanced toward the church door where the snow spun and tumbled on the wind. "With any luck the bishop and his man will freeze to death out there in the cold and save the King his trouble."

He took up the lantern and led the way to the door, slamming it closed behind us. In the sputtering light I saw the standing stones about the churchyard draw close like sentinels. There was blood on the church steps. I drew back in alarm, and Francis put an arm about me. "It is only Franke's," he said. "One of the bishop's men ambushed us and got in a lucky blow."

Franke grunted, clearly put out to have been bested. "It's no more than a graze," he said.

"I'll patch you up when we get back to the guesthouse," I promised. "It's the least I can do when you sacrificed your shirt for me."

We made our way back down the frozen street to the abbey guesthouse, the snow obliterating our footprints as soon as they were made. This time the gate to the courtyard stood open and the space was lit with flaring torches. A monk was shoveling snow to cover what looked like bloodstains on the ground. He looked at us with wide, frightened eyes as we passed.

"Nobody died," Franke said in response to my look. "I barely touched them."

"Dear God," I said, shuddering. "I hope we are safe here. I shall not sleep a wink until dawn."

Francis, too, seemed disinclined to rest. Once Franke was patched up and sent off on the only decent horse in the stables, Francis and I went up to the guest chamber. He paced the floor whilst I poured wine for both of us, passing a cup to him. He took it with a distracted smile, finally easing himself into a chair.

"You got what you came for," I said. "Once Franke delivers the papers to Gloucester, all will be well."

"I wish I believed that," Francis said heavily. "The King's marriage is invalid, Anne. That is dangerous information in the wrong hands."

"Did Stillington really tell Clarence?" I asked. "Of all the foolhardy things to do."

"He thought to profit by it," Francis said grimly. "Whatever preferment Edward has shown him, Clarence promised more. Archbishop of York, or even Canterbury."

I shook my head at such stupidity. "He will live to regret it," I said. "Or die for it, more likely." I sat down on the rug at Francis's feet and leaned into his warmth. "Who is the lady?" I asked. "The one whom Stillington married to the King?"

"The Lady Eleanor Butler," Francis said.

"But she is dead!" I said. I felt a sense of relief. "She cannot bear witness."

"Unfortunately," Francis said dryly, "she did not die until after Edward had married Elizabeth Woodville."

I snapped my fingers. "Even so. The King may dismiss any stories as no more than idle gossip and any papers as a forgery. In fact, if he were to destroy the papers, no one would be any the wiser."

Francis smiled at me. "You are always pragmatic," he said. "Would you have Stillington murdered to ensure he holds his peace? And anyone else who can bear witness to the truth?"

"Of course not," I said. "But Edward must deny it, for what is the alternative? He would have to put aside the Queen and remarry legitimately and beget another heir, and that will never happen. Better to destroy the evidence, allow a strong king to continue to rule and his son to come after him. Declaring Edward's children to be bastards would only serve to plunge us into further war."

Francis smothered a yawn. "I fully expect Gloucester to do just what you say," he said, "or to pass the papers to the King who will burn them without a backward glance. As for

Stillington, perhaps a spell in the Tower will persuade him to hold his tongue."

"I hope so," I said. I had no truck with the bishop who seemed to me to be a foolish, venal man, but I had some softness for the King's children and, more importantly, I knew what it was to have a disputed succession to the throne. Edward and his sons were our best, our only hope for continued peace.

I did not know then that Edward had less than a half dozen years to live.

Chapter 17

SERENA

Minster Lovell
Present Day

The smell of pizza greeted Serena when she arrived at Lizzie's house that evening. Although she'd agreed to come over for supper, she wasn't sure whether she could eat anything. Whilst Jack had gone into Oxford to do some research in the records office, she had spent the afternoon at the police station, running over her initial statement from the time that Caitlin had disappeared. It had been a bruising experience; her seventeen-year-old self's grief and misery had burned from the page even though it was a formal statement that Inspector Litton was reading aloud:

"'The last thing I remember was walking back from the dovecote that afternoon. I don't remember whether I saw Caitlin again after that… I don't remember anything else that happened that day. I wish I could… I've tried so hard… When I think about it, all I can see is blankness like a bright mist, so bright I have to shade my eyes.'

"'The interview was paused at that time as Miss Warren was in distress,'" Inspector Litton had read, looking up at her.

"Yes," Serena had said. Then, with irony: "That I *do* remember."

She'd told the police that she had recovered a little more of the memory of that afternoon, and that she had met Jack Lovell in the ruins on her way home. Inspector Litton had made a note to ask Jack to verify this and had said politely that she hoped this was a sign that Serena would remember more details. Sergeant Ratcliffe had smiled sympathetically, then walked her back to the reception as he had done the previous time. There had been no substantial progress on the investigation. The stumbling block was still the apparent burial of a twenty-first century corpse in the eighteenth century, a fact that forensics had been unable to disprove, which put Inspector Litton in a very bad mood.

"Serena!" Lizzie flung open the door before Serena had a chance to knock, and embraced her warmly. "How are you doing? Was it ghastly? Do you need a glass of wine?"

"I don't expect she needs another interrogation," Arthur, Lizzie's fiancé, said dryly. He smiled at her. "Come on in, Serena. Jack's here," he added. "I hope you don't mind?"

"Of course not." Serena could feel herself turning pink. "The pizza smells amazing." She turned the subject. "Is it homemade?"

"Arthur made it." Lizzie looked smug. "You know I can't cook."

"You're a good gardener, though." Jack had come out of the kitchen, a can of lager in his hand. "You grew the salad. Hi, Serena. How did it go?"

"There's no news." Serena accepted the glass of rosé Lizzie proffered, a nonalcoholic version to keep her friend company. "The police can't get beyond the whole issue of the burial."

She took a seat at the big scrubbed pine table. The kitchen, like the rest of the house, was gorgeous, an eclectic mix of the old stuff that Lizzie had inherited and bespoke modern design. Almost all the units and appliances were white and chrome.

"I know," Lizzie said, sighing, as she saw Serena looking. "They won't withstand the onslaught of children."

"Worth it, though," Serena said with a smile.

"Tell us how everything is going," Lizzie said, subsiding onto the bench next to her. "Assuming you're okay to talk about it?"

"I'm fine as long as you all are," Serena said. "I'm just disappointed, I guess. This morning I remembered some more stuff that happened on the day that Caitlin disappeared." Her eyes met Jack's for a moment, and he smiled at her. "But there are still big gaps."

"Don't be too hard on yourself," Lizzie said, squeezing her hand. "You've only been here a couple of days. There's plenty of time to remember more." She sighed. "At least recovering the memories doesn't appear to have damaged you in any way."

"Quite the contrary," Serena said, this time avoiding Jack's eyes, but very aware he was watching her. "It was…very interesting."

Arthur transferred two pizzas from a tray on the work top to the center of the table, and Lizzie immediately started to pull a piece off one of them. The rich smell of cheese, basil and tomato made Serena's mouth water, and she realized she had an appetite after all.

"Sorry," Lizzie said with her mouth full. "I'm hungry all the time."

"There are plates," Arthur said mildly, passing them to Jack and Serena, and pushing the bowl of salad toward her, too. "Don't hold back," he said with a grin, "or it'll all be gone."

"I gave Lizzie and Arthur the diary entries to read," Jack said to Serena as they settled down to eat. "The ones written by the eighteenth-century lady's companion. I thought it would be interesting to have their perspective."

Lizzie nodded. "She wrote well, that woman. And she deserved better than being stuck in that ghastly vicarage with the hideous Miss Wheeler. I wonder what happened to her?"

"I can answer that," Jack said. "I went into Oxford this afternoon with Zoe to talk to a few people and to do some background research. One of the things I did was go to the records office and took a look at the original copy of the diary." He helped himself to some salad. "The woman who wrote the diary was called Rebecca Shaw," he said. "She was lady's companion to Miss Wheeler, the vicar's daughter, from the late 1690s to 1708, which was when they found the body." He glanced at Serena. "A few months later she ran off with Mr. Anstruther, the land agent. That's why her diary was with the Wheeler family papers. She left most of her stuff behind when she eloped."

Lizzie gave a whoop. "Wasn't Anstruther the one Miss Wheeler wanted? Rebecca stole the guy from under her nose! Good for her. He sounded like a catch."

"It must have been pretty galling for Miss Wheeler," Serena agreed, "especially if she read the diary and saw her companion's less than flattering descriptions of her and her family. I'm surprised they kept the papers at all."

"They probably just got overlooked," Jack said, "bundled up with a load of other stuff and forgotten. Plus, in the nineteenth century one of the later members of the family was an antiquarian who collected everything he could find about the history of Minster Lovell. Maybe he read it and thought it cast an interesting light on his ancestors and the history of the village. Anyway, it was fortunate because I was able to read the diary alongside the original church records and the Reverend Wheeler's notes on the burial. All the reports do bear out that the body of an unknown woman, barely more than a girl, was found at that time and interred in the grave where Caitlin was found."

"Inexplicable," Serena said. "And yet the police agree. It has to have been Caitlin." She gave a shudder. "There's so much strange stuff going on that I'm starting to think I'm going mad. I mean, I don't rule out the paranormal as such, I just don't normally tangle with it to this degree."

"I don't think you're mad at all," Lizzie said bracingly. "You're as sane as I am." She caught Arthur's look. "Okay, I realize that's not a great comparison since I'm totally fey, but *you're* not, Serena. You're the most practical person I know. If you're starting to see ghosts and other stuff, then there has to be something *very* weird going on."

"Ghosts?" Jack cocked a brow at Serena. "You didn't tell me about that this morning."

"It was only one ghost," Serena corrected, "and just the once. Yesterday when I was in the manor, I thought I saw Caitlin on the stairs. She went out of the door into the walled garden—the one that's locked."

Arthur pursed his lips into a soundless whistle. "Do you think she was trying to tell you something? Or show you?"

"Or it could have been a manifestation of your own self," Jack suggested. "Perhaps it was *you* that you saw—you're trying to remember what happened to Caitlin and perhaps your unconscious mind is trying to prompt you."

"That's deep." Lizzie put her head on one side. "I thought that if you saw a doppelgänger that means you're going to die?"

"That's not helpful," Arthur said dryly. He pushed some of the mozzarella and arugula pizza toward Serena. "You'd better eat this whilst you have the chance," he said with a grin.

"Thanks," Serena said. "I suppose it could have been my own ghost," she said thoughtfully. "She was wearing a green coat, now I think about it, and that was mine, although Caitlin would often borrow it. And it's true that I am kind of beating up my mind about what happened, trying to remember… Perhaps it was a response to that." She shrugged, helping herself to the last of the pizza. Jack's suggestion was an intriguing one. She remembered one of the psychologists talking to her about something similar back when Caitlin had first disappeared. It had been called autoscopy and as well as being a side effect of anesthesia or drug abuse, she seemed to remember it could also be a product of a malfunctioning nervous system.

"I'll give it some more thought," she said. She looked at Lizzie. "Whilst we're talking about weird stuff," she said, "I asked Aunt Polly about Granddad's family history, after you did that psychometry on that spoon yesterday."

Serena saw Arthur swing around sharply. "Lizzie," he said. He sounded exasperated. "I thought we agreed you wouldn't do psychometry anymore—"

"It was an accident," Lizzie said. "You know how that can happen." She held out a hand to him and Arthur took it, his expression smoothing into resignation. Lizzie smiled at him, and for a moment they exchanged a very private glance. Serena looked at Jack, saw he was watching her, not Lizzie, and looked quickly away, aware that the color was rising in her face.

Lizzie cleared her throat. "Are you cool with this, Jack?" she asked. "Ghosts, time travel, psychometry?"

"I'm good." Jack grinned as he finished his beer. "I'm a journalist, remember? I've heard stranger things than this."

"Time travel?" Serena said sharply.

"I meant Caitlin," Lizzie said. "Lost in one century, found in another." Her face fell and she patted Serena's arm awkwardly. "I'm sorry, Serena," she said. "I didn't mean to sound flippant."

"Let's talk about the psychometry," Serena said. She wasn't sure she could get her head around time travel even though Lizzie was right; Caitlin's burial did appear to have been three centuries before her death.

"Serena and I were catching up over a cup of tea yesterday morning in the café at the manor," Lizzie said to Arthur and Jack, "and I touched a teaspoon that had a little crest on it. You know the sort of thing—they make them as souvenirs from everywhere from Paris to Bognor Regis."

"This one was from Shrewsbury," Serena said. "I recognized it as soon as I saw it. I went for a day trip there from school and bought the spoon for my grandparents. They used to collect them. I always thought it was an odd hobby but they loved them. There was a whole rack of them in the kitchen. I'm guessing my grandfather donated them along with some other bits and pieces when the charity bought the hall."

"There was no family connection to Shrewsbury, then," Jack said.

"I don't think so," Serena said. "I just picked it up for them because I liked it and because I knew they collected them."

"So what did you see when you touched it?" Arthur asked Lizzie.

"It was horrible," Serena said quickly, remembering how upset it had made Lizzie the previous day and noticing how pale she was now. "Don't make her repeat it. Basically she saw a child, a boy, who was dying, and experienced the grief and loneliness of whoever was with him at the time, probably my grandfather. I'm sorry—" She turned to Lizzie. "It was insensitive of me to drag it up again. I only wanted to let you know that I asked Aunt Polly if my grandfather had ever had a brother and she said he had, and that he had died young. She said he'd only mentioned it the once and that he never talked about family history. So that was probably it, and I'm really sorry I mentioned it now."

"That's okay." Lizzie's blue eyes were troubled. "I suppose that fits, except that the scene I saw really was a long time ago. Centuries, I mean, and it was in London…"

"In the Tower," Serena said. "Yes, you said that." She shook her head. "Well, I can't explain that—" She stopped.

"What is it?" Jack said.

"I don't know exactly…" Serena spoke slowly. "But you remember yesterday, Jack, when we were with my grandfather he mentioned 'what happened at the tower.' I think those were his words." She looked at him, troubled. "I wonder if it was *the* Tower rather than a tower he was referring to? The Tower of London?"

Jack nodded. "Your grandfather also mentioned lions and lilies," he said, "and those are part of the royal arms of England."

"Which I saw in the vision," Lizzie put in. "Oh, boy."

There was silence for a moment, then Jack reached for his phone. "I'm just looking something up," he said.

"Do you remember what happened when you gave the

spoon to your grandfather in the first place, Serena?" Arthur was holding Lizzie's hand. "I mean, did it seem significant to him in any way?"

Serena cast her mind back. "I do remember, actually," she said. "I remember it really vividly because although I was only a child, his reaction was…a bit odd, and that left an impression on me." She knitted her fingers. "I'd been meaning to wait until Granny got back to give the spoon to both of them, but she was out at work and Mum was hassling me that we needed to go home, so I just gave it to Granddad instead." She let out a long breath. "Well, he unwrapped it and sort of stared at it for what seemed like a long time and then he said, 'How very appropriate,' and laughed and hugged me really tightly. I was surprised—it was only a little thing, but it seemed to mean something big to him. But then Mum was nagging me to go, so I just hugged him back and we went home."

"Maybe he had some sort of connection to the place, then," Lizzie said.

"Maybe… Oh!" Serena pressed a hand to her mouth. "I've just remembered. Polly said that it was his stage name before he married. Yes—Richard Shrewsbury. Of course! That's what he meant by it being appropriate, though I didn't know it at the time."

"That sounds as though it fits," Lizzie said, nodding. "A stage name! Fancy. I didn't realize he'd been an actor."

"He did stunts in films and all sort of other exciting things, apparently," Serena said. "I've no idea why he didn't tell us, though."

Jack slid his phone toward Serena. "I searched on Shrewsbury and the Tower of London," he said. He spun the phone around so the screen faced her.

"'Richard of Shrewsbury, Duke of York,'" Serena read, "'born in Shrewsbury on August 17, 1473. Younger son of King Edward IV and Elizabeth Woodville. One of the Princes in the Tower, assumed to have died in 1483.'" She looked up. "I can't see what that has to do with Granddad."

"He's called Richard," Lizzie pointed out. "Richard Warren, aka Shrewsbury. Perhaps you're descended from the Plantagenets in some way?"

"Okay, but that's more than a stretch," Serena said. "It's more likely to be a coincidence. Granddad was fostered anyway. He didn't know his family history."

"He didn't *tell* anyone about his family history," Lizzie corrected. "He must have known it to tell Polly he had a brother. Maybe he just didn't want to talk about it if it was too traumatic."

"There's more," Jack said. There was an odd note in his voice. "I don't know if this is relevant, but look…" He pointed to the screen, where there was a list of Richard Plantagenet's titles.

Serena scanned it: Created Duke of York May 1474, Knight of the Garter the following year… Earl of Nottingham 1476, Duke of Norfolk… Then she saw it.

"'Created Earl of Warenne in 1477.'"

"Warren, Warenne," she said slowly. "Surely it has to be a coincidence?" She shook her head. "Besides, if Richard of Shrewsbury was one of the Princes who disappeared in the Tower of London, no one is going to be descended from him, are they? Wasn't he about ten years old? And didn't they find the skeletons of him and his brother buried beneath some stairs, or something?"

"Those skeletons have never been DNA tested." Arthur

stretched out his long legs and sat back in his chair. "Perhaps it was someone else. Perhaps Richard survived."

"The whole story of the Princes in the Tower has always fascinated me," Serena admitted, "but I still can't see a connection. I mean, if we had such an illustrious family tree, why wouldn't Granddad tell us?"

Jack had been scanning through some more articles on his phone and looked up, a dark lock of hair falling over his brow.

"There were some very persistent rumors at the time that Richard Plantagenet had survived and was spirited away after the Battle of Bosworth," he said. "There was a lot of complex political maneuverings going on that you'd need to read about for yourself, but essentially no one knows for sure what happened to him. So, there could have been a family story that your grandfather was descended from Richard. It would explain why he chose Shrewsbury as a stage name and maybe where the Warren name comes from as well." He looked dubious. "It's a pretty outside chance, though. Most family stories like that are just hearsay, distorted over the centuries."

Serena got up and walked over to the window, looking out over the dark garden and the twinkling lights of Burford on the hill below. Suddenly she needed space. What had Dick said to her only the previous afternoon when they had been talking about Caitlin?

I should have warned you. I should have told you both where we came from. I should have explained…

He had implied that whatever had happened to Caitlin was in some way connected with the past and with their family history. But how much did Dick remember now, how much did he understand? Serena looked out over the dark valley of the Windrush, where the little river wound its way downstream, through Minster Lovell and beyond to join the great flow of the Thames. That same river swept past the Tower of London and a room where, in Lizzie's vision, a boy had died and another had witnessed it in grief and loneliness. She wrapped her arms about herself. There were so many mysteries here. Was she letting her unhappiness at Caitlin's death and her determination to discover the truth behind it run away with her? The edges of reality were blurring. Nothing seemed simple or explicable any longer, and suddenly she felt exhausted.

"I think I'll go back now," she said, turning to the others. "I'm a bit tired and I've got to collect Aunt Pol tomorrow. Sorry I haven't been great company tonight. Thanks for supper—" she gave Lizzie a hug "—and for making me feel as normal as I can under the circumstances."

"You'll be okay driving back?" Lizzie looked at her anxiously. "You know you can always stay here if you want to."

"I'll be fine," Serena said with far more conviction than she felt. "Thanks for offering." She gave Lizzie's hand a squeeze. "I'll be all right. Really I will."

"Okay," Lizzie said, sounding far from sure. "I'll call you tomorrow."

Jack walked her out to her car.

"A lot to think about, huh?" he said when she was silent.

"It would help if something at least made sense," Serena said. "Between sealed burials and ghosts and the Princes in the Tower, I think I'm losing my grip completely. Which reminds me. I meant to ask earlier. When you mentioned the diary, you said there was an antiquarian in the Wheeler family who had collected all sorts of stuff relating to the local history of Minster Lovell. There wasn't a copy of a book called *The Lovell Lodestar,* was there? I think it's out of print and it was probably self-published in the nineteenth century, so it might be hard to get hold of."

Jack looked intrigued. "I'm sorry," he said. "I didn't notice. But it would be easy enough to check. Do you want to come with me to the records office tomorrow and see what we can find? If we aren't successful there should be a copy in the Bodleian Library."

"It's probably another wild-goose chase," Serena said, "but yes please, I'd like to find a copy. I think it was an old book of my grandfather's. It could be significant."

"Okay," Jack said. He put out a hand and brushed the hair away from her cheek. "Hang in there," he said, and then he was holding her just as she had wanted him to do since that morning, and it felt natural and right, and so much easier than she had imagined. For a long moment she stayed there, her cheek resting against his chest, their arms about each other, inhaling the scent of his body and feeling his warmth. When she drew back a little, she was smiling.

"What is it?" Jack asked.

"I remember hugging you that day in the ruins," Serena said. "You smelled of river weed and damp wool. Your choice of cologne has improved."

Jack laughed. "Hopefully I've improved all round since then."

"I want to go back," Serena said suddenly, pressing her cheek back against his chest, listening to the beat of his heart. "I want it to be like it was when we spent that afternoon together. I know it can't be, but it all felt so simple then."

Jack's arms tightened about her. "It's understandable to feel that way," he said, "when things in the present are so tough to deal with."

Serena was belatedly overcome with embarrassment. "I'm sorry," she said. "This is really stupid and needy of me. I'm sure I'm just suffering a nostalgia crush. Ignore me and I'll get over it soon."

"A nostalgia crush, huh?" There was a gleam of amusement in Jack's eyes. "Well, if that's what it is, it's obviously catching because I feel it, too."

Serena stared at him, at the curve of his mouth and the way the tousled dark hair fell across his forehead. Her stomach tumbled.

"I don't think my judgment's too sound at the moment," she said, answering the question that was in her own mind, "but..." She rested a hand on his chest. "Perhaps I should just trust instinct instead."

Jack's fingertips traced the line of her cheek, making her nerves flutter with anticipation. "You have good instincts," he said. "Believe in them." He threaded his hand through her hair, cradling the back of her neck, and his mouth came down on hers.

It felt perfect. It felt so perfect that for a moment Serena was overwhelmed by the rightness of it. It felt as though something she had not even been aware of losing had been rediscovered.

"Wow," she said shakily. "Damn my faulty memory. How could I have forgotten?"

She felt Jack smile against her mouth. He kissed her again, a brief, hungry kiss, then let her go. "When all of this is sorted out," he said, "perhaps we should give it another go."

Serena nodded. "I'd like that." She reached up to kiss his cheek, feeling the slight roughness of stubble against her skin. "I'll see you tomorrow," she said, backing away before she gave into the impulse to kiss him again. "Good night, Jack."

The warmth engendered by the kiss lasted her until she reached the main road. She felt fine for as long as she was driving under the streetlights' glare, but as she left Burford behind and the road took the ridge above the River Windrush the darkness closed in around her. She was tired and she felt suddenly lonely and afraid. There were so many thoughts, doubts and fears spinning around in her mind. She didn't want to think about any of them. Suddenly, she wished sharply that the police would simply tell her it had all been a mistake, that Caitlin had died of natural causes and that there was a simple explanation for her burial place within the church. That way, Serena was sure, she could forget everything else, persuade herself that her grandfather had been talking about things that made sense only in the world of his mind…

She turned down the hill toward Minster Lovell and the road narrowed and the trees closed in overhead, forming a tunnel of darkness. She was glad to reach the bridge where the sky opened up again and the water meadows stretched away to her right, the lights of the village pricking the night. Some creature caught the edge of the headlights and scuttered away to safety and Serena released a shaky breath, easing her fingers on the steering wheel. What was she expecting to see—the ghost knight racing her to the bridge, the gray lady flitting across the road, the ghostly dog stalking through the fields beside the river? She felt incredibly tense. She turned into the pub car park and relief washed over her to have reached safety. As she eased her car into a parking space the headlights cut an arc through the darkness, catching the edge of the ruined hall across the field and sending shadows racing across the lowering gray walls. Serena caught her breath. The light momentarily dazzled her, bouncing back from the stone, and she raised a hand to shield her eyes.

Then, in the same way that it had happened when she had seen Luna running through the ruins, she had a flash of returning memory. The cloudiness in her mind seemed to vanish, like the wind blowing away the mist, and she was back eleven years before, watching through the dark as a woman slipped through the shadows of the ruined hall and disappeared.

Serena sat quite still in the darkened car whilst the memory threaded through her mind, image after image, joining up at last to make a whole picture. She remembered Lizzie saying a few days ago in the café that Caitlin had been no saint and perhaps she had had a secret life. She remembered the shadow of doubt that had crossed her mind then because Lizzie's words had stirred up something buried deep in the lost memories of that last day. Now, at last, she knew what it was.

She had floated back to the manor that afternoon after seeing Jack. She'd wanted to find Caitlin and tell her all about it, but her sister was still out with Leo, and her grandfather wasn't at home, either, so she had kicked about the house, her mood gradually deflating. Her grandfather had come back at teatime and they'd eaten salad together—it was too hot for anything else—and Serena had covered for Caitlin, who had come back smelling of smoke and alcohol and disappeared off to their room.

"Leave me alone!" Caitlin had said when Serena had asked her what was wrong. "You wouldn't understand. You don't understand anything." And she'd thrown herself down on the bed and turned a shoulder to her sister.

Looking back, Serena felt a sharp pang of loss for both of them; for Caitlin whom she could see now had been struggling with late adolescence far more than anyone had realised, and for herself who had drifted away from her twin by slow degrees without even noticing. When she had gone up to bed a few hours later, Caitlin was asleep—or pretending to be—and they hadn't spoken. They had never spoken again, because when she had woken again, Caitlin was gone…

Serena felt oddly calm. There was no shock, no trauma as the amnesia receded. She ran carefully through everything in her mind again so that there was no likelihood of her ever forgetting it again. She fitted together each piece. She thought about how she had felt. She thought about Caitlin.

And then she cried, sitting in the car, looking out over the place where her sister had vanished, fierce, salty tears for what she had finally remembered and what she had lost.

Chapter 18

ANNE

Minster Lovell
June 1483

King Edward died suddenly in the year 1483. We knew, of course, Francis and I, that his marriage to the Queen had been invalid and the children illegitimate. We had seen the proof at Ashbury years before and knew that in law his eldest son Prince Edward could not inherit the throne. We had held our peace on the matter and been richly rewarded over the years. Francis had been made a viscount and was the right-hand man of his friend Richard, Duke of Gloucester. Now King Edward V had inherited and Gloucester was Lord Protector, I thought very little would change. I understood nothing.

The day that Francis told me that Gloucester was to take the throne was the day he smashed our existence to smithereens. He had ridden from London where the court and the city were in turmoil. I was in the potager garden at Minster Lovell when he came; it was late spring and the raised beds were groaning with the promise of a good crop. Already the colors of the peas and beans and cabbages were showing amongst the rich earth.

I had been unwell that spring. At first, I had hoped I was

with child. After seven years of living as husband and wife, I had begun to despair quietly. I was surrounded by sisters, cousins and friends who had growing families. I felt a failure, the barren wife, the butt of jokes, good for nothing. Francis never reproached me, yet our very silence on the matter seemed to drive me further away from him.

My mother, famously fertile, had been unconcerned when I had first sought her advice, a year after my removal to Minster Lovell.

"You are young still," she said. "Do not let it concern you. There is plenty of time."

Five years on and she was not so sanguine. She recommended a powder of mugwort and marshmallow root, and inquired delicately whether there was anything wrong with Francis. I thought not, though I had no means of comparison, and that spring my hopes were raised when I missed my courses for two months. I prayed fervently. In private moments, I even clasped the Lodestar to my breast and begged for a child, hoping that the holy relic would help me.

"I want a child," I whispered. "Give one to me."

However, it seemed it was not to be.

Francis came straight from the stables that day, striding into the garden and pulling me into his arms. I had turned at his step and my face, I know, had lit with happiness for even now my heart speeded each new time I saw him. But he did not speak. He kissed me and I sensed something in him I had not known before, a desperation and a conflict I could not understand, as though I was his last bastion against something terrible. When he released me, I raised a hand to his cheek.

"What is it?" I asked.

I had heard a little of the troubles that had followed the

death of the King. I knew that Elizabeth Woodville and her faction had not told Gloucester he was named Lord Protector in the King's will and that it had been left to Lord Hastings to send word to him in the North. Matters had only worsened when Gloucester had arrested the new King's escort at Stony Stratford and the Queen had taken the rest of her children and fled to sanctuary in Westminster Abbey. It felt to me as though King Edward's death had pulled a thread and now the entire tapestry was unraveling.

"The Woodville faction will not relinquish one iota of their power or influence unless they are obliged to do so," Francis had said at the time. "Gloucester is legitimately named Protector of the Realm yet they will not support him."

There was a legacy of mistrust between the two camps that could only augur badly for the future, I thought. Even as the new King, Edward V, was housed in the Tower of London, preparing for his coronation, it felt as though winter was coming rather than summer. Something was badly awry. I felt it and shivered deep inside.

Francis took my hand and led me over to the seat in the shelter of the garden wall. The stone was warmed by the sun and it was pleasant here, but the cold was already within me and would not be banished.

"Gloucester is to take the throne," Francis said bluntly.

I gaped at him, thinking that I had misheard. "What? Why?"

"It is the only way," Francis said, and it sounded as though he was rehearsing a piece he had repeated over and over in his mind in the knowledge he would need to hold fast to it forever more. "Only he is strong enough to hold the kingdom together. A boy king cannot rule the factions that threaten us." He looked down at our entwined hands. "Besides, you and I both know…the King's marriage was never legal. His children are illegitimate and his son cannot rule."

I jumped up. "It was legal enough for no one to mention it when the King was alive!" I said.

"Anne," Francis said. He spread his hands in a gesture of pleading. "That was different—"

"It was expedient, no more than that," I said cuttingly. I felt such rage that I could not understand it. Somehow it was tied up with the despair I had felt three days before when I saw the spotting of blood that indicated I was not to bear a child, not this time, perhaps not ever. I thought of the Queen in sanctuary with her children. What would become of them, denounced as bastards, their inheritance betrayed? They had lost their father and all the security they had known. Soon they would lose even more.

I pressed my hands together hard to still their shaking.

"Is Gloucester to make this public, then?" I demanded. "Did he keep Eleanor Butler's marriage lines all along so that he could claim the throne? Is it to be the basis of his usurpation?"

Fury flared in Francis's face. "You are not to call it that," he said. His voice was low, but his tone was colder than I had ever heard it before. "How can you not understand? Gloucester is the only one who can keep the peace! You yourself said as much when we were in Ashbury. You said we needed a strong king with a son to follow him! Now that Edward is dead, Gloucester is such a man." His shoulders slumped. "Prince Edward is no more than a child, a mere twelve years! We all know how badly it goes when a child sits on the throne. Besides, he is sickly and like to die—"

"Oh, well!" I could not help myself. "That makes the matter perfectly acceptable, then! Perhaps his little brother will oblige Gloucester by dying, too! Where is he now, Richard of Shrewsbury? Still with his mother, I hope, as befits so young a child—"

I stopped as I saw something furtive in Francis's expression, his gaze sliding away from mine as though there was something shameful he could not bear to reveal. But it was too late. I had guessed.

"No," I said, and it came out as a whisper. "Do not tell me that Gloucester holds both Princes."

"Richard is in the Tower with his brother," Francis said.

"Dear God, no." I wrapped my arms about myself. "That cannot be right."

"It is for their own safety," Francis said. He made a gesture of exasperation. "What are you suggesting, Anne? That Gloucester would harm his own nephews? He would never do such a thing. You know him for a fine and loyal man! How could you imagine it?"

"I only know that this is wrong," I whispered. "The Duke of Gloucester should not take the throne."

Francis leaped up and turned away from me as though he could not bear to look at me. Desolation swept through me and with it a kind of fury that Richard of Gloucester could do this to us, demanding Francis's loyalty and in the process weakening forever the ties my husband had to me. I understood well enough how we had got here. Francis and Richard had been friends in childhood and those bonds, forged through rebellion and blood, were so often the strongest. And Francis was the most loyal of men, the most constant. I knew that and loved him for it. Yet now, that very loyalty drove a wedge between us.

"What does Will Hastings think of this?" I asked, striving

to calm our quarrel. Hastings, the late King's Lord Chamberlain, was a man whose counsel I admired for he was strong, and able and farseeing. I could not believe he would support Gloucester's bid for power.

There was a silence, then: "Hastings is dead," Francis said.

"What? No!" I almost crumpled to the ground, but managed to steady myself, my fingers digging into the warm wood of the bench to keep me upright. "How?" I asked. But I already knew. He had opposed Gloucester's will.

"Oh, dear God," I said, half to myself. "Francis…" I looked at him. "This cannot be right," I repeated dully. "Did King Edward ask that his brother take the kingdom after he was gone? He did not! It is Gloucester's role to protect, not usurp!"

"It is the right thing to do!" Francis spun around on me. "Gloucester served his brother loyally and well and now he does what is best for England—"

I put my hands over my ears. Probably it was childish, but I could bear to hear no more of his twisted logic. Perhaps Francis was right, if one looked beyond personal allegiances to the greater good. I knew as well as any that the rule of a minor brought little but trouble. Even so, it stuck in my throat that a man who had been lauded as just and fair could now take so greedily for himself.

"You will be telling me next that Gloucester does not want to be king," I said, "and is only doing that for the greater good as well."

I walked away then. The tears blurred my eyes and clogged my throat. Each step felt like a step onto ever more uncertain ground, and each moment that Francis did not come after me felt lonelier than the last. I was at the gate when I heard him behind me and I turned to face him. We stared at each other over what was suddenly a yawning chasm. I felt shock and horror that we had been driven so far apart, so fast.

"Anne," Francis said. Once again, he drew me close to him and I did not resist. He rested his cheek against my hair, and I felt the misery of the world ease a little, for surely if we were united all would be well.

"I am sorry," he said. "You have ever been my guide and my conscience, Anne." He took a breath. "But now… I have to do what I feel is right." He let me go. It felt very final. I stood alone, feeling cold, and searched my heart to see if there was a way that I could simply forget what had happened between us; carry on as though it had never occurred.

Perhaps Francis hoped for that, too, yet the distance between us suddenly seemed unimaginably great. I felt despair and blinked back the tears from my eyes.

"Will you accompany me to London?" he asked me formally. "We should be there for the coronation."

I knew then that there was no way back. I had to either betray him or my own principles. I was his wife, bound to obey, and I did not want to put us to the final test and force him to order me.

"I will accompany you," I agreed.

He nodded. "Your cousin Anne asks to be remembered to you," he said very carefully. "She desires you to become one of her ladies-in-waiting when she is Queen. Both your mother and your sister Elizabeth have accepted the honor."

I hated them all then. I hated my mother for her Neville arrogance and her lust for power, and my sister for following her example. I hated my cousin Anne for choosing her ladies-in-waiting whilst the widowed Queen was hiding in sanctuary and Richard of Gloucester's enemies were barely cold in their graves. And I hated Francis for following Gloucester's star out of a loyalty I could only feel was blind.

"I shall not do that," I said steadily. "I shall never do that." And I turned my back and left him there amidst all the fresh promise of the summer.

King Richard III came to Minster Lovell Hall on his royal progress that summer and from there we all traveled through the Midlands and up to York. There was so much pageantry, so many feasts and entertainments, but they masked an ugly truth, which was that the country was not content with the usurper. There were men who plotted to free the King's nephews from the Tower of London, and to take the widowed Queen and her daughters from sanctuary. Rebellions blew up and were put down. Rumors spread like a plague. I felt as though we were skating, not on the thinnest of ice, but upon nothing but smoke.

The endless politicking masked another ugly truth as well, which was that my marriage to Francis was little more than a hollow shell now. We were always together at court yet never spoke of anything of significance. I wore the gowns of fine blue-and-crimson velvet and of white damask; I smiled and danced and played and sang, and all the while I waited for the quicksand to swallow us as it had so many others who had once been as close to the King as Francis was now.

My mother took me to task. "I do not understand you, Anne," she complained. "Your husband is the Lord Chamberlain and there is no man higher in royal favor. You have the world at your feet. Why must you be so dull about it? You do not even have the excuse of babes to distract you. You waste those chances that are yours." She looked at me with her blue

Neville eyes as though I should be grateful to be childless when she knew that it had snapped my heart in two.

That winter of 1483 we celebrated Christmas at court with much good food, wine, laughter and dancing even though—or perhaps *because*—the late King's eldest son, Edward Plantagenet, had died of plague in the Tower of London. Richard felt more secure on the throne than he had for a very long time.

"You are mistaken," I said coldly to Francis, when, unusually, he confided as much in me. "Edward's death changes nothing. The Queen has another son and any number of daughters, and have you forgotten the Duke of Clarence's son, too? Does he not have a better claim to the throne than his uncle?"

We stared at each other in mutual dislike and mistrust until Francis shook his head and turned away from me. "You are damned obstinate, Anne," he said. "Why can you not bend even a little to try and meet me?"

"Perhaps I would, if you use your influence to persuade the King to release his other nephew from the Tower," I said, hurt making me cruel, "instead of salving your conscience by teaching him swordplay and archery, and pretending that it is right that his uncle keeps him in captivity like a pet animal."

Francis walked out then and I was left with my grief that I had pushed him further from me still. Everyone was unhappy that year; it felt as though the country tiptoed on splinters of glass as matters grew worse and worse. Then the King's only son died and the court was plunged into mourning.

"There are rumors that the King is to put away his wife and seek another," my mother said waspishly to me. "No doubt your husband will do the same, for you give him scant attention and he is surrounded by the prettiest women at court."

I ignored her. It was true that there were many women

at court now who were younger and prettier than I was, including the King's nieces who, with their mother, had finally emerged from sanctuary at Westminster Abbey. It made for the most extraordinary brew of scandal and gossip. I felt as though I were looking through a mirror at a distorted image of what the world should be like, where two factions who hated each other with a deep and visceral hatred pretended to live in harmony. Something, I thought, was going to snap, and soon.

One day I was walking in the pleasure gardens, along the little winding paths beneath the sweet-scented trees. I walked alone because I had no appetite for company even though there were plenty who would have accompanied me had I given the word. Today, not even the sight of the climbing rose on the trellis, or the ivy entwined around the old trees could bring me a sense of peace. The air felt heavy, as though a storm was coming, and I sat down on a turfed bench beside a pool and closed my eyes for a moment.

A shadow fell across me, a woman, alone like me. I recognized her and rose, instinctively intending to curtsey, but she stopped me with a hand on my arm.

"Your Majesty," I said.

"I am Dame Elizabeth Grey now," Elizabeth Woodville said with the ghost of a pale smile. "I am the one approaching you for a favor, Lady Lovell."

I wished she would not. Elizabeth Woodville and I had never been friends, not even in the days when her husband had been alive, for we had clung fast to our factional loyalties. Now, though, she took a seat beside me and arranged the dove-gray folds of her skirts neatly. She was still almost as beautiful as she had been ten years before and still as cold. Her blue gaze appraised me, no softer than it had been when she was queen and I the wife of a minor baron far beneath her notice.

"I need your help," she said. "A time is coming when I shall need to know that my son is safe. I wish to entrust his care to you."

I gaped at her. Not only was she speaking treason, and every rustle of a leaf and every snap of a twig about us might indicate the presence of a spy, but her words made no sense to me at all. Richard, her son, was still in the Tower of London, kept safe from the world, so we were told, that he might pursue his education in peace, away from those who would use the Prince to further their own ambitious ends.

"Surely," I said, when I had regained my breath, "his uncle will see to his safety."

She smiled, a cold smile that moved her lips but failed to touch her eyes. "Of course," she said. She snapped off a leaf or two of sage from the plant beside us and rubbed them thoughtfully between her fingers. The smell of mint and bitterness was almost overwhelming.

"But should there come a time when he is unable to do so," she said, "then I ask you to take his place."

I stared at her. "I cannot see what I could do," I said bluntly. "I would have no power to protect him—"

She touched the Lodestar pendant at my throat, a light touch, almost as though she was afraid that she might vanish in a puff of smoke. "You have this," she said.

For a moment I stared at her in stupefaction. Then I remembered that Ginevra, when she had first given me the Lodestar, had been tirewoman to Elizabeth's mother, Jacquetta the witch. I put my own hand up now to cover the stone, as though to protect it.

"You know about the Lodestar," I said.

"I recognized it," Elizabeth said. "My mother tried to bind its power but it was too dangerous. Yet you wear it like a jewel."

"It saved my life," I said. "It is my talisman and I am its protector."

She turned those pale eyes on me again. There was something very disturbing about her gaze. For all that I wore the stone, it felt as though she was the one who could see the future.

"I have seen its power," she said. "I know it will save my son." She stood up. "Be ready," she said, "if either the King or I should send Richard to you."

She walked away from me down the winding path and I watched her go, watched as the brightly colored knots of courtiers parted to let her through, saw the curious glances, the sly smiles, and the calculations of those who wondered whether Elizabeth Woodville was still a force to be reckoned with. And then I sat there, wondering if it were true, if I had the power to protect another woman's child, and if I would be called upon to use it.

The distorted mirror smashed one day in the year 1485.

I had known that there would be an invasion; had known it from the very moment that Gloucester had taken the throne from his oldest nephew two years before. My only surprise had been that he himself had not had the wit to see it. Or perhaps he had, and he thought that he was strong enough to win. Whatever the case, in the spring of that year, news came of an invasion by Henry Tudor; Francis went to the south coast to oversee the provisioning of the royal fleet, and I returned home to Minster Lovell.

Francis came to me there one day at the start of August. I

had been working in the kitchen gardens for I found that being out in the open air was all that could lift my spirits these days. Outside, seeing the way that nature continued to turn regardless of the follies of men, gave me comfort and an obscure hope that one day the world might turn into the light again.

I was in my oldest clothes and had soil smeared across my apron and very likely my face as well. When I looked up from my weeding, a man and a boy were standing beneath the laden branches of the apple tree on the edge of the orchard. They were plainly dressed, like countrymen, like me, in fact. It was a moment before I recognized Francis and then I got to my feet, a little stiff from kneeling and hurried across to him.

"You should have told me you were coming," I said. "We are unprepared—"

He put out a hand to stop my flow of words. "No one must know I was here," he said. He touched the boy's back lightly. "I've brought Richard to stay with you here. The King commands it. Tell no one who he is. He will be safe here for a little." He took my hands in his despite their dirt. "Henry Tudor will invade and soon. If there is a battle…" He swallowed hard. "I have made provision for you, Anne. Two manors that will be yours alone, for you and any future children you may have should you remarry—" I made a move of protest, but he continued. "I will come back as soon as I may, but if I do not…" He hesitated. "I am leaving Franke to protect both you and Richard. He will guard you with his life."

"I am sure he will detest that charge," I said. I tried for a light tone, but my voice broke on the words. "He will want to fight alongside you."

There was nothing else to say. For two long years Francis and I had been estranged, and now that I was about to lose him, I regretted it bitterly. I had loved him since I was six years old and at last I saw that in doing so, I had expected too much of him. He'd told me of his imperfections, but I had held him to too high a standard. In my own way I had been as culpable as he.

I stepped into his arms and drew him close, and I thought: *Oh, how much I have missed this. What a fool I have been.*

Francis buried his face in my hair, and I felt the desperation in his touch and met it openly and with love as I held him to me. When we stepped back, I was crying and I did not care who saw it.

"I love you," I said. "Godspeed you safely back to me again." I wrapped my arms about myself and thought of Francis's words, of the provision he had made for me, of the children we had never had. That was the bitterest pill of all.

The boy had watched us in silence, and as Francis walked away, he looked at me with his mother's clear blue eyes and her impenetrable coolness. Richard Plantagenet, not even twelve years old, too young for all he had witnessed, too vulnerable to be at the mercy of this sort of fate. It was not a conscious decision, but in that moment, I wrapped him tight in a hug and after an initial resistance I felt him melt and he clung to me, a boy still in need of a mother's comfort.

"All will be well," I promised him. I felt like a tigress suddenly with one cub to protect. "I will guard you with my life and Francis—" I swallowed hard "—he will return. Francis always comes back."

Chapter 19

SERENA

Minster Lovell
July 2010

Something had woken her. She lay still whilst the last vestiges of sleep drained from her mind. The room was bright with moonlight that slid through a gap in the curtain and fell on the rumpled covers of Caitlin's empty bed beside hers. She knew her sister must have slipped out to meet Leo again. Where else would she be on a hot summer night? The knowledge, previously like sandpaper against her mixed-up emotions, mattered far less now that she knew Jack liked her so much. She gave a little wriggle of pleasure.

She was about to turn over and go back to sleep when she noticed that Caitlin's red leather knapsack was missing from the chair beside the bed. She felt a touch of anxiety then, and turning on the light, she saw that a few other bits and pieces had gone as well; the well-worn teddy from the pillow, Caitlin's beaded bracelet, her Justin Bieber T-shirt, her gold pendant and the book she had half-finished. She threw back the thin blanket and jumped out of bed.

A quick, furtive sort through Caitlin's drawer showed more items missing. Suddenly urgent, she groped for her shoes and slipped a coat over her pajamas although she wasn't in the least cold.

Down the stairs quick as a mouse, quiet as a thief, avoiding the creaking step, tiptoeing over the stone floor... She did not want to wake her grandfather. He would be utterly mortified to know that Caitlin was running away. He would think that he had done something wrong or failed in some way. Serena felt a pang of fear. She had to protect him from that. And Caitlin...what was she thinking? It was one thing to sleep with Leo, but it was quite another to run off with him... Her pulse quickened. She didn't want to interfere. She really did not. But if Caitlin was going to do something so foolish, so shortsighted, she had to make her see sense.

The latch of the door into the walled garden was very heavy, but it lifted silently and the garden outside was so bright white and black in the moonlight that it looked like a chessboard. She paused on the gravel path, listening. She knew that Caitlin and Leo had been meeting in the ruin of the old hall. Her sister had told her all the intimate details with the bright, confiding openness that had led to Serena putting her hands over her ears—too much information. But now she could see nothing, no one, moving in the landscape. The hall lay still and silent, the moonlight pitiless on its old gray walls.

It was as she was standing there that she felt the change come over her, first as a ripple of disquiet, then as a whisper of fear and finally as a clutch of terror. It was visceral and she felt it instinctively, in her bones. Caitlin was in terrible danger.

She looked back only once. The light was still on in her bedroom window, a warm reassuring glow, the familiar world as she had known it up to this point. She ran then, regardless of the loudness of her footsteps on the gravel, down the path and out of the gate. Caught up in urgency and terror although she did not know why, her legs were shaky and her heart was pounding. The tufts of dry summer grass tripped her and the stones scored her bare feet. She could not keep up the pace; already she had a stitch in her side.

Then she saw Caitlin silhouetted against the moon-washed walls of the ruin. Her sister was skipping lightly over the stones, smiling, happy, the knapsack in her right hand. Serena felt the clutch of terror again. She shouted.

"Caitlin!"

Caitlin looked up, pinned for a second in the bright glare of the waxing moon. Serena saw a shadow fall across her sister, a figure approaching from out of the dark. She was still running, the breeze on her face, the air tearing in her lungs, but she knew with despair that she would not be in time. She saw the figure raise a hand to take the bag from Caitlin. There was a struggle—she saw it only in snatches of light as the moon fell on the two of them. Caitlin had fallen and the other figure was standing over her and then there was a flash, brighter than the brightest fireworks she had ever seen. For a moment the entire hall seemed to be illuminated like a film set, but it was not the ruin that she knew so well. This was a different Minster Lovell, with tall towers and encircling walls and a water gate beside the river where a boat was moored… She saw Caitlin vanish, literally disappear before her eyes, and she screamed and screamed. Then the light grew like a great explosion and she raised a hand to shield her eyes and fell down and down through the dark.

"Thank you, Miss Warren," Inspector Litton said. She sounded utterly composed, as though she had heard many more improbable witness statements than this in her time. Very likely, Serena thought, she had. They were in the same bare little interview room as before, and Serena had just finished recounting her memory of the night that Caitlin had disappeared.

"It was good of you to come straight in this morning to tell us," Inspector Litton said.

"You look as though you haven't slept," the sergeant put in sympathetically.

"I didn't," Serena said. "Not much."

There was silence.

"If we could pick up on a few points?" Inspector Litton arched her brows.

"Of course," Serena said wearily.

"You say that Caitlin's knapsack had gone," Inspector Litton said, "and with it a few items?"

"That's right," Serena said.

"Check the original statements for that, Sergeant," Inspector Litton said. "I don't believe anyone mentioned it as missing at the time. And see whether the rucksack and any of the items Miss Warren listed were found during any of the searches."

Ratcliffe nodded, making a note on his empty writing pad in front of him. Neither he nor the inspector moved. They were watching her unblinkingly. It was slightly unnerving.

"You say that you thought your sister was intending to run off with Mr. Leo Whitelock, her boyfriend," Inspector Litton said.

"That was my initial assumption," Serena said. "They had become very close and…well, I couldn't imagine why else she would run away."

"Mr. Whitelock has an alibi for the night that Caitlin disappeared," Sergeant Ratcliffe said. "It was checked at the time. He was working at the pub and hadn't finished tidying up after closing time. The landlady confirmed he was on the premises."

"Speak to him again," Inspector Litton said. "And to the landlady."

Another squiggle joined the hieroglyphs on the sergeant's writing pad.

"You said that it was a woman's figure you saw approaching

your sister that night," Inspector Litton said to Serena. "Are you certain of that?"

"I'm certain of nothing," Serena said honestly, "but that was the impression I had."

The inspector nodded. "And you also said that when this person tried to take the knapsack from Caitlin there was a flash of light so bright that you were blinded by it. And when you looked again, your sister had vanished."

"No," Serena said. "I was still looking at Caitlin, still *seeing* her, when she disappeared." She shrugged a little helplessly. "I know it sounds absurd, but she really did vanish in front of my eyes. Or so it seemed."

"It's easy to become confused," Inspector Litton said dismissively, "especially when you are remembering something from a long time ago and—" her cold blue gaze considered Serena "—something that was evidently so traumatic—the murder of your sister—that you promptly erased the memory from your mind." She sighed, shuffling a few papers. "We'll need you to talk to a psychologist, of course—"

"If you're willing," the sergeant put in, earning himself a glare.

"But I think you will probably find that the bright white light was a figment of your imagination," the inspector finished. "A part of the trauma, the physical manifestation of the mind closing down, if you will."

"I see," Serena said, clamping down on the urge to tell Inspector Litton that evidently she didn't need a psychologist's input since she was such an expert. "I'm happy to talk to anyone you wish," she said.

"And we're grateful," Ratcliffe said warmly. "This can't have been easy for you."

"A pity you weren't able to get a closer look at the assailant," Inspector Litton grumbled. "That would have been really helpful."

"That woman has all the empathy of a crocodile," Serena said to Sergeant Ratcliffe as he escorted her back to reception. She couldn't hold it in any longer. "Don't the police have courses in emotional intelligence?"

"Inspector Litton's been on all of them," Ratcliffe said lugubriously. "You've either got it or you haven't." He shook her hand. "Thank you, Miss Warren. We'll be in touch."

"I'm sure you will," Serena said, sighing.

She felt cold when she was out on the street. Although it was almost April and the sun, when it was out, was warm, the morning sky over Oxford was a uniform gray and the wind was cool. She pulled her scarf more closely around her neck and buttoned up her coat. She'd texted both Jack and Lizzie to tell them briefly what had happened; Jack was in Oxford anyway and said he would meet her in St. Giles' when she was ready. Lizzie rang as Serena was walking up Cornmarket Street.

"Oh, my God!" she said. "You remembered! Are you all right, sweetie? How do you feel?"

"I'm okay, actually," Serena said, touched that Lizzie's first thought should have been for her well-being. "I'm exhausted but I feel…lighter, somehow. It's hard to explain. I guess I might run through a whole range of emotions in time, but for now it feels such a relief simply to remember."

"Well, please be careful." Lizzie sounded anxious. "Whoever killed Caitlin isn't going to be happy that someone is digging into all of this again, and they'll be even less so if they hear you witnessed her disappearance."

Serena resisted the urge to look over her shoulder. She didn't want to get paranoid. "We still don't know for sure that Caitlin was killed," she said. "And I could have misremembered. Inspector Litton thinks a lot of it could have been distorted by time and trauma. And I suppose she may be right. It was all a long time ago."

"All the same," Lizzie said, "just take care, okay? When is Polly arriving?"

"I'm picking her up at the station at midday and we're going to see Granddad," Serena said. "Jack and I are meeting up now for a coffee."

"Good," Lizzie said. "I feel as though you need to be under constant surveillance until this is all over."

"That could prove awkward," Serena said dryly.

She could see Jack in front of the Ashmolean Museum, the collar of his coat turned up against the breeze. He was reading something and had on a pair of ridiculously attractive dark-rimmed glasses that made him look both intellectual and sexy at the same time. Serena was smiling when she joined him.

"Hi." He shoved the book in his pocket and caught her hands, giving her a searching look. "I got your text. Are you okay?"

"I'll probably fall asleep if I don't get coffee soon," Serena said, "but I'm okay."

Jack nodded and tucked her hand through his arm. "There's a place just up here that's really cozy." He gestured to a small café farther up the road whose lamp-lit windows beckoned them in like something out of a fairy tale. "Here we are."

They settled in a corner of the upstairs, amidst dusty bookshelves, old church pews and farmhouse kitchen tables. It was still early, and there were only a handful of other people there.

"It's atmospheric here," Serena said, taking in the sloping

floorboards and sagging beams. "Eclectic, nice. I'll get the coffee."

When she came back upstairs with two cups of cappuccino and an assortment of homemade cakes, Jack had already spread out some papers and a couple of books across the table.

"Do you want to talk?" he asked. "About the police interview, I mean?"

"I'll tell you about it later," Serena said, stifling a yawn. "To be honest, I'd rather know whether you found a copy of *The Lovell Lodestar.* I'm ridiculously curious about it."

Jack laughed. "Fair enough," he said. He stuck his hand in the pocket of his coat and pulled out the book she'd seen him reading in the street. "Here it is."

"You found a copy!" Serena stared at him. "Did they have it in the records office? Did they let you borrow it?"

Jack shook his head. "I've got a mate who works in an antiquarian bookshop here in Oxford. I rang him last night to ask if he had a copy or knew where to track one down."

"Wow." Serena picked it up reverently, smoothing the plain blue cover. It was worn and faded, and when she opened the book, she saw the print was almost gone.

"It's very rare, apparently," Jack said. "It was a private printing, only a dozen of them made back in the mid-nineteenth century. The author was a local amateur historian called Oliver Fiske. He wrote a lot about the Windrush Valley and collected all the myths and legends of the area." He gestured to the other books and the sheaf of papers. "This is all stuff I've managed to gather together about his work. I thought it might be useful in some way, though I'm not sure how." He cocked his head. "You said you thought your grandfather had a copy. Do you want to tell me why it's so important to you?"

Serena nodded. "Granddad mentioned the lodestar to me," she said. "It was when I told him that Caitlin's body had been found. His precise words were 'It was the lodestar,' and then he said he should have told us where we had come from, how he should have warned us in some way." She shook her head. "I don't know what he meant and as you know, it's hard to understand what he's trying to say, or even to know if he understands himself. It felt odd, though, as though he was connecting something called the lodestar with our family history."

She picked up the book. "That night I saw a copy of this—*The Lovell Lodestar*—on the shelf in the pub. I think it was Granddad's own copy because I half recognized it and it was tucked away with some other books that had come from the manor. I meant to read it, but then Eve came along and asked me what I was doing and..." She shrugged. "Well, she seemed so curious I didn't want to tell her about it. So I went back to look for the book later and it had gone." She leaned forward. "The most bizarre thing was that the next morning, the book was on the fire and I'm almost certain Eve had done it deliberately."

"Why on earth would she do that?" Jack said. He was frowning. "I know she's a bit odd and very nosy, but that's very strange."

"You're telling me," Serena said with feeling. She ran her finger along the black lettering on the book's spine. "I must say I'm curious," she said. "What on earth can be in here?"

"Well," Jack said, "we can find out." He took a mouthful of coffee. "I've done a bit of preliminary research, but I haven't had a good look at the book yet. According to the legends, though, the Lodestar was a holy relic. When the church of St. Kenelm was established in Minster Lovell, the monks brought a treasure belonging to the saint for pilgrims to venerate. It was kept in a gold and jeweled box and was immensely precious."

"A relic," Serena said. "You mean like a bone from St. Kenelm's body or something like that? That's…extraordinary." She drained her coffee. The hit of caffeine cleared the fuzziness in her head a little. She definitely needed more.

"In the case of St. Kenelm it wasn't as grisly as that," Jack said with a smile. "Apparently, the Lodestar was a compass. Not the sort you or I would recognize," he added, "but something rather more basic—a flat plate, a pin and a needle of some sort. The earliest compasses were considered to possess magical powers because they contained lodestones, which attracted iron and pointed to due north." He tapped one of the other books on the table. "There's a historical encyclopedia of mining here," he said, "in case you wanted to read up on lodestones and their properties."

"I'll save that for the next time I have insomnia, thanks," Serena said dryly. "Just give me the top line on it."

Jack grinned self-deprecatingly. "I'm no scientist," he said, "but my understanding is that lodestone is a rock that's made of magnetite. Lodestones align themselves naturally with the earth's magnetic field, hence their use in compasses. Oh, and the polestar was often known as the Lodestar because, of course, it points to the north and has been used for navigation for millennia."

"With a name like Lodestar you'd expect it to be a jewel," Serena said.

"Well, it could be both practical and decorative," Jack said. He inclined his head. "The Ashmolean, just down the road, has a lodestone adorned with a gilt coronet that was donated in the eighteenth century, and apparently Sir Isaac Newton's signet ring contained a lodestone, too. They sound pretty cool. You can imagine why people might think they were magic."

He nodded toward her empty coffee cup. "Do you need another of those whilst we talk this over? It might help the thought processes."

He headed down the stairs and Serena reached for the book again and turned the fragile pages carefully. There wasn't much text and only a few hand-drawn illustrations: one was of the church, another of Minster Lovell Hall before it was ruined, looking exactly like in her grandfather's drawing, with the tower and the water gate still standing. She turned another page, skipping over Oliver Fiske's description of the legend of St. Kenelm, and came across another picture. She almost dropped the book.

"What is it?" Jack had come back, a cup of coffee in each hand. He put them down carefully. "You look as though you've seen another ghost," he said.

"Well, it's certainly a blast from the past," Serena said a bit shakily. "Look." She pushed the book across to him, pointing to the drawing. "This is what Fiske says the Lodestar looked like—that's based on hearsay. He admits no one in living memory had ever seen it."

"Yeah," Jack said. "A plate, a pin and a needle, is what he described but that... Is it an arrowhead?"

"I think it is," Serena said. "Jack—" she looked at him "—my grandfather had this...compass...on a shelf in his study at the manor when Caitlin and I were kids. I remember seeing it there."

Jack sat down abruptly. "Are you sure?" he said. "My God, I mean..." He ruffled a hand through his hair. "Did he know what it was? Did he ever say anything about it?"

Serena shook her head. "He kept it way out of reach. But I

noticed it because it was such an odd-looking thing and sometimes the arrow would spin around on its own." She reached for the coffee. "How bizarre," she said softly. "I always wondered what it was and why he kept it. One day I tried to climb up to reach it and he caught me and I got a good telling off." She met Jack's eyes. "He must have known what it was," she said slowly, "because he spoke of it only two days ago."

Jack nodded. "Do you know where it is now? Does he still have it?"

Serena spread her hands. "I've no idea. The only thing I know is that he seemed to think it was connected with Caitlin's disappearance—and our family history."

Jack put his cup down gently. "It says in the book that it was when the first minster church was demolished and a new one built in the thirteenth century that the Lovell family became the protectors of the treasure. That was because a number of people had attempted to take the treasure from the church and it was not considered secure there. Perhaps it was passed on from the Lovell family to yours for safekeeping? Or perhaps they stole it." He handed a copy of one of the loose pages over to her. "I copied this today," he said. "It's not in the Lodestar book for some reason, but in another work Fiske wrote. He listed the miracles performed by the relic when it was in St. Kenelm's church—various healing cures and so on—but he also recorded a couple of cases where someone tried to take the Lodestar and it apparently fought back to protect itself. It's something of a morality tale, I think—no doubt apocryphal but designed to reinforce the Victorian values on the evils of theft and the punishment you deserve if you go to the bad."

"'A young shepherd boy,'" Serena read, "'thinking to make his fortune, took the relic from its place in the church and made off with it. He had gone no more than forty paces when it struck him down and he was left gibbering in madness.'"" She looked up. "That's pretty fierce."

"Read on," Jack said. "Allegedly it even had the power to make people disappear—" He stopped abruptly. "Sorry," he said. "That was insensitive of me." He started to gather all the papers together. "I'm sorry, Serena," he said. "I should have thought of the parallels with Caitlin."

"No," Serena said shakily. "That's okay. This is exactly why I needed to know."

She saw puzzlement in Jack's eyes. She could feel her heart racing, so loud it seemed to echo in her ears. Her hands were trembling, too; the piece of paper shivered in her grip as she read aloud from Oliver Fiske's commentary:

"'One man even described what he had witnessed when the thief took the Lodestar:'

"'There was a flash of light, brighter than the brightest lightning I had ever seen, and with it a sound harsher than the loudest thunder. The whole sky was alive. The man vanished from before my very eyes as though he had been plucked by an unseen hand, and the light grew until I had to shade my eyes for fear of being blinded…'"

Serena put down the paper and it sank silently onto the pile on the table. There was no sound in the coffee shop but the muted conversation of the other customers, the clink of china and cutlery from downstairs and the faint hum of the traffic on St. Giles' outside. She looked up and met Jack's gaze.

"He's just described my exact experience when I witnessed Caitlin disappear," she said.

Chapter 20

ANNE

Stoke Bardolph
June 1487

Bosworth Field was not the end.

Francis was an attainted traitor. For two years Henry Tudor's men hunted him at home and abroad, whilst he took the role that had been the Tudors' before, and fomented conspiracy and rebellion, working to put the House of York back on the throne. They were hard years for me and for the young Prince Richard. I went back to Ravensworth where my mother, still the indomitable Neville matriarch, governed now in the minority of her grandson. I kept quiet and I kept Richard hidden whilst Franke went about seeking news of Francis, providing tiny scraps of hope to keep me fed; letters, messages, sparse but the promise that kept me going.

Men believed Richard to be dead. In the swirl of rumor and counter-rumor after the battle, knowledge of him was lost. Only his mother, Elizabeth Woodville, and I knew the truth—and Francis, of course. I knew not how any one of us could survive or build a life into the future unless the Yorkists retook the throne, and even then, I had fears that Richard, illegitimate or not, would always be seen as a threat. We took each day step by step, walking with the lightest tread so as not to give ourselves away.

Then Franke came back one day with the news that there was to be a rebellion, sponsored by Margaret of Burgundy, a rising against the Tudors by the remnants of the House of York. And so we came to Stoke Field, and to the last battle.

I had been in hiding since first light, concealed by the graceful fall of the willows that lined the river and dipped their branches low over the edge of the bank. The Trent ran shallow here, swirling over pebbles where the speckled fish darted and gleamed. The sun had crept around behind me and the light on the water almost blinded me. It was such a beautiful day to be alive.

It was certainly too beautiful a day to die.

I had been awake all night, waiting for the moment the first call of the blackbird pierced the darkness, schooling myself to stillness whilst my heart pounded so loud in my ears that I could barely hear the rustle of a mouse or the call of the owl out over the fields. When I slid from my bed of straw in the barn at the ruined manor that had once belonged to Francis's grandmother, I was stiff with tension and fear, walking like a broken puppet until my limbs eased a little. I left Richard asleep in the charge of Franke; they were safe here at Stoke Bardolph, or as safe as they could ever be, and Franke would guard Richard with his life, just as I would. I knew Richard would be angry with me for leaving him behind for he was almost fourteen now and fretting to be a part of this battle. I'd told him the time would come soon enough and for now he must wait. He had enormous patience for a child, that boy, learned in a hard school over the years. I loved him so dearly and he me; it was that bond that made him do as I bid him even though he chafed against it.

It was too dangerous to take the road. There were soldiers everywhere, rebels and king's men, so I slid like a ghost along hedgerow and tree line, following the curve and fall of the land down to the Trent. I saw only one man, a deserter crashing through the undergrowth, eyes wild as a hunted doe, running from the ghost of his own fear when the battle had barely started.

Francis had told us to wait for him at the manor, but I could never do what I was told. At times, though, during that long day, I wished I had. I had never been anywhere near a battlefield before. The hot heavy air carried the sounds to me, the jarring scrape of metal on metal and the cries of men; anger, fear, pain. I wanted to put my hands over my ears to blot it out, but I dared not for in the quiet only lay further danger. I had to stay alert. I hoped. I prayed. I needed to be here, not only because of a desperate need to see Francis again, at last, but also to know what I needed to do to protect Richard. I could not simply hide, deaf and blind to danger. I touched the Lodestar at my throat. It would be my last bastion, my last chance.

We have been fighting for as long as I have been alive, I thought. *Let this be an end.*

The sun on the river dazzled me even as the sounds of slaughter made me feel sick. The air quivered with the weight of death, so close, breathing down my neck. The sweat ran down my back, hot and cold, and the sun beat on my closed eyelids as though by shutting it out I could pretend none of this was happening, no more death, no more killing. The noise was intolerable. I wanted to run yet I had to bear it.

Perhaps I dozed as the hours spun out, for I awoke with

a violent start; a moorhen paddled away from the bank with much splashing, its movements jerky with terror. My heart raced. Someone—or something—was coming. I could see the ripples on the water. At some point whilst I slept, the sounds of the battle had ceased.

The ripple grew to a wake, lapping at the shore. I moved, stiff again from the hours of waiting, tiptoeing down to the edge of the river and pushing aside the willow curtain to look out. When Francis had told me that he planned to swim the river if he needed to escape, I had thought him a mad fool. Yet here he was.

He hauled himself onto the bank and I was beside him in a moment, a shoulder beneath his armpit as he struggled to pull free of the water. He had discarded his helmet but nothing else; his fair hair was plastered to his head, the water running in dazzling rivulets down his battered armor. Only the silver wolf, the blazon of Lovell, seemed to have escaped the blows.

"I told you to wait at the manor." He lay prone beneath the willows, panting for breath, scowling at me.

"I know." I was furious with him. It was odd to be angrier to find him alive rather than dead. And these were our first words in two years. We were quarreling already.

He made a sort of huffing noise. Probably he had no breath for anything else. "Why do you never do as you are told?"

"We're talking about this now?" I could not help myself. "When the battle is lost and you swim a river in your armor?"

He stopped my hands as I reached to unfasten the first buckle. "Leave it for now."

I paused. "You're injured?"

"No." He was short and I knew he was certainly in pain,

but he accepted my help to stand and even offered a word of thanks. I might as well have been his squire.

"I'm glad you're safe," I said. My throat closed with emotion. They were such inadequate words after years apart and a tumult of experience, but I felt utterly incapable of finding better.

"I'm hardly safe." Francis looked grimly amused. "Let's go."

He set the pace and I allowed it for his pride's sake. I asked no more questions. If the Yorkists had won, he would not have been here like this. It was as simple as that. I managed not to say that I had known all along that the battle would be lost, even though I had.

"How is Richard?" Francis half turned to look back at me.

"He chafes to be denied the chance to fight at your side," I said. "Francis, he is thirteen years old now. He wants to be involved—"

"He is the only hope for the future." He interrupted me. "Now, more than ever. You know his safety cannot be put at risk."

I wanted to argue. Richard of Shrewsbury was to all intents and purposes dead; we had promised his mother that we would hide him, protect him from Henry Tudor, the man who was now her son-in-law. She had lost one of her boys when Edward had died. All she wanted was for Richard to survive somewhere, somehow, in peace. It was not for him to reclaim his father's kingdom, not if he wanted to live.

The manor came into view suddenly around a curve of the river, squat and silent above the bank, gray walls, forbidding. Francis put out a hand to hold me back when I would have quickened my pace toward it.

"Wait." His voice was low, his breath stirring the hair by my ear.

"No one has come this way." I had told Franke to watch for us and signal if there was danger, and now I was fizzing with impatience to get Francis inside, into hiding, to an illusory safety. Nevertheless, his caution incited a rush of fear in me. I froze, ears straining for a sound, the snap of a twig, the soft footfall that betrayed an enemy was near.

After a moment, Francis sighed. I felt a little of the tension leave him. He allowed me to lead the way now, following as I ducked under the lintel of a door into a hidden corner of the courtyard. The air of desolation that cloaked the manor was tangible. Grass sprouted from the cobbles and a broken-down cart lay rotting in the sun. Shutters hung loose from the windows and the door was gone. Would it fool the King's spies? I hoped so. Yet I knew we could not stay. There would be time only for Francis to wash and probably not even to rest long before we would all need to leave. And there was nowhere to go. Francis was once again a fugitive and Richard was in even greater danger than before. We had come to the end.

I felt the Lodestar, warm against my throat. It had protected me and saved my life. What I was about to ask it was far beyond that and I could only believe, and hope, that it would see my cause as true and would answer me.

The door of the buttery opened abruptly. I saw Francis tense, his hand going to his sword. Light and color erupted; Richard hurtled past me then and straight into Francis's arms. I watched them for a moment, my heart squeezed with pain and joy combined. There was such a strong bond between them and had been since Francis had been his mentor during those days in the Tower. Richard loved me, too, I knew that, but his feeling for Francis was as simple as sheer, blazing hero worship.

Thank God he came back. I felt my heart give another tight squeeze.

I stepped past them to greet Franke. "All quiet?"

"I haven't seen a soul."

That was not necessarily reassuring.

"Was the field lost?" Franke spoke softly, one brow cocked in Francis's direction.

"Of course."

Franke's mouth turned down at the corners. "Then we should leave," he said.

"For pity's sake, give them a moment together first," I said. Francis and Richard were talking now, their heads bent close together.

"It is too dangerous to wait until after dark, when we can't see the enemy," Franke said shortly. "The King will know by now that my lord has escaped. Even if no one witnessed him crossing the river, his men will have checked every corpse on the battlefield."

"Francis and Richard need go nowhere to escape," I said, equally shortly. "I can get them away and no one the wiser."

I left him staring after me in bafflement and went to the other side of the hall to try to compose myself. I wanted no witnesses to my weakness. The end was coming and very swiftly now. I was frightened and unprepared.

The Lodestar seemed to vibrate against my skin as I took the chain from about my neck. It was warm against my palm, waiting. My faith in it was absolute. I knew nothing of where we might go or what might happen to us, but it had to be better than fighting and hiding and running forever.

Franke had gone to fetch water. Richard was helping Francis remove his armor now, performing the duties of a squire. I watched them for a moment, then closed my eyes and felt a tear trickle from beneath my lids.

Francis came to sit beside me. The wooden seat gave beneath his weight with a groan that threatened collapse. When I opened my eyes, he was wiping the water from his face with the cloth Franke had given him. The stubble on his chin and cheeks rasped against the rough material. Droplets clung to his eyelashes and the ends of his hair. He had yet to take off his gambeson, and the padded jacket was filthy and stained with sweat. I could smell the sweat on his body, too, mingled with the metallic scent of blood. It did not prevent me from wanting to throw myself into his arms just as Richard had done.

Francis leaned forward and brushed the tears from my cheek. "Don't cry." His voice was gruff. "We are not dead yet."

"I know," I said, "but this is the end now, Francis. You know it."

He opened his mouth to reply, but never got the chance.

"Someone comes!"

Franke yelled a warning from the doorway a second before I saw them. They were soldiers in the King's livery. They cut Franke off with one quick slash to the neck and he fell without another sound. I grabbed Richard's arm and thrust him into Francis's side and then I closed Francis's hand tight over the Lodestar relic.

"Take us to a place of safety," I said, and I prayed with my whole heart.

The room seemed to brighten with a blinding flash of light and I fell to my knees, covering my face with my hands. The ground shook and the walls began to fall, dust and stone flying. I felt as though I was falling down and down, through darkness. I came to myself in a pile of rubble with the kindly face of Father Hubert, the priest from All Hallows Church, peering at me through the devastation. Out in the courtyard the soldiers milled around seemingly as stunned as I.

I rubbed the grit from my eyes and the priest extended a hand to help raise me to my feet.

"I heard the terrible noise from the road," he said. "What can have happened here, daughter?"

I could not speak. All I could think was that I had failed, that the relic had failed me when I most needed it. Once it had saved my life; had I asked too much this time, when my prayers had been for others and not myself? Like Ginevra before me, all I had wanted was power for a good cause, and yet I had been punished beyond measure. But whilst the Lodestar had taken her away, this time it had taken the others and left me behind.

I looked around. Franke's body lay where he had fallen, bloody and dust-stained on the cobbled yard. There was no sign of anyone else at all.

"Lady Lovell?" I recognized the King's uncle, Jasper Tudor, dirt-stained, straight from battle, pushing his way through the troops in the yard.

"Where is your husband?" he demanded.

"I have no idea," I said. I took a deep breath and thought, *I am alone now. God give me strength.*

"I was waiting for him here after the battle," I said, "but as you see, your Grace, he is not here."

"Search for him," Tudor barked, glaring at me from beneath his brows. I drew closer to the priest and despite everything, despite all that I had lost, I felt my heart lighten a little, for I knew they would find nothing; not Francis, not Richard, both gone, never to be seen again. I remembered what Ginevra had said then: *When she stopped falling, she was in a different place, in a different time.* This time I had fallen into darkness, but they were the ones who had gone to a different place, a different time.

I pressed my fingers to my lips in a kiss. "Go with my love," I whispered. "And may God bless you always."

Chapter 21

SERENA

Minster Lovell
Present Day

"Serena, honey!" Polly enveloped her niece in a huge hug and a wave of Chanel. "It's so good to be here!"

"Here" was Oxford station concourse where Polly's perfume was mingling rather queasily with the smell of fried food and diesel. She was wrapped in an enormous faux fur coat, and her Californian tan was drawing considerable attention. She looked exotic, like a migrating bird blown far off course.

The station was also reassuring in its ordinariness. Serena, nerves still buzzing from the coffee and even more so from reading about the Lodestar, had never needed a dose of normality more.

"You look amazing," she said truthfully. Then, feeling a rush of affection, "It's good to see you, too, Aunt Pol." She took hold of Polly's smart wheeled suitcase. "What would you like to do first?" she asked. "Go and see Granddad, or go back to the hotel to rest?"

Polly looked at her out of the corner of her eye. "Would it

be wrong of me to put off seeing Pa until later?" she asked. "I feel so *grubby* from traveling and want to be at my best—"

"Of course," Serena said. She'd caught the slight note of uncertainty in Polly's voice.

She's nervous, she thought, and felt another burst of love for her aunt. It was only a few months since Polly had seen her father, but she knew he was declining all the time. It would be hard for her, not knowing whether Dick would recognize her or how he might be.

"We'll go back to Minster Lovell," she said. "The pub isn't exactly five stars, but it's comfortable and—" She was going to say welcoming, but she wasn't sure that it was. She also wasn't sure she wanted to be there at the moment when her mind was in such turmoil and she needed to think through all she had learned about Caitlin's disappearance. Not for the first time she wished she could talk to her grandfather. If only she knew what he knew.

"Thanks, hon." Polly slid gratefully into the passenger seat of the car. "The journey was fine, but I've been traveling for twenty-four hours and I'm exhausted." She closed her eyes for a moment, and Serena saw the lines of tiredness and worry beneath her immaculate makeup.

"Is there any more news on the investigation into Caitlin's death?" Polly opened her eyes again and looked out as they pulled into Frideswide Square and turned onto Botley Road. "Boy, this place has changed since I was last here! I like what they've done with the square and this cute little bridge over the river. Are we on an island?"

"Osney Island, I think," Serena said. "This is the Thames. There's no news on Caitlin," she added, "although, I've—" She stopped.

Polly raised her brows. "You?" she prompted.

"I've recovered my memories of the night Caitlin died," Serena said. She glanced sideways at her aunt. "I went to the police and told them this morning."

She summarized for Polly what she had remembered; the fact that she had seen someone else in the ruins with Caitlin that night, that Caitlin seemed to vanish before her eyes and that there had been a blinding flash of light. She didn't mention that she'd met up with Jack and they'd found out about the Lovell Lodestar; she wanted more time to read Oliver Fiske's book properly and think about what it might mean. She'd borrowed it from Jack, and it was on the back seat ready for her to take over to show her grandfather later.

"Oh, boy," Polly said when Serena had finished telling her the story, "that's the weirdest thing." She looked troubled. "Are you sure that's how it was, hon? What do the police think?"

"Unsurprisingly," Serena said, "they think that I imagined the bit about Caitlin vanishing and the flash of light. They think it was an illusion caused by the trauma. They do seem to accept that I saw someone with Caitlin that night, though, and that it was probably a woman, so I suppose that advances the case a bit."

Polly nodded. "And how do you feel?" she asked, much as Lizzie had done. "I'm immensely glad that it doesn't seem to have caused you any further trauma, but it can't have been pleasant for you recovering all those memories."

"It was very strange," Serena said honestly, "but I felt…as though I was ready for it, somehow. As soon as I was back in Minster Lovell, I started to remember things. My mind started to prompt me in different ways."

"Perhaps it was time for it to happen," Polly said heavily. "Perhaps it was time everything started to come out."

"I think it was," Serena said. "And I feel better now. Even if they never find out who was with Caitlin that night, and what really happened, I feel I've done what I can now. I've done my best for her. That makes me feel lighter in spirit, I suppose, if not happier to have lost her."

Polly nodded, and Serena saw her aunt surreptitiously wipe away a tear from her cheek. Then Polly closed her eyes and leaned back against the headrest. "Do you mind if I nap a little?" she said. "I know it'll probably make the jet lag worse but I'm so tired."

"Go ahead," Serena said. A splatter of rain hit the windscreen, and she turned on the wipers. They'd left the city behind now and were passing Farmoor Reservoir. Gulls wheeled overhead on the ragged breeze. She remembered she needed five pence for the toll bridge at Eynsham, but decided not to disturb Polly yet by reaching over for her bag. Her aunt was already sound asleep.

They joined the main A40 and bypassed Witney, Polly snoring gently in the passenger seat, snuggled down in her faux fur. As they came into Minster Lovell, though, Polly stirred and blinked awake.

"We're here," she said slowly, looking around. "This feels a little weird, kind of familiar, but deeply different at the same time."

"How long is it since you were here?" Serena asked.

"I didn't visit Minster when I came to see Dad six months ago," Polly said. "It must have been the year after Caitlin disappeared, I think, when Dad was talking about packing up and moving out of the hall. I do remember that it was a terrible summer—it rained all the time."

It was clear from Polly's face that she wasn't enjoying herself as she got out of the car at the Minster Inn. She viewed the old pub critically, and Serena immediately felt awkward.

"Would you rather stay at the Old Swan?" she asked. "It's more your sort of place. I only chose this one because it's closer to the manor, but we can move out if you prefer."

"No," Polly said slowly. "It's fine. There's just something about this place that feels…not quite right…" She shook her head sharply. "Ignore me. I'm just tired."

Eve was behind the desk as they came into the reception area and leaped up to check Polly in.

"I've put you in the Lady Lovell room," she said. "It has a four-poster."

"That sounds delightful, thank you," Polly said warmly. They fell into easy conversation, Eve admiring Polly's coat. "You'll feel the cold after all that lovely Californian sunshine…" And Polly telling her about selling real estate to the stars. "I sometimes get to sell a tropical island or two…"

She took her key with a word of thanks, politely refused Serena's offer to carry her suitcase up for her and set off up the stairs to her room, yawning widely. "I'll see you later, hon," she said to Serena. "I'll knock when I'm ready to go over to see Pa."

"Your auntie's very cool," Eve said, eyeing Polly's designer boots enviously. "Can I get you anything?" she added. "Lunch? A drink?"

Serena ordered a cheese sandwich, a bag of crisps and a glass of apple juice and went upstairs, carrying her tray. The door of the Lady Lovell room was already closed, and she couldn't hear any sound from inside. She wondered whether Polly had simply lain down on the four-poster and gone straight to sleep. It seemed likely. Polly had clearly been exhausted, and no wonder after the stress of the journey. Serena suddenly felt incredibly weary herself, drained by the interview with the police and all the emotional trauma of reliving Caitlin's disappearance. She curled up on the bed, leaning back against the headboard. There was so much she needed to think about.

An hour later Serena woke up to find that she had dropped off sitting upright on the bed, her sandwich half-eaten and the glass of apple juice still in her hand. She had a crick in her neck and had crushed half of the crisps into the bedcover. She got up, stretched and tidied the tray onto a side table. The sound of a door closing down the corridor made her wonder whether Polly had woken up, too, but when she looked out onto the landing she couldn't see anyone. She wandered along to the Lady Lovell room, but the door was shut and she decided not to knock.

The room service trolley was on the landing, loaded with used plates and cutlery, crumpled napkins and food wrappers. There was a strange, heavy quiet in the air, which seemed to make the stale smell of the previous night's food all the more pungent as it mingled with old-fashioned beeswax and dust, and an indefinable scent that Serena tended simply to call "old things." Something about the silence felt oppressive, and Serena found herself tiptoeing back along the corridor to her room to avoid making the floorboards creak.

The door of the laundry cupboard next to Serena's room stood open, the light illuminating the neatly stacked piles of sheets and towels that surrounded an old-style water tank at the back. Remembering the groaning plumbing, Serena wasn't remotely surprised to see an ancient cistern or hear it hissing softly. In contrast to the fusty smell of the pub itself, the linen smelled of windy days and fresh air, but even in the dim light, Serena could see that the floor of the cupboard was dirty with cobwebs and thick with dust.

A gleam of something blue caught her eye in the far corner of the cupboard. It was a vivid spark of color amongst the cobwebs, catching the light from the bare bulb overhead. Serena paused with her room key in her hand. She took a step closer, bending down to pick it up.

It was a bead. She rubbed the dirt from it and it rolled into her palm, glowing as deep blue as the sea. Serena recognized it at once. That glorious color was unmistakable. It was one of the beads from Caitlin's bracelet.

A whisper of suspicion crept into her mind. She found herself down on her hands and knees in the dust, searching to see if she could find any more. There was one, trapped between two old floorboards, and beyond it in the darkest and most hidden corner of the cupboard Serena could see something else, a battered corner of what looked like a knapsack with, incongruously, a teddy bear stuffed in the top.

All the air left Serena's lungs in a rush. She felt dizzy and put out a hand to steady herself against one of the shelves. Caitlin's knapsack, the beads from her blue bracelet, the teddy all hidden away here in a place that no one would ever find them.

Leo, she thought. Leo had worked at the pub. She was sure that Caitlin had been planning to run away with him. But the police had said that Leo had an alibi for that night. He had been working behind the bar...

"What are you doing?" It was Eve's voice, sharp and accusatory from behind her. Serena jumped violently.

"Oh, I..." She felt guilty, as though she had been caught trespassing. She scrambled to her feet.

Eve was standing at the top of the stairs, one hand resting lightly on the newel post. Her gaze, very dark and bright, moved to the beads Serena was still holding in the palm of her hand. There was a very long moment when time seemed to swing in the balance. Serena closed her fingers protectively over the beads but it was too late. The shock of realization hit her and a second later, Eve spoke again.

"You know, don't you?" she said.

"Yes," Serena said. Her mouth felt dry. Images were flickering through her mind like old black-and-white newsreel film; the same scene she had remembered the previous night, the same scene she had told the police, except that this time the woman with Caitlin's knapsack in her hand had a face. This time it was Eve.

"I saw you," she said. "That night in the ruins when you killed Caitlin. I saw a woman with her and I know it was you."

Eve looked at her. There was no expression on her face at all. "I didn't realize you had been there that night," she said. Her mouth flattened into a thin line. "That sodding knapsack," she said. "I didn't dare get rid of it. I thought the police would be looking for it and that they'd find out I was involved somehow."

The blood was pounding in Serena's ears. "Why did you kill her?" she said. "Why did you kill Caitlin?" She thought she was shouting, but the words came out as a whisper.

Eve's gaze narrowed. "I didn't mean to," she said. "We were arguing and it got out of hand." She gave a tiny, hopeless shrug. "I shook her. I don't really remember, but... I think I must have put my hands around her throat."

"You broke her neck," Serena said, remembering what Inspector Litton had told her.

Eve shrugged again. There was a hardness in her eyes. "Like I said, I didn't mean to. It was an accident. I only wanted her to give me the Lodestar."

Serena felt as though her throat was blocked. She swallowed hard. "You knew about that?"

"Of course I did." Eve looked contemptuous. "My family has lived here for centuries. I know all the old stories. We had a copy of that book, the one your granddad owned." Her voice changed, turned soft. "I even saw the Lodestar once, in the manor, when Mrs. Warren held an open house one year. It was in a glass case on a shelf in the study. I recognized it at once from the picture in the book. And I thought about it for years, thinking what it could do for us if only we could possess it. So I asked your sister to steal it for me."

"Caitlin wouldn't do that," Serena said. She felt a chill seeping through her skin, through her blood.

Eve's face twisted. "You think? She was keen enough when I said I'd report her to the police otherwise. She was always hanging around in here, panting after Leo, putting my license at risk with underage drinking. When I caught them in bed together, sky high on cannabis, I gave her an ultimatum. Said I'd give her and Leo the money to run off together if she'd steal the Lodestar for me. I told her to hand it over that night and I'd make sure he was waiting for her in the car, ready to go. The silly little fool believed me, too."

Serena felt nauseous. She'd known Caitlin was no saint, known she could be thoughtless and frivolous, but this wasn't the sister she recognized. Eve's description of her sounded so sordid. Perhaps her sister had got into drugs when she had got involved with Leo, but she'd also been naive and lovestruck. Serena could finally see that this had been Caitlin's tragedy—her sophistication had been brittle. She had no experience, only hopes and dreams. And Eve, Serena thought, was another one who had resented Caitlin's bright spirit and the butterfly nature that had seen her flit happily from one thing to another, rarely settling, carelessly kind, never intending to hurt anyone. Perhaps Eve had loved Leo, too, with his dazzling surfer good looks and his swagger. They had worked together; perhaps they had had a closer relationship before Caitlin had appeared on the scene. She thought about asking Eve whether she and Leo had been lovers and decided it didn't matter. The only thing that mattered was that Caitlin was dead, that Eve had killed her.

"So Caitlin thought she and Leo were running off on a big adventure," Serena said. She was clenching her fist so tightly that the bead was digging into her palm. "She must have been so excited and happy. What went wrong?"

Eve blinked as though it was an effort to remember. "Caitlin realized it was all a trick," she said simply. "When we met up that night in the ruins of the old hall she guessed I hadn't said anything to Leo and she refused to give me the Lodestar."

"So you quarreled and then you killed her," Serena said.

"I didn't mean to hurt her," Eve repeated. "I only wanted the Lodestar. But I grabbed her neck and she fell and then..." She frowned. "Well, the next thing I knew, she'd gone. Vanished! If you were watching, you'll know what I mean. You would have seen it, too! It was bright, like lightning or something." She shook her head. "I'd never seen anything like it."

"That was the Lodestar," Serena said. "I thought you said

you'd read the stories about it? You knew it was supposed to possess magical powers. Wasn't that why you wanted it?"

Eve pulled a face. "No," she said. "I didn't believe in that sort of paranormal crap." She put her hands on her hips. "I wanted it to sell. I've been nighthawking for years around here and other historical sites. I've uncovered masses of old coins and buckles and small finds but never anything really valuable. Then I remembered the Lodestar. Do you know how much antiquities are worth on the black market?" She cocked her head at Serena. "A piece like that, almost a thousand years old, would fetch millions."

"So where is the Lodestar now?" Serena said. She looked around. The paint was peeling from the wall of the corridor. The old water tank churned softly. The brightness of the day made the pub look what it was, sad and neglected, and the light falling on Eve's face illuminated her, too—her jealousy, her cruelty and her cupidity.

"You never had it, did you?" Serena said suddenly. "You never got your hands on the Lodestar. When Caitlin refused to give it to you, you tried to take it from her by force, but it cheated you."

Eve's eyes flared with a sudden fury. "Of course I never had it," she spat. "Do you think I'd be hanging around in a dump like this if I'd had the choice? Caitlin was holding it and I tried to snatch it from her when she fell, but it slipped through my fingers. The next thing I knew, Caitlin was gone and the Lodestar was gone, too. It was unreal. I was terrified. So I just grabbed the bag and ran." She took a step toward Serena. "All that trouble, all for nothing," she said. "And now there's you. What am I going to do about you?" She snatched up a knife from the service trolley and took another step closer.

The breath seemed to stop in Serena's throat. "Don't be stupid," she said. "It's too late. Too many people know—" But still Eve came closer, forcing her away from the stairs, trapping her against the wall with a flick of the wicked silver blade.

"Just take the Lodestar and go." Polly's voice cut across them, making Serena jump almost out of her skin. Her aunt was standing on the half landing at the curve of the stairs and she had clearly been out. She was wearing the faux fur coat and her cheeks were pink with fresh air, her blond hair mussed by the wind.

Eve spun around, the knife in her hand, as Polly came steadily up the final flight of steps and stopped on the landing in front of them. Serena saw that in Polly's outstretched hand was a misshapen arrowhead. It looked like the picture in the Lodestar book, like the compass Serena had seen all those years before in her grandfather's study. Polly was holding it out toward Eve. Her gaze was focused entirely on Eve, concentrated and fierce.

"You've taken one of my nieces." Polly's voice faltered slightly on the words and then strengthened again. "You're not hurting Serena. I won't let you. This was what you wanted." She extended her hand with the arrowhead flat on the palm. "Take it, and we'll all pretend none of this happened."

Eve stood frozen to the top step. Her eyes were huge, fixed on the Lodestar. "You're *giving* it to me?"

"It's cursed," Polly said. "It's dangerous. I just want it gone. Take it." She gave a little nod. "Take it," she said again.

Eve darted forward as though she could not help herself and snatched the Lodestar from Polly's hand. There was a moment when it felt to Serena as though everything was suspended on the edge of darkness; time seemed to stop and then to fold in on itself.

Serena knew what would happen next. Instinctively, she threw up an arm to protect her face. The flash was blinding. She was knocked to the floor amidst tumbling piles of sheets and towels, dazzled, lost. She lay there, winded, then reached out desperately and her hand closed around Polly's, and she clung on tightly for she did not know how long.

"Are you all right, hon?" When Serena opened her eyes, her aunt was sitting on the floor next to her, somehow looking as immaculate as she usually did. "That was a bit of a shock," she said mildly.

Serena started to laugh shakily, but it turned into tears instead, and Polly reached out for her and held her as though she was a child. "Hush," she said. "It's okay now." She rested her chin on the top of Serena's head. "It's over. She's gone."

Serena nodded. She knew that Eve had gone for good.

"Did Eve take the Lodestar with her?" she asked. She eased into sitting and pushed the hair back from her face. Somewhere down the corridor the fire alarm was ringing. Soon, she knew, people would arrive and there would be lots of questions.

"No," Polly said. "I have it safe." She opened her hand. Sitting on the palm was the black arrowhead. She looked up and met Serena's eyes. "The stone makes its own choices," she said.

"You sound like Granddad," Serena said. "Did you know about the Lodestar all the time?"

Polly smiled at her, but it was a smile edged with sadness. "I knew about the stone," she said, "but I never knew it was connected to Caitlin's disappearance. Not until I heard you and Eve talking just now."

She rubbed her eyes, suddenly looking very tired. "I'd never heard it referred to by that name. To me it was always Lady Lovell's arrow. Mum told me the story when I was a child. Anne Lovell, wife of Francis Lovell, had the arrow as a talisman. I don't know where it originally came from, but Lady Lovell protected the Lodestar and it protected her in return. When the time came, Mum said, Lady Lovell gave the Lodestar up to save the life of a child she loved." Polly's eyes were suddenly bright with tears. "Cute story, right? But I knew that little arrow wasn't to be messed with." Her tone was dry. "No matter it sounded like a fairy tale, the power was real enough. I always sensed that somehow, even when I was a child."

"Granddad knew it was powerful, too," Serena said. "He told me so. Yet he kept it in the study where anyone could have seen it."

"Hidden in plain sight," Polly agreed. "I think he thought there was no one alive who would recognize it for what it was. But Eve did—and she persuaded Caitlin to take it."

"I assumed that when Caitlin vanished, she took the stone with her," Serena said, "but it turns out I was wrong."

Polly nodded. "Like I said," she said, "the Lodestar makes its own choices. It belongs here at Minster Lovell."

"But if that's the case," Serena said, "how did you come to have it, Aunt Pol?"

Polly was silent for a moment, looking at the arrow. "I found it," she said. "I found it in the ruins of the old hall the last time I came home. I thought it must have got lost—dropped or thrown away when Dad moved out of the manor, you know—and so I just picked it up and tucked it away in my pocket for old times' sake. But it didn't feel right to take it away from Minster Lovell for some reason, so I popped it onto the sundial in the walled garden at the manor and forgot about it." She rubbed her fingers thoughtfully over it, and it seemed to Serena that for a moment the Lodestar quivered in her palm. "Then this afternoon a weird thing happened," Polly said. "I was so tired when I came up to my room, but for some reason I couldn't rest. I thought it was jet lag and that I might feel better for some fresh air, so I went out…" She paused. "I felt so strongly that I had to go to the manor. And then when I got there, I just *knew* I had to go to the walled garden and find Lady Lovell's arrow. But the gate was locked because they were renovating it and I couldn't get in."

Serena was remembering the girl in the green coat, the ghost she had seen on the manor stairs who had led her to the doorway into the garden. Leading her to the Lodestar…

"I didn't know what to do," Polly was saying. "I was in a sort of panic by now because I knew somehow that it was really important that I get that arrow and bring it back to you. And then someone came." She smiled. "A girl your age. She had red hair and she was *very* pregnant. I sort of recognized her—I think she used to be a friend of yours when you were young? Anyway, she had the arrowhead in her hand. All she said was 'I found this. You must take it to Serena now,' and handed it to me. I didn't know what was going on, but it seemed to make sense so I did."

"That would be Lizzie," Serena said. Her throat closed and she blinked back the tears. "She's fey that way."

"Well, thank God she is," Polly said with feeling.

Outside there was the wail of sirens and the flicker of flashing blue lights. A door crashed open. Someone shouted. Serena recognized Jack's voice, heard the pounding of his footsteps on the stairs. She scrambled up and held out a hand to Polly, who got to her feet a little stiffly, smoothing her skirt down.

"It's a shame the police didn't make it before Eve ran away," Polly said quietly. "They'll never find her now."

"No," Serena said. "They never will."

Then Jack burst onto the landing and hauled her unceremoniously into his arms. She was quite happy to stay there. She could hear his heart thudding hard against her ear, and his arms were tight about her. "Thank God," he said against her hair. "When Lizzie said she'd given you the Lodestar, I was afraid I'd lose you."

"Lizzie's amazing," Serena said a little shakily. "Between them, she and Aunt Pol saved the day."

There were more people on the landing now—it seemed as though there were hundreds of them: various police officers, Stuart from the café, some of the villagers and Ross, the barman. Serena drew away from Jack and saw Polly looking at them with a twinkle in her eye.

"And there I was thinking you'd told me everything that was going on, hon," she said. She held out a hand to Jack. "Hi, I'm Polly, Serena's aunt."

Jack looked very slightly disconcerted. "Hi. I'm Jack Lovell." He glanced at Serena. "Sorry, I—"

"It's okay," Polly said, smiling widely. "I understand. And it's good to meet you, Jack Lovell. Now—" she looked around "—let's get out of here."

"The others will be here in a minute, Granddad," Serena said, "but I wanted to talk to you on my own first." She settled Dick's chair under the big oak tree in the gardens of the manor and wrapped a bright tartan rug over his lap. The house was closed today, but the formal gardens had been opened specially for them, as had the walled garden, which was still under restoration.

It was a fortnight after Eve had disappeared and spring was most certainly in the air now, air that felt softer and gentler than when Serena had arrived back at Minster Lovell. Wild primroses peeped through the grass, and wrens scurried about their nest-building in the hedges. She had spent the previous two weeks tying up the loose ends of the investigation into Caitlin's death and Eve's disappearance with the police. Inspector Litton, with a confession witnessed by Polly and the evidence of the rucksack, had accepted Eve's guilt despite the anomaly of dating of the burial. There was an international warrant out for Eve's arrest, although Serena suspected that Eve might be in a place it could not reach.

She angled Dick's chair so that the spring sunshine warmed him and sat down on the cushioned bench opposite.

"I'm going to tell you a story, Granddad," she said. "I think you already know it, but it might help me get it straight—and accept it—if I say it out loud. And if I get it wrong," she said, smiling at him, "you can put me right, because you are the only person who knows the truth."

Dick smiled back at her, head slightly on one side as he waited. Serena had the strangest sense that he understood everything that she was saying to him although it was impossible to tell.

"The last few weeks," Serena began, "in between talking to the police—" she pulled a face "—I've been finding out about our family history."

She saw Dick's chin come up and his blue eyes seemed to focus on her even more intently.

"I'd never really thought about it before," Serena said, "and

I realized that it was odd, in a family where we all valued the stories of the past, we never spoke about our own history." She traced a pattern on the smooth wooden armrest of the bench. "Polly was able to give me some information, and I went online to look up birth certificates and other details. I found the record of your marriage to Gran in London in 1962, but there was nothing before that." She looked at him. "I knew that you had been adopted so I wondered whether Richard Warren was different from the name you were born with."

Dick shifted a little in his chair. "Richard," he said. "I was always Richard."

"Yes," Serena said. "You were always Richard, right from the beginning. There were lots of clues once I knew what I was looking for. There was the 'rose *en soleil*' engraving on the necklaces that you gave to Caitlin and to me. There was the name Warren. There were your drawings—the one of the Gyrfalcon—one of the emblems of King Edward IV—and those yellow flowers, which were broom."

"Plantagenet," Richard corrected. "*Planta genista*. It grows here." He gestured to the garden.

"Grandma grew it here," Serena agreed, "along with the *Rosa Alba*, the white rose of York. When I started to work all this out, I assumed we must be descended from Edward Plantagenet, Edward IV. But then I thought, if that were the case, why keep it a secret? It's the sort of thing that we would all know, even if it was only talked about within the family. It seemed odd."

A little breeze rippled through the oak tree where the first new leaves were starting to unfurl.

"In the end," Serena said, "it was understanding what had happened to Caitlin that helped me to work it out. How could

Caitlin possibly have disappeared eleven years ago and yet be buried in the eighteenth century? It seemed impossible yet not only was the archaeological evidence clear, there was even a witness account of it from 1708."

She saw Dick's hands clench together and leaned forward to lay her own hand over them. "I'm sorry, Granddad," she said. "I know it hurts to talk about what happened to Caitlin. It hurts you more than any of us, I think, because you blame yourself. You shouldn't do—Caitlin died because of Eve. It was Eve who killed her, not the Lodestar. We know that now."

Dick's head was bent as he stared down at her hand resting over his. Then she felt the tension leave him, and he nodded slowly.

"I tried to keep it safe," he said.

"I know you did," Serena said. "You kept it in a locked glass case on the highest shelf in the study. And then on the night Caitlin vanished you realized that the Lodestar had gone, too. You saw the flash of light and you knew what had happened." She squeezed his fingers. "You knew because you had seen it happen before, hadn't you? You were the only living person who had. In fact, I think you are probably the only living person who has *experienced* it."

Dick was gazing out across the garden as though he was seeing past the present to the Minster Lovell he had once known. "Anne sent us away," he said. "She sent us to safety."

Serena caught her breath. She remembered the story Polly had told her, the fairy tale about Lady Lovell and the Lodestar. She wondered who Dick had meant by "us."

"So it is true," she said on a whisper.

"The Lodestar possesses the power to move through time and space." She looked up to see that Jack was standing beside her seat. "You saw it do it with your own eyes," he said. Then, apologetically: "Sorry, but the others are coming. I thought I should warn you."

Serena nodded. She released Dick's hand and sat back. Although she had talked to Jack and Polly and Lizzie about what had happened, no one else knew the truth. "I think we're done," she said. "We both know." She smiled at Dick who nodded gently back. "We both understand."

Jack glanced across the lawn, where Nigel and Stuart were approaching with picnic tables and crockery. Behind them came Polly carrying a huge teapot, and Lizzie and Arthur with what looked like several plates of cake.

"Before they get here," he said, "there's one other thing you should both know." He paused. "You know that when Caitlin first disappeared, they took DNA samples from all males in the local area as part of the investigation?"

Serena nodded. "I remember. Dad was tested, and Granddad as well."

Jack nodded. "Well, before Eve allegedly ran off and put herself in the frame, I was talking to Sergeant Ratcliffe and he let on that they were planning on retesting your grandfather and father. He shouldn't have mentioned it, of course, but he's a mate of Zoe's and he knew I was interested in the forensic archaeology side. He said that there had evidently been some major flaw in the original DNA tests because when they put your family's results into the national database, it came up with a match that was completely impossible. Inspector Litton was absolutely livid."

"Why on earth?" Serena said.

"Because it was a close match for King Richard III," Jack said with a grin. "They had his DNA from the dig in Leicester in 2012, but I imagine they weren't expecting to match it to anyone in 2021."

A breeze stirred the branches over their heads and ruffled the edge of the rug covering Dick's lap. He was looking quite tranquil as though he had perhaps not even heard, but Serena knew that he had.

"Well," she said, "they won't need to waste resources on a second test now, will they." She stood up. "There's just one thing I wondered, Granddad," she said. "When you said that Anne Lovell sent you away, you referred to *us*. Who was with you?"

There was a long silence. Dick's gaze was vague and distant, and Serena wondered whether he had not understood her or remembered his original comment. His mind could have drifted away at any moment, and she had probably tired him with her questions. But no. Just as she thought she would never know, Dick looked up. He wasn't looking at her, though. He held out a hand to Jack and he smiled, so suddenly and vividly that he looked exactly as she remembered him before his illness.

"Francis," he said.

They had all had tea and several cupcakes and slices of Victoria sponge cake, and Dick was dozing comfortably in his chair, when Serena opened her bag and took out a little wooden box. She put it on the table.

"Is that it?" Lizzie said. She looked slightly anxious, Serena thought, as well she might.

She opened the lid. The Lovell Lodestar sat neatly on a bed of blue velvet, looking for all the world like what it was—a small, shiny black arrowhead. Serena's fingers shook slightly as she touched it. It felt smooth in her hand, and warm, and she thought she felt the tiniest vibration from it. She gave Lizzie a smile. "It's okay," she said. "I'm getting good vibes from it. And anyway, you don't need to worry. It entrusted itself to you that day when you gave it to Polly. You're not going to disappear in a flash of light."

"I wasn't worried for me," Lizzie said with dignity. "I'm used to these things. I'd just rather not lose you somewhere in time."

"Fair enough," Serena said. "But I have a sense we are all safe." She put the stone gently in its box. "It's back where it belongs," she said. "Back for good."

"Have you decided what you're going to do with it?" Polly asked.

Serena slipped her hand into Jack's. "We've talked about it a lot," she said, glancing at him, "because really it's Jack's decision. The Lodestar was entrusted to the Lovells centuries ago. They were the custodians of the relic of St. Kenelm. It was stolen from them and that was when it began its journey. Now it's home."

"It also feels important that it should stay here because of Caitlin," Jack said, squeezing Serena's hand. "It's the right place."

"I agree," Lizzie said, staring at the Lodestar as it sat innocently on its blue velvet bed, "but is that safe?"

"Well," Serena said, "we could put it in a museum because Eve was right when she said it's an ancient artifact that is actually worth a lot of money. It would have twenty-four-hour security and everyone would know that it was the Lovell Lodestar, and it was reputed to have magical powers. Or—" she looked around at the spring garden, the sun patterning the grass and the blue stars of the scilla flowers planted in a drift beneath the trees, "we could hide it here in plain sight.

After all," she said, looking at Polly, "it was in the gardens ever since you put it here, and we are the only people who know what it is. Let's keep it that way."

She got up and picked up the box. Polly stood, too, and went over to stand by Dick's chair. "Dad's dozing, I think," she said, touching his hand, "but I'm sure he'd agree with us."

They all walked over to the sundial, their feet sinking into the soft grass. It was a perfect late March day, the trees starting to show their new green and the birds chattering above them. Serena took the arrowhead from the box and slipped it onto the pin in the center of the sundial, and it fitted perfectly. Around the base of the pillar, on the lichen-covered stone, she could see the carved words she remembered:

Shadows we are and like shadows depart…

She felt the tears sting her eyes. Caitlin, she was sure, would always be with them, but no longer as a shadow haunting, a lost memory. She could once again be the bright and vibrant spirit they remembered.

She ran her hand over the bronze plate beneath the arrow. It felt warm from the sun. "Caitlin and I always loved the sundial," she said softly. "This is for her. To close the circle." The Lodestar quivered. It spun for a few seconds and Serena held her breath, then it pointed to the north. Across the garden a blackbird called with its piercing note. Dick dozed on in his chair. Serena slipped her arm through Polly's.

"The last daughters of York," she said. "How does that feel, Aunt Pol?"

"I'm damned proud of it," Polly said, "and I need another piece of cake."

Chapter 22

ANNE

Bermondsey Abbey
1495

The abbey is thronged with pilgrims today come to venerate the relic of the holy rood. They fill the church with their voices raised in worship. The guesthouse is bursting at the seams, and the abbey coffers are filling with gold from the rich and groats from the poor. On such a day as this I keep to my cell. I have no wish to be either a figure of curiosity to the visitors nor a distraction from their prayers.

I have lived here at Bermondsey Abbey for eight years, ever since I lost Francis and Richard after the Battle of Stoke Field. At first I was here with the Queen Dowager, Elizabeth Woodville, neither of us suited to the contemplative life, both of us locked behind these walls by King Henry VII because we were dangerous women. She was the unwanted mother of the Yorkist Queen, I the penniless widow of a Yorkist traitor. We were like two cats in a barrel, each other's torment and punishment, yet I missed her when she died.

I think about Francis every day. Each day I wonder where he is and what has happened to him and to Richard. I never expected him to come back for me. Ginevra told me, all those years ago, that the power of the relic does not work in that way. It cannot be bent to man's will. So I pray for them; and of course I hope, secretly, because hope is always the last thing to die.

It is hot for September and I long to be out in the fresh air, but only when I hear the bell for vespers and the monks' voices raised in chant do I slip outside into the cool of the evening to catch the last light in the gardens.

The grass in the orchard is cool beneath my feet. I walk slowly under the trees, the fruit heavy above my head, a tiny sliver of new moon captured in the branches. It reminds me of the day that Francis first brought Richard Plantagenet to me at Minster Lovell. Except that then the sun was bright and hot and there was still hope of restoration, no matter how battered and tarnished it was.

I do not see the figure in the corner of the cloisters until I am almost upon him. It is a pilgrim in jerkin and hood, a tall man and well made, loitering it seems with no particular purpose. The skin on the back of my neck prickles because along with the holy, the pilgrimage will always bring criminals to prey on virtuous men. This could be one such. When he reaches out to me, I draw back in alarm.

"Anne," he says. "At last. I have been waiting for you."

My heart leaps, for I recognize his voice. I am the one who has been waiting, it seems forever. It is impossible and yet here he is.

"Francis?" My whisper is so faint I am surprised he can hear, but he does, and puts back his hood to reveal himself in the faint moonlight.

"What are you doing here?" I ask stupidly. I feel confused, angry at the risk he is taking, disbelieving that he could be here at all. My mind is in utter turmoil. Is he real, or is he no more than a figment of my imagination, conjured up by longing? How can it be him?

"I have come for you," he says, as though it is that simple. "Did you think I would not come back?"

I stare at him in stupefaction, wondering if I had misunderstood all along, if he and Richard have only been in hiding, not far, far away in another time, another place.

"How can this be?" I say. "Do you have the pendant—the Lodestar?"

He shakes his head.

"The Lodestar is with Richard," he said. "He sent me back, just as you sent him and me away before."

"Then we cannot get back to him!" I am babbling, confused. "Where is he? You should not have left him alone and unprotected—" I stumble over my words, unable to understand.

Francis laughs. "Richard is a man grown now," he says. "He is ready to make his own way." He stops, and for a second I see sadness slide across his face. "We shall not see him again," he says, "but I know all will be well with him. He will be safe. I wish you could have seen him again, Anne, just once. He is a fine man. You would be proud of him, as I am." He cups my cheek in his gloved hand. "I will tell you everything when I may, but for now I am in haste for us to be away…" He puts his hands lightly on my waist. "Must I abduct my own wife from a monastery?"

"Yes," I say. "I do believe you must." I recognize his touch. My body leans into his. He feels the same, smells the same, and suddenly I am dizzy with love for him, my heart soaring. "Take me away," I say recklessly. "I do not care where we go or what happens, Francis. I have so missed you."

He grabs my hand and we run to the stables. There is a horse there, very fine, tied up and waiting. One of the abbey servants, an ostler, looks at us curiously, but I ignore him, heady with joy. Let him raise the alarm. They will not catch us. This I know.

"Where are we going?" I ask as Francis tosses me up into the saddle and settles behind me. "Do you have a plan?"

"Of course I do," he says. He sounds offended that I would doubt it. He urges the horse to a canter and we shoot out of the stables like an arrow, like a sword into the heart of light. Behind us the abbey bells ring out a peal, as though in celebration.

"You may remember from long ago," Francis says in my ear as we gather speed, "that your family had a castle, a place granted by the King of Scots to your father when he was a fugitive from the crown?"

"I remember," I say. "The Red Castle at Lunan."

"We go there," Francis says. "We go to Scotland." His arms tighten about my waist. "If God is willing," he says, his body hard and strong against mine, "then we will raise a family there. And if he does not so bless us, we will still have each other as we were always meant to do."

I lean back against him. For all the speed and the danger, it feels safe.

"The one thing about the Lodestar," Francis says, and I hear the warmth in his voice, "is that it was always intended to be a compass. It guides a man to his one true north. That was what I thought of, Anne, when I came back to find you."

The buildings of Bermondsey fall back, the hunched shadow of the abbey recedes against the night sky and the sound of the bells fade. The road is straight and empty and we ride for the North.

★ ★ ★ ★ ★

Keep reading for a special preview of
The Forgotten Sister

The spellbinding novel from
USA TODAY *bestselling author Nicola Cornick*

An unresolved mystery from the Tudor era will shape the lives of two women, centuries apart…

Available now from Graydon House!

Prologue

AMY ROBSART

Cumnor Village

They came for me one night in the winter of 1752 when the ice was on the pond and the trees bowed under the weight of the hoarfrost. There were nine priests out of Oxford, garbed all in white with tapers in hand. Some looked fearful, others burned with a righteous fervor because they thought they were doing the Lord's work. All of them looked cold, huddled within their cassocks, the one out ahead gripping the golden crucifix as though it were all that stood between him and the devil himself.

The villagers came out to watch for a while, standing around in uneasy groups, their breath like smoke on the night air, then the lure of the warm alehouse called them back and they went eagerly, talking of uneasy ghosts and the folly of the holy men in thinking they could trap my spirit.

The hunt was long. I ran through the lost passageways of Cumnor Hall with the priests snapping at my heels and in the end, exhausted and vanquished, my ghost sank into the dark pool. They said their prayers over me and returned to their cloisters and believed the haunting to be at an end.

Yet an unquiet ghost is not so easily laid to rest. They had trapped my wandering spirit, but I was not at peace. When the truth is concealed the pattern will repeat. The first victim was Amyas Latimer, the poor boy who fell to his death from the tower of the church where my body was buried. Then there was the little serving girl, Amethyst Green, who tumbled from the roof of Oakhangar Hall. Soon there will be another. If no one prevents it, I know there will be a fourth death and a fifth, and on into an endless future, the same pattern, yet different each time, a shifting magic lantern projecting the horror of that day centuries ago.

There is only one hope.

I sense her presence beside me through the dark. Each time it happens she is there, too, in a different guise, like me. She is my nemesis, the archenemy. Yet she is the only one who can free me and break this curse. In the end it all depends on her and in freeing my spirit I sense she will also free her own.

Elizabeth.

I met her only a handful of times in my life. She was little, but she was fierce, always, fierce enough to survive against the odds, a fighter, clever, ruthless, destined always to be alone. We could never have been friends yet we are locked together in this endless dance through time.

I possessed the one thing she wanted and could not have and in my dying I denied it to her forever. For a little while I thought that would be enough to satisfy me. Yet revenge sours and diminishes through the years. All I wish now is to be released from my pain and to ensure this can never happen again.

Elizabeth, my enemy, you are the only one who can help me now, but to do that you must change, you must see that the truth needs to be told. Open your eyes. Find the light.

Chapter 1

LIZZIE

Amelia and Dudley's Wedding,
2010

Everyone was drunk. They had broken into the wedding favor boxes early and were downing champagne directly from the quarter-bottles, lobbing chocolates at each other and throwing the beribboned scented tea bags into the swimming pool. Amelia, the bride, who had personally chosen the Rose Pouchong and Green Jasmine tea bags to match the scented candles, had stormed off in tears. Dudley, instead of going after his new wife, had jumped fully clothed into the pool, laughing maniacally.

Lizzie thought boy bands were the pits, especially Dudley's band, Call Back Summer, whom she secretly believed were just talentless entitled rich boys. She would never say that to Dudley, of course. He was her friend. But she wrote and played her own music and before they'd split up, her band had been way more successful than Dudley's.

Lizzie didn't drink. She hated it when Dudley behaved like her father, ringing her up when he was pissed, slurring his words as he told her she was his best friend in the world, that he'd love her forever. It was only because they'd known each other since the age of six that she put up with it. She had no idea why he had married Amelia anyway unless it was for publicity. He'd said he was in love, but Dudley was always falling in love with someone. It was a stupid idea to get married when you were only eighteen. Lizzie didn't intend to marry anyone, ever.

She stood up, unpleasantly aware of the sweat sliding down her back and turning her lace mini dress transparent as it stuck to her skin. Kat, her godmother, had told her it was bad taste to wear a white dress to a wedding, but Lizzie hadn't cared. The June sun was dropping towards the horizon now and the marquee cast long shadows across the lawn. Not a breath of wind stirred the sultry air. A band was playing on the terrace, but no one was paying any attention. Lizzie knew the partying would carry on long into the night. Dudley seemed to have an inexhaustible capacity for drink and drugs, but she was bored.

Stepping out from beneath the jaunty poolside umbrella, she was hit by the full heat of the day. She hated being too hot; it didn't agree with her redhead's pale, freckled skin. Suddenly the water looked very tempting. Dudley, seeing her hesitate on the edge of the pool, waved a soaking arm in her direction.

"Lizzie!" he shouted. "Come on in!" Beside him a number of girls splashed around, screaming. One was Amelia's younger sister Anna, who had jumped in wearing her bridesmaid's dress. Another was Letty Knollys, the girlfriend of one of Dudley's bandmates whom Lizzie privately thought was an even bigger groupie than Amelia.

Lizzie smiled and shook her head. Her curls would go even frizzier if she got them wet and there were bound to be paparazzi hiding in the trees to capture the wedding reception for the papers. Dudley would have made sure of that. She didn't want to be all over the red tops with mad hair and a wet see-through dress. She was too careful of her reputation for that.

She wandered off in the direction of the luxury portaloos. Evidently the plumbing at Oakhangar Hall, the ridiculously ostentatious wedding present that Amelia's father had bought for the bride, was not up to coping with two hundred celebrity guests. Nevertheless, the cool darkness of the entrance hall beckoned to her.

It took her eyes several seconds to adjust when she took off her sunglasses and then she almost fell over the enormous pile of wedding presents spilling across the floor. Beyond the gift mountain the flagstones stretched, smooth and highly polished, to the base of a grand staircase that curved up in two flights to a balustraded gallery. The soaring walls were paneled in dark wood and hung with tapestries. The whole effect was consciously mock-medieval and rather over-the-top, but Lizzie could see that it suited Amelia's Pre-Raphaelite style.

A huge black grand piano skulked in a corner beside the stair, its surface playing host to a vast display of lilies more suited to a funeral than a wedding in Lizzie's opinion. She muffled a sneeze as the pollen tickled her nose. In contrast to the roar of the party outside, the house was sepulchrally quiet. Except… Across the wide acreage of floor came the cascading melody of a harp, the notes resonating for a couple of seconds, then dying away.

Lizzie spun around. There was no sign of a harp, no sign of any instrument other than the piano. The cadence came again, higher, wistful, a fall of notes that sounded like a sigh. She moved towards the sound and then she saw it, on a little shelf to the right of the door, a crystal ball held in the cupped palms of a stone angel.

The crystal swirled with a milky white mist.

Touch me.

Lizzie stopped when her hand was about an inch from the crystal surface.

No. The urge was strong, but she knew what would happen if she did. Ever since she had been a small child, she had had an uncanny knack of being able to read objects. It was something she had grown up with so at first it had seemed natural; it was only when she had first mentioned it to Kat, who had looked at her as though she was a changeling, that she realized not everyone had the gift. "It's just your imagination running away with you," Kat had said, folding her in her embrace and stroking her hair, trying to soothe and normalize her, to reassure herself as much as Lizzie. "You see things because you want to see them, sweetie. It doesn't mean anything..."

Lizzie had never mentioned it to her again after that, but she had known Kat was wrong. Later, when she looked it up, she saw it was called psychometry. She used it carefully, secretly, to connect with her past and the mother she had lost as a child. The rest of the time she tried not to touch anything much at all if it was likely to give her a vision. She really didn't want to know.

The crystal was calling to her. She rubbed her palms down her dress to stop herself reaching out to obey the unspoken whisper.

"What did you see?"

Lizzie jumped. A boy was standing on the bottom step of the vast staircase, dwarfed by its height and breadth. He was staring at her. It was disconcerting; she hadn't known anyone was there.

"Nothing," she said. "I didn't touch it." She sounded defensive, which was ridiculous. She'd done nothing wrong and he was only a child. Deliberately she relaxed her face into the smile she used for the public.

"Hi, I'm Lizzie."

The boy looked at her as though he was trying to make some sort of private decision about her. It was an odd expression for such a young child; wary, thoughtful with a flash of calculation. It hinted, Lizzie thought, at a rather terrifying intelligence.

"I'm Johnny." He came forward and stuck out a hand very formally. Lizzie shook it.

"You're Amelia's brother. I saw you at the wedding." She recognized him now from the church, traipsing in behind the flower girls in Amelia's wake, looking as though he'd rather be somewhere else. Amelia's family had turned out in force for the wedding. They were all very close, a situation which Lizzie secretly envied.

"They made me be a page boy." Johnny sounded disgusted. He looked down at his miniature three-piece suit with loathing. Lizzie could hardly blame him. It was horribly twee. "I hated it," he said. "I'm six years old, not a baby."

Lizzie smothered another smile. "Life lesson, Johnny. People are always trying to make you do stuff you don't want to do. You have to stand up for your rights."

"Arthur says sometimes you have to do what other people want to make them happy," Johnny said.

"That's true," Lizzie acknowledged. She wasn't great at putting other people's happiness first. She'd had to struggle too hard for her own. She thought Arthur, whoever he was, sounded a proper goody-goody. "It's complicated," she said. "Next time, though, ask Arthur whether he'd like to be a page boy instead of you."

Johnny giggled. "Arthur's too big to do that." He cocked his head to one side. "Did you really see nothing in the crystal?"

"Not a thing," Lizzie said lightly. She remembered now that Amelia liked all the flaky stuff, though with the amount of drugs she and Dudley took sometimes they didn't need a crystal ball to see things. Lizzie didn't do drugs. She'd grown up seeing her father offer Ecstasy to his dinner guests along with coffee and mints. No thank you.

"The crystal called to you," Johnny said. "I heard it."

Okay, so he was an odd child, Lizzie thought, but then so had she been. She felt a tug of affinity with him.

"I thought I heard a harp playing," she said, "but it must have been the wind. That must have been the sound you heard, too."

"There's no wind today," Johnny said.

"Then it must have been the band," Lizzie said.

She saw Johnny watching her with those bright blue eyes and thought, *He knows. He knows I'm lying. How can he? He's only six.*

"Amelia says that the crystal speaks to her," Johnny said seriously. "Maybe that's what you heard. She says it has healing powers."

"That's nice," Lizzie said, wondering how many more of Amelia's new age philosophies her little brother had absorbed. Not that she could criticize. She might not like possessing woo-woo powers but she could hardly deny they existed.

"Johnny?"

This time they both jumped. A man was crossing the hall towards them, young, tall, unmistakably related to Johnny with the same lean features and dark blue eyes. Where Johnny had ruffled blond hair, this man's hair, however, was black, and unlike Johnny he looked good in a morning suit. Lizzie thought he also looked familiar and wondered if they had met before. There had been such a crowd in the church, and she knew so many people, but she couldn't quite place him. Perhaps she'd seen him on a billboard; he looked like a model.

His gaze focused on her, and Lizzie saw that he recognized her and, a second later, saw equally clearly that he did not like her. It was a novel experience for her to be disliked. She worked hard to be sweet and appealing. There was no reason to *dis*like her.

"Hi, Arthur," Johnny said. "This is Lizzie."

"I know," Arthur said.

Arthur Robsart, Lizzie thought, of course. He was not a model, but he did do something on TV, not that she ever had time to watch, and he had some impossibly glamorous fiancée who wasn't at the wedding because she was about to make it in Hollywood. He was also Amelia's older brother, or half brother, she thought—Amelia's family was almost as complicated as hers—which, she supposed, explained his dislike for her. Her heart dropped a little. She'd tried to be nice to Amelia; after all, she was Dudley's oldest friend so she should be Amelia's friend, too. But somehow it hadn't worked and evidently Arthur knew that and like some other mean people, thought she should get out of Dudley's life.

Johnny scrambled up from the step and held out his arms unselfconsciously to his brother, asking to be picked up. Arthur's face lightened into a transforming smile.

"Where have you been?" he asked, ruffling Johnny's hair. "Your mum's looking for you."

"I want to get out of this stupid outfit," Johnny grumbled, fretful as any ordinary six-year-old now.

"Come on, then." Arthur swung him up onto his shoulders. "Let's go and get changed." He gave Lizzie a cool nod, nothing more. Her heart dropped a little further, which was weird since his dislike mattered not at all. She was seventeen years old and she'd already learned not to care about other people's opinions. She'd also learned not to get entangled with handsome men. Or any men, for that matter; the life lessons she'd already absorbed would probably make even a psychiatrist wince.

As Arthur's footsteps died away, silence washed back into the hall and with it the plaintive echo of the crystal's song. Unwilling but unable to resist, Lizzie moved back toward it. The glass had turned a pale violet color now. It seemed too beautiful *not* to touch. And surely something so beautiful couldn't be dangerous.

Her fingertips brushed the surface of the ball. It felt cool and smooth, the drifts of mist within following the movement of her hand. Immediately, Lizzie saw a vision of the crystal sitting in the window of a shop in Glastonbury surrounded by a whole variety of other bogus magical items from joss sticks to druids' robes. She could see Amelia exclaiming in delight, pointing it out to Dudley who had his habitual expression of bored amusement plastered across his face. Dudley shrugged:

"It's total rubbish, but buy it if you want…"

Lizzie withdrew her hand. Psychometry gave her the ability to pry into other people's lives sometimes, but she really didn't want to know what went on between Dudley and Amelia. She absentmindedly rubbed her fingers over the lines of the stone angel's wings, tracing the intricate carving. It was a beautiful piece, the hands cupping the crystal ball, the head bent. As she touched it, she heard the thrum of the harp again, but this time it wasn't sweet and plaintive. There was a cold edge to it like shards of ice that sent a shiver down her spine.

The world exploded suddenly around her. She felt a rush of movement and a blur of color; she felt a hand in the small of her back, pushing hard, then she was falling, falling. There was a rush of air against her face and the lightness of empty space beneath her. There was fear screaming inside her head. Then, as quickly as they had arrived, the sensations passed. She was lying on the floor and people were buzzing around her like flies.

"What happened?"

"I heard her screaming..."

"Trust Lizzie Kingdom to try and steal the limelight today of all days..."

Lizzie sat up. Her head was woozy as though she had had too much champagne. Pieces of the crystal lay scattered about her in glittering shards, one of which had embedded itself in the palm of her right hand. It stung fiercely. She could hear Amelia in the background, wailing that Lizzie had broken her gazing ball.

The stone angel lay next to her, unbroken. Lizzie felt dazed, her mind cloudy, sickness churning in her stomach. *What the hell had happened?* She knew she hadn't smashed the crystal.

People were still talking. No one seemed bothered about helping her up. She could hear Dudley's voice: "For fuck's sake, what's the matter? It was only some cheap ornament." Amelia's wails rose above the chatter. Lizzie focused on keeping still and not throwing up. That would be the final humiliation. She felt like a pariah, abandoned in a sea of glass.

The crowd fell back a little, crunching the slivers of glass beneath their stilettos and hipster brogues. Arthur pushed through to her; he didn't say anything, simply held out a hand to help her to her feet. Lizzie grabbed it and scrambled up. She had no pride left. She followed him down what felt like an endless succession of dark corridors into what looked like an old scullery full of discarded wedding paraphernalia, piles of empty boxes and flower containers heaped up and left out of sight. This, Lizzie thought, was definitely the servants' quarters. She had been demoted from guest to unsightly wedding detritus along with all the rest of the rubbish.

Arthur was rummaging in a cupboard underneath a white ceramic sink. He emerged with a first aid kit in his hand. She turned her palm up so that he could clean the cut. The bleeding had stopped now, but the wound throbbed, even more so when Arthur dabbed at it with antiseptic. Lizzie suppressed a wince as it stung. He was so dour and exasperated, and there was no way she was going to show any weakness.

"I'm sorry," she said as the silence became blistering. "I really don't know what happened."

"Keep your hand still whilst I bandage it up," Arthur said. "It's Amelia you should be apologizing to," he added. "It's her wedding you've ruined."

"Don't be ridiculous," Lizzie snapped. Her hand was smarting, but not as much as her feelings. "If anyone has ruined the wedding it's Dudley, and that's not my fault."

"You think?" Arthur looked at her very directly and her heart did an odd sort of flip. He continued to wrap the bandage methodically around her hand and her wrist, as gently as before. Lizzie suddenly became acutely aware of his touch against her skin and by the time he had finished and tucked the end in she was squirming to escape.

"Thanks," she said, jumping up and heading for the door. "I'll just grab my bag and..."

Go. There was no way she was hanging around here any longer. She felt very odd.

Back in the grand hall, someone had swept up the glass and the place was empty. It was as though nothing had ever happened. Lizzie could hear the band playing and splashes and screams from the pool. The party had moved up a gear.

She called her driver who was there in three minutes. She was in such a hurry to get away that she left her very expensive jacket behind. Days later, when she finally emptied the wedding favors, tea bags and scented candle from her goody bag, she found that in the confusion someone must have accidently slipped the little stone angel in with all the other stuff. She meant to return it to Amelia, but after all the fuss it never seemed like the right time. Then she saw Amelia wearing her jacket as though it were her own so she never mentioned it again, but stowed the angel away in a cupboard. She knew it was petty, but Amelia had started it and the jacket was probably worth more than the ornament anyway.

Over the years she forgot about the stone angel, but she never forgot Dudley and Amelia's wedding. She tried, but there was no way she could ever forget a day that had ended with Amelia in hysterics and with blood on her hands. It felt ill-starred. It felt as though, sooner or later, something bad was going to happen.

Chapter 2

AMY

Stanfield Manor, Norfolk,
August 1549

I met Robert Dudley on a night of moonlight, fire and gunpowder.

The wind had a sharp edge to it that evening, summer already turning away towards the chill of autumn. It brought with it the scent of burning from the rebel camp twelve miles to the north. The sky burned, too, in shades of red and orange below the dark clouds, so that it was impossible to tell what was fire and what was sunset. They said that there were more than twelve thousand men assembled on Mousehold Heath, more than in the whole of Norwich itself, and Norwich was a great city, second only to London. Among the rebels' prisoners was my half brother John Appleyard, taken by our cousin Robert Kett, to help my father ponder whether his loyalty was to his king or to his kin. John's capture cast a dark shadow over our house but our mother made no plea—it was not in her nature to beg, not even for her children—and Father stood firm. He was and always would be the King's man.

"We will be fifteen for dinner," Mother said when I met her

in the hall. The servants were sweeping like madmen, some scattering fresh rushes, others covering the table with the best diamond-patterned linen cloths, the ones that Mother generally considered too fine for use. I saw the sparkle of silver: bowls, flagons, knives.

"There is an army of rebels twelve miles away," I said, staring at the display. "Is it wise to bring out your treasure?"

She gave me the look that said I was pert. I waited for the reproach that would accompany it, the claim that my father had spoiled me, the youngest, his only daughter, and that I would never get myself a husband if I was so forward. Pots and kettles; I got three-quarters of my nature from my mother and well she knew it; from her I had inherited a quick mind and a quick tongue, but also the knowledge of when I needed to guard it. Men say that women chatter, but they are the ones who so often lack discretion. Women can be as close as the grave.

But Mother did not reproach me. Instead, her gaze swept over me from head to foot. There was a small frown between her brows; I thought it was because my hair was untidy and put up a hand to smooth it. My appearance was my vanity; I was fair and had no need of the dye. My skin was pale rose and cream and my eyes were wide and blue. I knew I was a beauty. I wouldn't pretend.

"You are quite right," Mother said after a moment's scrutiny, with a wry twist of her lips. "You, of all our treasures, should be kept safe at a time like this. Unfortunately, your father insists that you should attend dinner tonight."

I gaped at her, not understanding. I had only been referring to the plate and linens. Seeing my confusion, her smile grew, but it was a smile that chilled me in some manner I did not quite understand. It hinted at adult matters and I, for all my seventeen years, was still a child.

"Your presence has been requested," she said. "The Earl of Warwick comes at the head of the King's army. They march against the rebels. He is bringing his captains here to dine with us tonight and take counsel with your father. Two of his sons ride with him, Ambrose and Robert."

My heart gave a tiny leap of excitement, which I quickly suppressed out of guilt. The Earl of Warwick was coming here, to my corner of Norfolk, bringing danger and excitement to a place that seldom saw either. It was a curious feeling that took me then, a sense of anticipation tinged with a sadness of something lost; peace, innocence almost. But the rebels had already shattered both peace and innocence when they had risen up against the King's laws.

"I'm sorry," I said. "About the King's army, I mean. It is hard for you, with John a prisoner and family loyalty split."

She looked startled for a moment and then smiled at me, a proper smile this time, one that lit her tired eyes. "You are a sweet child, Amy," she said, patting my cheek. Her smile died. "Except that you are not a child any longer, it seems."

She sighed. "Do you remember Robert Dudley?" She was watching me very closely. I was not sure what she was looking for. "He asked your father if you would be present at dinner tonight. No..." she corrected herself. "He requested that you *should* be present, which is a different matter entirely."

Her look made it clear what she thought of the sons of the nobility asking after a gentleman's daughter. I suppose she imagined that no good could come of it, despite my father's ambitions.

"I remember him," I said. I smiled a little at the memory, for a picture had come into my mind, a small, obstinate boy, his black hair standing up on end like a cockerel's crest, a boy whom the other children had mocked because he was as dark as a Spaniard. More cruelly they had called him a traitor's grandson because the first Dudley of note had been a lawyer who had risen high in old King Henry's favour and had then fallen from grace when the new King Henry had wanted to sweep his father's stables clean. It had all happened before I was born, before Robert had been born, too, but the ghost of the past had haunted him. People had long memories and cruel tongues, and as a result he was a child full of anger and fierce defiance, seeming all the more impotent because he had been so small and so young. I had secretly pitied Robert even whilst he had sworn he would be a knight one day and kill anyone who slighted his family name.

"When did you meet him?" Mother was like a terrier after a rat when she saw that smile.

"I met him years ago at Kenninghall," I said. "And once, I think, when the Duchess took us up to London."

My mother nodded. I felt the tension ease from her a little. Perhaps she believed that no harm could have come of a meeting between children under the auspices of the Duchess of Norfolk.

"You were very young then," she said. "I wonder why he remembers you."

"I was kind to him, I suppose," I said. "The other children were not." I remembered dancing with Robert at some childish party at court; Lady Anne Tilney had scorned his proffered hand for the galliard and so he had turned to me as second choice. We must have been all of twelve years old and he had spent the entire dance glaring at Lady Anne and stepping on my toes.

"They may be regretting that unkindness," my mother said

with another of her wry smiles, "now that his father rivals the Duke of Somerset for the King's favour."

A shiver tickled my spine like the ghosts of the past stirring again. I wondered whether Robert's father had learned nothing from his own father's fate. Why men chose to climb so high when the risk was so great was a matter on which I had no understanding. It was as though they enjoyed tempting the gods with their recklessness and repeating history over and again.

Mother's mind had already moved on to more practical matters, however. "Wear your blue gown," she instructed, "the one that matches your eyes. Since you and I are to be present we shall at least make your father proud even if we will be bored to distraction by talk of military strategy."

"Yes, Mother," I said dutifully.

"I'll send Joan to you," Mother said. "And don't lean out of the window to see what goes on outside whilst you dress." Seeing my blank look, she said with a hint of irritation: "Did I not mention but a moment ago that there is an army coming? There will be nigh on ten thousand men encamped in the fields beyond the orchard. I do not want you to become their entertainment."

"No, Mother," I said. I thought it would be easy enough to steal a look without being seen. The encampments, the fires, the horses, the food cooking, the scents and the noise… Stanfield Manor would be abuzz and it was impossible not to feel the expectancy in the air.

"Remember that soldiers are dangerous, Amy," Mother added sharply, "commoner or nobleman alike."

It seemed excessive to say "yes, Mother" again, so I nodded obediently and hurried away to the stairs, aware that her watchful gaze was pinned upon my back. There was nothing to dispute in what she had said, nor in those things that she had not put into words. I might be young, but I knew what she meant about soldiers and the way in which they snatched at pleasure with both hands in case it was their last chance. I did not want to be that prize, seized for a moment's gratification then cast aside.

Even so, I thought about Robert Dudley whilst Joan helped me to dress and started to plait my long fair hair. She was slow and methodical, her tongue sticking from the corner of her mouth as her fingers worked. My thoughts, my dreams, were the opposite of slow, skipping lightly from one place to the next. My memories of Robert were vague, but that did not stop me from pinning my dreams on him. What sort of a man had he become? Was he handsome? Would he like me? Even as I counseled myself to hold fast to my common sense, I could feel excitement bubbling through me.

"Keep still, Mistress Amy," Joan tutted as the braids slid from her fingers. "You are hopping about like a hen on a thorn."

It seemed to take her an age of pinning and smoothing and straightening, but finally she was done and I flew down the stairs. Yet when I reached the door of the hall I hesitated, stung by a sudden shyness at the sound of voices within. I smoothed my skirts, patted my coif, took a deep breath, but my feet seemed fixed to the flagstones. I could not move.

"Amy!" Mother appeared in the doorway, voice as sharp as a needle. "Why are you loitering there?" Her gaze darted past me, looking for trouble. When she found none, it did not seem to appease her.

"Come in." She flapped at me to go ahead of her.

The hall was hot. We did not need a fire in August, but

Father had ordered one lit anyway, all the better to show off the richness of his glass and silver. I wondered how the table bore the weight of so much food and spared a thought for the kitchen staff; Cook's sweat must have been liberally mixed in with the sauces. The servants were sweating, too, as they attended us, heat and nervousness making their faces redden and their hands shake. Father, never the most patient master, was snapping orders as though he were a general in the field.

"There is a space for you there, Amy—" Mother pushed me towards the center of the table where there was an empty place laid. I sat. She sat opposite me, watching me like a cat with a mouse.

I felt like telling her that there was no need for her vigilance. On the one side of me was an old man who looked as though he had last ridden to war alongside the late King Henry at the Battle of the Spurs. On the other was a younger man who was so fat I wondered at the horse that had to bear his weight and whether he had to be winched into the saddle. A swift search of the room, conducted surreptitiously as I took my seat, had told me that neither Robert Dudley nor his brother Ambrose was present. I felt disproportionately disappointed. The old soldier ignored me, sucking noisily on chicken bones and throwing the scraps to the dogs. The younger smiled shyly and poured wine for me.

At the head of the table Father was deep in discussion with Lord Warwick. The King's general was a fine-looking man, all the more so in his armor. He had presence and grace; I watched him as he talked, animated and at times fierce. I caught an echo of Robert in the proud lift of his head and directness of his gaze.

I picked at my food. The chicken was drenched in a sauce

that was too rich and heavy. I wondered if Cook was a rebel sympathizer and wanted to give the King's men a stomach ache. Not that they were complaining. They looked half-starved and only the presence of ladies prevented them from falling on each dish like dogs as it came out.

There was little conversation. The weather, the poor quality of the roads, the availability of horses and the fine taste of Stanfield-grown apples sustained us through several courses whilst I sat and sweated and reflected bitterly that I had wasted my hopes and dreams on a fantasy.

I escaped to my chamber as soon as I was able. Mother had no need to chivvy me out whilst the men sat late over their wine and their strategy. I took off my pretty dress and released my hair and lay down, but of course I could not sleep. I was too irritated; with Robert, who had asked for me and then forgotten me, with myself for building something out of nothing. Outside there was a cacophony of noise: shouting, hammering, horses, footsteps, sounds of urgency that now rather than exciting me only served to annoy me. After a while I realized that I was not going to sleep. That irritated me even more. I threw back the covers and strode to the window, pushing wide the leaded pane.

Outside, there was full moonlight, bright as day and yet casting the world in only black and white. It was the moon that preceded the harvest, except that the rebellion had thrown the harvest into disarray this year. The crops lay trampled in the fields and there would be no festival of celebration though there could well be a reaping of souls if not of corn. Instead of mummers and music, shadow men walked amongst the trees of the orchard. Smoke rose white against the bleached night sky and the air was rich with the smell of cooking and dung, a curious combination that caught at my throat.

There was sudden movement below my window. A man swung down from his horse, tethered it to a tree. I saw him in flashes of silver and black; the moonlight on his armor, his long shadow. He took off his helmet and took a deep breath of air, head back, shaking himself like a dog coming out of water. He was dark; the moon lit shades of blue in his hair like a raven's wing. Then he looked up and the light fell full on his face.

I must have made some involuntary movement that caught his eye for he turned his head sharply to look at me. The gesture was so familiar even though I had not seen him for so many years. Recognition tugged deep within me. He raised a hand in greeting. I saw the flash of his smile. He knew me, too.

I pushed the window frame wider. "Robert Dudley," I said. "You missed dinner."

He laughed. "I am here now." He set his foot to the climbing rose that grew beneath my window. The whole delicate structure shivered as he put his weight on it, the last petals of summer drifting down, and I leaned out farther to stop him.

"You'll fall!" I had no care for propriety, only for his safety. I did not see the ranks of grinning soldiers pausing in their drinking and their gaming to watch us. I saw only him. Already I was swept away.

"Never," he said. "You won't lose me, Amy Robsart. I'll not fall."

A cloud passed over the moon, red like blood from the fire on the heath.

Despite the cumbersome weight of the armor, he climbed fast, sure-footed, like a cat. He reached the window ledge and swung himself over and then he was in my room. A ragged cheer went up from the men below and he reached across me to close the window and banish them so that there was only the two of us there in the candlelight. He smelled of sweat and horses and smoke and the night air; it was exciting and my head swam.

We stood and stared at one another. His armor was dented and blackened by smoke. His face likewise was filthy with dirt and sweat. I put a hand up to touch his chest, but could feel nothing but the coldness of hard steel beneath my palm, so I raised it to his cheek and touched warm flesh. He was vital and vivid and all the things that my life lacked. His eyes blazed as he bent his head to kiss me.

That was how I met Robert Dudley again. By the morning we had pledged our troth and the seeds of our mutual destruction were already sown.

The Forgotten Sister
By Nicola Cornick
Available now from Graydon House